"Provocative and compelling, *Skylight* has a genuine 'ripped from the headlines' feel as it imagines a brilliantly realistic future that, given the book's animating premise, is as plausible as it is terrifying. You'll find yourself turning the pages faster and faster just to keep up with your heartbeat. It's the kind of story that envelops both your mind and your heart and has you constantly asking, 'What would I do in that situation?' Mr. Hopkins proves himself to be a masterful storyteller able to effortlessly blend politics and catastrophe into an incendiary mix that will fuel debate from all points on the political spectrum. Read this book on a night you don't need a lot of sleep. And leave a few lights on . . . just in case."

—ANDREA ZRIMSEK CROUCH
Award-winning journalist

"*Skylight* reads like a blockbuster movie. Exciting, fast-paced, unpredictable, and full of tension, it pulls the reader along from one dramatic scene to the next. And starting with its cataclysmic opening through to its final revelation, *Skylight* leaves readers pondering this chilling question: *what if it really happened?*"

—CAREY BORTH
Movie producer and director

"Kevin Hopkins has written a brave and beautiful novel—a journey of hope that takes us down two haunting paths. One path follows two of the main characters in the days immediately following the Catastrophe as they navigate through a rapidly collapsing society in order to return home to Southern California. The second path begins one year later, when most of America's coastal cities have become virtual armed compounds, overflowing with millions of lost souls desperately seeking the safety of lower altitudes. These two paths ultimately converge in one brilliant, uplifting moment—a moment that affirms that the human spirit has the capacity to overcome even the darkest of nightmares. In all, this is a vivid, eloquent, and unforgettable book."

—RON DI LORENZO
Film producer

"*Skylight* proudly joins such dystopian classics as *1984* and Cormac McCarthy's Pulitzer Prize-winning *The Road* as a warning sign of the future as it may become. More so than any other novel in recent memory, *Skylight* powerfully depicts the fragility of freedom and human dignity even in a country as steeped in liberty as America. The characters and their conflicts are vividly drawn, the action is breathtaking, and the harrowing images of a world gone over the edge will stay with you long after you have put the book down. No one who reads this ultimately uplifting novel will come away unmoved."

—DOUG BANDOW
National columnist, Forbes.com

"*Skylight* launches a powerful strike against the rapidly expanding culture of government intrusiveness and civil-liberties violations that have become such a growing threat to American democracy and freedom in recent years. In dramatic and sobering fashion, *Skylight* depicts the terrible human cost of an all-knowing, all-powerful government that callously ignores the basic principles of privacy, prosperity, and freedom that over two centuries have made America the beacon of hope and goodness for billions of people. *Skylight* is a very important book. Read it now. And tell all of your friends to read it. You'll never look at government's accelerating intrusion into people's lives in the same way again."

—BARRY GOLDWATER JR.
Former US Representative and coauthor of the Federal Privacy Act

"*Skylight* is one of the most exciting and thought-provoking political thrillers to come along in many years, so reminiscent as it is of the work of Michael Crichton. But more than that, it is also one of the most intelligent discussions yet of the trade-offs that our society faces between energy production and environmental protection that are usually never the focus of the news media. As *Skylight* makes vividly clear—in a way that most political discussions and media do not—we simply must have both. And *Skylight* goes on to offer a straightforward prescription for doing just that. The book's clarity and insights are a very valuable addition to the public debate on these vital issues."

—JACK COX
Political journalist & former Chief of Staff, US Congress

"So many novels depict technology in a negative light. *Skylight* is one of those rare novels that portrays technology favorably. In brilliant and powerful fashion, *Skylight* demonstrates that technology can be used to improve our society—and, one day perhaps, even save it."

—DAVID HOLLAND
Senior Vice President, Entertainment & Sports, Cisco Systems

"*Skylight* is a warning cry for the future as we never want it to be. Stark, riveting, and at times terrifying, Kevin Hopkins's novel paints a portrait of the consequences of environmental collapse in a way that is more dramatic, and yet more personal, than any work to date—of either fiction *or* nonfiction. But *Skylight* goes beyond the normal invocations for environmental common sense by showing us a *way out*—a conceptual approach to global policy that will uniquely satisfy advocates of both economic growth and environmental protection. This is a very important book, and is 'must' reading for anyone who is concerned about the future of our planet."

—NICK YATES
President, The Eco-Institution

"*Skylight* is a riveting novel from beginning to end that is guaranteed to keep you on the edge of your seat and reading long after you should have put it down. I highly recommend it."

—ERIK OLSEN
Author, *Quest and Honor*

SKYLIGHT

KEVIN HOPKINS

SWEETWATER
BOOKS
AN IMPRINT OF CEDAR FORT, INC.
SPRINGVILLE, UT

© 2014 Kevin Hopkins

All rights reserved.

No part of this book may be reproduced in any form whatsoever, whether by graphic, visual, electronic, film, microfilm, tape recording, or any other means, without prior written permission of the publisher, except in the case of brief passages embodied in critical reviews and articles.

This is a work of fiction. The characters, names, incidents, places, and dialogue are products of the author's imagination, and are not to be construed as real. The opinions and views expressed herein belong solely to the author and do not necessarily represent the opinions or views of Cedar Fort, Inc. Permission for the use of sources, graphics, and photos is also solely the responsibility of the author.

ISBN 13: 978-1-4621-1326-2

LIBRARY OF CONGRESS CATALOGING-IN-PUBLICATION DATA

Hopkins, Kevin R.
 Skylight / Kevin Hopkins.
        pages cm
 ISBN 978-1-4621-1326-2
 1. Environmental disasters--Fiction. 2. Death--Fiction. 3. Survival--Fiction. I. Title.
 PS3608.O657S59 2014
 813'.6--dc23
                         2013034835

Published by Sweetwater Books, an imprint of Cedar Fort, Inc.
2373 W. 700 S., Springville, UT 84663
Distributed by Cedar Fort, Inc., www.cedarfort.com

Cover design by Angela D. Baxter
Cover design © 2014 by Lyle Mortimer
Edited and typeset by Melissa J. Caldwell

Printed in the United States of America

10 9 8 7 6 5 4 3 2 1

*Dedicated to my wife, Mary,
my love and inspiration,
and to my son, Brandon,
my hope for the future.
May he inherit a world where
there is not so much darkness.*

A generous portion of the net proceeds from Skylight will be donated to organizations dedicated to preserving the Earth's endangered species—including humankind.

We are, along with everything else on earth, subject to the great cycle that controls the planet. . . . Sudden climate change is an established scientific fact. But . . . nobody has been able to study what happens during a period of sudden change, because we can only measure its effects, not observe the event itself.

—Bell & Strieber, *The Coming Global Superstorm*

For climate change optimists, California is indeed the golden state when it comes to aggressive policies designed to avoid catastrophic climate change. But as a new report [from the Lawrence Berekely National Laboratory] makes depressingly clear, even Ecotopia will fall far short of hitting a target of reducing greenhouse gas emissions 80% by 2050 without the invention of new technologies and imposition of more draconian green mandates.

—Todd Woody, qz.com

The United States alone can do next to nothing about greenhouse gas emissions. . . . China and India are growing so rapidly that their additional greenhouse gas emissions swamp any reductions possible in the U.S. today."

—Andrew Morriss, McClatchy News Service

Let us assume that the entire industrialized world—not just the United States—was to reduce [greenhouse gas] emissions by 80 percent below 2005 levels by 2050. . . . If we apply the widely accepted MAGICC climate model developed at the National Center for Atmospheric Research, the result is: by 2050, temperatures would decline by 0.1 degrees Celsius, and by a bit less than 0.3 degrees by 2100. How much economic pain is that worth?

—Dr. Benjamin Zycher, American Enterprise Institute

AUTHOR'S NOTE

Skylight is a work of fiction. A figment of the imagination. A bedtime horror story. It couldn't happen, not really. The science is mere possibility, the political response a matter of conjecture. It is, as they say, only a story. But in the midnight darkness, when all around lies in silence, I begin to wonder: what if the events described here—or something very close to them—did in fact take place? What would happen then?

Skylight was first conceived more than thirty years ago, during the energy crisis of the late 1970s, when the Arab oil embargo had forced Americans to endure long gas lines and home-heating-oil shortages and fears that dollar-a-gallon gasoline might become a permanent feature of their daily lives. Draconian measures like "no drive" days and government-imposed home-temperature limits were seriously put forward in those days by then-President Carter and others. As an ardent political watcher even then, I was left wondering: how would ordinary Americans' lives have changed had regulatory solutions like these been adopted as our answer to foreign-engineered energy crises?

Fortunately, these questions quickly became moot as the Arab oil embargo soon ended and gas lines and the home-heating-oil crisis faded into little more than a bad dream. Indeed, the eventual deregulation of US oil and gas prices in the early 1980s ushered in a generation of abundant, low-cost energy, with inflation-adjusted energy prices beginning a two-decade-long decline. A speculative novel based on the energy crisis that I wrote during these early years—a story called "An Act of State"—ultimately would be reenvisioned as *Skylight*. But

Author's Note

not in the coming era of energy surplus. In those days, the story had become an anachronism, of little interest to any but the paranoid, and I soon set aside, leaving it largely forgotten.

It was more than a decade later, when emerging environmental concerns had begun to occupy the minds of politicians and the public alike, that the story at last returned to mind. Global warming, climate change, and worldwide superstorms were fringe theories at the time, but their potential consequences were so catastrophic that even people who normally dismissed such dark environmental speculations began to press for clarification and understanding. And, most of all, for answers. For if humankind truly were subject, within just a few generations, to the prospect of life-ending atmospheric collapse, paying careful attention to our planet's ecosystem seemed to be more than a matter of good public policy. It was essential to our species' survival.

Skylight was reborn in response to a simple question: what *was* the answer to this challenge? Having spent most of my professional career in economics and public policy, I knew quite well the arguments and issues on both sides of the debate. But closer study soon revealed that neither side offered any real solutions. The environmental skeptics derided the science of global warming and atmospheric change, denying that fossil fuels, greenhouse gases, and climate change posed any real threat to humankind. To be sure, there was some merit to the skeptics' claims, as mounting evidence revealed that global temperatures were *not* in fact rising despite increasing CO_2 concentrations. And yet there was a more disturbing question: what if the skeptics were wrong? What if the environmental threats they derided turned out to be real? Was continued ignorance of the potential for environmental catastrophe really our most intelligent route to the future?

The answers from the other side, voiced at increasingly greater volume as the new century dawned, were hardly more reassuring. The tireless warnings of Al Gore and Greenpeace and others, along with brilliant fictions like Whitley Strieber's *Nature's End* and *The Coming Global Superstorm*, appropriately raised a call for alarm. If taken seriously, their grim portraits should have left even the most jaded partisan terrified. And yet, in reflective moments, the more rational of these environmental advocates reluctantly admitted that their most often-asserted answers—from carbon taxes to cap-and-trade to the greening of industry—were likely to be either too little too late, or else were so impractical that they never would be implemented.

Indeed, the unspoken flaw in the environmental debate is this. If the darkest predictions about global warming and climate change are indeed our planet's future, the steps that we must take—and must take *now*—are far more oppressive than has ever even been whispered in the public debate. If, as NASA's Jim Hansen claims, we truly do have only a few years in which to act, a little trimming around the edges simply will not do. If the atmosphere, as a growing number of scientists assert, is already slipping past the tipping point, we need to literally shut down our society, put an end to concerns about prosperity and personal freedom, and make species preservation—*our species'* preservation—our overarching goal, the economic and political consequences notwithstanding.

Anything less is a death sentence for life on Earth.

That is the bold and inescapable—even uncomfortable—truth: if the warnings of imminent environmental catastrophe are correct, then the solutions must be more far-reaching than even the most outspoken environmental Cassandras have been willing to concede.

And so we return to the question that gave birth to *Skylight* more than thirty years ago: what would the effects of such environmental electroshock be on ordinary people's lives? The economic recession and its aftereffects that gripped America—even the whole world—during the 2008–2012 time period have caused untold human heartbreak and misery. And yet these consequences pale in comparison to what would inevitably take place should an environmentally mandated global economic and democratic lockdown be imposed.

Hence the dilemma: either we blithely ignore the warnings and continue to do far too little to protect our global environment—and so invite the ecological disaster that so many claim is inevitable. Or else we do what avoiding these environmental nightmares would truly require, and cast a future that would make the recent economic crises feel like a frolic the park. It's a Hobson's choice if there ever were one.

Unless... Unless there were, in fact, an answer to our environmental dilemma that could satisfy the demands of both environmental protection and economic production. In other words, what if we *could* find a solution that preserved both our planetary environment and our personal freedom and prosperity. *What if?*

It is to that search that *Skylight* has long been dedicated.

But is it really a search worth making? Why should we worry? Even if the most ardent environmentalists are correct, any disaster is decades, even centuries, in the future. Isn't it? The truth is: *no one knows.* Could events even remotely similar to those depicted in *Skylight* ever occur? Maybe. Or maybe not. Again, no one knows.

But I offer this caution. One of the key distinguishing characteristics of complex systems like our planet's atmosphere is the manner in which they degrade. Systems that fail gradually are said to "degrade gracefully"; those that stop working all at once are said to "degrade catastrophically." Consider a prosaic example. If an old-fashioned vinyl record becomes scratched, it will still produce music, although with annoying clicks and hisses. On the other hand, if a modern digital music file becomes corrupted, it becomes completely unusable, and will not play at all. It fails completely, catastrophically. Or, more vividly, consider this: if a bicycle tire goes flat, the rider can continue to ride, albeit with some discomfort. But if a simple O-Ring on the Space Shuttle disintegrates, as happened with the US Space Shuttle Challenger, the spacecraft explodes, and all aboard are lost. Again, the system "degrades catastrophically."

The most important question of our time is this: *will our planet's environment degrade gracefully or catastrophically?*

I am convinced that we no longer can wait for the answers to this question to unfold. As a parent, as a lover of our world's endangered species, and as an ordinary citizen of our Earth, I know that we must act, and that we must act *now*. But in so doing, we must act in a way that actually *solves* the problems that confront us, not that only moves us a few steps in the right direction. We must act with prescriptions that actually can be *implemented,* not merely with impressive-sounding catchphrases that do little more than score political points. Most importantly, we must act in a way that actually acknowledges the real consequences of those actions for the lives of ordinary people. People who have little voice in the political processes that control their fate, who live not only amidst the relative prosperity of the United States, Western Europe, and Pacific Asia, but also in the impoverished and economically struggling regions of Africa, Latin America, and many other parts of the world.

Author's Note

The time has come to recognize that safeguarding our future environment is absolutely essential. But so is preserving the freedom and prosperity of Earth's people. Both must be protected, and neither can be sacrificed, else life may be scarcely worth living.

It is to achieving these mutual and vital goals that *Skylight* is humbly offered.

Will we yet act in time? For the sake of my son, and for the billions of other children born and yet unborn, I pray that we will.

—Kevin Hopkins, February 2014

ACKNOWLEDGMENTS

Few books are the result of the author's efforts alone, and that is certainly the case with Skylight. And so I would like to briefly express my gratitude and appreciation to all those who helped this story make the long journey from conception to publication.

I first would like to thank all those current and past employees at Cedar Fort, who more than anyone made this publication possible. Justin Kelly, my original editor, was kind enough to see the promise in Skylight, and made extremely valuable editorial suggestions that greatly improved the pacing and style of the book. Alissa Voss, Cedar Fort's fiction editor, reviewed the entire manuscript in detail, and offered numerous substantive suggestions that, in the end, made a critical difference in the story's quality and appeal. Melissa Caldwell, Cedar Fort's senior copy editor and typesetter, took over management of the project in midstream and expertly shepherded Skylight through the final stages of production. Katreina Eden, Cedar Fort's vice president, helped to resolve the important production issues that greatly improved the book's physical appearance. Kristen Reeves did an exceptional job in executing the graphics despite having to deal with a very persnickety author. And Kelly Martinez, Cedar Fort's marketing guru, offered and continues to offer valuable insights and guidance in marketing and promoting Skylight, especially through social-media channels.

Outside of Cedar Fort, my first debt of gratitude goes to Erik Olsen, a good friend and Cedar Fort author who provided the introduction to Cedar Fort and without whose generous assistance Skylight might still be waiting for attention. Jack Cox, my good friend and colleague, has been a brilliant mentor in the subject areas addressed by Skylight, and was instrumental in many other key respects that helped make the book what it became. I also would like to express my deep appreciation to all those listed in the first three pages of the book who were gracious enough to offer kind words about the novel, including Doug Bandow, Carey Borth, Jack Cox, Ron Di Lorenzo, Barry Goldwater, Jr., David Holland, Erik Olsen, Nick Yates, and Andrea Zrimsek-Crouch. Special thanks go to Andrea Zrimsek-Crouch, who also read and offered valuable suggestions about important parts of the book. Kristen Lindstrom read an early draft of the manuscript and suggested a number of very helpful editorial improvements. And Martin Artiano was a true friend and colleague, who made many valuable contributions to earlier versions of the story.

Finally, I would like to express my deepest gratitude and love to my wife, Mary, who was exceedingly patient throughout the lengthy editing process, and who offered (as she always does) very wise and insightful editorial and production suggestions; and to my son, Brandon, who amazes me with a writing ability whose potential exceeds anything I could have hoped to achieve in my youth. Our faithful cat, Layah, sat with me many long hours while the editing took place, and our equally faithful dog, Casey, gave up many periods of playtime so that the book could be completed on time. Lastly, I would like to thank my Heavenly Father, whose continuing inspiration and love makes every miracle possible.

CHAPTER 1

Like an aneurysm that erupts in a young and healthy heart, the horror begins in a time and place unexpected. Is there some clue that I missed? Some precaution I could have taken?

Even with the benefit of hindsight, I do not know.

All I am certain of is this. As the day winds toward its tranquil close, it is as perfect as any day I have ever known. The sweet highland air, alive with cookouts and chimney smoke and the coming season's chill. Lawns so recently green, dusted now with the yellow and brown leaves of slumbering maples. The Rockies in the distance, capped by an early snow. And high above, a sky that soars beyond sight, a blue canopy brushstroked with gentle clouds and the passage of birds on a wing. It is a master's rendering: still life in the mountains.

Yet somewhere in this tableau, we can also be found. The six of us, friends paired off with friends, trading dreams and memories as if the demands of the city never again would intrude. Jeannie—my wife of fifteen years—stands at the barbecue grill with our friend Ray Stanford, whom I've known even longer, blackening the steaks for our dinner. Sara Stanford and I move about in the background, setting the picnic table as carefully as if it were a corner booth in a five-star hotel. And in the sprawling yard beyond us, our two girls practice their soccer skills, racing past each other with the infinite energy of youth, any thoughts of next week as distant as another planet. We are here. We are together. We are *alive*. That is all that matters.

For who knows when we will see each other again? Tomorrow, Jeannie and Cassie and I fly back to Los Angeles, bowing to the edicts of school and work. This is our fifth visit to Denver since Ray and Sara migrated here to the city's eastern edge, and like all of our trips it ends too soon.

Someday, we keep telling ourselves, we will move here too.

I overhear Ray making this pitch to Jeannie, as he always does when our sojourns draw to a close. It is a fruitless quest, and he knows it. Yet inevitably he tries. "Sure you can't stay the weekend?" he asks, his voice coming over the girls' whoops and shouts.

Jeannie glances at our ten-year-olds as they pass the soccer ball between them. Darby Stanford is gazelle-fast, the athlete of the two. Cassandra Fall is bookish and quiet, prettier than Darby but even less agile than on our last trip. Our parental pretense dismisses what we already know: her future does not lie on the athletic field.

But tonight, for one last time, they'll both be stars.

Jeannie smiles at Ray's question and nods toward me. "Ask Babbitt over there," she tells him. "He says he has to get back to the office."

"On a Saturday?"

She shrugs. She knows how hard I had to press Fran Amalfi to let me leave for this long.

"You'll be back up for the baby, won't you?" asks Ray.

"Sure. At least Cassie and I will be. Martin too, if he can get away."

Ray shakes his head, then returns his attention to the steaks. "Man works too hard," he mutters, peering back up at Jeannie. "You really ought to get out of that city while you can, Jean. That air can't be good for you. Or Cassie, for that matter."

"And where would we go?"

Ray spreads his arms wide. "Here. God's country. You'd be amazed what the mountain air can do for you." He offers a broad, self-effacing smile. "Look at me," he says. "I'm positively blooming."

I step over then, carrying a huge bowl of freshly mixed barbecue sauce. I hand the bowl to Jeannie to let her work her culinary magic on a sizzling rack of grilled chicken, then pat Ray's bulging belly with the back of my hand. "You're blooming, all right," I tell him, turning with mock warning to Jeannie. "Don't let him start. Last time he was sending us flyers for *weeks*. Remember?"

Without warning, the girls' soccer ball comes bounding over then, jarring the bowl from Jeannie's hands and sending barbecue sauce raining in all directions. I retrieve a wet cloth from the side of the grill and begin wiping the red sauce from her apron as the two girls race toward us, chasing after the ball.

"Hurry *up*, Daddy!" Darby calls to her father as she runs past. "We're gonna be late!"

Cassie trails behind her. "Yeah, hurry!" she jeers. "Darb's afraid she's gonna—"

I grab Cassie's arm as she sprints by, and she tries to pull away. "What do you say to your mother, Cassie?"

"Leggo! I'm winning!"

She squirms again, and I fake-struggle to hold her. She knows the game—we've played it so many times before—and smiles penitently at me. It's a prize-winning smile, one of the great treasures of my life. I dab her pixie nose with the end of the cloth I've been using to wipe off Jeannie's apron, leaving a bright red spot in its place. "We're almost ready. Go get washed up."

And that's when it happens.

"Martin, what's that?" Jeannie asks, looking up. I crane my head toward the sky just in time to see a black spot materializing above us.

That's odd, I think.

Slowly, the speck comes into focus. I realize that I'm watching a bird. A crow, maybe, or a sparrow. It flails earthward, dropping slowly, before flying a few yards more. Then it falls again, wildly thrashing its wings. Against what? The wind? There is no wind. Yet the bird stops each time, hanging there in midair, flapping its wings as if trying to balance itself on an invisible perch.

It succeeds only briefly before resuming its fall.

Poor thing.

Then its resistance gives way for good, and the bird plummets lifelessly into a bush at the far edge of the Stanfords' lawn.

"Oh, gross!" Darby calls out.

"Yeah," adds Cassie, darting forward. "Last one there has to eat it!"

"Stop it, girls," Ray says, halting them in their path. "Leave it alone. Now go get ready for dinner."

The girls slump away at Ray's command, denied the opportunity to inspect what must have been the most interesting mystery to cross their lives this entire week. They sit sullenly throughout dinner, nibbling at their food and barely speaking. But by the time we leave for the soccer field, their pouts have morphed back into glee. They pass the ride in devilish delight, speculating about the tiny creature's strange and unexpected fate. I have volunteered to drive Ray's van while he talks on his cell phone, and with the girls seated behind me I'm treated to their whole discussion.

Cassie is convinced that the bird was killed by a larger one. "Most probably a vulture," she professes.

But Darby insists it was murdered. "By some boy," she concludes. "He must have hit it with a stone or a stick or something."

This possibility moves the young minds into gear, and the girls proceed to demonstrate just how this dumb boy must have acted in his pursuit of the defenseless bird. Their performance grows louder with each rehearsal until Sara finally intervenes, suggesting that the bird might have eaten something poisonous or had a heart attack.

But the girls brush off the suggestion without a moment's thought. They take a vote between them. And in this, the dumb boy does not fare well. He is convicted of birdslaughter in the first degree.

▼

By the time we reach the soccer field, perched high on a mountainside bluff overlooking Denver, all of us have forgotten about birds, dead or living. Our minds are fixed on the contest ahead—a practice game for Darby's community soccer team. The coach has been kind enough to let Cassie play so that she would not have to sit alone on the sidelines. Jeannie had argued against it at first, worried that Cassie's debilitating asthma, like her own, would be aggravated by the thin mountain air. But Cassie's inhaler remained idle throughout a week of backyard scrimmages. That fact—abetted by Cassie's tears when her mother first told her she couldn't play—persuaded Jeannie to change her mind.

Now, as we find seats in the old wooden bleachers, we see that we have made the right choice. Parents, grandparents, siblings, and friends surround us—all beaming with the pride of possession. And there on the field, Cassie is as much the center of attention as the other girls. Had we kept her beside us on some frail and imagined precaution, no words would have smoothed the hurt.

It turns out we had little to worry about. For most of the first half, Cassie is more spectator than participant. She defers to her teammates, never taking her eyes off the racing, tireless, tumbling Darby.

Perhaps Cassie's natural shyness is taking over. Or perhaps she just doesn't want to make a mistake.

As the half nears its close, however, she has forgotten to be self-conscious. She runs along behind Darby, following in her friend's quick footsteps, trying with little luck to keep up. But on this grand evening the soccer gods are with her, and her form makes up for what she lacks in speed. A pass. A blocked shot. Another pass. Each perfectly executed. Even from the distance of the bleachers, we can see her glow. Moments later, when she passes to Darby for the score, it's all huzzahs and high fives, and she and Darby are the Pirate Twins again, out to conquer the world in twos.

But their conquest will have to wait. The referee has blown his whistle, bringing the first half to a close.

"Outstanding job," Ray pronounces between gulps of soda several minutes later. We're walking back from the concession truck, an old ice-cream wagon parked at the top of the hill behind the bleachers. "I still can't believe it. *Three* goals."

I take a bite of my hot dog, savoring its hickory taste against the crisp mountain air. "Yeah, I remember when Darby couldn't even *catch* the other girls. Too bad the rest of the team's got their feet stuck in concrete."

"Yeah, too bad," Ray says, pausing to light a cigarette before we head up. "And I hate to say it, Chief, but it looks like Cassie's moving in slow-mo too. Darby's beating her pants off."

I shrug aimlessly as we move on, but come to a quick stop again when my foot lands on a small mound that squishes softly beneath me before firming. I look down to see what it is, thinking it might be a fast food bag with the contents still inside, or some other discarded item.

But I'm wrong. It's a dead bird.

There's something odd about it, but in the moment I can't think what it might be. So I simply wipe my shoe across the grass to clean its sole and turn back to Ray. "What'd you say?"

"I said Darby's beating the pants off Cassie tonight."

He's right, of course, but there's no sense admitting it. "Cassie got her looks from her mother. She had to get something from me."

Ray smiles. "Maybe you shouldn't have been so generous."

We've reached the steep and rickety bleachers and I step aside. "Don't let an old man hold you up," I tell him.

His smile comes again, but broader now—all the sweeter because Ray knows I'm twice as fit as he is. He takes another gulp of his Coke and, with a flourish, charges up the steps. "I'll tell 'em you—"

Suddenly, he stops.

Grips the railing.

Pulls on the air as if he can't breathe.

He turns, and I see his face. There's a quick, anguished look of fright—the kind of look that men must wear when death, so long denied, finally steps through their door.

Then in an instant the look is gone, replaced with closed eyes and a deep gurgling cough.

"You okay, buddy?" I ask, catching up.

He stares at me for several seconds before saying anything. Then there's an answer, but it's not at all the sportive reply I'm used to.

"Must have gone down the wrong way," is all he says.

Less than thirty miles away, our future is being foretold in a way that I won't realize until long after it is too late. Had I known what was happening, I would have bundled all of us off in that moment. Abandoned our pleasant pursuits in the interest of safety and survival. Chosen another eternal course. I would have done anything but what I did. But I had no way of knowing what was about to happen.

Nor, it seems, did anyone else.

I was able to piece this much together third-hand, many days later. The information came from a man named Derek O'Brien, a friend of my work mate Mike Mesoto's. O'Brien—an engineer with the government's Storm Prediction Center—was working in Denver on the night of Cassie's soccer game. As Mike would later tell me, O'Brien was using his quarterly visit to Denver to ply his charms on a hard-to-get colleague named Nancy Caldwell. O'Brien, as he later admitted, was far more focused that night on the chemistry of human relationships than he was on the chemistry of the air.

It may not have been the wisest choice.

"Courtside seats to the Nuggets!" O'Brien entreats Caldwell, in Mike's retelling of the night's events. "You can't pass that up."

"Hmmm," comes Caldwell's reply. She pauses and sips her tea. "Is dinner included?"

"Sure. Your choice. Wherever you wanna go."

"Great! There's a restaurant in Paris I've been dying to try—"

Their repartee is interrupted by a third person, a scraggly-haired computer jockey named Augie. He sits as he always does in front of a bank of computer screens. "Hey, Nance," he calls over his shoulder. "You gotta see this."

"Later. I'm negotiating."

Augie rolls his chair over, slapping a computer printout in her hands. "Well, negotiate *this*. We're picking up instabilities all over the map."

This gets her attention. Augie rolls back to his workstation, and Caldwell and O'Brien step over behind him.

"O-2 saturation's down all along the Rockies. And as far south as Albuquerque. See?"

"Yes, I see it."

"The numbers have been bouncin' around all evening. Like I told you earlier. But now they're goin' haywire."

"Those numbers don't make sense," murmurs Caldwell, scanning the maps that glow on the banks of computer screens.

"They are what they are."

"Check the satellites."

"I *did* check 'em, sweetie. The numbers are readin' right. But the O-2 . . . Man, it's just gettin' zapped."

Caldwell and O'Brien stand in silence, studying the monitors, framed by a massive 3-D electronic US weather map on the wall behind them. The map's Mountain West region pulses with shimmering waves of yellow and red. The waves rhythmically billow and descend, like some baleful aurora.

"I've never seen anything like it," says Augie.

Caldwell shakes her head. "Neither have I." She turns to O'Brien. "Derek, check with Salt Lake. I want to know if they're seeing the same thing."

"On it." He turns to leave.

Caldwell looks back to Augie. "I don't like the looks of this."

Augie zooms the map closer until only Colorado is visible. The yellow and red waves roll relentlessly toward Denver.

"Well, whatever it is," he says, "it's headed straight toward us."

▼

When Ray and I return from the concession stand, our wives are waiting for their coffee, huddling in light autumn wraps like caterpillars snuggling in their cocoons. A chill has blown over the field, and I wish for their sakes that we had brought a blanket.

"This will help," I say to Jeannie, handing her the largest of the coffees, the cup I had intended for me. She takes it, but there's a rebuke in her eyes. "Sorry," I tell her, seeing the game has already resumed. "Long line." But her concern remains. "Something wrong?"

"The other girls ran right past Cassie."

"It's only a game, hon. Besides, she's—"

Jeannie crosses her arms, watching her daughter. "I think we should take her out."

"Take her out? Come on, Jeannie. She won't have another chance to play all year."

"Running around in this air isn't good for her, Martin." It's the same argument as before, and I start to protest. But there's a firm shake of her head: her no-appeals look.

Cassie doesn't know it yet, but she's made her last pass of the night.

"Okay," I say to Jeannie. "I'll tell the coach."

She relaxes. "Thanks."

I turn to go, but I've barely taken a step when I hear a loud thump off to the left. It sounds incongruously like a stray basketball bouncing down the bleachers. Then a woman screams nearby, and my head snaps toward the sound.

An old man lies crumpled on the bleacher steps, facedown. Blood trickles from his forehead.

I'm almost sure he isn't breathing.

As I watch, flickers of red and yellow wash over him like a scanning light. I glance up in search of the light's source, and I notice something I don't expect. Luminescent curtains of red and yellow are rapidly forming and disappearing across the vast expanse of the once-dusky sky.

It can't be the Northern Lights. Not this far south.

But I can't chase the thought. The fallen man needs help. I edge toward him, but another man—middle-aged and rotund—is there ahead of me. He bends over the older man, checking for a heartbeat. Then he's up again, kneeling and calling out. "Someone get—"

He stops. Begins to gasp. In fright? In shock? I can't tell. Then his hand goes to his chest, and I see the same look of terror that crossed Ray's face only moments before.

I have no idea what is going on. But I don't have time to think about it. Another gasp is coming from behind me, and not one of pain. It is one of maternal dread.

I can summon only a single image: *Cassie.*

My eyes instantly go to the soccer field, now shaded with the same flickering red and yellow glow that covered the man on the stairs. For the briefest second, I see Darby and Cassie in the glow's midst, chasing an opposing team member who races ahead with the ball. Our girls sprint after her, determined to catch her before she reaches the goal.

Then Cassie trips and falls. She quickly climbs back to her knees, but only for a second or two. Then, all in one slow motion, she stumbles. Falls. And then lies there, facedown on the night-cooled ground.

And without the faintest whisper, that is where she stays.

Not moving. Lifeless.

Just like the man on the stairs.

Somewhere amid the chaos, I turn to Ray. "Call an ambulance," I yell. But he is already reaching for his cell phone, rushing down the bleacher stairs so that he can hear above the rising buzz of the crowd.

In that same instant, I turn and rush toward the field. Bounding. Hurdling. Flying down the steps. I know this because, in later times, I will see the scene in my mind from the opposite side of the field, from above, from all angles. But through the lens of the present, I am not bounding or racing. I am drifting. Flailing. Struggling to reach my daughter. Pushing as if through something solid, able to penetrate only a few feet at a time. My mind wills me forward, but my body—a disembodied self, it seems—won't follow.

In real time, my travel surely consumes only seconds. But measured against the tortoise clocks of dreamtime, it takes me years to reach her.

I am not even aware that I look back at Jeannie in the course of this flight. But I must, because she is there in my later recollections. She is standing there, trying to pull away, trying to chase after me. But Sara is reaching after her.

Clawing after her. Unwilling to let her leave.

I do not understand why the wife of my best friend would be making such an imposition at a time like this, and only later will I come to that knowledge. For now, it is my last vision of Sara Stanford, and it is framed by a question mark.

Eventually, somehow, I make it onto the field and sprint toward Cassie. When I reach her, I turn her over, inspecting her eyes. They are dull. Empty. Unfocused. Like a plastic doll's.

I bend my ear to her mouth.

Nothing.

Somewhere over the silence of my numbing mind, voices intrude in desperate snatches.

"What's going on?"

"Where's my daughter?"

"Did somebody call an ambulance?"

But the voices only distract me, and I shut them out.

Cassie is still not breathing.

I rip away her jersey, the fabric tearing like a wet sheet of paper. Her tiny chest is exposed. Motionless. I try to remember the dance of artificial respiration, learned so many years ago from my days on the Force. The steps come back to me in rapid flashes. From a film. From a demonstration. From somewhere.

Pinch the nose. Tilt the head. Breathe.

I hope I'm remembering right.

But my own breaths come with a cough, and I have to turn away before trying again.

"Come on, Cassie! Come on—"

My plea is broken by a soft thud. I turn to see a middle-aged woman, white-faced with terror. She has tumbled down beside me, and is trying to crawl to some imagined safety. One hand plows at the earth. The other plows at her chest.

For a second her eyes bore in on mine. Her voice is a moan. A rumbling. The sound a person buried alive might make.

"Help me, please!" she calls out. "I— I can't—"

Beyond her, a few others collapse to the ground. Fighting for breath. Fighting back pain. But they can't concern me. Not now.

Just Cassie. I turn away and look back to my daughter. Breathe into her again.

She gasps, finally taking in air. Once. And then again.

It's a splinter of hope.

In the distance, a siren wails. It's low at first. Almost imperceptible. But for someone who is listening for it, it can only represent one thing.

Salvation.

The soccer coach is standing a few feet away, frantically funneling girls to their parents. I look up at him. "Where's it coming?"

He doesn't hear me, or doesn't understand.

More urgently: "Where's the ambulance going to come!"

Without looking up, he jabs his hand toward the parking lot high up behind the bleachers.

I breathe into Cassie again and am rewarded with more fragile coughs. Then I hoist her into my arms and race for the hill. The siren is closer now, only a block or two away. As I run, I desperately scan the field for Jeannie. I can't find her.

All I see are the people around me, deluged by this flooding sea of fear.

Choking. Running. Screaming. Lying on the ground.

Why?

I sprint past them. But I'm quickly stopped by another scream, this one coming from just off to my right.

The shriek of a terrified little girl.

Darby.

"Darby!" I call out. I reposition Cassie so that I can carry her in one arm, then hold out my hand to Darby. "Come on. We'll find your folks."

Where are Ray and Sara?

Darby clutches my hand, gripping it with the strength of terror. We run on, dodging parents and relatives streaming onto the field, detouring around others who have fallen.

"Hold on, honey," I say aloud, to both Cassie and Darby. But I'm not sure either one hears.

We're behind the bleachers now, and I see an emergency call box mounted on a rusted stand. Six, ten, a dozen people crowd around, as if the device were a totem. A rescue from this nightmare. Others lie on the ground. Not moving. Felled in their tracks.

Behind them, in a clearing where there are fewer people, another man lies. Fallen to the ground like the others, his cell phone dropped to his side. He looks straight at me as I rush past, peering out with hollow, lifeless eyes, as if his eyes could really see.

A tear drops to my cheek at the sight. Then another. I have to fight to keep from crying. The best I can do is to shield the view from Darby.

Ray Stanford deserved a better end than this.

What is going on? my mind blares. But I still don't know. I have no idea.

I feint toward Ray, but in the same instant I know that it's useless. Darby's cries seal the choice, turning me around, propelling me. Their shrillness is so piercing that they almost drown out the caw of the siren as the ambulance pulls into the parking lot up the hill. I carry Cassie up the concrete steps toward it, my throat starting to parch. Darby trails behind me, fighting to hold onto my hand. Screaming. Panting. Struggling for breaths of her own.

Two paramedics—overweight middle-aged men—leap out of the ambulance as we near the top. One meets me a few feet down the steps, reaching out for Cassie. "Did everyone decide to die at once!" he blurts out as he sweeps her away. "We've had fifty calls in the last five minutes."

"Just move it!"

"Right," he says blankly, scrambling back up the steps. The rear doors of the ambulance are already open, and he bundles Cassie in. Just then, I look around to see Jeannie reaching the top of the stairs— a small fragment of relief amid the deepening confusion. Her eyes are red with grief. She too is breathing in great heaving rasps.

"I couldn't get on the field!"

My own eyes brim with tears when she says it. I let go of Darby's hand and wrap my arms around Jeannie, my lips kissing her hair. I close my eyes for the briefest instant while I'm holding her, and then break away.

We'll have time for this later. Right now, we have to get out of here.

"It doesn't matter, sweetheart," I tell her. "Get in the—"

She nods toward Cassie. "Is she okay?"

"She's breathing. That's all I know."

The paramedics have finished loading Cassie into the back of the ambulance. They hook her up to the oxygen unit, then leap out, one calling to the other: "Let's go!"

Jeannie's breathing is more labored now. I catch the attendant's shirt back, nodding toward my wife. "Take her too."

"Sure. Get in, lady. We're out of here."

Jeannie's control vanishes then, and she bursts into tears. "Martin, Sara's—"

She can't finish. I nod, guessing with dreadful certainty what she must be trying to say. I can only motion toward the open doors. "Go ahead. We'll be right behind you."

I still have the keys to Ray's van, and I pull Darby toward it. "Come on, Darby," I tell her over coarse, heavy breaths. The van is just a few cars away, but it seems like forever. By the time I'm inside and have seated Darby beside me, the ambulance is already a block and a half ahead of us. But the vehicle's lights are strobing and the siren blaring, and the road to the parkway is a straight shot. It's easy to catch up.

Or it would be under normal circumstances. But now isn't normal. Several cars have crashed along the side of the road. A few are tipped almost straight up into the drainage culverts. Others are sprawled across the lanes. Ray's van isn't easy to maneuver in the best of times, and running this obstacle course, I fear, is beyond its capacity. More than once, the engine threatens to stall on a switchback, and the tires emit loud savage squeals with each spin. But through some grant of good fortune, we make it to the parkway.

The ambulance—with my wife and daughter inside—are only half a mile away.

I steal a glance at Darby. She sits there pressed beyond tears. Beyond all horrors that her tiny mind could imagine. I have never witnessed it in a person this young, but I know that she must be veering toward shock.

I wonder, for an instant, if she will make it through.

"Are you all right?" I ask, my eyes fixed on the road again.

Over anguished, rapid breaths she cries, "Where's my daddy?"

A long pause. "He . . . stayed back to help."

My mind goes back to Sara then as she must have looked, having fallen to her knees on the wooden bleachers. Her hand reaches out to Jeannie, who stands there. Not knowing what to do.

Get up, Sara. The ambulance is here. Come on.

And then I envision Ray, who must have finished his phone call before dropping to the ground, ignored by others lost in their own private hells.

Let's go, Ray. Grab Sara and pile in. I've got Darby.

I shouldn't think about this now, I tell myself. Can't think about it. Or I'll lose control too.

Up ahead, the ambulance speeds on.

"It *hurts*!" comes the tiny little voice from beside me. I look down to see Darby grabbing at her chest, her once full breaths now great empty gulps.

I notice finally that I too am starting to fight for air.

Dear God, what is going on?

"Hold on, Darby," I manage. "We're almost there."

Now, something even stranger happens. We have just passed a mangle of three or four vehicles crashed along the center divider when up ahead the ambulance has begun to slow. And then weave. And then—

"What the—"

I can't finish. My mind is riveted, trancelike, on the ambulance. It jerks back and forth across the three lanes like a wild whipsaw. A sports car roars past it, almost hitting it. But the ambulance doesn't react. *What's happening?* A steering failure? A blow-out? I can't see.

The ambulance continues to slow. Maybe forty, forty-five miles an hour now. But it's still swerving. There's no control. No pattern in its motion. It hasn't hit anything yet, but the luck doesn't last. The vehicle scrapes hard against the center divider, then lurches back across the parkway and veers toward a concrete abutment holding up the overpass.

I grip the wheel of the van, jerking from my trance just in time to brake. The skidding ambulance passes within feet of the front of the van, angling hard toward the abutment. I spin the van to the left, out of the ambulance's path, trying to slow. As the explosion of the vehicle's metal against concrete erupts from behind us, the brakes finally catch. The van skids, fishtailing this way and that, and for a moment I fear it's going to roll. But at last we stop, facing the wrong way down the parkway.

Disoriented, I look around. Try to get my bearings. Then the images around me become clear, and I race the van with the last of its power to the shoulder, gunning it until we're a few feet from the mass of steel that used to be the ambulance.

I'm gasping now, just like the fallen woman on the soccer field. Gasping as much from fright as from the lack of air. Beside me, Darby is moaning, a low turgid sound. She's motionless. Hardly breathing at all.

I lift her into my arms and barrel out the door, stumbling as I try to force back the jackhammer pain in my chest. As we step out of the van, the fluttering red and yellow lights from the darkening sky roll over us, bathing us in their funereal glow.

In seconds, we're at the ambulance. I peer into the front seat from the driver's side, and then instantly cover Darby's face. The driver's head is smashed into the steering wheel. Blood is everywhere, covered over by the stench of death.

There won't be any help here.

I pull away and carry Darby to the rear of the vehicle, mumbling an incoherent prayer that the other medic—and Jeannie and Cassie—have made it through the crash alive. I see at once that the force of the collision has jarred the back doors open. One door hangs limply in space, the other a few inches from its catch. I pull it the rest of the way open, but am not ready for what I see.

The medic and Jeannie are both slumped over, like puppets dropped in place by their master. They're not breathing. Not moving. Next to them, Cassie lies on the stretcher, the oxygen mask fallen away from her face.

In the background, the monitors hooked up to her register a steady, demonic hum.

The lines are all flat.

"Jeannie . . . Cassie . . ."

My body starts to shake. My mouth trembles. I'm falling apart now. I know it. But I refuse to believe this sight in front of me. I hurtle into the ambulance, carrying Darby with me. I prop her up in an open space on the floor and turn to Jeannie. Grasp wildly for her wrist. Feel for a pulse. Then I place my hand near her mouth, checking for breaths. But there is nothing.

Nothing at all.

"Please, God!"

I gasp again, choking wretchedly. Hardly able to breathe even the quickest breath. I turn my eyes to my dear Cassie. She lies there, in the awful repose of death, beyond even the help of angels. I bring my face next to hers. My lips kiss her forehead as tears stream down my cheeks like blood. I wail some piercing animal cry as my mind careens out of control. Over the edge.

I have no idea what to do.

At last, a sliver of reason returns. There may yet be hope. I reach for the oxygen mask that had slipped away from Cassie and place it back across her face. Cover her mouth. Its air rushes in, full of the promise of life.

But the oxygen only collects in the mask, unconsumed.

Please, Cassie. Breathe! I command her, as if the command alone were sufficient.

But it does no good. There is no life left to recapture.

She is gone.

The sobs come next. Loud. Heaving. Convulsing. My control slips further from me—

Darby.

The thought enters my mind unbidden. I look away from Cassie and peer down at Darby. The barest signs of life flicker in her eyes. But they too are ready to flee. I lift her limp body toward the air canisters, bending my ear to her mouth. Snippets of breath come, but wanly. Vanishing. *What do I do?*

There are no choices left.

I hesitate, but only for a moment. Then I do what I must. Automatically, robotically, I grab the oxygen mask that had been Cassie's and fix it over Darby's mouth and nose.

I can't even see her through my tears.

I spy another mask then, dangling uselessly from the bank of oxygen tanks. I pull it away and stretch it toward Jeannie. It's over her mouth and nose in an instant, hiding all of her face except for her eyes.

The eyes. They peer over the edge of the mask. Beseeching me. Pleading with me like Ray's.

But they are also lost. Empty. Far beyond life.

Just like his.

In the background, I hear the oxygen tank's monitor again. The tank is hooked up to Darby now, and the monitor beats out the sounds of her fractured breaths. Its sounds fill our tiny chamber like a kettle-drum, its beeps the clanging of cymbals.

But from Jeannie, there is only silence.

I pull the mask away from my beloved wife and breathe into her mouth, trying to administer the same magic that prolonged Cassie's life on the soccer field what seemed like eons ago. But from Jeannie, there is nothing. Only my own fading breaths.

"Breathe, Jeannie! *Please!*"

No response. I try once more, offering my life for hers. But I've nothing to trade. I can only stare at her, filled with an agonizing fright, struggling even to catch my own breaths.

The pain.

The press on my chest is an elephant's foot now. It bears down on me, the weight of a thousand beasts. But still the breaths won't come. There is nothing more I can give to my wife. Nothing more I can give to my daughter. Almost nothing more I can give even to myself.

Nothing.

And I don't even know why.

Good-bye, Jeannie. Good-bye, Cassie.

I do the only thing I can. I take the mask that would have been Jeannie's and strap it across my own mouth, gulping its burst of oxygen in huge, desperate swallows, praying for this nightmare to end.

I'm breathing quickly now. Gasping. But this time, the air flows in. My lungs fill. My breaths slow. My heart races, ready to explode.

In some lost moment, my hand reaches out to take Jeannie's. I pull it to my chest and hold it with all my strength in a hopeless wish to keep her with me. Then I find Darby's tear-stained face and press her head toward me. Listen to her still-frail breaths. Urge her back to life.

I look over at her. Her breaths are there: a miracle. Slowly, they become more measured.

Her color, back from the pale of death, is returning.

That's it, I say in silent thoughts. *Breathe, Darby. Just breathe.*

I lean back, holding Darby close to me as I gorge myself on the oxygen tank's precious bursts of life. But my mind is lost now to unimaginable fears. Confused and helpless. *Disbelieving.*

I'm not here. Not in this place.

This can't be real.

I'll wake up soon, I tell myself. I know it. I'll wake up in an hour or so, and reality will return. *Our* reality. We'll be sitting at the picnic table again. The six of us, friends paired off with friends, trading dreams and memories. Just as we were this afternoon. Living the life we were supposed to live. Talking. Eating. Laughing. Nothing changed. Nothing.

Nothing at all . . .

▼ ▼ ▼

We awake to a city of death. When we finally open our eyes, it is to horrific visions. Night terrors. Recollections of last, catastrophic minutes.

But we are the lucky ones. At least our eyes open.

In this city, on the morning after, half a million pairs of eyes do not.

For a moment, I am aware of none of this. I am concerned only about my sight. My eyes cannot focus. They have been sewn shut by endless tears from the night before. A hazy translucence is all that I can manage.

Have I gone blind?

The worry lingers as I try to force my eyelids apart. Gradually, and with much effort, light is permitted to enter. Bright light. The light of the sun. A beacon of salvation. From where I am reclining, I can see slivers of sky. It is brilliant beyond imagination. I don't think I've ever seen it this blue before. So calm. Even peaceful.

This vision, I will later realize, is the last instant of peace that I will feel for many months.

For the moment, the memories of last night are lost to me. Like one waking in the midst of a fractured dream, I don't know where I am. My only sensations are pedestrian ones. The sharp pain in my back. The tingling in my legs. The parched aching of my throat. I feel warmth beside me, accented by a dulcet rustling. Like tree leaves waving in a gentle spring breeze.

Or the sleeping breaths of a small child.

The warmth beside me begins to take form at the thought, and I turn my head. At first, a patch of tousled straw-colored hair is all that I see. It must be Cassie. My sweet Cassie, drinking the dreamy sleep of little girls. Daughter perched against Dad. What could be more perfect? Are we on another campout like those that our family has taken so many times in the past? Or on a backyard stargazing adventure that segued into morning because neither of us wanted to break the night's spell by heading inside?

Amazingly, this many minutes into waking, I do not know the answers to these questions. I still do not know where I am.

And then, all at once, the images from the night before begin to race toward me. Like the black pyroclastic stream rushing out from a vengeant volcano, they slam me back against whatever wall I'm leaning against. Slam me so hard that my head richters with a thousand cracks. There is no order, no sequence to this onslaught. Only rapid, malefic images, flashed for a microsecond before each is consumed by another.

The successive images begin to grow more vivid, each more brutal than the last. There are familiar faces. Familiar scenes. But they are all distorted in some macabre, Dalian treatment. I recognize them all, and yet I don't recognize any of them. Their broken, twisted form makes them seem so foreign. So unremembered.

So unreal.

But not for long. The memories cascade over me, and their meaning with them. My back stiffens. My body and legs arc with fire. My breaths accelerate—quick, machine-gun breaths, like those of a man gasping for air. Perspiration breaks out on my brow and slips down into my now wide-open eyes. Burning them. My arms, my whole body, starts shaking.

Jeannie! Cassie! I scream in my mind, not voicing the words. Not even able to.

No! No! No . . .

And then the tears come. Loud, heaving sobs, even worse than last night's, leaving me more breathless than before. The sobs are loud enough to wake the little girl beside me. I feel her small hand touch mine, and then she grips it. "Daddy! Are you okay?"

The words, the thin and frightened voice: they are a shot of morphine. I stop myself then. Force myself to calm. Damp down the pain as my breathing slows and deepens. The quaking slakes, and my sobs yield to teeth clenched so hard that I'm amazed my skull doesn't crack. I know now—with a certainty flayed of even a millisecond's hope—that this scared little child is not my own. She is not my precious Cassie. And I am not her father.

But I am all that she has. And she all that I have. For the memories have come back. In full force, and with complete clarity. Ray is gone. Sara is gone. Jeannie and Cassie are . . .

I can't even finish the thought.

"I'm all right, sweetie," *I say to Darby, although I'm not even sure my words are audible.* "I'll be all right." *A pause.* "We'll be all right."

She says nothing at this, but only grips my hand more tightly. I place my other hand on top of hers, and we sit there. Not moving. Not speaking. Finally, with great effort, I push aside thoughts of my own loss. Their departure's brief window lets me focus on Darby.

I wonder, in that instant, what she must be thinking. How this lost and anarchic world must seem to her. Are her fears and her pains as overwhelming as my own?

Or does she even know?

I expect her tears to come any second, but they do not. Her breaths remain steady. I feel no fear from her, only calm. I breathe it in, this calm of hers. Steel myself against the hysteria lurking just below the surface. Will myself toward the same graceful state.

I cannot believe that I am drawing strength from a ten-year-old.

But I know: her calm must be only imagined. Perhaps she doesn't remember. Not yet anyway. Or perhaps she has only slipped back into sleep.

Amid these thoughts, a fleeting rationality returns. I must be the strength. Not her. I can't let myself fall apart like that again. I tell it to myself. Command myself, really. I cannot do that again. I have a responsibility now.

A responsibility to this frail and beautiful child. The only person left from a glorious lost world I once knew.

A world that is now lost forever.

The silence goes on. Though I still have not looked into her eyes, I can see in my mind her moonglow smile, the memory of a smile shaded now with the tears that I know will arrive all too soon. My arm stretches across her shoulder as we sit awkwardly next to one another, two frightened souls in a world that never was intended to be. I feel an overwhelming need to press Darby close to me, but am reluctant to do so. That act alone might be enough to awaken her to the brutal reality that I wish I could keep hidden from her forever.

But they can no longer be held back, these memories from last night. I hear her tears finally come. They are hesitant gasps at first. Then a slow, streaming flood. She pushes closer to me, gripping my hand harder, as if the force of her grasp could help her resist all that has happened. I hesitate for but a second, and then I squeeze back. Assure her that someone is still here.

It is a commitment and a promise—our hands gripped together like this. And with this simple gesture, I know: there is now no turning back.

My left hand slips down her shoulder and presses against her arm, pulling her toward me. We sit uncomfortably for long minutes, she not able to speak because of her sobs, and me not knowing what to say.

Then at last—in the back of this vehicle that once held the lives of those I loved the most—we embrace. Like the father and daughter we once were in separate families, we have been joined together as one.

For now. For the future.

For as long as the heavens will allow.

CHAPTER 2

I am recalled to life by a conspiracy of time and circumstance. As the weeks have wound on, pain has yielded to anesthesia and anesthesia to boredom. I am still empty, hollowed out from within. But I am no longer immobilized by my grief. And so when the opportunity to leave presents itself, I am ready to take it.

I am ready to return to the living.

For the past ten months, my routine alone has sustained me. I rise into the inkwell blackness that colors our nights, an hour before the first rays of sunlight steal through the portals along the corridor. With my black-market pistol in hand—always in hand—I take the long and winding walk to the facilities. There, surrounded by anonymous others, I relieve myself of the cheap beer and medicine-tasting water consumed the evening before, then wash away the night's deposits of sweat and grime. There are no showers here, but I have a secret hoard of soap and washrags that I collected in strategic trades during the long months after the Catastrophe. They prove sufficient to the job of washing up.

At length, I return to the small compound that I share with Dagger Santos, a fellow refugee from the early post-Catastrophe days. A black ex-mechanic who now survives mainly by arbitrage, he hustles the streets at night and deals his take long before dawn to the immigrant merchants below. On most mornings, I awake to find him lying face-down on his cot, snoring loudly enough to wake the dogs.

He is an associate of convenience, nothing. And I for him. Nevertheless, I grant him the respect of silence as I dress, pulling on one of the now-ragged work shirts and pairs of overalls that I rescued from my house almost a year ago. Then it's a half hour's walk to the job site, where I arrive well before sunrise, ahead of the others so that I'm assured of work that day.

For as long as I can recall, our assignment has been to dig ditches for the new sewage network. Next month, we start laying the pipelines—corrugated steel monsters manufactured in China. It's a task more backbreaking than the digging. But with the Gold Coast's population still growing by a million a month, our work is the only break against pestilence. Or so we are told.

Still, like most of the work crew, I suffer the indignities of the harsh labor for purely selfish reasons. The extra ration coupons I earn are my graft. My mite of control. They are all I have to make sure that Darby Stanford is well taken care of.

After what happened—after they took her away from me—it's the least I can do.

By sundown, our work is finished. The night crew comes on, and I return to the compound. Dagger Santos is awake by then. If I've managed to smuggle some beers, we'll play a round of chess or argue over the imaginary NBA season that could have been. Then he is off for the anarchy of the streets, and I wish him well. One day, I know, I'll wake up to find that he didn't make it back.

Not that it matters. One day I won't be back either.

For me, that day comes sooner than I would have guessed. Because today I have a visitor, and she is asking me to go with her. If at first I resist, it's only because of the look that comes to her face when our eyes meet. It's a grim and unwanted reminder of what I once was.

And of the terribly long distance I have to go before I return.

▼

Here is how I imagine it must look when she finds me. She has made the uneasy journey from the entry gate, and now stands before the long climb of concrete stairs—the pathway to my home. She starts up, taking one slow step at a time. On either side of her passage, vagrants recline in their slumber, occupying their hard, sculptured seats as if they were thrones of fortune. The hopeful among them have their faces exposed, waiting for the warmth and promise of the new day's sun. The others wrap themselves tightly in discarded parkas and cheap plastic, hiding their tear-stained faces and praying for a break from the elements. For the winds blow cold at night, and savage rains often come with the dawn.

Life can be rough, even fatal, in the unprotected zones.

At last, my visitor reaches the top of the stairs. She stands there warily, her eyes a periscope, deciding which route to take. As she weighs her options, her throat begins to fill with the aura that envelops her, the medley of the masses, taken in as if it were oxygen itself. She tries to throw it off, but the foul medley remains, each chord distinct. The tang of weeks-old sweat. The stench of stale urine. The toxic clouds of flatulence. The decay of human lives. Intermingled, they are the aroma of the living, and those of us who live here accept it as the price of survival. We have had time in any case to grow accustomed to it, and the smell no longer affronts us. Only new arrivals and the occasional visitor seem to take note, and some react worse than others.

This woman falls somewhere in the middle. She doesn't come close to retching as so many do on their first encounter, but she finds each nauseous breath less tolerable than the last. The experience inspires a brief sacrilege.

She wishes, for an instant, that she weren't breathing at all.

But only for an instant. The woman—mid-twenties, cautious, determined—is the fount of practicality. She will do what needs to be done. Her name is Alison Leary. She is the assistant to the Council's director of operations, and she used to work for me. She also was a friend of mine, in the days when I risked having friends.

I'm sure she must be recalling those times. Given what she sees before her, it's all that could tip the balance in my favor. And so she chooses to continue. She traverses the wide concrete walkway that leads into my corridor, then enters the cavernous tributary a hundred or so paces down from the inlet where I live. Her eyes go immediately to the corridor's walls. To the ceiling. To the unseen ends. The corridor is huge—probably thirty feet up, at least that far across. But it's not the dimensions that startle her. It is what the corridor contains.

People.

Nothing but people, jammed four and five deep against the concrete walls.

Stretched out beyond sight in both directions.

She takes a moment to let her eyes focus in the predawn light that filters in from behind her. The visions assault her. A young Salvadoran woman holds a sleeping infant, aimlessly stroking its head. A group of three-year-olds play with toy cars and trucks, reliving a past of which they have only the palest recollections. A boy, not yet ten, sharpens a knife against a stone, preparing to face down men of ill intent who might cross the path of his younger sister. An elderly couple rest in each other's arms, forced to replay the life they've had together rather than plan for the years ahead.

These are only some of the hundreds who appear before her as she begins the long trek down the corridor. Singles. Broken families. Alliances of chance. In another time, they would be easy to categorize. The homeless. The city's destitute. The victims of poverty. Their possessions alone would mark them. Ragged mattresses and old lawn chairs. Fractured radios and receptionless TVs. Books with torn covers and shirts with torn collars. Shopping bags and grocery bags: the treasure chests of spent and discarded lives

These people *are* victims. She knows that much. But these are not the sepia-toned faces of the inner-city poor that watch her passage. They are the faces of the middle class. Faces of the American Dream gone bad. There is a residue of defiance in them, mixed in with shame and disbelief. *If we lived our lives as we were supposed to,* their expressions seem to ask, *then why are we here?* Some of the faces look up when she passes, their eyes seeking her favor. Perhaps their owners think that she is here to rescue them, that she is the messenger of hope they have been waiting for.

She chooses not to meet these glances, but stares at her feet instead. It is safer that way. And as a balm for her conscience, she is no doubt right. But averting her eyes has a cost. The shadows deepen the further she goes, and it's harder to see the obstacles in her way. She finds herself tripping over jutting legs. Stumbling into storage crates. Sending water jugs and ration cans crashing to the floor. Angry stares accost her in response.

"Sorry," she apologizes to no one in particular. "Excuse me. Sorry." But the apologies bring her no offers of assistance. And that is what she needs most.

She has no idea where she is.

Up ahead, sitting in the ruby glow of a gas lamp, an old, stubble-faced man winks his eyes open just long enough to take in her display of grace. A smoldering cigarette hangs from the corner of his mouth, dropping ashes on torn and faded khakis. He doesn't brush them away. Doesn't even stir.

His eyes are closed long before she can reach him.

"Pardon me, sir," she says, stepping delicately among bodies to shake the man awake. "Excuse me. I'm sorry to bother you." She thrusts an old photograph into his line of sight. "Do you know this man?"

He studies the picture without a trace of interest.

"Please. Have you seen him?"

"Dogs," is his laconic reply.

"Excuse me?"

"Dogs," the old man repeats. Then he shuts his eyes again to ward off further queries. A wan smile comes to his lips. "You'll see."

She doubts that she will. But then she spies a large alcove a few dozen yards down the corridor. She can just make out the curve of a large dog's snout pushing up against a chain-link fence, as if the beast were trying to smell its way to freedom.

Perhaps the old man isn't crazy after all.

She approaches the alcove. Gingerly at first, and then more boldly, pressed on by the certainty of conquest. Her destination. *At last.* The dogs are there, not just the one but two—fierce black Dobermans the size of small ponies. They're both at the fence, growling low guttural warnings and baring their teeth like switchblades.

She edges closer. Then peers through the fence, her sight aided by the light from an opening down the way. What she sees is a home, or the travesty of one. A wire is draped across the compound, host to several work shirts and overalls. A battery-powered bulb is suspended from the ceiling by an exposed and tangled cord. A washtub stands in the back, filled with brackish water. Provisions are scattered about, mixed with some books, a small gas stove, a battery-operated radio. In the back, a chessboard is set up on an orange crate, suspended in mid-game.

But what draws her interest most are the two men lying on their cots. One—the bigger of the two—lies on his stomach, snoring like a speedboat. The other, considerably more haggard than the last time they met, is on his back, staring at the ceiling with tired and empty eyes.

She steps toward the fence. "Martin?" she calls out in a stage whisper. "Martin Fall? Is that you?"

But she doesn't get to finish. The dogs, ever my faithful protectors, start barking like mad.

▼

I am not asleep when she arrives. I am not sure that I have slept during the night at all. But I must be lost in some fugue of self-revulsion, the kind that occupies so many of my mornings. For it is not until I hear the dogs' violent protests that I become aware of the woman's presence.

"Popeye! Sinbad! Shut up!" I snarl, rolling over to determine the source of their outburst. Obediently, the dogs fall to silence. I pull the thin blanket around me to cover my naked torso, then sit up on the edge of the cot. Though I've grown accustomed to the dim filtered light of the corridor, it still takes me a few seconds to recognize the person standing in front of me.

"Alison?" The words come out slurred over my morning palate, limned with confusion.

As I wait for her response, I am suddenly aware of how frayed my cot and blanket are. My face is unwashed and unshaven. My thinning hair is still dabbled with dust from the night before. I'm dressed in the clothes I sleep in: a worn and muddy pair of overalls, a sweat-stained undershirt, and a pair of work socks that are years past their prime.

How offensive—how hideous—must I look to her?

"Oh, Martin. You look terrible," she confirms. But there's no bitterness in her voice. No critique. Only sadness.

"Thanks," I tell her. *Thanks a lot.*

She recoups with the flicker of a smile, but it comes too late to hide her sorrow. "How are you?" she asks. "How have you been?"

What can I say? Nothing that isn't a lie. I just shrug. "What about you? How's life in the Palace?"

Are we really making casual conversation in this cesspool?

"It goes on," she answers. "We're doing the best we can."

"The best you can. Well, that's good news for all of us, I guess."

And now what? Does she expect me to invite her in for coffee and a Danish? Is she really this hardened?

I rub the sleep from my eyes and see at once that she isn't. It's the same Alison Leary that I know from before, still solicitous with concern. And still looking barely old enough to vote. The smattering of freckles around her big, innocent eyes. The petite childlike figure. The teased and mousy hair that looks as if it has been styled by the wind.

And the innocence, shrouding her in a veil of absolute trust. As if, even amid our disintegrating surroundings, the world still works as it should.

But today she looks uncomfortable. Even guilty. Perhaps she feels out of place standing there in her crisp navy blue suit, the silk sky-blue blouse, the two-hundred-dollar Givenchy scarf that Mike Mesoto and I bought for her birthday the month before the Catastrophe.

Or maybe it's just the shock of seeing the man that I've become.

But there's no sense being rude to Alison. I'm responsible for my being here. Not her.

"Give me a second," I say, less churlishly. I turn and grab a work shirt from the overhanging wire, slip it over my shoulders, and pull the overall straps on top of it. Then I step to the fence.

And suddenly it occurs to me that she may be bringing news of Darby. A tinge of panic wells up. "Why now?" I ask more urgently. "Why are you here?"

Her answer is not what I expect.

"Fran needs to see you," she says.

My relief comes as a loud mocking laugh. This request is so absurd that I don't care if I wake Dagger Santos from his sailor's dreams.

Fran Amalfi was my boss at the city's energy office, where I used to work, in the days when I still held a respectable job. I haven't spoken with her in almost a year. Why she would want to see me now, when she surely has so many other important matters to attend to, is beyond even my most fervid imagination.

And yet, when Alison tells me why, her visit suddenly makes sense. I am less surprised than I would have thought.

"She wants you to come back, Martin," Alison tells me.

I just stare at her for a moment. "She should have thought of that ten months ago."

"She *did* think about it. Mike and I both tried to get you back."

She has touched a nerve. Opened a subject I don't care to discuss. I close my eyes, the anguished memories flooding in. "I needed time, Alison."

"I know you did. And I also know that when you finally tried to come back, Erthein shut you down, said you were no longer any use to him."

A grunt. "Guess I'm still not, am I?"

She doesn't say anything to this. Neither do I.

"Come on, Martin," she protests. "I have to bring you to her. It's my job."

"Well that may be. But it's not mine. Not anymore."

"Don't do this to me. Please."

I don't know what to say. And so I just stand. In silence. Staring blankly.

Why is this so hard? It's what I want, what I've waited for. Isn't it? A way out of this place and all that it represents? All that it recalls?

Why do I resist?

Alison watches me, trying to decipher my reluctance as well. I see the hurt in her eyes. And the grief that's more than professional.

I don't need this. Not today. Not ever. I should just ask her to leave and set off on my morning routine.

But I don't. Something in her eyes tells me that her visit is a gift. One that I should not—*cannot*—refuse.

It may be the last chance I have.

I sigh in defeat.

"Okay," I tell her. "Just wait outside. I'll be there in a minute."

▼

We're standing in the corridor across from my compound shortly afterward. The first rays of daybreak are slipping in through a crack in the ceiling a few yards away. Which means the morning work crews have already started to gather. If I don't leave now, I may not receive an assignment. That means no ration coupons for the day, and nothing to barter at night.

But I stay anyway. And let Alison deliver her pitch.

"I couldn't do the job now," I tell her minutes later, after she's played out her best arguments. "I wouldn't be any use to Fran. Even if I tried."

"And what use are you here?"

"I keep out of the way. That's something."

She glares at me. "The noble martyr. Thanks for your help." But her anger won't hold. "I'm sorry," she says, shaking her head. "I didn't mean it that way."

Unfortunately, I know she's right. "Forget it."

"Won't you at least come talk with her?"

I shake my head again but say nothing.

"Just listen to what she has to say," Alison presses, sensing an opening. "If she's wrong—if you *don't* think you can help—you're back here in an hour. I'll bring you back myself."

A long sigh. I watch her, knowing I've already made my decision. And knowing it's the only one I *could* make. "I'm not promising anything."

"Of course not," she says. "It's still your choice. Absolutely. Your choice." She waits for a reaction, but there is none. And so she hurries on, like she always does, a cover for her nervousness. "So here's the plan. I'll come back this afternoon, give you time to get ready. I'll meet you out front. Two o'clock okay?"

She turns to leave before I can tell her otherwise. But she has gone only a few steps when the question comes to me. I'm surprised I didn't ask it sooner. "How did you find me, Alison?" I never told anyone at the Council where I was.

She stops. Turns slowly. But her answer is rushed. "I asked the Children's Bureau. They told me where you were."

My frown is automatic. Even an allusion to Darby is an accusation. "I couldn't keep her."

"It wasn't your fault, Martin."

"Really? That's not what they said."

The words come back to me—haunting me—from the last time I saw Darby, on the first of a dozen fruitless visits to the sprawling government orphanage euphemistically called The Children's Bureau. Even a personal appeal from Fran Amalfi during those long weeks of waiting was not enough to return Darby to me.

"I just have a few questions for you," the antiseptic young man told me on that day as he prepared to lead me down the hall to warehouse of interrogation cubicles.

The questions seemed hostile, as if they were meant to deny.

Had I ever been charged with a sex crime?

Did I regularly spend time alone with children who were not my own?

Did I own a home with barred doors, a security system, and at least eight-foot-high exterior walls?

Was I fully employed with no risk of termination?

Had I cried or yelled at anyone in the past thirty days?

Was I on medication?

Should I be?

In the end, my answers proved unsatisfactory. My application for guardianship, which only an hour before had seemed a formality, was denied.

"You can file an appeal in twelve months," the young man told me as he steered me toward the exit. My protests turned to anger, but to no avail. "Do that and you'll only make matters worse for yourself," he scolded. "And for her. We have to protect the children. I'm sure you agree."

I look back at Alison then, forcing the dark memories away. There's a hesitation in her eyes now, as she has watched me these long seconds. I can tell she is wondering what I must have been thinking that could have turned my own expression so foul. And wondering how she should respond. Should she take what she's already won? Or gamble and risk losing it all?

But it's no longer business that drives her.

She steps closer and takes my hand. "Did I ever tell you how sorry I was?"

"I know, Alison," I answer. "I know."

She looks at me with her big, sad eyes. Then offers a hug that's less platonic than I'm sure she intended. "If it means anything," she says into my shoulder, "I still am."

▼

She's gone before I have a chance to reply. But I follow her exit just the same. First with my eyes. And then in my mind.

She trails back down the corridor, more sure-footed than before. When she reaches the exit stairway, she mounts it without looking back. Then she descends the narrow concrete stairs in a sluggish slump-shouldered gait, certain she has failed. She no longer allows the smells to insult her. Doesn't even look around. If she did, she would see the occupants of the hard, plastic seats peering up at the rising sun. Almost in wonder. As if the morning's amber rays were a revelation each time they arrived.

In a way, they are. Many of these people have not seen the glow of electric lights for nearly a year.

Soon she's at ground level, making her way through a sea of people, packed together on the artificial grass like a concert crowd that's stayed too long. They lie under sleeping bags. Under ragged blankets. Under old curtains and linings from packing crates. Whatever protection they can find.

Gradually, this ocean of souls gives way to rows of jury-rigged wooden stands that line the exit path like game booths at a run-down carnival. The owners—most of them Asians of uncertain ancestry—are already at work setting out their wares, trying to score a windfall profit before the competition is ready to deal. Some of them step out as Alison nears, brandishing their irresistible offerings. Rusted tin crosses and paperback mysteries with just a few pages missing. Week-old poultry only a day or two past rancid. Lottery tickets for a prize that will never be drawn. Bargains all, they assure her. At any price.

She turns them down, waving them off like a swarm of unfriendly bees. But the peddlers are not discouraged.

Soon there will be more than enough to take her place.

A few hurried steps more, and she is finally almost out of this foreign land, her failure left permanently behind. The exit gate looms ahead. In seconds she is through it and out into the streets. The peddlers, the sleepers, the malodorous masses have receded into a forgotten past. They can offend her no more.

It's just sunup, and already this has been a terrible day.

She stands there for a moment, in the shadow of a hundred-foot "A" girded by its ever-present halo. Collects her thoughts and prepares to return to her world—a world at once separate from and yet the biggest part of the one she has just left. As she steels herself for what lies ahead, she catches a glimpse of a red-lettered banner hanging from the high wall behind her.

She must have missed it on her way in.

"Voluntary Resettlement Area 14. Los Angeles Division. Western Orange County Sector," it reads. She shakes her head, numbed by the recollection. It couldn't have been too long ago that this place was known by a far more inviting name.

The Stadium at Anaheim, it was called.

Home of the Angels.

▼ ▼ ▼

The phone systems, like much of the rest of the city that used to be Denver, are dead. The complex switching systems and networks of cell towers have finally ceased to function. They were overloaded last night by useless frantic calls, and have now been abandoned by the technicians who once maintained them. I try random numbers on my cell phone every half hour, but am greeted only by quick foghorn blasts followed by thunderous silence.

The response is the same on the landlines and pay phones I have tried.

But the van's radio is working, and so I spend several hours listening to it while Darby sleeps in the seat behind me. I realize what I am doing with this pedestrian routine. I am simply trying to bring myself back to some sense of reality.

Or at least to narcotize my pain.

Darby and I had spent the rest of the night near the oxygen tanks in the back of the ambulance, praying that our supplies would last until morning. I awoke just before dawn to a terrifying discovery. In my tortured sleep, I had somehow ripped off my oxygen mask. But after a few fevered breaths, I realized that its magic potion was no longer needed. The air outside was once again as breathable as it had been in that distant world long before last night.

Nevertheless, I decided it best to submit to caution. And so Darby and I remained in the rear of the ambulance, masks firmly affixed and oxygen flowing.

Until morning came.

Now we have moved to the van, and she lies propped against my rolled-up jacket in the backseat, covered by a wool blanket that I found in the ambulance's storage compartment. We are parked once again on the freeway, directly in front of the ambulance, having just returned from a short and fruitless drive during which I searched for a working phone. We are fortunate in one respect, however. Although the van was apparently scraped by a couple of careening cars during the night, it is otherwise unmolested. And the gasoline tank still registers full.

It's some small measure of encouragement. At least Darby and I will be able to depart the city without problem.

Whenever our time arrives.

That time may be further away than we would like. The local radio stations report that the roads out of Denver are jammed, all but impassable. The National Guard has been called in to begin clearing the congestion but *won't reach the city until late afternoon at the earliest. Public conveyances are also no longer an option. The Denver and Colorado Springs airports have been closed until further notice, and the intercity bus lines have been shut down. Now that the initial terror has passed, people are being urged to remain in their homes and off the streets—at least until the government has assessed the damage and put new security procedures in place.*

This information is delivered to frightened and anxious listeners by reporters who are clearly trying to contain the fear in their own voices. Many of these journalists, it seems, are unused to speaking on the air.

And none are used to covering tragedies of this magnitude.

The only voice of authority appears to be that of the state's lieutenant governor, who had been in Miami for a transportation safety conference when the tragedy began. Now he is en route to an undisclosed location, well outside the state.

Meanwhile, nothing has been heard from the governor. The leaders of the state legislature. The mayors of Denver and Colorado Springs. There are rumors that they were among the million-plus Coloradans who died last night.

But the rumors—like so much else on this morning after—remain unconfirmed.

National news reports add little clarity or hope. The President has spoken to the country twice, declaring a national state of emergency and dispatching military troops to the affected areas. He has urged listeners to avoid panicking, emphasizing that calls for martial law and the invocation of the National Emergency Broadcast System have been rejected.

For now.

But his appeals for calm are belied by the quaver that an attentive listener can hear in his voice. And by the hushed reports that the President and his staff already have relocated themselves to the secure bunker far beneath the White House. Facing similar calamity, world leaders join the American president in choreographed calls for patience—even as they too flee for the personal safety of their seaside resorts.

Dispatches are also beginning to filter in from throughout the country and from around the world, and they are as uniformly grim as those from nearby.

We learn what we would expect: Denver was not the only city hit by the atmospheric catastrophe. Salt Lake City, Albuquerque, Reno, El Paso, and other US cities above 4,000 feet in altitude were equally devastated. Santa

Fe, New Mexico; Mammoth Lakes, California; and Aspen, Colorado, were rendered almost lifeless.

Indeed, if there is any positive news amid this horror, it is only that the residents of cities below 3,000 feet appear to have been spared.

Overseas, the civil infrastructure has broken down in many developing countries, preventing the outflow of official news. But images transmitted by cell and satellite phones from Mexico City, Lima, and the mountainous Chinese provinces show streets littered with uncounted masses of the dead.

Twelve million deceased in the United States, 80 to 120 million worldwide: these are the numbers most frequently heard. But they are nothing more than guesses.

Concerning the questions that loom above all others—what happened, why, and whether it will happen again—there are no answers. Commentators offer predictable speculations, ranging from global warming to freak superstorms to the revenge of an angry God.

But the truth is that no one knows anything.

I listen for a few minutes more, the words gradually fading into meaninglessness. I finally turn off the radio and sit in the last unfettered silence that I will experience for some time.

Even the most tragic of catastrophes can numb the mind and spirit into anesthesia, and I need to remain alert.

In any event, I have more urgent matters to attend to. A rustling from the backseat tells me that Darby is beginning to awake, and that means I cannot delay the inevitable any longer.

It's time to move on.

CHAPTER 3

I think Alison is surprised when I'm standing outside the stadium to meet her later that afternoon. I'm surprised too, but for a different reason. She arrives in an automobile, something I haven't seen this close up in a long time. I thought they were permitted only for emergency situations and visiting dignitaries.

I can't imagine that either description applies to me.

The car is a Cubic, a tiny box-shaped import designed more for profit than comfort. It's a sparkling azure blue, its only embellishment the emblem stenciled on either door. A pair of stylized hands—one white, one black—clasped together atop the scales of justice. This is the seal of the Los Angeles Citizens Council, the new governing body for Los Angeles and the surrounding counties. It is where Alison works. And where I would be working too if I had stayed on.

As the car slows to a stop, I climb inside. Alison gives me a long and probing glance, and I realize that I must be failing inspection again. Even cleaned up, I look little better than a vagrant.

"See, you're back to normal already," she says after a moment, and I'm grateful for her lie. This time, at least, I tried to look decent.

"I'm glad you think so," I say as she sends the Cubic sputtering from the curb. It's an odd feeling, being transported again by some force other than my own. "How'd you manage this? I thought they'd been outlawed."

A conspiratorial grin. "They have been. For most people."

"You must be pretty important."

She laughs. "Not me. *You*. I wouldn't qualify for a skateboard."

She's silent for a moment and lets the comment settle in. I can tell that she's still nervous in my presence. But it doesn't take her long to start talking again, in the breathless run-on cadence normally reserved for new loves and moments of sheer terror. "Everything's changed since you were there," she rushes on. "You wouldn't believe it. The whole city looks up to Fran like she's some sort of god. I mean, here she is, a year ago, not even a third-rate bureaucrat in a city office no one had ever heard of. Now she runs the place. Not just the office. The whole city. And Erthein's gotten to be such a pain in the you-know-what. I mean, he was always that way. But now he's got the title to go with it. And Rooker, well, he just strolls around like—"

She stops as she catches me eyeing the gas gauge. "Oh, don't worry," she quickly adds. "It uses hydrogen." A beat, and then the grin again. "Even Fran wouldn't push her luck that far."

Knowing Fran Amalfi as well as I do, I'm not so sure. But that's not my concern right now. I'm here with Alison, chatting with an ease that I'd almost forgotten. In this moment I feel almost human again.

It's good to know it's still possible.

"So why does she want to see me?" I ask at length.

The nervousness returns, this time washed over with a wave of tension. "You'll see."

"Problems?"

"I'd rather let Fran tell you about it, if that's okay."

I watch her, scanning for a hint. "Things *haven't* changed, have they?"

A pause, then a poorly hidden look of defeat. "Look where you've been living, Martin. All those people . . . Do you really need to ask?"

And it strikes me then in a way that it hasn't before. Things haven't changed. Not only inside the stadium, but on the outside too. The city—what I've seen of it—does seem to be locked in some grim stasis, like a patient on permanent life support. The same food wagons. The same ration coupons. The complete absence of what we used to call luxuries. And the absence of much else besides.

Even the millions of people who still have jobs and their own homes, I've heard in whispered rumors, have to scrap for food and medical supplies just like the rest of us who live on the streets or in fetid communes like the stadium.

"Those poor people . . . I figured by now—" I begin weakly, but don't finish the thought. Even as I speak, my mind is drawn back to the stream of government announcements in the weeks following the Catastrophe. The emergency declarations. The news and revelations from the atmospheric research labs that I preyed upon to keep my mind away from more personal losses. Yet even as I think back to those half-remembered days, my eyes go to the despondent neighborhoods that surround us, and I see in morbid clarity the stories the news reports didn't tell. This is the farthest I've been from the stadium in months, and it feels as if I'm looking at the city for the first time.

This isn't the Orange County that I knew in the years before.

Other than an occasional fire truck or food wagon, the streets are devoid of traffic. They are filled instead with trash and people. Along the sidewalks, families huddle in tents and cardboard shelters. Their hollowed-out eyes are set against soot-washed faces, their glances home to the same lost expressions that greet me every day in the stadium. The faces peer up as we pass, wondering at this odd engine in their midst. But then they see the Citizens Council seal on the vehicle's side, and they quickly look away.

After a year, I wonder, *is there still nothing the city can do to help them?*

The rows of stores behind them are just as desolate. What commerce remains along these streets has been reduced by shortages and government decree to islands of insufficiency. Most of the buildings are padlocked, their windows broken, their iron bars contorted into impassable shapes never intended by their makers. Stores without such protections were torched and looted long ago and have become little more than charcoal caves. At the few shops that are open—a liquor store, a thrift shop, a lottery agent, a government surplus store—the lines wind around the block. Their patrons, with little to trade but their last shreds of dignity, leave with bags almost as empty as when they entered.

It must be easier to shut down a country's production, I presume, than to find new ways of getting it going again.

I start to ask Alison about the long lines of people when another image steals my attention. Up ahead looms a video screen the size of a billboard, encircled by waves of ill-clothed people maneuvering for a better view. With the car's window shut, I can hear only echoes of sound. But the vision itself tells me all I need to know. An attractive Asian woman in a coral suit with matching pearls and earrings is reading from a teleprompter as maps of the city flash behind her, intermixed with images of the Citizens Council seal.

It's apparently time for the afternoon report.

"Those are new," I say as we drive past.

"They were Fran's idea," Alison answers with a frown. "Something to keep people's spirits—"

As she speaks, she is interrupted by the buzzing of her cell phone sitting in the cradle on the car's dashboard. She reaches over to turn on the speaker. "Hello?"

"Leary?" comes the voice across the phone. Even over the static, I recognize its owner. Mike Mesoto. The man who used to be my deputy. "Leary, is that you?"

"Hope so. Where are you, Mike?"

"The refinery over on Carson. Is our friend with you?"

A smile. "If you mean Martin, yes, he's right here."

I turn away. It has been longer than I care to recall since I've felt the warmth and friendship of this man I was once proud to call my best friend.

I wonder. When I see him, will I fail to measure up to him as well?

I can't look at Alison at this moment—can't let her look at me—so I fix my eyes outside. I see that we're leaving the county's residential streets and climbing up a northbound freeway on-ramp. It strikes me then that I have no idea where we are. I used to know every major freeway and surface street in Los Angeles—no small accomplishment for a metropolitan area the size of a small country—and now I can't remember a simple freeway entrance that I must have traveled dozens of times.

And then I realize something else: I can't even clearly recall the face of Mike Mesoto, whom I once saw almost every day of my life. His image comes to me only in fragments of features that never cohere. It's amazing how quickly a mind, burdened by impossible trauma, must learn to forget.

But it really doesn't matter. I'll see his face in person soon enough.

"Great," I hear Mesoto telling Alison as I turn back. "I'll see you out front."

"No, we're heading downtown," says Alison. "To see Fran."

"She can wait. You need to be here."

I start to cut in, but then hesitate. Now that the moment of contact is here, I wonder what hurdles time and circumstance have placed between me and this man. But I brush the concerns away. I've nothing more to lose.

"Mike," I say, leaning into the phone. "This is Fall—"

The coarse and cheerless voice is suddenly alive. "Hey, *compadre*! I'd given you up for dead. How are you?"

The emotion in his greeting is genuine and welcome. "Good question," I answer honestly. "I wish I knew. Listen, having to deal with Fran will be unpleasant enough. Worse if we're late. We'd better head downtown first and see what's up."

A pause. "*I'm* what's up," says Mesoto.

"What's that?"

"*I'm* the reason Amalfi called you in. I told her I needed you."

That figures. I didn't think it would have been Fran's idea. "At least she's started listening to you."

"Not in a million years, my friend. Not in a million years." A pause. "Anyway, you need to be here, *novato*. You'll definitely want to see this before you talk with her."

"Okay. If you say so." I turn to Alison. "Change of plans, I guess."

"All right, Mike," she says into the phone. "We'll see you there."

She turns the phone's speaker off, and I look outside again. I see that we've been driving on the northbound freeway, headed downtown. I'm scouting for an exit so that we can make our way onto the southbound lanes when I feel the car begin to slow. I look over to see that Alison is making a U-turn in the middle of the sixteen-lane thoroughfare. In seconds she's headed south, going the wrong direction against traffic.

Or she would be, if there were any traffic.

"It's quicker this way," she says.

I shake my head, smiling. Same old Alison.

But there's another feeling mixed in with this one. A feeling that lasts for a few seconds before the past takes hold again.

It's good to be back again.

▼

Minutes later, we're riding west on the 405, about fifteen minutes from Carson, and the layout of Los Angeles is starting to come back to me. But it's surreal—*un*real—like a movie set abandoned after a long-forgotten filming or a new house before anyone has moved in. We've passed a half dozen buses, a National Guard convoy, a couple of police cars. And that's all. I can remember driving this stretch of road late at night, when it was jammed worse than most freeways are during rush hour. Or *were*, I should say.

These days, the only rush hours take place on other continents.

But I see that there's been some consolation from our collapse. The yellow haze that for years covered the Los Angeles Basin like a funeral shroud has finally lifted, replaced by an endless blue dome as bright as the time before man. It's hard to believe we're in a city that, by last count, has grown to 80 million people. In fact, from the berth of this deserted freeway, the only signs of life are the inevitable drone squadrons gliding just above the horizon. And, much nearer, a black billow of smoke filling a corner of the sky a few miles ahead.

"What's that?" I ask Alison, nodding toward the smoke.

"It's where we're going."

"The refinery? Why all the smoke?"

"That's Mike's surprise. You'll see when we get there."

But instead of heading on, she guides the Cubic off the freeway and onto the tarmac of an isolated service station at the base of the exit ramp. The grounds are hardly promising. Abandoned cars, vandalized and stripped for trade. Gas pumps lying prostrate on their service islands. An empty Coke machine, its jimmied face swinging back and forth in the wind. The waiting-room window shattered and ground into dust.

"Looks like they're closed," I offer, wondering why we are here.

"Looks like it."

She reaches behind her seat then and hands me a large cardboard box. I open it. There's a gray suit inside. A white shirt. A striped tie. Shoes and socks.

She glances across for approval. "I thought you might like to change," she says, "before you saw Mike again."

▼

I retreat to the back room of this desolate building that used to be a service station. The inside restroom is so foul and desecrated—and its stench so oppressive—that I cannot even step through its door. So I decide to change clothes in the stockroom.

It doesn't really matter. No one is going to be stopping by for gasoline.

As I begin to remove the frayed and faded clothes that I wore from the stadium, I am taken back to another time almost a year ago when I entered the back room of another gas station, much cleaner and more well-kept than this one. That station's back room was a small apartment, not a stockroom, and it was filled with so much pain and grief that I can barely summon its image without tears coming to my eyes. Darby was with me then, and Pepper, and at least some small measure of hope. It was there, right outside that room, that I met Dagger Santos. The awareness instantly comes clear, as it has so many times since then. Were it not for that man's intervention, neither Darby nor I would be alive today, much less in Los Angeles. It is one small, saving grace that I have to be thankful for.

But I also know this. If I make the choice that now lies before me—if I return to this life that I once had—it is unlikely that Santos's and my paths will ever cross again.

I stop at this thought, and cease buttoning the freshly pressed white shirt that Alison has brought me. I almost give up the game in that instant, almost decide to return to the stadium and to the harsh but predictable life that is all I have known for the past ten months. And that is precisely what makes a return to the stadium so enticing. Hard as that life has been, in the stadium I've had nothing left to lose. Here, on the outside, the risks are far greater. Even the few entanglements I have already invited—Alison, Mike Mesoto, my renewed thoughts of Darby—loom with costs so personal and so great that I wonder if I can even accept them.

But in this brief space of contemplation—in which returning to the stadium suddenly seems the better option—a vision from the previous week comes to me. Overwhelms me, really. Consumes me. I stand there shaking for a moment at the thought.

In the end, the vision proves enough to force me to go on.

This is how I experienced the incident the week before, the vision that arrested me then and that remains with me now. It was a cloudy, sunless morning, and our work crew was standing in the midst of a garbage dump, stretching out endlessly in every direction, several city blocks wide. A lumbering crane was lifting a huge drainage pipe overhead while colorless, fungible workers like myself roamed about, clearing away the human detritus that routinely infected such foul refuges. Squatters. Treasure-seekers. Lost and broken families who had set up tents among the rubble, hoping that the squalor itself would ward off those who might seek to molest them.

The crane turned and rolled forward, unrelenting and unforgiving, yielding nothing to those in its way. One of the work crew had tried to persuade an immigrant family to flee their ripped and tattered tent, but the family was recalcitrant, unmoving. The crane rolled on, the tent in its footpath. At the last instant, the tent's occupants fled, wailing harsh curses in some foreign tongue that I did not recognize. The crane was undeterred. Its awful treads pushed on, grounding the immigrants' leavings in the dust. The tent. A cook stove. A plastic doll. The shards of a surrogate life.

All crushed.

And now indistinguishable from the blanket of garbage below.

Several yards away, on a promontory of rancid waste, two workmen stood watching, clothed in protective orange suits and gas masks to guard against the fell surroundings. It wasn't for the workers personally that these precautions were taken, of course. With sixty million people unemployed in the Los Angeles area alone, human inventory was expendable, easy to replace. But if these workmen were to take ill en masse while on the job, most of a day's work could be lost. In a city now ruled by the artifice of efficiency, such an outcome was unacceptable, one to be avoided at all costs.

The orange-suited workmen thus waited, safe from the waste's toxic fumes. They were positioned on either side of a ten-foot-wide pipe that had already been welded into place, just above the garbage line. The workers signaled the crane's driver, who began carefully lowering the suspended pipe into alignment with the one on the ground. As the new pipe descended, I joined several other workers below the descending pipe, ready to perform the fine adjustments that would allow this metal hulk to slip seamlessly into its companion.

Presently, the task was before us, the new pipe only feet away from its destination. And that's when I saw it, peering out from the pipe on the ground. A small face, that of a young boy, not more than three or four years old.

"Hold it!" I yelled across to the man who was directing the crane's operator. In seconds, the new pipe jerked to a halt, swaying from its chains twenty feet above us.

I climbed up the walls of garbage, angling up the incline for surer footing, and finally reached the lip of the pipe that was already in place. Once there, I could see that it was not just the boy inhabiting the shadowed pipe, but an entire family. Probably more than a dozen people. Their dark faces marked them: immigrants from the south, no doubt. They backed away as I approached them, moving more deeply into the cavernous pipe. Children and adults alike huddled uselessly behind pieces of cardboard and scraps of metal, hoping that these unexpected intruders would quickly disappear and leave them be.

"You've got to get out," I called out to the pipe's occupants.

From the chattering that emerged in the silence, I could tell that English was not their language. But neither was their chatter in the dialect of fear. They murmured with defiance, only retreating further into the pipe's endless blackness.

I looked behind me then to see that our work crew's foreman—a towering, grease-stained trucker sucking on a foul cigar—had climbed up to the rim of the stationary pipe. "What's the problem?" he demanded. Then he too eyed the family that had backed away, almost beyond sight, into the belly of the pipe. He was instantly furious. But the furor was directed at me and not them. "Get out!" he snarled at me. "*Now!*"

I hesitated, looking back at the slivers of fright that now streaked the faces of these lost souls within the pipe. But I had no time to think. The foreman reached his bulky arm up into the pipe. Grasped my wrist. Then pulled me out of the pipe in one violent move. Were it not for my reflexive quickness, I would have fallen facedown into the garbage mound below.

"Hose 'em!" the foreman barked to a group of nearby workmen. "*¡Andale!*"

I could do nothing now but look on, bearing the weight of the foreman's harsh and punitive stare, as three workmen hoisted a huge fire hose toward the pipe. They aimed the hose down the pipe's center. Then they signaled to a fellow worker, who spun the wheel that regulated the water flow. In an instant, a fierce blast of sewage water filled the pipe, echoing off the metal like a dying beast. Assaulted by the fierce stream, the pipe's residents staggered blindly forward toward the mist-covered daylight. As they neared the pipe's end, workmen reached in, ripping the squatters from their footing and throwing them mercilessly onto the garbage heaps below.

The foreman looked on, his expression one of efficient satisfaction. Success had been achieved, and our work could proceed. With the pipe on the ground now cleared of its debris, the crane began once again to lower the new pipe in place.

I could not bear to watch, could only look away.

In anger. In sympathy. And in shame.

This can't go on, I told myself, with no idea how I might ever make it right.

As I close my eyes now, in the rear of this abandoned service station, the vision grips my throat, and it takes several seconds to cast it away. But I am finally recalled to the present. When I open my eyes again, the garbage dump is gone. The squatters' frightened faces are gone. The work crews are gone. Only the revulsion remains, and it is half a memory, like a receding headache or yesterday's bad news. I am back in a foul-smelling stockroom, half-dressed and taking far too long. But a commitment—some inchoate sense of purpose—has taken root in me that was not there before.

It is enough to shake me from my torpor. And I return, methodically, to buttoning my new white shirt.

▼

Soon I am in the car again, seated uncomfortably next to Alison. Even by the time we reach the refinery, I haven't adjusted to the suit. I used to dress like this every day. But now the clothes feel bulky and unnatural, like a second skin or the armored vest that I wore in the years when I was a street cop. I'm amazed the suit even fits. I've lost twenty or thirty pounds in the past year, but the work on the digging crew has padded the muscles of my arms and chest to the point that nothing but the baggy work shirts slip past my shoulders. Alison must be a good judge of clothes.

But not of temperature. It feels like a cauldron in here, and I start to ask her to turn down the car's thermostat when I realize the heat is outside, surrounding us. We've pulled into a parking lot that overlooks the refinery, and I can see clearly what, from the freeway, I had to imagine.

The refinery, squatting a couple of hundred yards away, is a monster of a complex. Its pipes and pumps are joined in such a jumble that even the architect must have forgotten what was connected to what. But today, it's harder than usual to make sense of the structure. For the complex is covered over by great rolling clouds of smoke rushing out from its core, and hidden by mountains of flames shooting toward the sky. In the cacophony of fire and sirens, the firefighters' commands are lost. And so are their hopes.

This, I gather, must be Mike Mesoto's surprise.

Alison pulls the Cubic beside a battered van that, like her vehicle, bears the official seal of the Los Angeles Citizens Council. We climb out, and I'm standing on the pavement in time to see a man step around from behind the van. He's about my height and weight and looks as careworn as I feel. His drab sienna suit—thrift-shop couture to begin with—lies limply across his broad, pulled-back shoulders. He wears the same blue oxford shirts that he always chooses, turned a splotchy turquoise now by cheap powders and harsh bleaches. The loosened tie, a canvas of discordant colors, is even more the statement of a fashion agnostic. Only a bright chrome bracelet that he wears on his left wrist appears to have been acquired within the last ten years.

I think, as I look at him, that Alison should have dressed him as well.

But she couldn't have done much with his face. There's a hardness in his eyes that I don't remember, a callus over the memories of what he's seen. The hardness is all the more striking because, as Alison told me, this man has lived in protected housing the entire post-Catastrophe period, and so has suffered nowhere near the loss and deprivation that most of us have. Even his creased and pockmarked cheeks seem more etched than when I saw him last. The jowls droop a bit more. The hair is thinner.

Perhaps, I decide, I have been the fortunate one after all. At least the scenes I have witnessed inside the stadium have been the same from day to day. For this man, the world he inhabits has been endlessly tumbling downward in one long dark spiral, each new image a mockery of the last.

Then he approaches, and the hardness and wear slip away, dispatched by the luminescence of friendship. Mike Mesoto, director of operations for the Los Angeles Citizens Council, flicks his cigarette to the ground and comes up to greet me. His hand is outstretched, his crooked smile warm and welcoming.

"Hey, you haven't been livin' so bad," he says, his eyes taking in my new attire. He gives me a broad, warm *abrazo*, holding it for several seconds. Then he steps back, still gripping my shoulders. "Good to have you here, *compadre*. We've missed you."

He drops his arms then and nods toward the flames. "How do you like our little welcoming ceremony?"

"A small marching band would have sufficed."

The smile again. "Ah, at least the humor is back. That's good news." He steers me a few steps away, out of Alison's hearing. "Seriously, how are you doing, my friend? I feared the worst when you disappeared. Tried to find you for weeks, but no luck. I'd hoped you'd pull through. I knew you would." A beat. "Are things any better for you now?"

"Yeah, some days are," I tell him, after a moment. "Some aren't. I guess this is one of the better ones."

"That's good. Get out of that stadium, so Alison tells me, it'd turn anyone's day around." He eyes me sympathetically. "Well, you look healthy, anyway."

"I look terrible and you know it, Kemo. But thanks for the thought."

I'm watching him, glad to be looking at this rugged face again. But we've talked around the edges long enough and there are no more words to say that don't lead closer to the past than I want to go.

Time to get down to business, if that's what I'm here for.

I turn toward the flames. "Calimex never was very good at handling this stuff, were they?"

"Today isn't one of *their* better days, if that's what you mean," Mesoto says. "But the oil companies won't take the blame for this one."

"Why not?"

"This puppy was set."

"Set? Really?" Have conditions descended so low, I wonder, that people are cutting off their own lifeline? The only source of fuel for the food, medical supplies, and the few other amenities that companies are allowed to produce? I look askance at Mike "How do you know it was set?"

"Call it a hunch," he says drily. "This is the fifth storage tank that's blown since August."

"A pretty good hunch, then. Bad timing for you, though."

He grunts. "Tell me about it. I go to bed every night wishing you still had this job."

"I don't."

"No, well . . . This doesn't look very good for the director of operations, you know what I mean? Just another dumb Chicano who can't do his job, that's what they say."

I think about what I've just learned, trying without success to come up with a better alternative. "You're sure it's not an accident?"

But Mesoto has already turned away. He stands with his back to me, watching the demolition across from us in bitter silence, his body silhouetted by the war-dancing flames. He lights another cigarette—one of few ecologically safe brands, I presume, that people are still allowed to smoke.

As he takes his first puff, the refinery coughs up a new explosion from deep within, sending great swells of smoke tumbling skyward and firefighters rushing for cover. In the seconds it takes for the jolt to reach us, the shock waves spread throughout the building. A charred bank of pipes on the refinery's far wall recoils, stalls for an instant, then springs back. But its rusted braces won't hold, and the pipes start to slant away again, then fall in a slow graceful arc to the asphalt below. They land in an eruption of thunder and ashes.

And I'm thinking: *It's a wonder the whole block isn't on fire.*

"What did you ask a moment ago?" Mesoto says after the din has subsided.

"I said, what about accidents? They happen sometimes."

"Sure they do," Mesoto grumbles, his back still toward me. "Accidents, they happen all the time these days. Especially when some *pendejo* leaves a trail of nitro lying around."

He takes a long pull on his cigarette, then turns back to face me, the flames of the explosion still burning in his wearied eyes. "Someone is blowing up fuel tanks, novato. On purpose. *That's* why Fran wants to see you."

He motions toward his van. "Come on, my friend. Show's over. It's time to earn your keep."

▼ ▼ ▼

My first task on the morning after is to attend to the morbid protocols of the burial arrangements. In normal times, were a spouse or a child to die, one would hold long and somber meetings with unctuous funeral directors, planning the burial ceremonies with all the delicacy of a contract negotiation. What color casket would you like? Wood or metal casing? Silk or rayon lining? What about the headstone—will it be a single or double? Would you like our premium maintenance package, with fresh flowers ten times a year?

When I buried my father several years ago, I became convinced that questions like these were meant to allow the bereaved to purchase some small recompense from their grief and guilt more than they were to help ensure the dignity of the deceased. Jeannie and I weren't offered that many decorator choices when we bought our new home. My father loved football, almost never missed a game. I could imagine him calling from wherever the dead go, urging me to sign up for the Mega Sports Burial Plan, complete with an in-casket flat screen TV and 100 channels of cable.

But there will be no luxury burial plans today, no funeral directors we can summon to dress the bodies. The few local morticians who survived the night surely would have been pressed into service already, pulled in countless agonizing directions by desperate families seeking their help. Other funeralists, less civic-minded or just afraid for their own lives, long ago would have joined the desperate on their trek out of the city.

Not that I could have contacted any of them even if I had wanted to. The phones still do not work, and I had not thought to inventory the local funeral homes before we left on our vacation.

And so I consider our options. It doesn't take long, for the options are few. I can leave the bodies to the cold anonymity of public disposal, or I can take them with me. If I do the latter, I will have to transport them in the van. There is no other choice, distressing as it may be. The ambulance no longer runs, and there are no trailers about that I could attach to the van even if I had the tools.

I close my eyes for a moment, contemplating the inescapable, eviscerated by the chore that I seem forced to choose. Jeannie. Cassie. Ray. Sara. They all deserved better than this, but it is all I can offer them. I was unable to do anything to help them last night. Providing them with a private if simple burial is the least I can do.

The decision made, I step out of the van's front seat, where I have been dazedly listening to the radio, and I open the passenger door behind me.

Darby lies in the backseat, stirring in her half-sleep, but her eyes are not yet open. I gently lift her into the front seat. She looks up at me then. Her eyes are tear-stained and red, but her face is otherwise expressionless.

I kiss her forehead and hold her close for a moment. Then I strap her into the seat and bundle the blanket around her, carefully positioning her so that she cannot see into the rear of the van. It is becoming chilly outside despite the bright noonday sun and the wind is starting to pick up, so I put on the jacket that had served as her pillow. The mere act of once again donning the leather jacket that I wore at the soccer game brings back a rush of memories. They stop me for a moment, and I lean rigidly against the side of the van, arms outstretched and choking back tears. At length and only with prayer and great effort, I am able to command the unwanted recollections to depart.

I cannot afford their distraction. I have work to do.

Closing Darby's door, I return to the rear of the ambulance, which remains parked directly behind us. I unlock the vehicle's battered doors that I had closed and secured the night before. Averting my eyes from Jeannie's and Cassie's lifeless bodies that now lie beneath white sheets, I check the vehicle's storage compartment. I am gratified, in some small macabre way, to find half a dozen body bags there.

They will be the final raiment for those I loved.

When I was younger, I served briefly as a field medic in the Army, and so I know the procedures. But I do not have the steel heart that I did in those days, and I break down repeatedly as I try to slip the bodies of my wife and daughter into the dark green bags. Somehow, I am able to complete the task, and stand in silence for a few moments before I move them. Then I carry their lifeless forms, one-by-one, into the back of the van.

I return to the ambulance and survey its rear chamber one last time, collecting supplies that might prove useful in some as yet unimagined future. The last two oxygen tanks. A few oxygen masks. A variety of medicines and instruments. Some rope and tape and other sundries. I place each of them on the floor in front of the van's rear seats. Then I climb into the van's driver's seat, willing myself to calm. I have a responsibility to Darby now, and it is an obligation for which I am deeply grateful. Floating in the pain of incomprehensible loss, that obligation is all that keeps me sane.

I am able to start the van again without difficulty, and we drive the few miles back to the soccer field. We must arrive on autopilot, for I cannot remember having guided the vehicle to this destination nor having witnessed the road or scenes along the way. When I finally return to awareness,

I have pulled the van into the soccer field's parking lot, and I quickly spin it around so that we are facing away from the body-littered field. Darby fell back to sleep on the ride here. But should she wake before we leave, I do not want her to see the place where, not too long ago, she and Cassie had raced through their own private heaven.

I turn off the van's engine and drop the keys into my pocket, then collect the body bags I will need for Ray and Sara. Sara is unexpectedly light, despite her pregnancy, as if her spirit had left nothing but a hollow shell when it departed. Ray is as heavy as I would have expected, but I hardly notice. My daily regimen of push-ups and heavy lifting has kept my arms and back strong. It is only my heart that is weak, and I desperately look away from my friends' faces as I slide their night-chilled bodies into their respective green bags.

There is some small relief. This time, at least, I complete the task without breaking down.

I carry their bodies back to the van and lay them, for a moment, on the nearby grass. Like a porter packing a trunk for a long trip, I carefully reposition the quartet of bags so that Ray's and Sara's are on the bottom and Jeannie's and Cassie's are on top. Then I climb into the front seat and mumble an incoherent plea for heavenly help—the closest to a prayer I can manage at this moment—before once more starting the engine.

In minutes, we are on the road again. The six of us—the living paired up with the living, the dead paired up with the dead—heading on in silence toward Ray and Sara's home.

CHAPTER 4

Mike and I are in the old Council van a few minutes later, heading north on Avalon Boulevard, with Alison trailing behind us in the Cubic. Mike is driving, since he knows the way, and has jammed a disk into the van's CD player to accent our trip. It's an obscure Latin instrumental with swaying sensual rhythms and machine-gun congas, which I normally would regard as annoying. But today I find I just want to sit back in the seat, absorb the music, and try to forget.

But the notion won't hold. I'm slipping back to the last time that I was in a van. Suddenly, my thoughts aren't of the music anymore.

I was afraid this peace was too good to last.

Then it's shattered completely by the booming interventions of my friend. "Get out of the way, people!" Mike Mesoto growls from somewhere in the present, blasting the vehicle's horn and hailing me back from my memories.

I look up to see that we've gone deeper into the city. The street ahead is awash in people—far more than I have seen gathered in one place since leaving the stadium. At the distant edge of our sight line, a crowd presses forward into a ragged semicircle. We draw closer, and the crowd resolves into its tattered constituents. I can see grime-faced spectators pushing past one another in constant flux, cheering and goading, angling to gain a view of some performance at the semicircle's center. I'm reminded of a scene I once saw in London's East End, with tourists sandwiched together around mimes and magicians plying their talents. I try to envision what cast of entertainment these beleaguered residents might find worth their time.

As I wonder, my eyes inevitably go to the children, as they always do these days. Barely waist-high to the crush of adults, they dart in and out of the congested forest of legs, playing hide-and-seek or trying to pick pockets, as if there were anything in these frayed and empty pockets left to steal. Their clothes are torn and dirty. Their hair unkempt. Their bodies unwashed. I have come to accept all of this. But what strikes me most are their delicate and brittle frames. These children are so thin they look like little matchstick kids running about. I can only imagine how hard it must be for their destitute parents to try to feed them. If they have any parents at all.

At least Darby—locked within the confines of The Children's Bureau—has three healthy meals a day.

Or so I'm told.

I cast the disturbing thoughts aside and scan the rest of the scene, looking for solace in this sea of desolation. Off to the right, a Council Medivac unit is set up under the fractured arches of an abandoned McDonald's. Harried paramedics distribute bandages and aspirin to the long and winding ranks of the ill and infirm—partly because this is all the government allows them to dispense, and partly because it is all they have. In the middle of the road, a band of squatters sit immovably in a circle of wind-whipped tents, lodging their own hopeless protest against Nature's having routed them from distant homes. Closer on, a group of preteen boys, their faces painted the color of human skulls, crouch behind discarded sofas in some sort of game, launching stones and shards of glass at each other, screeching and punching the air when they score a hit.

As I watch these images, I realize: these people live every day of their lives like this. Their paper freedom from cattle pens like the stadium notwithstanding, they are as isolated from the world that Mike and this van and my new suit of clothes represent as prisoners of conscience are in their own country. Indeed, I suspect that many of these people, consumed by the diurnal chores of navigating the anarchy that surrounds them, have stopped caring whether forces of order and authority even remain.

As if proving the point, almost no one looks up at the sound of Mesoto's horn as our van grinds to a halt before the gathering mob. So he blows the horn again, leaning on it, until the blast echoes off the walls of the crumbling apartment buildings that line the boulevard.

This time, he draws a rash of suspicious and angry stares, and two or three large stones thud hard against the van's side. They're followed by a cracking sound directly in front of us that quickly forms a silver starburst on the windshield. All at once I'm not thinking about us. I'm thinking about Alison, driving along behind us in a tiny car with all the protective integrity of a bread wrapper. I hope she's able to turn around and find another route.

"We shouldn't have come this way," Mesoto mutters. He glances in the rearview mirror, and I turn to look behind us. The people who had parted earlier at the sound of Mike's horn have flowed back into the street behind us, blocking any rear exit. Seeing this option blocked, Alison pulls the Cubic so close to the van that she bumps us. It's a weak measure of safety, but the only one she can take.

Mesoto blasts the horn again, two or three more times, as he continues edging the van forward, and eventually the Avalonians see that he means business. Young and old alike push to the outside lanes, clearing a path for the van even as they open a breach in the semicircle of spectators gathered on the left side of the road. As we drive by, I'm offered a brief glimpse of the show they have been watching. At first I block out what my eyes observe. But then the vision comes to me, in sterilized clarity, after we're already past. I'm thankful I can't look back, thankful that I can't hear the mournful whelps of pain.

I have never seen a group of twelve-year-olds butchering a dog before.

We are soon past the gathering and onto a relatively empty stretch of the boulevard again. But it is several minutes before I can say anything. I just sit with a lead ball in the pit of my stomach, wondering how the city could have descended this far, how it could have fallen so fast. The stadium I can understand. The confinement, the meager rations, the unaccustomed setting: these are the natural ingredients of distrust and savagery. But on the outside, where people can make their own way . . . I guess it's not what I had expected.

"I didn't know things had gotten this bad," I say to Mesoto, after the first wave of nausea has finally passed.

"Worse, my friend," he says. "In many places, much worse. We lost two cars in North Hollywood last week. Put Keith Jennings in the hospital." A pause. "You remember Jennings?"

"I remember him," I answer. Jennings is a careless and arrogant sort, and that probably contributed to his misfortune. But it doesn't excuse what happened.

"He'll walk again," Mesoto adds. "Maybe."

As Mesoto goes on, I turn to look back at Alison, suddenly fearing that she might be verging on a similar fate. But I see that she too has made it through the crowd unharmed. *Thank goodness,* I think. Still, it wasn't very smart.

I look back to Mike, and it takes a moment for me to recall what we were talking about. *Jennings.* I ask, "Was he hurt that bad?"

"Not as bad as some of those *cabrones* wanted, I'm sure of that." A beat. "We're trying to help them. But most of them, I think, see *us* as the enemy."

I just shake my head, not caring to hear any more details. "They're frustrated, Mike," I tell him. "They're scared. You can't blame them for that."

"I know they are. And I don't blame them. They're suffering terribly. All of them. I just wish they wouldn't vent their frustrations on us, that's all." He pauses and turns to face me. "We're all scared, you know? This thing could come back any day, and we're all scared. But if we can't do our jobs, it's bad for them too."

A frown. "Look around you, Mike. It's *already* bad for them. You're still driving a car. You eat when you want to. You live in a secure building somewhere. These people probably spend every day fearing for their lives. Fearing for their children. Fearing that every piece of bread or bowl of cold soup they eat might be . . ."

And then I stop, letting my words trail off, warned by his silence. And I'm thinking: Listen to me. Here's a guy—a *friend,* no less—about to go on the unemployment line because some idiot's torching fuel tanks, and I start lecturing him like some self-righteous jerk.

"I'm sorry, Mike," I offer. "I forgot who I was talking to. I've spent a lot of time talking to myself lately, I'm afraid."

"No, no problem." He pauses briefly, reflecting. "But you're right. Things could be worse. Twenty million *Mejicanos* come here in the last ten months, two or three times that many people from around the US. We couldn't figure out how to handle these problems *before* they got here. Now, with the power cutbacks, the restrictions—it's almost impossible."

He reaches out, his big hand snapping off the CD player, the rhythms that minutes ago were a blanket of calm now only a distraction. As he pulls his hand back, I notice the slightest tremor. Perhaps he's been gripping the steering wheel too tightly.

"You know what I keep thinking, *amigo?*" he goes on, taking his eyes off the road just long enough to make sure he has my attention. "I saw a movie once, about a prison that got real crowded—you know, six, eight guys to a cell—and the warden just kept taking things away. Privileges. Food. That kind of thing. But they were prisoners, you know, so no one really listened to them gripe and moan. No one cared. They just put up with it, made up their own rules, kept all their anger and rebellion inside. Until the warden told them no more television on Friday nights. He had his problems, you know, not enough space, not enough guards. But that did it. The prisoners went nuts. They killed each other. Killed the guards. Killed the warden. Burned the place to the ground."

A pause. "It wasn't just the television, you know. The men were ready to fly over the edge. Whatever came next, one more piece of bad news, that would have done it." He pauses again, running a soiled rag across his broad, sweating brow. Then he glances back at me. "I think about that movie sometimes," he says. "We take away one more thing, and maybe that's it. Maybe they go flipping crazy out there and kill us all."

He slows to round a corner just then, and I see that we've finally reached downtown. Here, the crowds have thinned considerably, warned off by the barricades across the streets and sidewalks, the heavily armed patrols, and the thick iron security gates at the fronts of office buildings. Mike maneuvers the van through an opening in the concrete barriers, flashes an electronically coded pass card, and is waved through by a bored police officer. It's only then that I realize we must be nearing Council headquarters, though I don't remember it being this way.

"Some days," Mesoto is saying. "Some days, I wonder why it hasn't already started. Why there aren't riots on the streets every night."

While he was talking, I was wondering the same thing. "Hard to get up the energy, I guess, when you're worried your next breath could be your last."

"No kidding," he says, and looks over his shoulder into the rear of the van. For the first time notice a regiment of oxygen tanks standing upright along the van's walls, an oxygen mask attached to each one.

"Standard issue," he says.

"Yeah," I reply. "Just like Amex. Don't leave home without it."

▼

Several blocks later, we pull up to a towering office building, one of the banes of modern architecture—all glass and mirrors and luminous reflections. The broad plaza outside the building's entrance has been paved with granite, and through the building's quadruple glass doors I can see a five-story lobby that runs all the way to the back. The building looks familiar, but I can't place it. I can only presume that, whatever its former function, it now houses the Los Angeles Citizens Council.

A glance at the sign by the entry tells me I've made a good guess.

I can remember when the Council occupied less than half a floor in the old brick-and-concrete administrative wing of City Hall. But those were the early post-Catastrophe days, when the Council was a paper successor to the city's energy office, before an aggressive director named Fran Amalfi decided to test the limits of the federal rules. Thousands were starving, she argued. Old diseases were running rampant again. Migrants and homeowners were killing each other for the right to their homes. Steps were needed, she asserted. Action had to be taken. Serious action.

I lived through those times, but my mind was in such a fog that I can't remember how much of what she said was true. But enough people apparently believed her—or were pushed out of the way—for in three months' time she had brought within the Council's ambit all the powers that the new laws allowed. In the process, so I'm told, she turned the Council into a model for its counterparts in the nation's other cities.

I wonder if—amid all this success—she realizes how little things have really changed.

"You've moved," I say to Mesoto, as he brings the van to a halt near the plaza's curb.

An indifferent shrug. "We needed the space."

"You've got that, all right."

And yet there's more than just office space. A crowd of hundreds fills the plaza ahead, blocking passage as completely as the residents of Avalon Boulevard had. But these people are wearing business suits and sport coats, not the worn and tattered raiment of the street. They remind me of nothing so much as the homeward-bound masses departing downtown Los Angeles in years past—and this, I realize, is what they must be. These are the Council staff, the city bureaucrats, the mid-level managers in essential industries. *The employed.* They probably know of places like Avalon Boulevard and the stadium and North Hollywood only by way of late-night rumors or morning-after body counts.

But the throng before me does recall one other such gathering I have seen in the less-privileged parts of the city today, for these favored flocks have stopped on their journey home to hear the news of the city. I follow their watching eyes high up the Council building, and see that one whole wall of glass has been given over to a public video screen. Three stories high and perhaps twice as wide, it's the big brother to the one I saw along the road outside the stadium. This time, an African-American gentleman of exquisite couture and indeterminate age anchors the newscast, backed by a Hispanic woman and an Asian of uncertain gender. I just shake my head. Political correctness is alive and well, even in the worst of times. I suppose it's good to know that some things don't change.

Mesoto, who has been watching me absorb these sights, calls me back to the present with a back slap and a crooked smile, nodding toward the building's upper stories. "Ready to face the lions, *amigo?*"

I manage a chuckle. "Not a good question for someone who's spent the last ten months in a stadium."

"No," he says, "I guess not." He hands me a white magnetic keycard. "You'll need this to get in the building. Fran's office is on the fortieth floor."

I must be grimacing, because he quickly adds, "Don't worry. It runs the elevators too. Some of us don't have to walk."

I turn the card over in my hand, studying its blankness, and its power. "White gold," I murmur, slipping it into my pocket. "What a great idea."

▼

The elevator to the fortieth floor opens onto a corridor that is configured more for effect than function. There are twelve-foot ceilings, passageways wide enough for Army troops to practice their marching orders, thick imported carpets the color of the winter sea, and magazine-sized bronze signs posted every few yards declaring: "This building is 100 percent solar-powered." As I walk along in the silence and the emptiness, the last rays of sunlight glint off the solar reflectors on the roof, streaming in through the corridor's skylights and filling the passage with a golden haze that lights up the motes of dust like sequins. I'm convinced by this display that I must be elsewhere. This can't be the same city, in the same juncture of time, in which I awoke this morning.

At length, after winning passage from the gatekeepers at two Army-staffed security stations, I reach the end of the corridor, a circular foyer of mauve and marble whose centerpiece is an imposing set of double doors. Dark walnut, lettered in what in other places would be imitation gold, but what, in this structure, I suspect is the real thing. The letters capture my eyes at once, the name an all too familiar one: *V. Francine Amalfi*, the nameplate reads. *Director, Los Angeles Citizens Council.* My destination.

I open the door and step inside.

The reception area is as richly appointed as the hallway. Deep pile carpeting, an eggshell white that bespeaks a sizable cleaning budget. An old English horseshoe desk holding sentry a dozen footsteps inside the entrance. Burgundy tweed sofas shaped to the curving walls on both sides of the desk. A gallery of framed exhibition posters from a lost and forgotten age, flanked by formless, flowing oils. *Objets d'art*, crouched like cockroaches on every flat surface, so hideous they have to be expensive. A prison of pretension.

"May I help you?"

The voice belongs to the receptionist, a slender African-American man with closely cropped hair and piercing eyes. He looks up at me like a security guard, assaying my intrusion as pleasantly as he would an infestation of vermin.

"I'm here to see Fran," I tell him.

"Your name?"

"Martin Fall." I say it without emphasis or rancor. Though there was a time when that name meant something in these quarters, when I didn't have to offer it at all, that is clearly no longer the case.

The attendant peers down through eyeglasses so narrow that they must be worn only for fashion, and studies what I take to be a list of the day's appointments. He looks up after a moment. "Yes, you're on her calendar," he says. "But you're late. She's already in another meeting. Take a seat. It may be awhile" The tone is peremptory, and the invitation isn't a request.

I decide not to press the issue, and slump back into one of the sofas. Behind the desk, I now notice, are two doors. One, a double door, is closed, and I assume that this is Amalfi's office. The other door is open, and I first make out the voice, and then—as he moves into view—the figure of Barry Erthein, Fran's executive assistant. Erthein—late twenties, dark-complected, barely five-foot-five—is a nasty little man who compensates for his lack of stature by filling up with his own importance. And when his personal cachet falls short, he borrows liberally from Amalfi, a line of credit that has won him few friends. At an office Halloween party a few years ago, an anonymous donor honored him with a Halloween mask custom-made to look like Amalfi, and Erthein seemed to regard everyone around him with suspicion and contempt from that day forward. It was just as well: the rest of us were quick to return the favor.

I catch his eye as I'm watching him, hoping that he might be able to speed things along. But he doesn't acknowledge me, and merely goes on about his business. He has been on the telephone, and now is talking to someone in his office—a woman, I think—but whoever it might be is blocked from my view.

So I wait. Fifteen minutes pass, and I step to the desk to ask the receptionist when Fran will be able to see me. I am told—reprimanded is more like it—that when Ms. Amalfi is ready, I will be the first to know. I suggest to the receptionist that he at least tell her I'm waiting. But I am informed that this is an unnecessary interruption, and that I should return to my seat and wait.

And so I walk past him, toward Erthein's office, and the man is so startled by my unwonted disobedience that he can only turn and stare. In seconds, I am in Erthein's lair, standing just inside the doorway. Now I can hear the other occupant's voice distinctly, and it *is* a woman—well-dressed, middle-aged, and intensely unhappy—standing on the near side of the room.

"I've told you fifty times already!" she fairly shouts. "Are you even listening? You killed my husband!"

"And I'll repeat what I've already told *you* fifty times, Mrs. Forrester," Erthein tells her, oblivious to my presence, speaking in careful tones that reveal that even his vast store of affected patience is running out. "We did not kill your husband. We did the best we could."

"You refused to treat him! It's the same thing!"

"This city—this *country*—does not have the resources to treat everyone. Especially low-priority cases like your husband. As I'm sure you know. We have to make choices." He moves to stand beside her, placing his hand on the woman's shoulder to steer her out. "Your husband was terminally ill. There was nothing we could do."

"He had *pneumonia!*"

"Not according to our records."

"Your records are wrong!"

"Our records are correct, Mrs. Forrester. Our computer systems are set up so that we *don't* make mistakes like that. I can show you triage nurse's report if you like. He was terminally ill. We couldn't help him. But there were others we *could* help."

She's breaking into tears now, and a small fist beats limply against Erthein's chest. "You can't do this to me! He was all I had."

"I know, I know," Erthein says. "It's hard for all of us, and I'm truly sorry this had to happen to you. I really am." He gently grips her shoulder again and turns her so that she moves—under his control more than hers—toward the exit. "I can't bring your husband back. But the Council will pay for the cost of his funeral. I'll make sure of it. It's the least—"

Now, just feet from the doorway, Erthein finally sees me, and I can tell that he's struggling to hold his anger. He nearly pushes the grieving woman through the portal. "Clifford," he commands the receptionist. "Please help Mrs. Forrester complete the reimbursement forms. Then I will see *you* when I'm finished."

Erthein comes back to face me and then just stands there, as if it were ten minutes and not ten months ago that he last ushered me out of his office. He doesn't even offer his hand.

"What can I do for you, Martin?"

"I'm here to see Fran. As I'm sure *you* know."

"She's busy. Why don't you have a seat—"

I am just at the point of deciding whether to collar this man or to walk out of this building—and this life—for good, when I hear a breezy, intimate greeting come from behind me, securing the peace.

"Hello, Martin," the voice says. "Thank you for coming."

I turn to see Fran Amalfi standing at the outer edge of Erthein's office. She extends her hand to take mine, her smile falling somewhere between cordial and cautious. I take this moment to study her and am not surprised by what I find.

Fran is as she was. Tall and slim and neat. The sides of her thick auburn hair are pulled back, held in place by a small pearl-studded barrette. She wears a fitted white jacket over a pleated knee-length black skirt, slit high. Heels and stockings also, black as well. Her face is attractive and angular, with wide dark eyes that as some point in the past year have been transformed to ocean blue. She has a pretty mouth, but it's a bit too small, almost pursed. If Avon ladies were androids, I am thinking, Fran Amalfi would be their prototype.

"Come in," she says, ending my assessment and leading me away. "Were you waiting long?"

I hesitate, scowling sideways at Erthein, but say only, "A few minutes, that's all."

"I'm sorry for the delay. Some of these people can be a real nuisance. I shouldn't have kept you."

We're in her office in seconds, and now it's her turn to examine me. She gives her verdict quickly. "You look—well, frankly, a lot better than I'd expected, Martin. I hope that means you've been well."

"Oh, I've been great, Fran. Terrific."

"Good, good. I'm glad."

If she needs me as much as Alison said, I suspect she's not really focusing on these meaningless pleasantries. But neither am I. I'm looking around this world that she inhabits and feeling more distant than ever from the life I was living until this morning. Everything about this office—and about Fran—is perfectly normal in a pre-Catastrophe sense, which is why I find it so disconcerting. A plush blue-gray carpet, warmed by exotic Oriental area rugs. A polished mahogany desk. Glass and marble side tables, burgundy leather sofa and chairs, track lighting, fresh flowers. A sleek desktop computer and flat-screen monitor and, behind the desk, a blackboard-sized LCD screen. Four telephones. An entire wall of glass overlooking the city. A bathroom. A bar befitting a small party, with a refrigerator and ice. And, above them, rows of bottles—Chivas and Gordon's and Seagram's and imported brands I've never even heard of. No food vouchers needed here. No gas lamps, no oxygen masks. Nothing that would indicate the world was the least bit different than it was before. The sensation blows over me like a chill breeze.

And then, all at once, it has a name. *A museum.* I'm in a bloody museum. This office, this whole building. *The World As We Knew It: Exhibition and Commentary.* Even the people are relics. Erthein with his tapered suits and matching ties and pocket squares. The receptionist with his mannequin eyes and pre-programmed answers. Fran with her pearls and pursed lips and *Working Woman* wardrobe. Straight out of Madame Tussaud's, or the Museum of American History. I'm amazed I wasn't charged admission.

"Nice space," I tell her in a mocking, disbelieving tone.

"It is, thanks," is Fran's level reply. "Sempra was kind enough to turn it over to us when we outgrew City Hall." She's at the bar now, setting out glasses, selecting drinks. "Still scotch?"

"It would be if I could get any."

She offers a weak smile at this, one that says we both know my last comment was out of order, so why don't we just move on? She hands me the drink and takes a sip of hers, a sparkling water with lime. "Sit down. Please."

I have been waiting for the official invitation, but I've already looked around the room to locate my spot. If you work for Fran, she sits behind that oversized desk and you sit across it in the chairs with the too-short legs so that you have to look up at her, securing her advantage. I no longer work for her, and so I move to a leather chair facing the sofa and slide into it before she has a chance to direct me elsewhere. In fact, she's already taken a feint toward her desk and has to turn back and retrace her steps.

Even so, I notice, she's still smiling. That unnerves me, because smiling is an aggressive act for Fran Amalfi. I remember a housecleaning she presided over when she was director of the city's Energy Office. Scores of pink slips, from division heads down to janitors, all in the interest of efficiency. She smiled from start to finish.

And now, as she sits, the smile vanishes, as naturally as if she had been practicing the maneuver for weeks. "What a lousy day," she sighs. "Barry and I give up an hour every afternoon to deal with the special cases, and there's always more at the end of the day than when we started. We just don't have the time." She sighs again, then takes a long sip of the water-and-lime. "Comes with the territory, I guess."

"I guess it does."

A final sigh, and then the smile again. The game begins. "But you didn't come here to listen to me complain, did you?"

As she says this, she crosses her legs, and the slit in her skirt flexes open, revealing a little of her stockinged, well-toned thighs. She lets her foot rock slowly, drawing my eyes to the black heels and her porcelain ankle: all of her body parts are weapons. If I thought of her as a woman, this would be a distraction, a temptation. As it is, it's just a delay, a petty annoyance.

"Why *did* I come here?" I ask her.

"To help me, I hope." A pause, and then: "I want you to come back, Martin."

Good old Fran. Her voice hushed, she leans toward me, her eyes locked on mine. If a person affects certain mannerisms long enough, I wonder, are they still disingenuous?

"Mike told me about the bombings," I answer without emotion. "He's as good an ops man as I ever was. You don't need me."

"Mike needs help, Martin. He's a fine person; I'm not saying he isn't. But I don't think he can handle this one by himself."

"He knows this business as well as I do. *Better* than I do, frankly. That's why I hired him."

She doesn't respond to this right away, just compresses her lips and lifts herself from the sofa, silently stepping over to the wide window that looks down on the city. She stands there, with her back to me, her glass held an inch or two from her mouth.

"He needs help," she repeats, as if I'd said nothing. "We have to find out who is responsible for these bombings, and we have to *stop* them. Without the oil, we don't even have the *capacity* to produce what these people need. And that's just not fair. Those people down there, Martin, those people have a right to keep what little they have left."

And there it is, the reason for her move to the window. It's time for me to rise as well.

"Don't patronize me, Fran." I've set my drink down and am standing there, confronting her, when she turns around. "Your job, the Council's whole reputation, are on the line, and you're desperate. I can understand that, even if I don't care one whit about either one. You're scared someone is going to snatch this office and confiscate your private bar and move you into a tent—that's fine. Just say it, because I'll believe it and we can go on from there. Just don't lay it off on some talking point about 'the people,' or I'm out of here."

"Don't you even care about what happens to them?"

"Of course I care. I care more than you can imagine. I've lived with those people for most of the past year. I've seen how their lives have been blown apart in a way that you'll never know." A beat, and I stare into her. "I'd do anything to end this nightmare for them. For all of us."

"And now you have the chance."

"We'll see. But assume you're right. As long as what I'm doing really helps them, I'll stay—*if* I stay—as long as it takes. But the moment I find I'm protecting you and this office and not them, I'm gone." A beat. "Am I making myself clear?"

She says nothing to this. But as she watches me, her smile slips into a sneer, which means we understand each other. *Good.*

"I want you to find out who's behind this," she says, conceding nothing but this one small skirmish.

"So what makes you think Mike can't handle it?"

"It's a big job. He's got to coordinate with the police, the utilities, the private security firms. Not to mention the Federal energy officials who practically live here now. And he's got to start coming up with *answers*. Nothing against Mike, but he just doesn't measure up."

"And I do?"

No smile, no sneer, just business. "You used to. That's all I know."

And with that, she has opened the wound again. I'm glaring at her, unable to respond. Why does this single, unguarded statement anger me so much? She's right, of course. Things aren't the same anymore—*I'm* not the same anymore. Old news. But now someone else is saying it. And here I stand, with hurt and resentment in my eyes, providing her with the proof.

Uncharacteristically, she doesn't seize the moment. "Look, I know what you've been through," she says. "You suffered a terrible loss that none of the rest of us can even begin to fathom, and we're all sorry for you. *I'm* sorry for you. But life goes on, and I go on, and right now I have eighty million people to worry about and a government in Washington that's telling me what I can and can't do and ten thousand brainless scientists who still can't agree on exactly what happened or why or whether it's going to happen again."

She moves to her desk, flips open a control pad, and presses a couple of buttons. The wall screen behind the desk comes to life, flashing a glowing graphic map of the continental United States. The states are outlined in green, the cities in red, the mountains in blue. The map is otherwise undistinguished, except for the raven-black ovals that cover large sections of the mainland.

"That's our beloved country, Martin," she goes on. "I'm sure you've seen the reports. Everything above twenty-five-hundred feet is still at risk, and everything above five thousand is uninhabitable. Those people outside don't have anywhere else to go."

"But the situation's stabilized, hasn't it? That's what I've heard."

"There haven't been any more oxygen wipeouts in the last ten months, if that's what you mean. And no one in the government is forecasting any for the future. But no one predicted the first one either. Or the second. So where does that leave us?"

She turns off the map, and the image of the United States disappears into nothing. She just stands there, propped up against her desk, and for the first time I see there's a weariness in her eyes. Uncertainty, too. This isn't an act: this is the real Fran Amalfi. It's a glimpse that comes only at the end of long defeated days like this one, and it lasts only until she's ready to speak again.

"The world doesn't change overnight," she pronounces. "That's what everyone from the President to the Energy Secretary to the head of FEMA keep telling us. 'Things will improve if you're patient. In the meantime, you've just got to keep cutting down on emissions, cutting down on greenhouse gases, cutting down on fuel use.' And so that's what we do."

She walks back and slips to the sofa, draining the last of her drink. The scarf around her neck is askew, and a few strands of her hair have slipped from the grasp of her barrette. But she doesn't move to fix them. I'm not even sure she notices.

"We've cut back industrial production and pushed fuel use in the Basin down to a quarter of what it was six months ago, and we're going to *keep* pushing. Most of the other big cities have done the same. But who knows how long it will be before the air's back in balance? Even with all that we've done, the oxygen ratio is still too low in some places for birds to breathe, much less people."

A pause, and then the summation. "And so the Feds tell us to keep cutting back. Well, we're doing what we can. But then the bombings come along, and we lose three months' worth of fuel reserves and half our refining capacity, and now—like I told you—we can't even produce what little the law allows. We can't run a city like that, Martin, not for very long. And especially not with all these people. *That's* why we have to stop the bombings. And we have to do it soon. Or oxygen will be the least of their worries.

"That's it," she says, her hands outstretched in petition. "That's why I need you back. It's your call."

And then she's silent. The sparring is over, the arguments finished. She has left me with a request, and a decision.

I'm too spent even to draw it out. Though it's Fran I'm watching, my mind is on the faces that lined the corridor outside my compound at the stadium. On the children of Avalon Boulevard. On the little girl I used to know from that long night in Denver who had lost so much, yet whose eyes were filled every day thereafter with more love and trust than I could ever hope to supply. They—and not Fran—are my jury, and their sentence is one I cannot appeal.

At length, I merely nod in response to Fran's offer. It is a soundless gesture, one whose meaning she instantly understands. With that, her smile comes again. Tight. Triumphant. Relieved. She extends her hand and I take it, showing nothing. For that is what I feel.

Without ceremony, I bid her good-bye and walk out toward the night.

▼

"How did it go?" Alison asks as she drives us away from Council headquarters. I don't bother to ask where we're headed.

"It went. We got past the niceties in a hurry."

"And then what?"

Alison pauses. Hopeful. Expectant. I let the silence go on for a few seconds and then answer flatly, "I guess I'll be hanging around for a while."

At this, I see the barest glimmer of a smile come to Alison's face, the uplifted corners of her mouth shadowed in the moonlight. She waits for a moment, hoping that I will elaborate. Eager, I am sure, for the specifics. When I don't say anything, she seems to form the question with her lips, but decides not to voice it and simply settles back behind the wheel. She knows this is my time, this quiet passage, and she chooses not to take it from me.

I look around as we make our way down the empty street—the same street that, just a few hours before, was host to hundreds of anxious duty-bound city employees watching the evening news. Now, the video screen high up on the Council building is blank and silent. The employees have returned to their fortified homes and apartments, and the streets have been blocked off with steel retaining walls and concrete security bunkers. The city has fallen into another fitful, dreamless sleep, and we are all that remains.

This is a new experience for me, moving through the city's night-darkened quarters. It's peaceful in a way. The few streetlights in use, maybe one out of ten, are lit at half-power. The buildings are all dark. The area is completely abandoned except for the contingents of Army troops patrolling the streets. Yet the scene is threatening too. For beyond the relative safety of this isolated government enclave, I know, must hide millions of angry, desperate, what-have-I-got-to-lose people. People crammed into dark rooms or hallways, or couched invisibly against the cold stone walls, waiting only for a reason.

Tonight, at least, I won't be among them.

But we are in their country in minutes, past the official government barricades, on our own for who knows how many blocks. Almost nothing changes, right at first, except for the subtleties. Now, when I glance at the office buildings with the big iron gates, I see shadows huddled at their base, people wrapped in weathered blankets and guarded by the hope that they will wake to see another day. Up above, the streetlights become one in fifteen, then one in twenty, then none at all. On the sidewalks, every few blocks, I spot a security patrol with their neon armbands and bright orange helmets. They walk in groups of four—always at least four—a few steps behind packs of dogs that are even more intimidating than the men's automatic rifles.

The stadium, I decide, was safer, more inviting than this. There, at least, you knew your chances.

"Nice spread upstairs, isn't it?" Alison says at last.

Her voice brings me back, but it takes me a few minutes to decipher the question.

"Fran's office," she explains. "Pretty impressive. Upsets a lot of people, though."

As she says it, every detail, every nuance of the office comes back to me. "I'll bet."

"She even has her own house, did she tell you that? A real house, with a lawn and a garage and outside lighting. Can you imagine?" A beat, then the wry smile again. "Not everyone suffers."

"Everyone in her own way, I guess. I'd wager she feels as oppressed as the rest of us."

"Maybe. But at least she doesn't have to wear one of these." Alison lifts her left wrist in front of her, and for the first time I see that she is wearing a chrome bracelet that's a match for the one on Mesoto's wrist. It must have been hidden under the sleeve of her jacket. "You'd probably have one too," she says, if Fran weren't afraid it would scare you away."

"What is it?"

"A PMD," she says, but the acronym means nothing to me and I reply only with an empty stare. "A personal monitoring device," she goes on. "It tells the Council where you are at every moment, what you're doing, who you're with. They say it even transmits your phone conversations to some listening station out in Victorville. It's humiliating as can be. But it's probably the only reason there isn't more violence and looting than there already are."

"But no one in the stadium has one."

"I'm sure they don't. Neither do most of the people living on the streets. 'The proles.' They actually call them that, can you believe it?" She shrugs. "Some people don't matter, I guess. The rest of us, though—those who still live amid some semblance of civic order and who have access to resources that actually could do the city harm—we *have* to wear one. It's a small price, they say, for government housing and medical care and luxuries like—"

Suddenly, from all around us, loud pulsating Klaxons sound, their deep bass chords piercing our bodies like X-rays. Alison breaks off her thought and her face washes with concern. She angles the car to the side of the road and turns on the car's video screen.

"What's that noise?" I ask.

"Just a minute," she says. She's all business now, the playfully sardonic Alison of moments before stashed away, her attention focused fully on the video screen. Almost immediately, the screen flickers to life with the image of a worried young soldier.

"This is Leary," Alison says into the device. "What's the vector?"

"We're still checking," the soldier replies. "We don't have a visual yet."

Alison's eyes go to the skies as the man speaks, peering into the moonlit darkness, and then to the streets. Up ahead, several street people emerge from the shadows and look toward the sky as well. All around them, the Klaxons continue to blare. As I look on, I realize: as much as I cherish her as a friend, I also know that Alison is coolly efficient, enormously capable at what she does. Especially in times of crisis. It is one reason why she has survived during Fran's rise to the top while so many others have not.

"I'm on Santa Monica just east of Fairfax," I hear her explaining. "Where can I pull in?"

The soldier pauses and looks away, tapping keys on an unseen keyboard. Then he turns back to the screen. "There's a substation about twenty blocks ahead. But I don't know if—"

He stops. Alison looks around, puzzled. A few seconds later, I notice it too: the Klaxons have gone silent.

"False alarm," the man on the screen says, in obvious relief. "You're in the clear."

"Okay, thanks," Alison says, as she turns off the video screen and pulls the car back onto the boulevard. As we roll slowly on, the crouched shadows from before have materialized into human beings, standing in doorways and behind porches. They glance warily at us as our car goes by, then turn again to watch the skies.

And that's when it all becomes obvious. "Air warnings . . ." I mutter, almost to myself.

"Yep. Happens every few days," she explains. "The slightest change in the ambient O-2 and the alarms go bonkers. You don't want to be out there if it's the real thing."

It's then I notice the bank of oxygen tanks lining the backseat of Alison's tiny, trunkless Cubic. I turn away from them and glance back outside, letting my eyes gradually return to the people standing alongside the street. Some of them are crawling back into their hiding places, but not all. Those that remain stand as if on guard duty, holding weapons of convenience. Iron pipes. Boards with protruding nails. An occasional black-market hunting rifle. All trained on passersby, ready to use.

"I'm not too thrilled about being out here right now," I tell her, after a moment.

▼

We finish the drive in silence. A few blocks later, I see that Alison is pulling the Cubic up to a security gate outside a large fortified apartment complex. The guard—an older Army Colonel type with a fatherly face and shadowed eyes—shines a flashlight into the front seat, then skims it along the vehicle's floor and backseat. The search complete, he takes Alison's proffered identification card and runs it through the card reader. In seconds, her photo is displayed on the guard's computer monitor, along with enough biographical information to fill a small novel. The guard clicks through several screens, then types some notes into his computer

"Evening, Miss Leary," he greets her. "Be going back out tonight?"

"No, we'll be staying."

He enters another notation into his computer and hands back her card. As he leans forward, I see a row of forty-round carbines lining the walls of the guard post. Pretty heavy artillery for an apartment complex.

"Good thing," the guard says, nodding toward the Council logo on the car door. "One of these jobbers was firebombed in Culver City last night. Best to keep in."

"Uh-huh," Alison says absently, taking her card. "Thanks for the tip." She rolls up the window and steers the car through the parking lot toward an underground garage.

"Staying?" I ask her as the guard post fades behind us. "What do you mean?"

"We're home. What do you think?"

"You live here now?"

"*We* live here. Your apartment's right down the hall from mine. Courtesy of Fran." She shrugs, as if embarrassed by this largesse. "She moved most of the mid-level staff here a few months ago."

"Better than the street, I guess."

"Yeah, a lot better," she answers, but this time her grin has returned. "Like I said, not everyone suffers."

▼

We reach the apartment—*my* apartment—a few minutes later. I see that it's nothing special by pre-Catastrophe standards. A tiny, cube-shaped living area. A kitchen no bigger than a walk-in closet. Some spare rental-quality furnishings. A solitary lamp with a bulb so dim that the moon, shining in through the curtainless window, provides more illumination. But I'm not complaining. After the stadium, it looks like Bel Air.

Alison takes my hand and leads me into the small bedroom to finish the tour. I step to the closet, almost by reflex, and slide open the door. I find what I expect. A couple of suits. A half-dozen dress shirts. Some casual clothes. An entire wardrobe. It's nice, I appreciate it, but I'm not taken in. I know it's nothing more than a bribe.

"Fran's pretty thorough, isn't she?" I say.

"Actually, I picked out the clothes." She reaches into the closet, selects a suit jacket, and holds it up against me. "Like it?"

She's smiling, obviously pleased with her choice. I let her enjoy the moment, then take the jacket from her hand and hang it back in the closet. She's watching me, a hopeful expression on her lips. I try to thank her, but it doesn't seem right, even though I know it is.

And suddenly, I feel the familiar symptoms of withdrawal gathering within me. I step to the room's lone chair and sit down on it. I want badly to shake myself clear of the barriers, to respond normally to people whose only intentions are good. But I am in some foul purgatory now, only a few rungs above the hell of the past ten months, and it's the best I can do.

As I'm sitting there, lost in my thoughts, Alison moves behind me. I feel her small hands start to work on the muscles of my shoulders. How long has it been since someone touched me, laid hands on me, in a gesture of affection? I'm not sure I want to remember.

"You'll feel better after you rest," she tells me. "You must be totaled."

But her hands continue to knead my shoulders. Pressing. Relaxing. Gliding over the surface. Sweet Alison. She always does exactly the right thing. Impressive in itself, all the more impressive because she does what you *don't* expect, what would seem inappropriate if you stopped to think about it or had it offered to you. Alison's special gift.

I say nothing as she goes on, hoping she can feel my gratitude as the tension in my muscles slakes in response to her touch. At last, I grasp her hand in mine, thanking her. She holds my hand for a moment, squeezing it softly in return. It is a parting gesture and a promise. And then, after a quick and polite good-bye, she is gone.

But her gift remains, comforting me. The silence—the isolation—tonight will be less punishing that it could have been. For a few brief hours anyway, I can forget all about the past and think only of the present.

Like a wounded war veteran, I am being eased back into the world.

▼ ▼ ▼

*T*he drive to Ray's house is one of the most wrenching I have ever made. When I served in the Special Forces, many years ago, I was responsible for leading what the generals euphemistically called "cleanup missions." My squad would enter a bombed-out village, scouring the still-burning ruins for caches of weapons, intelligence plans, surviving enemy combatants. Death was everywhere in those towns: the remains of guerrillas, soldiers, terrorists, army captains. Their bodies were charred and broken just like the imploding buildings they were trying to flee, their corpses littering the streets and alleyways along with the pulverized bricks and blasted concrete that were all that was left of once-humble structures.

This was war. It was to be expected. It was all of a piece.

But then, one dark morning, the story was different. We were assigned to inspect a distant village that, the whispers of infidels told us, had been raided by the troops of the government whose land we were charged with defending. There were rumors of wanton destruction that our own generals refused to believe. Some said the whispers were a diversion, a setup. Others claimed the voices came from those who had executed the deed themselves as part of a deadly propaganda ruse. But the generals sent us anyway, on a mission to prove the rumors wrong. It was our job to comply.

When we disembarked at the village's edge, the first thing we noticed was the silence. There were neither birds nor insects on this day nor any kind of noise, though one would usually hear the rustling of a distant engine, the voices of covert commandoes barking orders, the staccato of shuffling footsteps. But in this village, on this morning, there was nothing.

We entered slowly. The just-dawning sunlight danced with the uplift of heat and sand, painting the sides of buildings with shifting amber waves. The shadowed alleyways that ran beside them heaved breaths of stillness. Like a decommissioned army base or a museum façade, the village was without life, without spirit. Yet it was perfectly preserved, not a curtain nor a crate out of place.

And then I saw it. The image was fleeting at first, easy to miss. A scar on an otherwise undisturbed surface. A dark-skinned man's hand, protruding from a half-open doorway, lay flat against the wooden floor. Motionless. I flagged my men to take cover, raising my weapon in a single swift cut, ready to fire. But no action would be needed. From this new angle, we could plainly see the body attached to the hand, the snaking riverlet of blood like a funeral ribbon around the mufti shoulders.

Dead.

Then, in slow revelation, the other images came. A woman with armfuls *of laundry, splayed behind the rear of a small hut. Two old men, collapsed beneath a small wooden table, one with a cup still gripped in his weathered hand. A group of children, not long ago playing a game of marbles, now lying around the edge of a chalk circle, as if angling for a better view. All of them dead where they lay, in pools of congealing blood. And not even a bullet hole visible in the surrounding clay and stucco walls.*

I think about that scene now as I drive along the surface streets on the eastern edge of Denver, with Darby sitting silently beside me. On this gloriously bright afternoon, when the city should be alive with activity, there is nothing. The buildings are pristine. The restaurants' hanging signs swing rhythmically in the soft breeze. The stores are open for business, their sale and promotional signs beckoning pre-holiday shoppers. But no one passes through the doors. Ghosts have little need for commerce—and ghosts are all that inhabit this city on this day of otherworldly light.

Ghosts, and those they left behind. As it was in that early-morning village on a lost continent far away, the images that stay with me are those that come last. I look more closely and see that this city is not as empty as it seems. There, in a curio shop: the aging proprietor. Slumped over a table, having taken his last breaths while tallying the receipts from the day before. The elderly couple in a car, sitting in the bank drive-through, there to make a deposit that will never be registered. The portly auto mechanic, bent over the sputtering engine of an old Ford, endlessly seeking a malfunction that will not be found. And the playground—oh, the children on the playground, just like the children in the village . . .

I have to look away then, forcing my eyes, tunnel-like, on the road ahead.

"Don't look, honey," I whisper to Darby in a husky, barely audible voice. But she is now fully awake, fully alert, and my caution does no good. For her eyes take in the scene completely, though with an oddly detached expression, as if she were watching an old horror film she didn't quite understand.

"Don't look," I say again, more steadily this time. "We're almost home."

And then comes the question that I've been dreading all morning, dreading with the inevitability of death. But I am so spent, my mind so overwhelmed with the chaos of loss and uncertainty all around us, that even when the question is uttered, the most I can summon is a single tear.

"My mommy and daddy are dead, aren't they?" comes Darby's small, all too matter-of-fact voice.

"Yes, sweetie, they are," I tell her, after a moment, in an almost silent whisper.

CHAPTER 5

I envy Fran Amalfi's faith in me. I came before her a man whose mind has been suspended for nearly a year in the tortured dreams of Denver and its aftermath. How can I possibly be of any help to her? It's true that I once held the post Mike Mesoto now occupies, and so I know much of the city and its procedures. It's also true that I've kept my powers of thought and reasoning from permanent decay by reading histories, novels, philosophy. Whatever I could trade for or steal. There were many sleepless hours to fill, crouched in my corner of the stadium beside the flickering oil lamp, and many memories to be kept at bay. I must have gained something from this.

But is it enough? If what the city faces in the wake of the bombings is of the urgency Fran describes, can a man from the outer provinces return with answers even remotely sufficient to the challenge? I have no way of knowing. But I am ultimately sustained by a play on the old saw: in the country of the frantic, the patient man is king. I have nothing but patience. Nothing left to fear losing. Nothing to tilt my loyalties one way or the other. This, I decide, must be my only advantage.

Either that, or Fran is more desperate than she is willing to let on.

For now, I focus on myself, and see the evidence of recovery in my new morning routine. I wake not to the speedboat snores of Dagger Santos nor to the wailing of babies terrorized by the dark. I awake instead to silence, stark and almost holy. When I look up, it's with surprise. For I am lying on a bed, not a cot, and the bathroom is only feet away. I walk naked toward it and step under the shower, letting the lukewarm spray run over me like a waterfall. I wash my face and shampoo my hair and lather my body with the scented soap, and I do it all slowly. I had forgotten that such pleasures existed.

When I'm finished, I towel down before the full-length mirror and study the changes in my body. The hardness. The leanness. The deep tan on my arms and face. I shave, with a new razor and a new blade and real shaving gel, and use the aftershave and deodorant that Alison has left for me. And then I dress, relishing the indulgence of choice: suits, shirts, ties, shoes. As I'm struggling in the reflected light to knot the tie, I notice something else. On the living room table: a basket of fruit. Not for sale. Not for barter. Not for distribution. Just for me. Alison must have left it for me on her way to work.

I step over, peeling and biting into an orange, overcome by the familiar yet exotic taste. I feel strangely like the first sketch of a man who used to do all of these things naturally, in the ordinary course of affairs. Now I'm doing them again, almost without thinking. I'm surprised, after my long time away, that's it's this easy to come back. Too easy, in fact. I don't deserve it.

Suddenly, recalling those helpless souls on the street for whom this fruit basket would be a treasure beyond gold, I feel a stab of guilt that tells me I *don't* deserve it. In that moment, I almost walk away, leaving the rest of the fruit untouched. The guilt pierces more deeply then, but as the seconds go on, the pain of conscience abates. I finally push the thought away completely, taking solace in the hope that, if we stop the fuel-tank bombers—if we are successful in Fran's mission—millions will have more food to eat once production can return to post-Catastrophe normal. Yet in the same instant I am reminded of the residents of the stadium, for whom the fight against starvation was constant even in the midst of putatively normal production.

And I wonder: will what we're doing—what *I'm* doing—make any difference at all?

For now, there is no time to brood over such matters. Mike Mesoto will be here in half an hour to collect me for the day's events, and I need to steel myself for the work that lies ahead. And so I take another orange from the fruit basket and step quietly to the window, where I watch the city end its slumber, wait for Mike's arrival, and think of other things.

▼

Three hours later we are in the air, cresting the Hollywood Hills and careening over the vast residential plain of the San Fernando Valley, northwest of the city's center. Our transport is a glass-bottom helicopter emblazoned with a bright gold-and-blue corporate logo—a stylized sun rising behind a row of jagged mountains. The logo is the emblem of the Golden West Power Company—the Los Angeles Basin's major power producer and the site of our morning's visit.

This is the first time I have been in the air since my family's flight to Denver, one year ago this month. Within days of that trip, air travel became a luxury reserved for emergency relief teams, public officials, and those who were sufficiently well-connected to secure the needed government permits. I was not one of the privileged few, and so I remained earthbound. I am not sure this was a punishment.

Looking out over the Valley, I see arrayed before me the harvest of the mass migrations that the Catastrophe incited. It is a view that, in a way, is even more sobering than what I saw on my rides with Mesoto and Alison down the city's streets or even during my months in the stadium. From this vantage point, the picture of the present no longer comes in fragments, but in full perspective. I feel like the lunar astronauts must have felt when they saw the Earth for the first time when rounding the far side of the moon. Before those voyages, our globe was a sprawling, teeming home with endless borders and endless powers of recuperation. Infinite, in a way, in all directions. Afterward, it was just another small and insignificant planet, easily left for ruin.

At least for those of us living in the affected zones, events seem to have proven that dark possibility correct.

But what I see below me is devastation of a different kind. We are flying low enough to make out the contours of blocks upon blocks of what used to be middle-class neighborhoods, and at first I notice little amiss. Most of the homes and apartment complexes are still standing, and the streets are clear enough to give passage to buses and horse-drawn carriages, to delivery wagons pulled by horses or teams of men, to Citizens Council supply trucks.

Below us, children play on abandoned school playgrounds. Families tend vegetable gardens in the corners of their yards. Neighbors band together to build new shelters for the unending flow of migrants. In fact, if you ignore the overgrown wilderness of charred wood and ashes that used to be Encino and Sherman Oaks and Studio City—areas that must have suffered the same man-made conflagrations that visited so much of the nation in the weeks following the Catastrophe—you might think that the Valley's residents had fashioned some semblance of community, even livelihood, out of the forces that have sent other parts of the country into virtual collapse.

But look more closely, and the picture becomes a piece with what I have already seen. This is no happy-faced Ecotopia of the kind imagined by fabricators of fairyland dreams. It's a portrait of people contending without relief against the hidden evils of both Human and Mother Nature—and against the anarchy that erupts like a simmering volcano when neither remains subject to civil control.

This struggle is written in the images that come to the eye only after the more optimistic impressions have been taken in. The lawns and courtyards that have been given over *en masse* to migrants in sleeping bags and lean-tos. The vast tent cities that spread out across the parking lots of what used to be shopping malls and schools. The thousands of others who lie crammed in garages and under park pavilions—the best accommodations they can manage. The police cruisers and Army convoys that wind endlessly through the once-peaceful middle-class streets. The gunfire and street fights that shred the last fading hopes of the morning peace. The continuous lines that form at the government stores and canteens that are even longer than I have witnessed elsewhere.

I look at all this, and I think, *If this is paradise, it is a dead man's version.*

But what I can't see—the invisible images—stay with me long after the visible ones are gone. The hunger that hides in the stomachs of the children, who race on the playgrounds not to chase their dreams but to escape their hunger and their pain. The fatigue of the spirit that comes from ever-present shortages of the simplest necessities—and from the small and nearly forgotten perquisites of life, like music and magazines and toys and motion pictures, that have long since been forced out of production. The darkness that looms beneath the rooftops each night, like a blackout of the soul. The chance of random violence that lies behind every strange and desperate face. The uncertainties of why and what and what's to come. And perhaps most of all the remembrance of what was and will likely never be again.

In the end, this is what overwhelms me, what compels me to look away from the landscape below. I have driven through the worst of the America's inner cities in days gone by, through the Watts and Harlems and Anacostias and the projects of Chicago, when those broken-down neighborhoods were penitentiaries of unchecked lawlessness. I have seen machine-gun fire on the streets of Miami and the drive-by shootings of the urban drug wars that claimed target and bystander as one. I have taken the life of a nineteen-year-old Puerto Rican boy, his mind obliterated by angel dust, who would have killed me with my partner's revolver if I hadn't shot him first. I have watched television reports of the desolate poverty and inadequacy elsewhere, the bleak tragedies of Bangkok and Rwanda and Ethiopia and Kolkata. The names and places come back to me, when I think of them, like a catalog of horrors. They are an inventory of all that went wrong in a world where, we were told, we were doing far too little to set things aright.

But then I look out across the Valley, at the vastness of the grief and struggle that now knows no geographical or political boundaries, and I come to a stark realization. Today, this is as good as it gets in our own metropolises, almost a year after our course was bent back on itself by the whims of nature and the laws of man. Our shining city on a hill has become a faint and dimming wasteland in the valley, and yet we are still a place of refuge. We are still called on to feed the world, and we can't even feed ourselves. Under these circumstances, how long can our illusions last? How long until the frail walls of safety and order and subsistence collapse altogether? What do we do when our whole country becomes Kolkata?

▼

Eventually, I return my attention to the inside of the helicopter. Mesoto is sitting in the seat beside me, in the rear of the craft, dragging nervously on a cigarette. His fatigued and bloodshot eyes are fixed on his briefing book, although I am not certain he is actually reading it. I skimmed my copy on the drive to the helipad and thumbed through it again while we were waiting for takeoff, searching for some great store of wisdom. But I found little that I hadn't learned from the conversations of the day before. I wonder what Mike expects to take from it.

"Am I missing something, Mike?" I ask him.

My question takes a moment to register. When he looks up, he's still lost in whatever thoughts have been barricading his mind. "Missing what?"

"The book. It's just a rehash of the bombings. You already said the teams didn't find anything at the sites."

"Right, nothing. No surprise there. All five of the tanks were blown up the day after they were filled. Did I tell you that? For maximum explosive power, I guess. Anyone planning his protest that carefully would've made sure to cover his tracks. We didn't find a thing." He takes a long pull on his cigarette, then grinds it out. "No, the real question, *amigo*, is this. *How do they know?* How do they know when the oil is being shipped? How do they get past the security systems? How do they do all of this without being seen? This isn't like spiking a tree in the forest or pouring sand down a bulldozer's gas tank. It takes a lot of information that most people don't have. And can't get."

"Couldn't they get it from the shipping companies?"

"Not unless there's a conspiracy a mile wide. Five different shippers, five different brokers, five different trucking companies. Hard to believe they're all bent." A pause, and he lights another cigarette. "No, the information is coming from inside. I'm sure of it."

The response to this comment comes not from me, but from the man sitting in front of us, in the seat next to the pilot. "Haven't we been through this before, Mr. Mesoto?"

The speaker is James Alan Rooker, director of the Information Services Office for the Citizens Council. It's a green-eyeshade division that once merely monitored the area's fuel supplies. But now—in the wake of the new energy laws—the office controls the allocation and use of all fuel and electric power throughout the Los Angeles Basin. Unlike the far more public Amalfi, Rooker accumulated these responsibilities with no grand proclamations and no pretenses that he might not be up to the task. He simply accomplished what was needed, asking no one for permission to do his job, and finding his own way around obstacles when they were set in his path. Though only in his thirties, he carries himself like a much older man, silently keeping his own counsel. With his lank frame and preference for trench coats, he gives off the air of a CIA analyst, or maybe a deep-cover spy.

Yet he is no spy burned by years in the cold: his manner reveals as much. His thinning blond hair, combed back in aggressive strokes, descends below the point that either diplomacy or bureaucracy would deem proper. His lips seem fixed in a permanent fleer, speaking their impolitic judgment without the burden of words. And his eyes. His eyes are watchful, yes. But more than that, they are home to conviction. There is a spark of defiance residing there, a nucleus of the unpredictable hidden behind the veil of formal courtesies. Most of all, there is the unapologetic certainty that he is right, at all times and in all things. He is not a man troubled by shades of gray.

"As I recall," Rooker says crisply to Mesoto, closing his own briefing book and turning in his seat to face us, "my division has implemented every security measure you've recommended. The altered code sequences. The secure transmission links. The reduction in the number of people with access to shipping data. And none of it has had the slightest impact on the bombings. Am I right so far?"

It's a false pause, and Mike doesn't answer. We all know that what Rooker has said is correct.

"As for the facilities themselves," the information services director continues, "the Council has doubled the on-site security detail at every major fuel-storage site. We've assigned new field operatives, and we rotate them every week. We've ordered shippers to take one of our own people with them on all major fills. And we've even arranged for the fire department to send out special hazard teams after each fill to make sure there are no combustibles or accelerants lying around that might feed an explosion. Please correct me if I misspeak on any of this."

"You don't," Mesoto says. "It wasn't the shippers and it wasn't the storage tank operators."

"Nevertheless, five newly filled tanks have been hit—exactly one day after they were filled. Even someone with inside information would find it hard to breach such stringent security barriers that often, don't you think?"

Again, Mesoto doesn't answer, and Rooker goes on. "Need I add that you also restricted access to the sensitive areas around the storage tanks so severely that our own ground crews have started to complain? And not without reason, since none of your measures have been successful."

"*Yet*," Mesoto insists. "They haven't been successful *yet*. And unless *I'm* mistaken, Mr. Rooker, barring ground crews from the fill sites was your recommendation, not mine."

"That's right. It was," says Rooker evenly. "Don't misunderstand me. I'm not taking issue with any of your actions specifically. And I agree: somebody on the inside has to be involved. But we need to know who that somebody is, and how he's getting access. And we need to know it *now*. Not after a dozen more fuel tanks have blown."

There is a tense pause. "You've seen the list of possibles," Mesoto says slowly. "It's long, but we'll get through it. We have surveillance on most—"

"Yes, I've seen the list," Rooker cuts in. "And do you know what bothers me about it? You've excluded your own people."

Mesoto glares at the man for a moment, but his answer comes in a calm, almost indifferent tone. "Shall I also put *myself* under surveillance, Mr. Rooker?"

I'm surprised that Mike is taking this challenge with such equanimity. Normally, in situations like this, his face would be flushed, his voice hardening with anger. Maybe he anticipated this confrontation, or maybe he's already written off this job and just doesn't care. Or maybe, I think, some of his affected strength is aimed at *me,* as if facing down Rooker is meant to prove that Mike is still in control.

But his restraint is too forced, too much like submission, and the advantage quickly slips back to Rooker.

"No one is questioning your loyalty *or* you competence, Mr. Mesoto," the information services director concludes. "Nor that of your people. But then I'm not the one signing your paychecks. For your own sake, you might want to start showing some results."

And with that, Rooker turns back around toward the front of the helicopter. He opens his briefing book again, his side of the discussion completed. Mesoto merely sits for a few seconds, searching for a response. But before he can answer, the craft's radio crackles to life, followed by the pilot's voice. By the time the interchange between pilot and ground control is finished, Mike's moment is gone, and he merely slumps back in defeat.

▼

"Golden West tower," the pilot announces. "This is Golden-One. Do you copy?"

"We copy five-by-five, Golden-One," comes the Golden West air controller's reply. "You're cleared for landing on the north helipad."

The clearance given, the pilot banks toward the right, and I find myself looking outside again. All at once, Mike's dispute with Rooker is overwhelmed by what I see before me. We're flying toward the Sierra Madres, the great forested mountain range along California's central coast, and by now we must be just a short distance north of Ventura. I had known that Golden West was constructing a solar-powered electrical plant in this mountain range—a mammoth facility intended to serve all of Ventura County as well as the San Fernando Valley and much of northwest LA. I had even participated in some of the early planning meetings for the new generating plant. But when I last visited the site more than a year ago, the company had finished only the administrative and research wings and part of the transformer housing. At that time, the proclaimed "miracle of innovation" looked like nothing so much as an ordinary gas-fired plant, and a modest-sized one at that.

Now, suspended here in midair, I feel as though I am passing through a time warp. The mountains all around us are swathed in low rolling clouds, leaving only a few ragged peaks to pierce the shimmering cover. Up ahead, between two of these peaks, a high plateau sits just above cloud level—an island in a sea of white. I can see buildings of some sort strewn along the length of the valley, but can't resolve them into anything concrete. They're just a long filament of reflected sunlight strung out between the two mountaintops, looking like the stuff of fantasy, like a shimmering castle, or a magic kingdom.

But gradually we draw closer, out of the angle of the reflected light, and I can see that it's not a castle at all, but something even more incredible we're approaching. The solar plant has been transformed from an artist's conception into a life-size working facility. The more conventional power-plant structures—the administrative and research wings, the fuel storage tanks, the transmission towers, the huge steel dome that houses the transformers and generators—are massed together at the south end of the valley. This much I could have forecast from my earlier visits. What I couldn't have predicted, even with the optimism of the artist's sketch, is the immensity and otherworldliness of the solar array.

Imagine an igloo the size of a ten-story building. Now, imagine the igloo's half-cylindrical entrance stretched out not just for a few feet but for nearly a mile, and you'll have a fair image of the outlines of the Golden West solar plant. The body of the imaginary igloo contains the transformer housing and administrative offices, while the mile-long half-cylinder serves as the foundation for the solar collectors. There must be hundreds of these billboard-sized panels attached lengthwise along this cylindrical shell, in neat and orderly rows that run from the transformer housing all the way to the half-cylinder's northern end. As many panels as there are, though, there are hundreds more blank spaces along the shell where other panels await installation. As we veer toward a landing, I notice that each of the already installed panels is aligned at an angle that passes just over the helicopter, toward the ten o'clock sun. But as the day progresses, I recall reading, these panels will tilt on their axes to remain in the sun's direct line of radiance, swiveling continuously toward the west until the sun sets over the ocean. Then slowly they will return to face east by morning, where they once again will greet a new day's sun.

"It's amazing," I say aloud to no one in particular, as the reality of the image settles in. "The whole solar array was just bare rock a year ago."

I'm surprised when there's an answer, even more surprised when it comes from Rooker. This is the first time he has addressed me directly, other than a hurried greeting and the obligatory courtesies, since we climbed into the helicopter.

"What's amazing," he says, "is how fast they could work once the government picked up the bill."

I look up to see that he has turned in his seat again, and is facing me with an expression as easy and collegial as if we were brothers-in-arms. Perhaps he has spent all of his hostility on Mesoto. Or perhaps he's merely trying to compensate for his insolence before.

"The Feds paid for this?" I ask. I knew the government underwrote Golden West's solar research, but the utility was supposed to build the construction costs into its rate base. "When did that happen?"

"A few weeks after the Catastrophe," Rooker says. "Congress had already sunk three bills into it. With fossil fuels out the window, the other twenty were a gimme."

"And it's online?"

"Barely." A scowl. "The plant's running at eight-percent efficiency. Three months on, and it still consumes more energy than it produces. Heckuva bargain if you ask me."

I'm looking out at the plant as the chopper traverses the length of the cylindrical shell, wondering how a facility this massive could produce so little electricity. Forget the San Fernando Valley. At this rate, most of Ventura would have to look elsewhere.

"What's the problem?" I ask. "Why can't they get their efficiency up?"

"Big plant. There's five hundred thousand miles of wiring between the collectors and the transformers alone. Most of the power leaks out before it ever reaches the switching stations." A sneer. "One of the things Congress didn't have time to think about, I guess."

He digs into his stack of notebooks, and hands me a thin folder with the Golden West logo on the front. "Never fear. Our good friend Mr. Farraday promises the plant will be generating enough electricity by this time next year to power half the Valley." The sneer again, and with it the certainty that this promise is worthless—and that Rooker alone knows it. "What do *you* think, Mr. Fall? Can we take that promise to the bank," he asks, in a manner that begs no answer.

And I don't give him one. I've been away too long to know whether Rooker's concern is genuine or whether he's merely waging a surrogate war against Farraday. It's easy to guess why he might be upset at the solar plant's low output. The less energy there is to allocate, the harder his job becomes, and the more pressure he's under—from Amalfi on one end, and from bureaucrats in Washington, D.C., on the other. His position can't be a pleasant one.

Still, for some reason I can't yet name, his protests seem almost forced, his real grief against the plant's operators left unspoken. And in the end, that is what bothers me the most. I'm not being asked to like the man. And I doubt that I ever will. But I *am* expected to trust him, to rely on what he says.

And at this point, even when I have no concrete reason to think otherwise, I'm not sure how much I can.

▼ ▼ ▼

When Darby and I finally make it back to her family's home, the house looks just like it did when we left it, less than twenty-four hours before. The porch lights are incongruously shining, despite the mid-afternoon brightness. Her pink bicycle stands undisturbed on the front patio. Pepper, the Stanfords' two-year-old black Lab, lies patiently on the doormat, relishing the warmth of the sun and waiting for his family to return. It's a scene out of Norman Rockwell, captured for this last fleeting moment, soon to be lost to some distant and fading past.

I park the van in the driveway and turn it off, glancing around the neighborhood. In my frayed memory, this quiet cul-de-sac is filled with life. Fathers and mothers coming home from work. Neighbors chatting and exchanging recipes and weekend hunting tips. Teenage boys playing basketball while taunting their too-eager younger brothers. Babies in strollers looking around in wonder. A scene of tranquility and peace. When I actually saw those scenes I can't remember. But now they are all gone.

I am thankful at least for at least one mite of mercy, however: none of the dead are outside to greet us.

I press the van's garage door opener, and the lumbering, three-car-wide door swings up. I step out and open Darby's door, telling her gently what she already knows: that we are home. She nods slowly, her eyes closed, but she does not move. I realize how painful this arrival must be for her, and so I say nothing more. I merely reach in and lift her out of the passenger seat and carry her into the house. Energized by this arrival, Pepper sprints from the front porch and slides into the garage behind us. He barks excitedly, begging us to nuzzle or play with him, unaware that we are all that remain of what was once his grand dominion.

We're inside in seconds, and the house is as pristine as it was yesterday. Sara always was a meticulous housekeeper. And while one can spy a stray dog toy here or there, or one of Ray's annoyingly apocalyptic survivalist magazines lying around, the rooms sit in nearly open-house condition. Having spent many happy evenings here, I know my way to the back and carry Darby to her bed. "Would you like something to eat?" I ask her when we arrive. There's a barely perceptible shake of her head. "Would you like to rest a while?" A shrug. "Why don't you rest then," I suggest. "And then take a bath. It'll make you feel better."

It's the best I can offer her at the moment, although I know it does little good. I pull her bedroom door closed and then walk back to the family room, where Pepper jumps up to greet me. He curiously sniffs my hands and then starts licking them, and I realize that these are smells and tastes that are surely unfamiliar to him. I suspect that the fragrance of the dead will become much more common for all of us as the days go on.

I fill Pepper's empty bowls with food and water, and he digs in excitedly. Then, lying back in the recliner, I pick up one of Ray's magazines. Its cover blares: "Prepare Now for the Next Disaster!" I aimlessly leaf through it, hoping that at least a few people paid attention to the once hyperbolic and now prescient warnings. But even as I let the thought filter in, I realize how physically and emotionally spent I am. It's only a few minutes before my mind has given way to a deep and fitful sleep.

When I awake, the family room is dark, and the digital clock on the microwave informs me that it is just past seven. I close my eyes again, commanding the fog of sleep to depart, and soon am well aware of where I am. I slowly climb out of the chair and go back to check on Darby. She is lying on her bed, still in her soccer uniform, breathing softly in deep and oblivious sleep. I cover her with the faded Barbie throw that she treasures and then let her rest.

I know I should shower, start packing, take care of other tasks that demand my attention. But instead I walk back into the family room and turn on the television, wondering as I do how long the electricity in this now-ghostly city will continue to flow. Sitting in the translucent darkness, I watch the flickering displays of tragedy play across the screen on the few news stations that are still broadcasting. Horrific scenes never meant for the family hour intercut with the ragged and worried faces of news anchors. Gone is the authoritative calm, the quiet arrogance of superior knowledge, that once infected so many of this class. It turns out they are human too.

Scientists and politicians appear seriatim to rehearse one theory after another. Many come prepared with charts, with maps, with satellite photographs. But these visual aids do little to prove their case. The only commonality in all of their observations, it seems, is a description of the undulating aurora that we ourselves briefly noticed last night, and that also reportedly appeared above many of the cities around the world that suffered the greatest loss of life. But other than postulating that the wavering light show resulted from some chemical imbalance in the air, none of the talking heads can assert with any confidence what it means.

Other guests debate the random consequences of the oxygen wipeouts. How did some people survive and others didn't? Why did most dogs and cats make it through but horses and cattle were almost obliterated in the affected areas? Some commentators suggest that geographic fluctuations in oxygen density—over areas as small as a neighborhood block—might be responsible. Others speculate that those with greater lung capacity had an advantage over those whose lung function was impaired. But even the advocates of these views admit that they have no proof to support their theories.

Oddly, the most definitive statement comes from a scientist whose key mark of distinction is the profession of his own ignorance. "We knew something was coming—it was inevitable," he opines. "But even with the best scientific models available, no one could have forecast this specific event. It proves once again that what we know—or what we think we know—remains far less than what we don't."

The man's explanation is suddenly interrupted by the station's "Bulletin" graphic. In seconds, the news anchor returns. Her expression, if anything, is more somber than before. "We have new numbers just in from South Dakota," she says, speaking matter-of-factly, as if she were reading nothing more momentous than the latest election returns. "There are now 125,000 deaths confirmed in that state, bringing the total number of lives taken by the Catastrophe to more than 18 million in the United States, and to some 78 million worldwide."

The rest of the words she speaks—the local tallies, the rescue efforts, the contesting explanations—slip past me like a cold breeze that blows through so quickly that one wonders if it were only imagined. The numbers have grown too large by now to have any meaning: no one can comprehend such figures, nor the death and pain they represent. All that can be felt are the tremors of the individual stories, the personal tragedies, the individual lives lost. It is only then—for the first time since Jeannie and Cassie and Ray and Sara died—that I think of all of the millions of losses experienced by other people in other places. How can these decimated families cope? I wonder. How can they go on?

But in the moment I summon them, these other tragedies are forced away, the visions of these anonymous misfortunes almost instantly replaced by my own. I close my eyes, hoping for some relief, but the visions only grow stronger. I see myself looking down at Cassie as she lay on the soccer field, breathless and dying. She just lies there, not breathing. My own breaths quicken at the recollection of her tiny body as it exhaled its last rushes of life.

And then, suddenly, the train is rolling again. My body starts shaking. My breaths race impossibly fast. My head pounds like a jackhammer. The pain is exquisite. Unbearable. In an instant, my body is past control. I *uselessly grip the arms of the chair, so hard I can feel the faux leather ripping beneath my fingernails. Then lift my hands to fold my throbbing head in their grasp. At last, like a release, my tears gush forth—great heaving sobs that leave me gutted, hollowed out from within. I gasp for breaths then. Breaths that, for the moment and for no cause outside myself, will not come.*

I do not know how much time passes, but eventually the sobs subside. My breaths return. And I manage to regain some sense of control. But the control is a sham, the spasm of a remnant muscle after a body has long since died. For I know I am beaten. Conquered. Burned from the inside out. The memories admit no escape. And they never will.

But with that awful knowledge comes a thin thread of hope. For I know that the pain, as great as it is, can grow no worse. It too can be conquered: I will learn over time to hold it back. I have my duties and my obligations, and they will get me through.

This, I silently vow, will be the last time I allow myself to break down.

Steeled in that instant, I finally come to terms with the chore that faces me. Nighttime is here, and the excuses I made to myself earlier have lost their power. I arise. Wipe my face with a cold damp cloth. And pull the heavy gardening gloves from the drawer where I know Ray keeps them.

I have work to do. And it's time to get to it.

CHAPTER 6

In seconds, our helicopter settles onto the helipad at the northern end of the Golden West solar plant. We've landed next to a wide stone plaza edged on three sides by the peaks of the Sierra Madres—a high platform that offers a mountaineer's view of the tops of the pines poking through the low cloud cover. Only on the far side of the plaza do the works of man intrude, in the form of the entrance to the half-cylindrical shell that supports the solar arrays. A half-moon-shaped wall three stories high, the shell's entrance is painted in warm earthen hues and framed with greenery. But set up against the majesty of the mountains, it still manages to look like an old army Quonset hut.

Gathered in the shadow of the entrance, a white-coated technician lectures a group of Chinese businessmen, their hair and jackets whipping in the wind. Three other men stand a few feet away from them, conversing in more intimate tones. An older Chinese man, round-faced, weighted with authority. A Hispanic man in his late twenties with dark longish hair and a menacing air that's helped along by the revolver bulging under his suit coat. And a tall, tailored gentleman, transformed by his height and silver hair into the center of attention. This is the only person on the plaza I recognize, and I have not seen him for more than a year: Stuart Farraday, chairman and chief executive officer of Golden West Power.

As the chopper's blades slow their spin and we climb out, Farraday breaks off his conversation and he and the young Hispanic man stride over to meet us.

"Mr. Mesoto, good to see you again," Farraday says, extending his hand and warmly grasping Mike's. The hand and greeting go next to Rooker, a shade less warmly. Then Farraday turns to me and hesitates, more in examination than uncertainty.

"I believe you know Martin Fall," Mesoto intervenes.

"Yes, yes, of course," Farraday says. "We've met several times." Farraday now takes my hand and his eyes hold on mine, eyes of understanding and compassion. "I was sorry to hear about your wife, Mr. Fall. And your—son, was it?"

"Daughter," I say, over the unwanted lump in my throat.

"I'm so sorry. Terrible tragedy. Just terrible." He pauses respectfully, allowing the moment to play out and then lets his businessman's mien take control again. He nods toward his companion. "This is my executive assistant, Luis Rojo," he says. "I think you'll find him most helpful."

Rojo doesn't step forward but merely nods, whether out of arrogance or deference, I can't say. But it gives me a moment to look him over, and up close he is not as threatening as he seemed from a distance. He has the build of an athlete, hard and sleek and not a trace of fat, and radiates intensity like a man with a fever. But his face is gentle, almost saintly, and his eyes watch with the mute and passive interest of a priest. Still, it's an odd and unsettling combination. Though I know nothing about the man, I don't think he would be my first choice as a desert-island companion.

Farraday looks on during this moment, clearly trying to discern my thoughts. But he lets it pass and brings the preliminaries to a close with a sweep of his hand. "Shall we go inside, gentlemen?"

We head toward and then through the shell's entrance, into the half-cylindrical passageway beneath the solar arrays. The immediate sensation is one of stepping into an endless tunnel. Stretched out before us is a mile-long walkway, covered the entire distance by an industrial-yellow traction mat. Deep pits line both sides of the walk, pits filled with braids of electrical cables, walls of gauges and lights, and the huge creaking motors that tilt the solar panels to track the sun. Arched above all this is the tunnel's translucent shell. Through it, the shadowy undersides of the forty-foot solar panels are visible, black slabs looming against the late-morning sky.

Farraday leads us down the long corridor, through a rush of activity. Groups of technicians stride past, carrying toolkits, electrical equipment, blueprints. A crewman drives a motorized dolly that holds modular sections of a solar panel, individual pieces small enough to fit on a desktop—yet quite heavy, judging by the effort that a few of the men are expending to lift them. Beyond them, other workers climb fixed steel ladders that pierce the shell and open out onto the curving roof. Over this clatter comes Farraday's voice, proud but restrained, as if the fact of his accomplishment were emphasis enough. "You're looking at the future, gentlemen," he says, indicating the solar panels and the pits filled with motors and cables. "One hundred percent clean energy. No waste heat. No greenhouse gases. And no hydrocarbons. A power source even the most hardened environmentalist could love."

He takes a few steps more, the restraint now so pronounced that he sounds like a kindly museum docent. "And the best part is that access to this kind of power doesn't depend on accidents of history or geography. A few days of sunshine a month is all that's needed to run a plant like this. And so almost every city on the globe can have as much clean, renewable power as they want."

There's a rumbling from behind me. "All courtesy of Golden West Power," I hear Rooker mutter.

"What was that?" Farraday asks, stiffening.

"I said, all courtesy of Golden West. Your firm will be responsible for building all of the plants you're talking about, I presume."

"Of course we will, Mr. Rooker. We invented the technology. We own the patents. And we're the only company qualified to do it." A beat. "Does that bother you?"

Rooker replies with the sneer that I have come to expect. "It hardly makes you a disinterested observer."

"We *aren't* a disinterested observer, as you're well aware. We've invested more than three billion dollars in this technology, and we intend to get some of it back." He pauses, regarding Rooker with his own parcel of disdain. "Or does that bother you too?"

At this, Rooker looks on defiantly but says nothing. It's up to Mesoto to break the tension.

"Perhaps we should get on with the meeting," he says.

Farraday lets his glare linger on Rooker for a few seconds, and then he's calm once again, the kindly museum docent returned. "Yes, I think we should."

▼

The meeting proceeds as planned, but with little apparent purpose Mesoto begins by briefing Farraday on the Council's security measures, a presentation to which the power-company chairman listens quietly but with an air of impatience, as if these were matters internal to the Council and not worth his time. Farraday's own operations director, a wiry milquetoast of a man with an irritating habit of twirling his moustache with his thumb and forefinger as he speaks, adds to the collective annoyance by describing Golden West's security procedures in such numbing and irrelevant detail that Mesoto himself rushes the man to conclusion. A superfluous walk-through of the rest of the plant follows, and then we return to debate, well into the afternoon, the various ways in which the Council and Golden West might work together to stop the bombings. Like the politician that he is, Farraday moves even this discussion to his advantage. The injury emerges as all his, the responsibility for resolving the problems solely in the hands of the Council. It's not hard to see why Mike might feel frustrated at the meeting's end.

Rooker, to my surprise, says little during this time. Only when we tour the plant does he show any interest—and then, I presume, only because the plant's own security infrastructure takes on more meaning when it is seen rather than merely discussed. Several times he stops to examine the solar panels, inspect the surveillance network, and ask questions about the security rotations. But when we return to the conference room, he makes no use of this information and defers to Mesoto to defend the Council's position.

Luis Rojo, though supposedly Farraday's chief assistant, is even less a participant than Rooker. He spends the entire meeting sitting silently at the end of the conference table, looking like a man whose mind is elsewhere. His only signs of life come intermittently when he retrieves an apple from the fruit tray set out for lunch. With a pearl-handled pocket knife, he removes the apple's skin in one long, winding ribbon, then carefully slices the fruit into wedges before spearing them and bringing them to his lips. His movements are so fluid and precise, the act of eating becomes a work of art. But his contributions to our discussions, like Rooker's, are nil.

As the afternoon winds on, I find myself wondering why these two men even bothered to show up. Or why even Farraday did, for that matter.

And then I know. Just as we're standing to depart, Farraday motions us back into our seats. "One more thing, gentlemen," he says, tossing a thick green-bound document onto the table. "Perhaps you've read this."

"Many times," Rooker replies. "I wrote it."

"Yes, I know. Every time the federal government has cut fuel shipments into this region, your allocation rules have placed that burden disproportionately on what you call 'fringe services'—like finishing construction on the LA solar plant."

"You've made your opinion quite clear on that issue, Mr. Farraday. We have—what is it?—something like forty filings from you in just the past six months."

"And you'll *keep* getting them until this matter is resolved. If this solar plant is the main hope for bringing our city's energy supplies anywhere close to normal—as you and Amalfi have both said—then we can't delay its completion any longer. For *any* reason."

Rooker looks on calmly, saying nothing for the moment. He is a man of supreme confidence—one whose arguments have no foil and his position no imperfections—and he wears his disrespect for those who disagree with him like a thousand-dollar suit.

"Let me ask you something," he says at length. "You do realize we're in the middle of a little crisis, don't you?"

Farraday only frowns at this, as if this line of discourse were more of a waste of time than Mesoto's briefing. "I'm well aware of the extent of the crisis, Mr. Rooker. Probably more than most."

"I'm not sure you are. This isn't some—what did you call it?—some 'bureaucratic field day,' I believe it was," Rooker says, checking his notes. "I don't like this allocation business any better than you do. And I don't particularly enjoy closing down factories or confiscating private generators or telling people they can't drive their cars. But until we understand exactly what happened and what we can do about it, we have no choice but to err on the side of caution. Otherwise, we may wake up one morning and *none of us* will be able to breathe. Ask me about your allocations then."

The chairman sits expressionless through this, but the hardness from before has taken over his voice again. "Get to the point."

"The point, Mr. Farraday, is that this city doesn't have the fuel to give you, and you wouldn't be allowed to burn it even if we did. You're already ten percent over your emission allowances for the quarter as it is. Your *federal* emissions allowances. Not ours."

"And this plant, Mr. Rooker, is ten *weeks* behind schedule—thanks to your allocation rules. We haven't even been able to break ground on the Orange County or Riverside plants yet."

"I know," Rooker says. "And I know it's difficult having to operate within these restrictions. But you and your friends in Congress should have thought about that before they passed the new energy controls. Washington won't allow us to burn enough fuel in this city to produce the barest minimum of consumer goods and services—little luxuries like food and medicine and purified water—much less to power a factory to build your solar panels."

"Which is precisely why cutting allocations for our solar plants is so myopic. Every barrel of oil you divert from us is one more kilowatt of clean, non-polluting electricity we can't produce."

"All right," says Rooker, leaning back with crossed arms, meeting Farraday's intransigence with his own. "Let's assume you're right and that our top priority *should* be increasing power output from your solar plants. If that's what you're really interested in—and not just building more of these monstrosities to peddle overseas—why don't you try increasing your conversion efficiency?" A pause, and his voice fills with judgment. "Or is that too much to ask?"

Farraday's diplomatic façade starts to crack at this, his face reddening. In the same moment, Mesoto looks across vengefully at Rooker, as if to silence him before the skirmish erupts into a full-fledged war—and undoing what minuscule agreement Mesoto was able to achieve during the day's discussions. But the exchange strikes me more as a topic that should be aired than it does a mere flexing of egos. and so I cut in before Mike can say anything.

"It's a fair question," I say to Mike, then look to Farraday. "What about it, Mr. Farraday? Are you stuck at eight-percent efficiency forever?"

Mike offers me only a steely glare as I ask the question, and now he's ticked off at me too. *Sorry, buddy*, I think. *Guess you shouldn't have asked me along.*

His diplomatic façade returning, Farraday promptly dispels the moment's animus, offering a calm, concessionary reply. "Of course we're not," he says. "Before long, this plant will be operating with a conversion efficiency of more than thirty percent, as the report Mr. Rooker is holding makes clear."

I can see Rooker's own anger building at this, but I press on. "And when will that be," I ask Farraday. "Next month? Next year?"

"As soon as we can make it happen. Look, I don't mean to sound evasive, but you have to understand, with a plant this large and complex, it takes time—"

And now Rooker has boiled over. "Almost ninety million people have died!" he bursts out as he stands, his arms pressed to the table in the stiffness of rage. "And thousands more are dying on the streets every week! How much more time are you going to waste!"

"The Catastrophe is *over*, Mr. Rooker. The problems with the atmosphere are *past*."

"Are they?" Rooker sneers. "What crystal ball have you been reading? We have *no idea* whether the Catastrophe is over or when it will strike again. We don't have *any* time to waste!"

Amazingly, Farraday just shrugs at this. "You're a very pessimistic man" is all he says. "But let's all agree that time is critical. So instead of lecturing me about how to run my plant, why don't you and your Council get off your collective hind ends and do *your* job and find out who's behind these bombings. *Now*." He turns to Mesoto, his hostility building. "And that goes for you too, " Farraday says. "There's no reason your office can't protect a few dozen fuel tanks. These eco-freaks who are blowing them up—whoever they are—are probably just a group of dope-headed flakes without a brain in their heads. They're intellectual *midgets*. And you can't be *that* incompetent."

"We've got electromagnetic fences, retaining walls, and an army of security people at every plant," says Mesoto. "And security cameras every thirty feet. We're doing the best we can." He finishes with an attempt to be stern, but he ends up only sounding defensive.

"We'll see, Mr. Mesoto. We'll see. But I'll tell you something—and this goes for you too, Mr. Rooker. If we don't have the fuel to get this plant and the Orange County and Riverside plants up to full power by the middle of next year, those precious people you and Ms. Amalfi profess to care so much about won't be breathing—"

Abruptly, the conference room door swings open, and Farraday turns, scanning for the cause of this interruption. I look up and see a woman standing in the doorway, her hand gripping the knob. She's Latina, tall, probably in her early thirties, dressed in a white lab coat. Striking, even in her genderless attire. But if she's embarrassed at having intruded on our meeting, she doesn't show it.

"I'm sorry," she says evenly, eyeing Farraday. "They said your meeting was over." And with that she closes the door and disappears.

I look back to catch two expressions at once. Farraday is merely irritated, the expected reaction of a man whose professional privacy has just been violated. But Rooker's response is something else entirely, both more surprising and harder to explain. There's an unmistakable look of unease that comes to his face in the instant that his eyes meet those of our visitor.

But then the look is gone, and I'm not sure I even saw it.

"We seem to have some problems in the lab," Farraday says calmly as he stands to leave. "We'll have to resume this discussion another day. I hope," he adds, directing his words toward Rooker, "in a more civil atmosphere."

And he turns to go. Rooker endures this parting shot without word or expression, banking again on silence as his best defense. But he's clearly less composed than he was a moment before. Mesoto takes the meeting's end with a loud sigh of futility, now that the last opportunity for achieving consensus with Golden West are gone. The only man unchanged by this event, in fact, is Luis Rojo, who sits with perfect aplomb at the table's far end. After a moment, he casually reaches for another apple, then begins to shear away its skin with his pearl-handled pocketknife in slow, surgical strokes, leaving the long red ribbon to fall, like a luminous cascade of blood, to the table below.

▼

"Completely useless," Mike Mesoto informs me, when at last we're alone, hours later. "First, Farraday and his *flojo* won't give us squat for assistance on the bombings. Then he wastes half the afternoon with his worthless show-and-tell. And then when you put him on the spot on the efficiency ratings, his *chica latina* calls him out of the meeting." Mesoto stares down into his beer, repeating his assessment, but with less fervor this time. "Completely useless."

"Helped along by our own Mr. Charm," I add, taking a pull on my beer. Mesoto only grunts at this, and I'm thinking back to Mike's conciliatory gesture after the meeting, his invitation to Rooker to join us for drinks. The information services director brusquely declined, making it clear that he had better things to do and better people to spend his time with than a couple of blue-collar stiffs who can't shoot straight. "I'd forgotten what a pleasant person he is."

"The times are made for his kind," is Mesoto's grudging answer, and then he is silent. After a moment, he looks up, idly scanning the bar. I follow his eyes, taking in this setting that is an oasis only by comparison to the streets outside. Amalfi closed most of the city's dining establishments shortly after the Catastrophe, but allowed several of the bars and nightclubs to stay open in the belief that some form of public respite was a necessary sedative for keeping the public's rage below the boiling point.

As I look around, I decide that she was probably right. The bar is jammed with working-class men and women narcotized by the despair and deficiency that rule their daily lives, trading their last ration coupons for the bittersweet taste of oblivion. They crowd in tens and twelves around the small round tables originally meant for four. Stand blank-eyed and motionless against the walls like witnesses at an execution. Huddle as closely as they can to the squadrons of oxygen tanks stationed in the corners, like desperate penitents seeking the proximity of a heavenly totem. In the anemic light of the flickering candle stubs that are the room's only illumination, their faces are masks of quiet portent, as if their owners stood here waiting to march toward some inexorable death.

And yet I wonder: what would these people—and the thousands like them in the city's other open bars—be doing if they *weren't* inside? Would their own oblivion be enough to satisfy them? Or would they feel the need to take others with them?

I turn back to Mike, not wanting to think about it, and see that he is regarding me with a look of defeat that is almost a match for the funeral watch that surrounds us.

"You know, maybe I told you this," he is saying. "A long time ago, when I first applied to the police academy, I was rejected. Top third of my class, two years in criminal justice, cruised through the physical. But they cut me anyway. Did I tell you about it?"

"No, I don't think so."

"Really got me down, that rejection. I packed my bags the next day and went to stay with my grandparents in Mérida. Miguelo—my grandfather—told me I got turned down because I'm a *cabezon*."

Mesoto takes a long drink and slumps back in his chair, but I don't interrupt. If you know Mike, you know he'll get to the point soon enough. And he won't reach it any more quickly if you try to rush him.

"I tell Miguelo he's crazy," Mesoto resumes after a moment, in his slow what-do-I-care cadence. "Los Angeles is loaded with *Mejicanos*, I say, got lots of Hispanic cops. But they're not *cabazones*, he tells me." A pause, a change of direction. "You ever see a picture of a Mayan Indian, *amigo*?"

I shake my head. I probably have, but I don't remember. It doesn't make any difference anyway. Mike is about to tell me what I need to know. He always does.

"They look a little like me," he goes on. "The shape of the head. The eyes. In Mexico, people can tell. If you look like a Mayan, they call you a *cabezon*. It makes them feel they're better than you. Lots of *cabazones* in Mérida. They hear it all the time. But I grew up right here in LA, so it never occurred to me until Miguelo told me." Another pause, and the mug goes to his lips, but he doesn't drink. "Now, when I say something dumb or someone makes me feel like an idiot, that's what I think to myself—*cabezon*. Funny how that happens."

I study him, finally understanding where this was meant to lead. "You're talking about Farraday, aren't you?"

"You noticed it too?"

"Yeah. Hard to miss," I tell him sympathetically. But frankly, I hadn't thought about it until this moment, how it would look to Mesoto. I guess I should have been watching with his eyes instead of my own. "He screwed you big time today, didn't he, Mike? I'm sorry I didn't realize it soon enough to do you any good."

"You did what you could, and I just tried to shut you up so we could be done with it. But it wouldn't have mattered what you did or didn't say. I feel like a *cabezon* anyway." He lets out a frustrated sigh. "What did Farraday have to gain by it, *amigo*—making me look like an idiot?"

"I've been asking myself the same question," I lie. "I don't know. The bombings may not have cut back his allocations as much as he says, but they certainly haven't helped. And after today, Rooker isn't going to give him the time of day." I take another swig of the beer. It's flatter than Kansas and refreshes like dry heat. But it's better than the water, which tastes like Clorox. "I don't know what he expects to gain, Kemo. He undercuts you, and it only slows down the investigation."

"Maybe he thinks I'm in over my head, that the job's too much for me. Maybe he wants someone else in my place." A bitter pause. "You know, I'm beginning to wonder if he isn't right. I *am* in over my head. I can't even come up with a motive for what's going on, much less a method."

"I thought the motive was obvious."

He snorts. "*Tal vez*. At least that's what Amalfi, Rooker, Farraday, and everyone else says. 'They're eco-terrorists, crazies. They just want to stop us from burning any fuel at all.' Well, maybe that's it. But I've been thinking. What the bombers are doing, it hurts us, yes, for a while. At least until we get more oil shipped in or an old refinery back online. But if they really wanted to send us back to the stone ages, if they wanted to keep us from burning oil altogether, they'd bomb the food factories, blow up the electric generators, do a hundred things that would make it impossible to use the oil even if we had it."

He finishes his beer and then stares into the empty mug for a moment, collecting his thoughts. In the silence, from somewhere outside, comes a low, barely perceptible moan. Like the howl of a dying dog or the wail of a distant siren. I can't quite make it out.

"And something else," Mike continues, his voice washing away the sound. "The bombers—they wouldn't care so much if people were killed. Right after the Catastrophe, you know, people in some places totally lost control. Blew up oil derricks, car factories, that sort of thing. They killed dozens, maybe hundreds of people. Indiscriminately."

"And these bombings haven't?"

"Not a one. Three people hurt, that's all—and they weren't even supposed to be where they were. Whoever's doing this is being unbelievably careful." He shakes his head, and the sigh comes again, more defeated than before. "It just doesn't add up. If these *imbéciles* were really trying to send us a message, they'd be all over the video screens right—"

"Wait, Mike. Hold on," I say, raising my hand to silence him. The sound from the distance has become clearer now. Unmistakable.

"It's only a siren," he says.

"It's coming this way."

He listens. "Yeah. So? There are sirens all the time these days. Fires. Bombings. Arsonists. People with nothing better to do. Probably more fire trucks on the street than food wagons."

He goes on, but my thoughts are elsewhere. I'm looking around the bar. A man at a pay phone, trying to get a dial tone. A couple making out in a dark corner. A fight ready to erupt at a table across the way. Nothing out of the ordinary, and yet disturbing for that reason alone. *Too* ordinary. Like the inside of an airliner the moment before it blows apart.

And still the siren comes closer.

"It's right down the street," I say.

"Sounds like it." But now he's looking at me in an odd sort of way, like someone might regard a mental patient who has stumbled into a board meeting. I'm sure he's wondering what has taken hold of me. Frankly, so am I.

"I have a bad feeling about this, Mike," is all I can tell him. "Let's get out of here."

"Sure, if you want." He lumbers to his feet, grudgingly following me but not knowing why. "Never get a table this good again, though."

But I'm past listening, thinking only of the front door. We elbow our way through the crowd, drawing a few irritated stares, a few challenges that fall dead on inebriated lips, but no blows. It doesn't matter. In the suddenly panicked state I'm in, I'd flatten anyone who tried to stop us. Right now, for some reason I can't explain, I have to get out of here. Maybe it's only the claustrophobia, the feeling that I can't breathe. Or my own foul memories of the crush of patrons in a diner north of Flagstaff, so many lifetimes ago. Or perhaps it's other memories, even more deeply buried. An approaching siren that recalls the wail of an approaching ambulance. A crowded bar that recalls a crowded soccer field. Maybe that's what it is, why Mike doesn't notice anything amiss. He wasn't there; I was. And for a man with such haunted memories, with the experiences I've endured, it's a natural reaction. Completely understandable.

And it vanishes as soon as we're outside.

I breathe heavily, exhaling the panic's last rush. We're standing on the sidewalk, in front of the doorway of the bar. The sensation of claustrophobia, the imperative of departure, is gone. I feel pretty stupid.

"Better now?" Mesoto asks.

"Yeah, sorry. An attack of the willies, I guess."

"Must not be used to all the people," he says with a smile, pulling a cigarette package from his pocket. As he does, the siren blasts again, giving me a quick shudder, and I peer toward the end of the street to see a fire truck racing through the intersection, directly toward us, its siren blaring.

Apparently, the siren's sudden outburst has startled Mike as much as it did me. He has fumbled his lighter, which has fallen to the sidewalk and skidded toward a drainage culvert. We're both bending down to retrieve it just as the fire engine passes. At that moment, there comes from the bar behind us an explosion so deafening and heat so enveloping that we forget all about fire trucks and fallen lighters. The blast is so powerful that it knocks us both forward, and we're tumbling toward the pavement, forced to our knees by the rush of scorched sulfur air.

I look back then toward the bar. Anxious, not yet comprehending, trying to see what happened. The bar's front wall is as it was, wood panels with a bad paint job. The only changes in this façade are the now-shattered windows and the triangles of glass dusting the sidewalk below. But visible through these fractured portals, past the flapping blackening drapes, are the bright strobes of destruction. There's nothing but red inside. And, behind the red, pale gray shadows turning to black.

And the roar. A suffocating roar pours out over us, spilling down the street like a floodwall. It is the fire's war cry, punctuated by the fading, banshee screams of the victims within.

And then, in moments, there is only silence.

I'm too stunned to grasp the magnitude of this horror, the mere seconds that kept our own lives from being extinguished along with those of scores of others. My sole impulse is to rush inside, to try to help, and I'm not even thinking about what the consequences might be. But I've gone only a step or two when I feel my arms locked up behind me, held in the grip of a man stronger than I am.

"Hold on, *novato*," says my companion. "Not a thing you can—"

And then, all at once, there's another blast from inside, even more thunderous than the first, its payoff more vile. The whole front wall of the bar has become a mural of flames now. The fingers of fire lick toward the roof as the thick jets of heat reach out to embrace us. I remember the rows of oxygen tanks lining the bar's interior, and I realize that the fire must now have consumed them as well.

There are no shadows this time moving about within.

I'm back to my senses in that moment. Mike and I are stumbling, then careening across the street. We pull up on the far side of a rusted mailbox, out of the heat's grasp, away from the view of destruction. Only the kaleidoscope of ruby lights playing on the wall of the building in front of us reminds me of the inferno that we have left behind.

That and the fire engine. At the other end of the street, its siren roaring with the fierceness of an awakened beast, the truck has turned around, and its crew speeds toward a mission in which they can have no hope of success.

"You all right?" Mesoto asks me.

But I've turned back to look at the bar. I'm thinking of the man at the pay phone. Of the lovers in the corner. Of the cheery little blonde with the Southern accent and too-sweet smile who served us our drinks. They're dead now, every one of them.

"Better than those people," is all I can say.

Mesoto doesn't answer right away. He merely lifts another cigarette from his pocket, lights it with a match, and takes a long listless pull. His eyes settle on mine—weary, vanquished, almost beyond the point of caring—and then he blows out a slow stream of smoke from the corner of his mouth.

"These days, *amigo*," he says, "I'm not so sure."

▼ ▼ ▼

I am standing in Ray's basement, in front of a wall of personally enhanced and probably illegal weaponry, when my cell phone rings.

It is the middle of the night. I have just ventured into the Stanfords' cramped and poorly lit cellar, having showered and, before that, completed the eviscerating duty of burying those I loved. The ground on Ray's property was hard but not impenetrable—the first freeze of autumn had not yet set in—and Ray owned a selection of shovels and picks that were worthy to the task. It was ironic and yet sadly fitting that Ray and Sara would be buried in the backyard of this house that had been their dream for more than a decade. "It's where we'll spend our glory years," Ray had once boasted. As for Jeannie, she would find her final resting place immensely unpleasant given how much she disliked the cold mountain climate. But at least she would spend the eternities with her daughter and her friends. And besides, she was long past feeling.

Almost as much as I am.

My grim duty discharged, I turned to my next task: preparing for our trip southward. I had made the decision during the long hours consumed by the burials that our best course would be to return home to Los Angeles. I knew no one here in Denver other than the Stanfords. Knew little about the city. And, like Jeannie, I wasn't eager to face the harsh winters that were would soon descend on the Rockies. At least in Los Angeles, I had a job, a home, some modest possessions, even a few friends—amenities that would help distract my mind when my thoughts ventured too close to the edge. Denver was Darby's home, of course—it was almost all she had ever known—and I also had to consider what would be best for her. But so many of her friends were surely gone by now that their loss might be more painful here than it would be if she were a thousand miles away. A new life would never compensate for what she once had, but at least it would give her the opportunity to heal. Something, I suspected, that would be difficult for her to do if she remained here.

Darby was awake when I stepped back inside the house, after completing my work in the backyard. She did not ask what I had been doing, and I did not tell her, although I suspected she already knew. With the act unspoken, perhaps it became less real, less permanent. So I quickly turned to more pedestrian matters, asking if she were still tired. She shook her head. Hungry? The same response. Darby was always a talkative girl, much more so that Cassie. But she had settled into a regime in which words were no longer her allies. That was all right. Each of us deals with our grief in our own way. She would talk when she was ready.

I brought in some suitcases from the garage and asked Darby to fill two or three of them with whatever clothes and toys and personal items she wanted to take with her. I added that we probably wouldn't be back for a while, but it was an unneeded reminder. I suspected she knew all too well that this would be the last she would see of the home where she had spent so many happy years.

I rummaged through Ray's closets to find a few clothes that would not be too awkward for me to wear—coats, work shirts, winter boots—and washed out the meager inventory of socks and underwear of my own that I had brought for the brief trip. Ray's extensive tool collection came next, along with an assortment of household implements that might prove useful. For a survivalist, Ray's stocks of emergency food storage were scattered at best, but there were a couple of cases of MREs and a well-furnished pantry that would provide more than enough food even for a week-long drive. And then, of course, there were the weapons. I had no idea what to expect once we were on the road, no fixed beliefs of what the trip might be like. But an uneasy sense of warning prodded me to caution. I decided to take them all.

That decision made only minutes before, I am in the process of removing Ray's lethal cache from the gun cabinet when I hear the ringing cell phone. It is so startling, so unanticipated, that I stand confused for a moment, trying to identify the once-familiar sound. I had tried dialing the phones throughout the day before without success—Ray's landline was still dead as well—but had given up since beginning the burials. Now, in the middle of the night, I am as startled by the phone's sudden return to life as I am by its timing.

It's probably a solicitation call, I think with a quick, mordant stab.

I answer tentatively. "Uh, hello."

"Martin! Oh, Martin! Thank goodness you're okay! I've been trying forever to reach you. All the lines have been down."

"I know," I reply. It's Alison Leary, sweet Alison Leary from the office. Mike Mesoto's and my assistant. If anyone were calling, it would be her. Mike hates to talk on the phone and Fran and Erthein and Rooker and the rest would be too focused on dealing with the crisis to take the time to wonder about me. Although frankly I'm not sure how busy they would be, since the air shortages apparently spared Southern California.

Busy enough, I soon find out. "It's been crazy here, just crazy," Alison goes on, intruding on my thoughts. "And all those people. I saw it on the news. It's everywhere. I feel so terrible. I cried all night."

Me too, I reflect, but don't say it. *But I'm thinking: why are we having this conversation? I appreciate your concern, Alison, I really do. But can't this wait until morning? I have a lot to do. A lot to think about. Can we call it a night?* Of course, I say none of this either. Alison is one of the most genuinely caring people I have ever known, and she has always taken a proprietary interest in Mike and me. I'm grateful that she made the effort to track me down, grateful for the sound of her voice, although it's more human contact than I really care for at the moment.

"Well, at least you're okay, Martin. I'm so relieved. When are you coming back?"

"I'm leaving today," I answer. "I'm driving. They say the airports are still closed, so I imagine it'll take a while."

"Probably so. But watch the roads, okay? I hear they're—"

And then I lose the connection. Once more, the phone is dead. But I can guess what she was going to say. *Crowded*. Yes, I know. Thank you. The roads are crowded. I saw it on the news too.

But I live in LA. I'm used to it.

I stare for another instant at the once-again lifeless cell phone, waiting without expectation for it to ring again. I try redialing Alison's number, but the call doesn't go through. At length, I place the phone back in my pocket and begin to collect Ray's firearms. Within a short time, the packing will be done. I can take a break then, and rest for a few hours.

And then, finally, we can be on our way.

CHAPTER 7

"The luck of the streets," Mesoto tells me, pronouncing his verdict on our timely exit from the bar. I accept his explanation because I don't want to talk about it. But I'm almost as disturbed by the manner of our survival as I am by the nearness of our demise. There was more to my premonition than claustrophobia or memories of Denver, I'm convinced of it. But what? I have no idea. Maybe Mike's right after all. Maybe it was nothing more than dumb luck.

Still, I want to be left alone with my thoughts when I reach my apartment. I'm even rushed with Alison when she stops by within minutes of my return, bearing bandages and burn cream. I sit quietly while she ministers to the places where embers burned through my clothes, then I hurry her out with only a quick good-bye when she's finished, claiming fatigue and a bad headache. I even forget to thank her for the fruit basket from that morning, although it sits in front of us the entire time. I silently promise myself that I'll make it up to her when I see her again.

But I wonder, even as I make this pledge, whether I'll remember it by morning.

For my mind is already veering toward overload. The sight of the San Fernando Valley, where Jeannie and Cassie and I lived for nearly a decade. The solar plant, appearing like a ghost on a site where—the last time I saw it—there was almost nothing. The hostility between Rooker and everyone around him. The random chance of the explosion and fire, and the equally random chance of our survival. Taken together, they are too much to bear in a single day, especially for someone still trapped in the corrosive mesh of the past. I need to decompress. I need to forget. I need to sleep.

But it turns out that all I can do is lie in bed and stare at the ceiling. After an hour or so of this useless exercise, I step into the living room, pull a chair up to the window, and just watch the night. As I sit there, I can't shake the feeling that I'm looking at California as it might have appeared a million years ago. The sky is overcast, leaving only the land to paint images on the eye. But there are no images. No movements. No proof of the present except for a single cluster of white lights, miles in the distance. A hospital maybe, or a factory on emergency shift. All of the other buildings are dark, and in the shadows they look more like the works-in-progress of an apprentice god than they do the finished structures of man. The only accents to the scene, in fact, are pools and pinpoints of fluorescent red strewn throughout. I decide that these must be the campfires of cavemen, or the vengeant signatures of primordial lightning. Or perhaps they're nothing more than the fiery aftershocks of human violence, like the bomb blast I saw tonight.

And that's it—that's all I can see. Beyond these few specks of light, there's only black. And even where there is light, the black grows to consume it, spreading like an aggressive cancer until the eyes refuse to register anything but the darkness. It does not take long before the scene itself becomes claustrophobic, and I give it up. Suddenly overcome by exhaustion, I retreat to the bed, hoping for my own taste of oblivion before the morning calls me back to the world of the present.

I find that release at last, after nearly an hour more. But it is an uneasy respite, filled with dreams of fire. The visions begin almost at soon as sleep comes, and they begin with black, left over from my vigil at the window. Then, moments later, the fires arrive. The black background of my dreamspace silently gives way as these rolling flames start slowly from the bottom of my vision and whip upward in long lazy strokes toward the top. This piling of flame upon flame continues until all I see before me is a flickering curtain of red. I muse in that moment that I must be watching the whole of Los Angeles falling victim to the same fate as the bar.

But then this fiery sheet gives up a small opening, like a space of sky when the clouds are blown apart by the wind, and a dark metallic object appears behind the flames. I can't tell what it is at first. But the flames gradually pull back and the object itself grows larger, or at least more distinct. I have seen this image before, I realize. Eventually, I am able to dredge the moment from my memory. I am looking at an oil refinery being consumed by flames, a dreamer's copy of the one Mike showed me in Carson barely two days ago.

Yet even as the image comes to me, it starts to break apart. Like the charred bank of pipes attached to the disintegrating refinery that we witnessed in Carson, pieces of this imagined structure separate and fall away. But instead of slanting outward, they tumble inward toward the image's core, collapsing in a slow graceful arc. The fractured pieces reach the images' center and then vanish one-by-one, as if vaporized, until only the skeleton of the imagined structure remains. Then it too crumbles under the force of gravity, and there is nothing left but the flames . . .

. . . and all at once I'm awake, sitting bolt upright. Sweating profusely even though I left the bedroom window open. Breathing hard, my chest pressing inward like a heart attack. I try urgently to recall the dream. What was it? As if in answer, the images slowly come back to me. The flames. The refinery. The disintegrating pipes. The whole complex being taken over by the fire until nothing remained.

I have to call Mike!

After a single ring, he answers—grumbles, really—and then I'm off, still half-asleep but focused, like a blind man in a tunnel, heading unveeringly in one direction.

"Mike," I say in a rush. "It's Fall. Listen, I know it's— I don't know, two, three o'clock. Doesn't matter. Can you meet me downstairs in— Yes, I'm okay. Now would you listen? Meet me in half an hour, all right? I'll tell you then."

My fervor urges him awake. It may not be a completely one-way conversation. I'm sure he must say something. But I have the presence of mind only to grasp my own words, and by the time I hang up, I cannot recall a single word he has said.

But it has to be that way. I have to ring off. To retrieve the dream in its fullness before I lose it. To bring back the certainty that infused me when I awoke—a certainty that shook me from deep inside as I sat there in its afterburn.

Yet even as the images come back to me in the room's revenant silence, I'm not sure I want to know what they mean.

"You figure all this out in your sleep, *amigo*?" Mesoto asks as I slide into the van's front seat.

"Figure *what* out?"

"The bombings. You didn't wake me up at three o'clock in the morning to go wind-surfing, I know that." He rams the van into gear and we barrel through the apartment's security gates and out into the street. "What's on your mind, Martin?"

I tell him I want to go back to the Carson refinery. He stares at me—to make sure I'm serious, I think—and then turns south toward the freeway without saying a word.

It is several minutes before he asks me to explain.

"What do you think you'll find?" he asks, once we're speeding along the empty thoroughfare, after I've rehearsed the dream. "I thought I already told you. My men have been all over the place. There's nothing left but walls and pipes."

"That's just it," I tell him. "The walls and pipes—they're still there."

"Yeah. So?"

"You remember the Long Beach explosion, about ten years ago?"

He nods, and I'm sure he's recalling the memory, just as I did during the minutes while I was waiting for him—visualizing the force of the blast, reliving the impact that it had on the surrounding property. And on us.

I had been called to Long Beach that morning because a fire had broken out near the refinery's main fuel tanks, one of which had been filled just two days before. I had brought Mike with me, and we were less than a mile away when the first tank blew. Within seconds, a wave of heat rolled over us so intense that nearby trees were bowed and scorched and our car felt like it was being microwaved. The facility—the whole surrounding block—was leveled. Fifty-five people died that morning. And the refinery? Forget walls and pipes. On the third day, after rains finally extinguished the flames, there was nothing left of the once-towering structure but a big black hole and a few charred fragments of iron and steel.

The Carson explosion was nothing like this.

"The tanks at Carson," I say. "They were about the same size as the ones at Long Beach, weren't they?"

"A little bigger, actually."

"And the main tank at Carson—the one that exploded—it was full, wasn't it?"

"Yes, of course. That's the whole point. The *malvados* bombed it the day after—"

Now he sees where I'm headed, and he looks across with grave and sudden interest. All at once, the torpor has gone from his eyes.

"And you're *sure* it was full?" I press him.

"The Carson operator checked the tank level that morning when he logged in. And I checked the central computer afterward. The tank was listed as full and it read out as full."

"I don't think it was, Mike. It couldn't have been. Or Carson would be a crater by now."

He gives a thoughtful pause. "You're right about that, *novato*," he says, pushing down on the accelerator, as anxious now to be there as I am. Even with the sluggishness of the vehicle's hydrogen fuel, the van chugs to fifty, then sixty miles an hour.

We're there in twenty minutes, well before I have a chance to finish the mug of black-market coffee that Mike has been kind enough to bring along.

▼

The next several minutes are passages of light and silence. First, there is nothing in front of us but shadows layered on shadows, indecipherable even to the well-trained eye. Then the dim oval of light from Mike's flashlight blinks on once we're safely past the security perimeter and finds its way to the tall chain-link fence hastily erected the day before as a means of discouraging scavengers. The light plays over this fence, a spotlight in search of its target, until a lock comes into view. The light dances around its target for a few seconds and then holds. Now a pair of hands enters the oval, brandishing a set of bolt clippers. With two rapid snaps, the lock is fractured and is left hanging haphazardly on the links, its defenses nullified. The breach is complete.

The push of a hand comes next. The gate creaks open, and we step through.

Inside the complex, the light continues to track ahead of us, over the blackened remnants of the refinery fire. There are girders and pipes. Bricks and concrete blocks. Broken-off sections of pumps and gutted electrical housings. But mostly there are unrecognizable pieces of metal and hillocks of debris. We wind around these and finally reach the far side of the operations office, now bombed-out remains slumped in the darkness like the ruins of Dresden. The light finds the edge of a steel wall, scarred but otherwise intact. Almost imperceptibly, the light moves along it, slowly and to the right.

"That's it," Mesoto says in a hushed voice.

And now the light closes in, centering on a metal panel held in place by a quartet of screws. But no screwdriver will pry these bolts lose, we see at once. They have been welded shut by the heat of the blast.

"Hand me the hammer and chisel," Mesoto says, and I pass them to him. With short, compact strokes, he sets about dislodging the plate from its mounting, attempting to do so as quietly as possible. But the first several tries prove feckless, and the plate remains as firmly fixed as when he started.

I watch this lack of progress, wondering now that we're here if it was even worth our coming. "You sure the gauge didn't melt?" I ask him.

"If I thought it did, would I be out here freezing my butt off?" Then less bitterly: "The casing's made of the same stuff as the black boxes on airplanes. It'll be fine." I move in closer just as he's swinging, and the hammer misses the chisel, banging against the wall. "Hold the light steady, will ya?" he says. "Gonna turn my hand into hamburger here in a minute."

"Sorry." I refocus the flashlight. "Listen, I don't mean to keep asking, but you're sure the gauge showed full?"

"No one looked at it directly, if that's what you mean," he answers as he continues working. "Only happens once a month during the regular inspections. But the lines go straight to the refinery's server and to the Council's central computer downtown. No way the signals could get scramb—"

This time, the chisel slips out of place, sliding across the metal plate and gouging Mesoto's palm. He emits a deep guttural gasp of pain, grasping the injured hand. "Give me a rag or something."

I look down, spy an oil-stained cloth in his toolbox, and pass it on to him. Just then, there's a tinkle of sound from the other side of the refinery. A sound like pebbles being tossed. Or someone walking on gravel.

"What's—" I start but am immediately called to silence.

"Shhh!" Mesoto snaps. I turn off the flashlight and we freeze. After a couple of minutes, there's nothing more. Mike nods for me to turn the light back on.

"Operations chief killed by his own security guards," he mutters as he sets the hammer and chisel to the plate again. "Great way to end a career. Let's put this *niño* to bed and get outta here."

He's hitting harder now, despite his injured palm and the risks of noise, just wanting to finish. The peal of the hammer against the chisel echoes off the steel walls on either side of us, sounding like great metal thunderclaps.

"So let me get this straight," he says as one corner of the panel finally breaks free. "If both the Council's computer and the refinery registers said the tank was full—but it wasn't—then somebody messed with the data files both here *and* downtown."

"Or rigged the transmission box."

"Right. Jimmied it so that it sent out signals that said the tank was full when in fact it—"

Suddenly, the hammer drives the chisel all the way under the metal plate, snapping all of the remaining screws at once. The plate jumps away from the wall as if it had been pushed. Mike doesn't notice what's happening, and I have to jerk his hand away before he gets his fingers sliced.

"Watch it, *cabezon*," I tell him, "or you'll lose the other one too."

"Thanks," he answers. But even as he says it, the incident's gone from his mind. The control box is open to view, and he's peering inside. I move the light forward, brightening our view. All we can see at first are rows of circuit boards connected with an infinity of colored wires. But one wire near the front has clearly been soldered on, and we follow it with the flashlight as it winds into a corner half-hidden by the circuit boards. A box the size of a cigarette package is parked there, held in place by twists of electrical tape.

"*Oh mi querida madre,*" Mesoto murmurs.

"If that means feedback loop, my friend, you're right on target."

His eyes form the question. He doesn't bother asking it."

"Used to be big items with the power thieves," I explain. "Long time before you came on board. Hook this little beauty up to an electric meter. Send in a signal from the outside. Make the meter read whatever you want it to—*whenever* you want it to."

"Or make a fuel-tank gauge read 'full' even if it's almost empty."

"You got it. Just enter whatever data you want into the system. And since this gauge feeds both the refinery *and* the central computer, no one notices anything amiss until the tank runs dry or time comes for the monthly visual."

"And by then the fuel tank's already blown."

"Bingo." I hold the light closer, examining the details of the box. "Uh-oh."

"What is it?"

"Oh, this is a gem, Mike. A real gem."

"What is?"

"You know the transmission boxes the power thieves used? We called 'em 'buzz boxes' because the codes were sent in by short-wave radio. Each box had a tiny little antenna that allowed it to pick up the signal from anywhere within a few hundred feet. Quick and easy." I point the flashlight toward the box. "What do you see?"

He cranes toward the box. "No antenna, that's for sure."

"Nope. If this puppy really is a transmission box, there's only one place that signal could be coming from."

He pauses to consider this. "The central computer."

"The central computer," I say, shifting the light toward the soldered-on wire that leads from the downtown transmission cable to the box itself. "This is serious stuff, Mike. To get the central computer to recognize a new input line like this, you'd have to change the internal configuration files. Only three or four people in the whole Council have the authority to do that."

He frowns as he realizes what that means. "Are you thinking what I'm thinking?"

"I'm thinking," I say, "that it isn't Stuart Farraday you should be worrying about." I take the hammer and chisel from his hands and drop them back into the toolbox. Mesoto just stands there, not wanting to believe.

"Come on, Kemo. Get your butt in gear. We've got work to do."

▼

It's after five o'clock in the morning before we've gathered in the Council's computer room and logged on, using Mesoto's private access code. Mike had called Alison as we were driving back in the van and had asked her to meet us here. Now she's sitting at the computer console listening to our instructions while Mike and I peer over her shoulder. She has called up the data files for the fuel tanks—files that summarize the transmissions from the tank gauges like the one Mike and I just inspected at the refinery. Rows upon rows of azure figures scroll up the monitor's face as we watch.

"Hold it," Mesoto says, after a moment. "That's the one. Tank 242. Do a history."

Alison enters the commands. "Almost empty three nights ago," she says. "Full the next day."

"The day of the shipment," I muse.

"Right," says Mesoto. "Let's do another." He glances at his notes. "Try number 365."

Alison logs the command, and a new table of numbers jumps to the screen. "Empty August twelfth. Full August thirteenth."

"The day before the explosion?" I ask.

Mesoto nods. "Right again."

We go through the others, and the results are the same.

"They all check out," says Mesoto. "All the tanks turned full when they were supposed to. Like nothing was wrong."

"Except the tanks *weren't* full."

"Right."

"Which means the fuel was drained from the tanks immediately after they were filled."

"Obviously," says Mesoto.

"Or maybe it never made it into the tanks in the first place."

Another nod. "Even easier."

But I'm thinking, *If the fuel didn't go into the tanks, it had to stay in the tanker trucks.* "Your drivers?" I ask. "They still fill the tanks themselves, right?"

"Sure, just like always. Not much to it. Just hook up the hose and wait. Then keep moving in fuel trucks, one after the other, until the gauge reads full. The lead driver oversees the whole operation."

"Then what happens?"

"The drivers take the excess back to the harbor and dump it in the reserve tanks."

"You still keep records on that?"

"Of course we do," Mesoto says, sounding a little peeved. "All the lead drivers have to fill out a report. I already looked. The numbers check out."

"Call up the file anyway. I want to see something."

Mesoto nods curtly toward Alison, knowing this is a futile exercise, but knowing also that it's not worth the fight. Alison compliantly enters the codes, and in a few seconds a new bank of data rolls up the screen. It's all a morass of names and numbers, meaningless out of context.

"Get rid of everything except for the five sites that were bombed," I tell her.

A few more keystrokes, and five records are all that remain. The comparisons among them are easy now—and disconcerting. The drivers. The crew members. The watch officer at the storage tanks. Even the keypunch clerks who input the data. They're all different. The only commonality is the receiving tank—Oil Reserve Number 8. And even that could be a coincidence, since so few of the harbor's reserve tanks are still in use.

But it's all we have to go on.

"Did you see this, Mike?" I ask, pointing to the display.

He shrugs. "So what? We got auditors looking at these reports every day. They keep track of what goes in and what goes out of each tank. If the numbers didn't add up, we'd know right away."

"Yeah," I say, frustrated. "If the numbers were right."

"What do you mean?"

"It still works like this, right? After the driver dumps his extra fuel in the reserve tank, he writes up his report and brings it back to the Council? Then some Joe down in Receiving types the data into the computer, and the auditing staff cross-checks the data to make sure everything's in agreement. That it?"

"That's it."

"And the auditors work from the data that's in the computer?"

"Of course. They don't go through the original paperwork unless there's an error in the data."

"Yeah, that would explain it . . ."

"You think someone intentionally entered the wrong data?" Disbelieving. "Five different clerks?"

"No," I say. "But what if someone changed the data *after* it was entered? Say the driver dumps a thousand barrels into the reserve tank and the clerk types 'one thousand' into the computer. But before an auditor has a chance to review it, someone changes the numbers to make it look like all the fuel was pumped into the refinery tanks and *nothing* went back into the reserve tank."

"And then that same someone draws the thousand barrels out of the reserve tank and doesn't file a report on it?"

"Gotcha."

"Sounds pretty thin."

"Yeah, but think about it. And you'd have to steal the fuel only from a single reserve tank. Plus, the numbers would add up—and the best auditor in the country couldn't find anything wrong unless he went back to the original paperwork. We could be losing thousands of barrels of oil and we'd have no way of knowing it."

A grunt. "Maybe," he says. "But you're forgetting something, Chief."

"What?"

"Only one person in the entire Council can authorize a change in the resource files once the data's been entered."

"Yeah? And who would that be?"

"Our friend Mr. Rooker."

I look at Mesoto, expecting this answer, almost jubilant in the discovery after Rooker's belligerence the day before.

"I was counting on that," is all I say.

▼ ▼ ▼

While Darby finishes packing, I map out our route to Los Angeles. There are only two realistic choices. Taking I-70 west to Utah and then down I-15 to Los Angeles would be the faster of the two. But it also would involve spending several hours crossing the Rocky Mountains— even longer if the traffic is as heavy as the reports suggest. Should another air shortage occur, we could be in serious, maybe fatal trouble, our own small store of oxygen tanks notwithstanding. Even if we could survive the air shortage ourselves, thousands of others would not. Our van would be jammed on an endless mountain highway, unable to move. With winter approaching, even one bad storm might make it impossible for us to walk out. It would be weeks before anyone would find us.

Counseled by these dark prospects, I opt instead to head due south down I-25, through Colorado Springs and Pueblo and into New Mexico—a state that I haven't visited in decades. The last time I did, I was a young boy, riding in the backseat of the family station wagon, playing baseball cards with my brother and not really paying attention to the scenery. But I vaguely remember seeing long stretches of flat highway surrounded on all sides by endless rocky desert. While boring then, the lower elevations would be a godsend now. Of course, we'll have to circle around Albuquerque. Not only does it sit at a much higher elevation, but that death-ridden city is likely to be as inhospitable as Denver is. Other than that small detour, however, our journey to Southern California should be uneventful.

My only real concern is whether we will be able to find enough fuel along the way. I listened to the news at midday, and what I heard was not encouraging. A growing number of service stations along the Mountain West freeways have exhausted their gasoline supplies and are shutting down—or else are being taken over by Federal authorities in order to conserve fuel for more essential uses. Fortunately, Ray kept a 50-gallon reserve fuel tank at home for his riding mower and snowmobile, and I've drained what I could into several steel containers. I'll have to carry them inside the van, which isn't the safest thing to do. But it's better than running out of gas in the middle of the southwestern desert.

At length, Darby is finished with her preparations. She has filled four suitcases and a backpack, mostly with dolls and toys and books, but with a few clothes and toiletries as well. She has also chosen to bring along a three-foot-high stuffed penguin that, she once told me, her dad had bought her at Sea World a few years ago. It's almost the size of another passenger, but I don't question her choice. We have room, and her memories are all that she has left. In fact, her luggage fits in less space than I was planning on. I was able to position all of it atop the food supplies and camping gear and gun crates in the back of the van, leaving the front two rows of seats free for the two of us. And for Pepper, the Stanfords' black Lab. He sits on the seat next to Darby, seeming more excited than usual at our pending trip. For him, I suppose, it's quite an adventure. In any event, he will be a welcome companion for Darby. And for me as well.

We finally pull out of the driveway just before three. The sun is sinking in the afternoon sky, but we'll be headed south most of the way, and so it shouldn't be glaring in our eyes. I already know—as Alison reminded me—that the roads will be congested. But the latest news reports said that traffic was at least moving, and so I'm hopeful we'll reach the New Mexico border by midnight. Once there, we can rest for a while. Then, as long as we don't run out of fuel, we should be able to reach Arizona by the next evening. Finally, in just two or three more days, we'll be home.

Home. With this unending horrific past behind us.

We begin our journey, moving slowly and deliberately, not bowing to the urge to rush. The Stanfords' neighborhood is as quiet as it was when we arrived yesterday afternoon. Too quiet. There are no signs of life other than a pair of large dogs prowling the street, stopping every few yards to inspect the dozens of dead birds that fell to the ground two nights ago. Dogs and dead birds. But no people.

Then, as we pass a cul-de-sac just before the main road, I see the first evidence of human life. A city garbage truck sits idling in the middle of the asphalt circle as a quartet of workmen toss big garbage bags into the rear of the truck. I find myself wondering, with all that's happened, why would garbage collection be so high on the city's priorities? Sanitation? Maybe. Disease is sure to set in when trash remains uncollected for a long time. But I think: it's only been a couple of days.

Puzzled, I drive on, and shortly afterward we pass another lifeless cul-de-sac. Within it sits another garbage truck, with another crew at work. But this time, I see that it isn't city garbage collectors I'm watching. It's soldiers. Army men with dour faces and black armbands on their right sleeves. And then I notice something more. As I look on, a group of Marines exits one of the circle's houses, carrying a pair of greenish-black bags. They're not trash bags. They're body bags. This isn't a trash-collection operation, after all.

I quickly drive on before Darby can see.

In minutes, we reach the entrance to the freeway, having passed several *more garbage trucks and Army convoys along the way. The on-ramp is backed up as expected, nearly two city blocks, and so I resolve myself to waiting the ten or fifteen minutes I estimate it will take. But my guess proves low: it takes forty-five minutes for us to reach the freeway entrance. Then, as we roll toward the on-ramp, I notice something strange: while the cars on the street leading up to the freeway are pressed together bumper-to-bumper, there's only an occasional vehicle on the on-ramp itself.*

And then I see why. A US Army truck sits astride the freeway entrance, and a trio of uniformed soldiers are stopping cars as their drivers prepare to enter the freeway. That's odd, I think. I have no idea why they would be doing this. But when a soldier young enough to be my son approaches our car, I compliantly slide down the window. "License and registration," he demands, polite but firm.

Automatically, I pull my license from my wallet and the van's registration from the glove compartment and hand them to him. He quickly scans them. "They don't match."

What that's supposed to mean? I wonder. And then I realize: of course they don't match. This is Ray's van, not mine. Are they looking for stolen cars?

"No, sir, they don't," I reply, suddenly choosing my words very carefully. "The van belongs to my friend Ray Stanford. He and his wife died Friday night." I pause, clenching my teeth. Steeling myself. "So did my wife and daughter." I nod back toward Darby. "This is the Stanfords' daughter, Darby. I'm taking her to safety."

The soldier peers in, looking at Darby. He isn't exactly cold and unfeeling, but he's efficient, by-the-book. His mechanical expression is enough to send a quick flash of chills down my back.

We're not even out of Denver yet, and already our path is blocked.

"Does she have any identification?" the young man asks, interrupting my thoughts.

I look back at Darby, thankful that I had the presence of mind to bring her birth certificate with me. "Darby, hand me the brown envelope in the backseat pocket, please."

She does, and I pass them to our interrogator. The soldier reviews the birth certificate carefully and then hands it back. "The address isn't the same," is all he says.

Of course it isn't the same. Darby was born in Los Angeles.

"I need an address that matches the vehicle registration," the soldier goes on.

Suddenly, I feel the panic start to rise within me. "Why do you need the address?"

"Rules, sir. I'm sorry."

"Please. She's just a child. Can't we go on?"

"No, sir, you can't. I'll need a matching address. Or else you'll have to turn around."

I'm thinking quickly now, desperately, having no idea what other item we might have in the car with the Stanfords' address. I didn't think to bring along their utility bills or Ray's driver's license or even one of his stupid magazines with a mailing label on it. I had no notion I would need them.

There has to be something in the car! *I flail in my mind.* I stab my hand into the glove compartment, randomly pulling out papers, glancing through them without even really looking. Nothing. Then I pull open the center divider. There's a McDonald's gift card. A gas coupon. A pair of sunglasses. A few odds and ends. But no identification papers. Nothing with the Stanfords' address on it. Come on! There has to be something! I sweep my hand across the dashboard, gathering only dust. Can we really not even get out of Denver?

And then it strikes me: Pepper. *"Pepper, come here, boy!"* I call into the back. Our canine companion jumps into the front seat, directly onto my lap. I place my arm around his shoulders, grasping for his name tag with my free hand. There, in metal relief, is the name "Stanford." Then Pepper's name. And then, miraculously, the Stanfords' home address.

I show the tag to the soldier. He examines it, then makes some notes on his notepad and hands the hastily scribbled form to me. "Use this if you get stopped again. You can go."

I look down at the form. "Travel Authorization Certificate," it reads, in official government type. I stare at the gray certificate for a moment longer, then place it securely in the glove compartment. A deep breath comes, and then another. I snap the glove department closed, then pull the van the rest of the way up the on-ramp.

But even as I do, for the first time in two days, I am not thinking of Jeannie and Cassie. I am worried about Darby and me. And wondering not when—but whether—we will ever make it home.

CHAPTER 8

The relief that I felt hours earlier, a mirage of emotions to begin with, has disappeared long before we're sitting in Fran Amalfi's office later that morning. What remains is a vague sense of unease, like the feeling that came over me in our last minutes in the bar. This isn't the way the investigation was supposed to turn out.

Perhaps I should just leave now, I think, *before the lines start forming at the gallows.*

But I stay, more as a support to Mike than as an emissary for any cause of my own. We must look like the wrath of Herod, we two, slumped before Amalfi in the chairs with the too-short legs. Black-eyed and sleepless, Mike is battered by doubt and I by indifference. But Fran receives us just the same, sitting behind her desk with all the manufactured composure of her public persona, poring over the documents we've given her as casually as if they contained nothing more foul than the latest reports of death on the streets. I must admit: she wears her shock well. Only Barry Erthein, bending down beside her to survey these papers, betrays any hint of anger, and that anger seems to be directed more at Mike and me than at our unexpected quarry.

"I'd say 'congratulations,'" Amalfi says as she looks up, "but I don't think I like what you're telling me."

"It's hard to read it any other way," Mesoto replies. "You've got all the original forms signed by the drivers. They're dumping full tank-loads into the reserves, yet the computer says the trucks came back almost empty. You can interview the drivers if you want, but you'll get the same story. I'm sure of that."

"And there's no record of any withdrawals from the reserve tank?"

"Nothing that isn't accounted for. But somebody must be taking the fuel out. We checked the level an hour ago, and it's right where the computer says it should be."

Amalfi considers this. "So you're saying the bombings are nothing more than a cover for stealing fuel?"

Mike doesn't answer right away. He looks decidedly uncomfortable, as if forced to draw a conclusion he's not yet ready to make. I wait for a few seconds to give him time and then cut in. "No, I don't think we can say that, not yet," I tell Fran. "We know the fuel tanks that were bombed weren't full and that somebody went to a lot of trouble to make us think they were. We also know the extra fuel vanished within twenty-four hours after being put back in the reserve tank. Beyond that, we're only guessing."

"Meaning?" asks Erthein.

"Meaning we don't know why or how or where the fuel went. Maybe it's being dumped into the ocean for all we know. It's just too early to say."

"Still," Erthein presses, "we know a whole lot more than we did two days ago when you came back on the scene. Taking nothing away from your accomplishment, Martin, I can't help wondering exactly what Mr. Mesoto has been doing these past three months."

I have to hold back a surge of contempt to keep from responding to this remark with the venom it deserves, but I suspect that my intervention would only make Mesoto look worse. And so I look to Mike to see if he'll mount his own defense. Surprisingly, it's Amalfi who comes to his aid.

"Barry," she tells her assistant, "we're trying to resolve this problem and I appreciate any contributions you can make. But if what you have to say doesn't serve that purpose, please do us a favor and just shut up."

Erthein is so taken aback by this slap that he doesn't even react. Now it's a leer of satisfaction that I have to restrain.

"So where does that leave us?" Amalfi goes on, turning back to me and to the business at hand, leaving Erthein to stew.

"At the food-processing plant."

"Okay, explain."

I'm reluctant to answer. Not because it wasn't my idea, which it was, but because Mike doesn't need me to steal his show any more than

I already have. But with Fran waiting and my knowing the details better than Mike, I don't have any choice.

At this point, it strikes me, I seem to have done a lot more harm than good to Mike since I've come back, and my barely suppressed self-revulsion starts rumbling back. All at once, I just want to be done with this job and be out of here.

"We've changed the date listed," I tell her, "for the next major shipment for the Century City food-processing plant—"

"From what to what?" Amalfi asks.

"From the end of the month to tomorrow afternoon. We've also programmed the database so this new information will appear only in response to Rooker's login—and only at his terminal. If a transmission box shows up at the plant, we'll know who ordered it."

"And there's not a box there now?"

"No, there's not," Mesoto says. "We checked that too. But I'd wager my next paystub that there will be tonight."

"I guess we'll see," Amalfi says. She gathers the documents on her desk and hands them to a grim-faced Erthein, who has been reduced by her scolding to silent hostility. "I know you've both come to some pretty firm conclusions about Rooker. But just understand, I'm not there yet. Rooker's smart and he's also careful. If he wanted to draw down our oil supplies—for vengeance, for money, or whatever—he could have found a much easier way to do it. So you're going to have to come up with a whole lot more proof than this."

"Of course," I answer.

She gives a tight, resigned smile to this, the expression of a person in complete control—but one no longer quite sure what she's in control of. "And one last thing," she goes on. "I know this may not be high on your own list of concerns, but Rooker's been working sixteen hours a day for the last year creating the fuel-allocation system. In some ways, that's all that's held this city together. I don't want to lose him if I don't have to, and I certainly don't want to hang him if he's innocent. So do what you have to. But let's keep this quiet and let's keep it clean. Is that understood?"

We both nod.

"Good. If the transmission box does show up tonight, then we'll meet tomorrow morning and decide where we go from there. But if it doesn't, I'm going to have to tell Rooker that someone has stolen his access credentials. And unless he has a good idea of who *that* might be, we're no closer to an answer than when we started." Another pause, and then the tight smile again, weaker than before. "Not a pretty picture either way."

She rises with this remark, letting us know that the meeting is over. "This may be your only shot, gentlemen, so no mistakes. And bring me the bad news when it's done."

▼

The rest of the day is a wash, its only redeeming feature the fact that we don't have to deal with Amalfi or Erthein again. Nor, thankfully, do we cross the path of James Alan Rooker. Mike and I spend the time in the field, both of us moody and withdrawn, inspecting the earlier bombing sites to determine if transmission boxes had been installed there as well. But the debris at these sites has long since been cleared away—or at least bulldozed into mountains of incoherent charcoal—leaving us with only the Carson refinery to inform our judgments. It's not much to go on, and I'm already beginning to have my doubts.

I return to the apartment complex well after the sun has set, dragged down by these sour thoughts, and force them off me only with the press of obligation. Mike and I have to venture out to the food-processing plant only a few hours from now in order to test our theories about Rooker. I'm hoping I can devote the time until then to the recuperative ministrations of sleep, or at least lose myself in some drab and mindless novel for a while. It's a weak medicine at best, but an attractive one. Too soon, I know, I'll have to be alert again.

I climb the long flights of stairs to my apartment. But when I reach the tenth floor, I find that I'm not walking toward my own unit but toward Alison's. I do not make this move consciously nor with any intent. But I also don't turn away when I realize where I'm headed. More than sleep, I decide, I need to hear a human voice, one raised neither in anger nor in despair, words offered as if they had no import beyond the moment of their speaking. I am enervated by these burdens, small as they are, that I have so quickly reassumed. I could use a little of Alison's faith and spirit.

But then I arrive at her door, and I'm uncertain once again. I've forgotten the etiquette of intrusions like this, having been too long removed from a world in which privacy and propriety were matters of concern. Besides, she's probably asleep herself, since she'll be joining Mike and me at the processing plant. I should just walk down the hall toward my own apartment, I tell myself, and try for the rest that I'd planned on. But I knock anyway. Because now that the moment is here, I really don't know how well I will pass the next few hours if left on my own.

Alison answers the knock almost immediately, as if she were waiting for me. She opens the door wide, her robe wrapped loosely around her, welcoming me with a smile of gentle friendship. I mutter a greeting and take her proffered hand as she leads me in. Then I walk past her, choosing silence as the safest response. I'm still not sure why I'm here. When was the last time that I wanted just to visit with someone, to be with them, to talk or merely sit without speaking? The company of others is something that I have come to suffer—an accommodation to survival. Now I seek it outright, which used to be natural, but it no longer seems that way. It feels awkward, like a new suit that's too tight or a discussion on a subject that has moved beyond one's understanding. I don't know what to say.

But I'm thinking, *Do you know what's happened to me, Alison, since you picked me up at the stadium? I had a dream, and I think Mike and I may have this explosion problem all worked out. But I'm not sure he wants me in his face anymore because now I'm the hero and he's the same quiet plodding* cabezón *that Amalfi and Erthein always thought he was. And I'm not sure Fran wants me around anymore either because if I'm right about Rooker, I've messed up her life too, and she's left as a queen without her court. And did I tell you that Mike and I survived the explosion last night only because I still can't endure the memories of sirens and crowds? Did I tell you how much it sickens me to suddenly be a person of privilege again when others around me—millions of people I don't even know— have so little? Did I tell you how much I already want out even though I'm hardly back in? Did I tell you all this?*

No, I didn't tell her. And I don't do it now. Instead, I take the drink that she pours for me—scotch, hard and straight, the way I used to like it—and walk over to the window. I stand there for long moments looking outside. Not really seeing. Not even thinking. Just letting my mind clear. When I finally speak, it's only to tell her about my day, and then only when she asks about it. But my answers come in grunts and monosyllables, and eventually she decides that I just want to be left alone.

It's another ten minutes before I turn around.

"Thanks for the drink," I say, draining the last of the scotch and setting the glass aside.

Alison has moved to the sofa and is sitting there, looking up at me. "Fran's private stock," she says, smiling. "I've got access to more than computer files."

"No wonder Mike keeps you around."

I meant it as a quip, a meaningless joke, but the forced humor comes through more as sarcasm. Either Alison doesn't notice or she ignores it, I can't tell. But suddenly she's the one who's contemplative. She takes a sip of her lime and soda, hiding her question behind the curve of her glass, then finally gives it voice. "Is he going to keep *you* around?" she asks.

I don't say anything to this, not right away. I just step to the end of the sofa so that I can see all of her. She's sitting with her back against the armrest, her legs curled under her, watching me with her soft mouth and sleepy eyes. Under her robe, I now see, she is wearing an oversized cotton pullover with pink flowers sketched across the chest, a match to her pink socks and slippers.

"He probably would," I tell her at last. "But I think I'll save him the choice."

She looks up, not comprehending. Or not wanting to. "What do you mean?"

"This isn't going to work, my staying on. Not for me anyway. I don't know what I want, but this isn't it."

And now she's no longer curled up on the sofa, but standing. She steps beside the sofa, facing me. "You *can't* leave, Martin. You'd only—"

"I can and I will," I say sharply, far more harshly than I had intended. Then just as quickly, I back off. Alison doesn't deserve this, not after my rudeness last night, not after her kindness throughout my return. "Look," I tell her, "I've done what Fran asked me to do. I've found her Mad Bomber and she can do the rest. I'll stay around for a few days to tie things up. But then I'm gone."

"And where will you go?" she asks, her voice hardening in protest. "Back to that dung heap where I found you?"

"No," I say, "not there." I give a morbid chuckle. "Although that place did have one advantage. It made it hard to sink any lower."

She has moved so that she's standing inches in front of me now. Her eyes peer up toward mine, her sadness and anger a mixture I don't care to confront. I look away, my eyes focused beyond her toward the dark end of the room, just somewhere else so that I don't have to meet her gaze. But I don't move away. Her small hands go to my shoulders, holding me there. I have no choice but to look at her.

"They're not coming back, Martin," she says softly, after I've resigned to face her again. "Jeannie, Cassie, Ray, Sara—they're all gone. You can mourn them for the rest of your life. Beat yourself up every day and every night. They're not coming back. But Darby could be here. Tomorrow, if you wanted. I have a friend there who just got moved upstairs. I'm sure she could arrange it."

I close my eyes at this, recalling too clearly the moment that I last saw Darby's confused and frightened face, watching after me through the thick waiting-room window at the Children's Bureau. And with those images come something else: the arrows of accusation. Painful. Eviscerating. No, I didn't want to leave her. I had no choice. The men with white coats and whitewashed smiles took her from me. But they were right in what they did, I realized long ago. I couldn't take care of her. Not the way she needed. I had no home. I had no job. I had nothing left inside to give her.

"And I'm here too," Alison speaks into my darkness. "That's something."

I wait, not moving. Then I open my eyes again and see that Alison is still looking at me, with—what? Compassion? Sympathy? Longing? *This isn't right, Alison,* I want to tell her. *This is a part of the past. Something I gave up long ago and cannot resurrect. Something left behind as permanently as childhood. I'm sorry, that's just the way it is. Please don't make me say it.*

And she doesn't. She breaks away and steps back into the tiny kitchen to refill my drink. When she returns, she's talking of other things. Safer things. Things about Mike. About Amalfi. About the old scratched CDs she found in the back room of a burnt-out music store. Through this, she repositions herself at the end of the sofa. I watch her as she speaks, so intently at times that I see her lips move but don't really hear the words. The effect is almost calming, and I realize that the instant of panic is gone. For a moment I'm at ease again. And I'm thinking, in silent wonder: *Alison, amazing Alison, you always do it right.*

"Would you like to hear one of them?"

It takes a few seconds for me to understand that she's talking about the CDs. I nod. *Yes, whatever you want, that would be fine. Anything to preserve this moment.* She lifts herself from the sofa and steps to the CD player that must be yet another bequest of privilege. I notice now that she must have removed her robe when she was in the kitchen, and as she moves, the soft material of the jersey pulls tightly against her, outlining with translucent clarity her petite form beneath. I avert my eyes from this when she steps back from the magical music machine, its output tinny and grating but a rare and sensuous pleasure all the same. When was the last time I heard music? I can't even recall.

While I am considering this question, Alison returns to the sofa and sits there again, apologizing for the poor quality of the sound. But I'm not listening to her, just to the music, experiencing another sensation that I had almost forgotten.

"You might want to slow down on that a bit," she says. It's only then that I notice that I'm nearly through my second drink. She's right, of course—as I'm sure I'll discover in a few hours, when the three of us are huddled in some shadowy corner of the processing plant, examining the handiwork of Rooker's minions. But for now I need the drink's benevolence. Need it because suddenly I'm feeling something that has been absent from within me since that long dark night in Denver.

And what is it? I ask myself. I sit down beside Alison, letting my subconscious direct me. I study her face in the music's soft, smoky haze. What is it that I feel? Not passion, I think, nor physical need. Not really. I have known both of these in abundance in my life, and this sensation is neither. It is more like a chosen desire. A desire for closeness with another human being. For oblivion of a different kind than I'm accustomed to. And for pleasure too. A pleasure, like all of the pleasures I once knew, that have long since been abandoned.

I wonder why Alison has provoked this reaction in me. And I wonder even more whether it is worth the inevitable price. I know it can't be. I know, even at this late moment, that I should just walk out and leave the situation as it is, like a rare work of art contemplated but untouched.

But I don't leave. I don't leave because it is Alison, and because I want this too. And so I stay, and let it happen.

I reach out to touch her face. Run my fingers along her forehead. Brush back a stray lock of hair. She smiles at this and closes her eyes, but she doesn't move. I glide my fingers down her temple and to her cheek. She takes my hand then and guides it to her mouth. Holds it there, gently kissing my palm. My hands go to her shoulders and I slowly pull her toward me. Her eyes are open again, her lips parted. I kiss her mouth, absorbing the feeling of my lips on hers, and then I kiss her chin and her neck and her mouth again. I do it all gently, delicately, as if she were a porcelain doll, or an imagined love from a long-lost dream. Gradually, the kisses grow deeper, more caressing. Our bodies are pressed against one another's now, and she grips my shoulders, pulling us together even more tightly. On some forgotten cue, my own hands respond, wrapping around her back, enfolding her.

She pulls back in that moment, takes my hands from behind her back, holds them in her own. Then she stands and pulls me up to join her, our arms circling around each other. She kisses me again, more passionately. I know what comes next, and through these minutes, from somewhere inside me, a plea for resistance—for self-denial—remains. But it finally grows weak and slips away, because the rest of me has decided against it.

We make love there on the couch, slowly, almost reverently. There is no sense of time in those moments. No sense of place. No sense of the world outside. There is only the fullness of the present, and we consume it all, drawing in each other's sounds and taste and smell with deep, lasting breaths, reacquainting ourselves with humanity. When at last we're done, we lock ourselves together. Hold each other. Silently. Without words.

Because there is nothing left to say.

At length, our emotions spent, we let ourselves fall away from each other. But not too far. She shifts onto her side and looks down at me, smiling softly. Her eyes peer in at mine and mine at hers, and we kiss for a final time.

And then, in this exquisite fragment of peace, we sleep.

▼

The telephone's sharp ringing awakens me. But this isn't my apartment and so I lie still, resisting the impulse to answer. I feel Alison, whose sleeping body has been stretched out against mine, roll off the edge of the mattress. *When,* I wonder, *did we leave the sofa?* As she steps to the phone, my eyes gradually adjust to the room's dead-of-night darkness. I see her slender robed body framed against the wall, an outline without interior, the mere shadow of a form.

She is saying something I can't quite understand. And then: "Yes, he is," in a soft bedside tone. I'm sure now that Mike is on the phone, and that he has asked if I am here. Then "no problem," which means he is probably on his way, and that we need to get ready.

I don't hear her hang up the phone.

She steps back to me and brushes my forehead with her lips. Then she runs her fingers along my cheek, almost as if she were telling me good-bye instead of good morning. She does not say anything for several seconds. I look up at her, and reach out to take her hand.

"It's time," she whispers, then turns away before either of us can do more.

I let her go, a necessary sacrifice. For Mesoto's call has brought an end to our hours of peace. It is time, for now, to return to the world outside.

▼ ▼ ▼

In normal times, Ray once told me, he could drive from Denver to Colorado Springs in just under an hour. During the evening rush, when I-25 was packed with commuters headed back to Castle Rock, the Springs, or points further south, the trip might take twice that long. But today, our journey has already consumed several hours, and we haven't even reached the main part of the city.

I hadn't expected travel to be quite this slow. In fact, after we entered the freeway on Denver's suburban east side, we were able to move along at twenty to thirty miles per hour. It wasn't the usual highway speed, of course, but it was faster than I had been counting on. I spent a good share of that part of the trip recalculating our drive time to Los Angeles and figured that we might be able to shave a day or more off my original estimates.

Then we reached I-25 South, merging with the traffic from Denver's center city and the northern and western suburbs, and traffic began to crawl. And then it stopped altogether. We sat on the interchange between the beltway and the main southbound route for more than an hour. When we finally edged onto I-25, we were able to move only in spurts, coasting for a tenth of a mile or so and then braking to a jarring halt. And then, whenever movement would resume, I always started slowly, never revving the engine, not wanting to waste even the smallest amount of gasoline. I even turned the car off a few times in order to conserve fuel. Despite these precautions, however, the inevitable occurred: our once-full tank was now nearing empty.

I was so focused on the congestion and the sinking gas gauge during this time that it wasn't until we were halfway to Colorado Springs that I noticed something odd. It was the second day after the Catastrophe. I would have anticipated that most Coloradans who were leaving the Denver area already would have done so. And with more than a million people in the region having lost their lives, there shouldn't have been that many people heading southward anyway. Yet the freeways were jammed.

I was puzzled by the unexpected exodus until I looked around more closely, and then I saw why. Most of the vehicles on the road were not even from Colorado. The license plates read Wyoming and Montana, North and South Dakota, Minnesota and even Canada. Hundreds from Canada—Alberta, Saskatchewan, Manitoba, and provinces further north. Some vehicles were from the high-altitude Canadian Rockies, and so their owners' southward migration might have made sense. But the elevations of many of the departure points were lower than the places to which the drivers were headed. What did they have to gain by leaving their homes?

I glanced at some of the other travelers' faces as we sat amid the endless line of cars and trucks, of vans and RVs. I could see the emptiness of loss, of course, and the fear of what was yet to come. That much I could have guessed. Some people—not just the mothers and children but even some of the men—were weeping as they drove on. Others stared blankly out the window, peering toward the sky—wondering, perhaps, when the atmosphere would deliver its inescapable death sentence yet again.

But in other faces, I saw something I had not anticipated. A sense of resentment. Of animosity. Of escalating impatience. Confined for hours on this almost motionless freeway, these weary travelers certainly had a right to such emotions. But the occasional steel-eyed glances and hostile stares looking back at me or at other drivers told me something else: that at least some of these southbound itinerants seemed to be angry at the very fact that there were others on the road, that their flight to safety was being blocked by selfish fellow travelers.

Where was the charity, the good will, the sense of brotherhood that always had followed other natural disasters?

Yet maybe what I thought I saw—and the motivations I ascribed to others whose losses surely were as great as my own—were nothing more than illusions, dark and unflattering interpretations borne of my own long and frustrating hours on the freeway.

Encouraged by this possibility, I take the chance to look around again. The sun has long since set, and I can see the passing faces now only by the grace of the moon and the few interior car lights that have been turned on. The reflections and smoked windows and towers of hurriedly packed belongings make it even more difficult for me to clearly see inside the vehicles than before. But what few expressions I can make out appear to be little different than what I would have encountered during a pre-Catastrophe rush hour.

Nothing to see, *I tell myself.* Just move on.

And so I put my earlier observations down to a fatigued and desperate mind. In that moment I realize, for the first time in hours, how tired I really am. I spend a few minutes trying to deny it, but ultimately am forced to admit that we can't stay on the road for much longer, even with the certainty of falling even further back in traffic. The conspiracy of low fuel and encroaching sleep will compel us to find refuge somewhere, at least for a few hours. It's not an option I prefer, leaving the freeway as night deepens and unknown threats lurk in every shadow. But it's the only choice we really have.

I look back at Darby, thankful that she is asleep again. She read aimlessly for a while during the afternoon. Played listlessly with some dolls. Brushed Pepper's napped fur probably far more than he wanted. Mostly, though, like so many other children I have seen along the way, she just stared out the window, no doubt thinking about her parents. About Cassie. About the many other friends she has lost. The one thing that she did not do was cry. This surprised me, because I know her pain must be immense. But all of us handle our grief in our own way, and I felt it best to leave her to her own methods of coping.

As I am looking back at her now, a flickering wave of amber light suddenly washes over her. I am transported for a panicked instant back to the night of the soccer game, when the entire soccer field was bathed in skylit red and yellow. But this color is more abrupt and more intense. It can't be the sky.

I turn around to the front of the van to spy its source. Half a dozen vehicles ahead of us, flames are arcing toward the sky from what looks like the cab of a semi. If there were an explosion, I didn't hear it, or else it just didn't register. But now the car next to the semi bursts into flames as well, the crimson fire shooting several yards into the air. And with it comes a shattering explosion that I cannot ignore. Was there an accident? A car overheating? A fuel leakage?

From this distance away, I cannot tell.

I glance at Darby again. The explosions have stirred her to restless movement, although she is still asleep. I am grateful she isn't watching this scene. Though it probably would be more interesting than worrisome to her—an exciting break from the tedium of the van ride—it's still not worth risking other, less pleasant possibilities.

There are some times when boredom is not the worst option.

It's in the middle of these thoughts that I hear it: a loud, piercing sound. At first I think it's only a tire squealing. But then the sound's identity routs itself into my mind: a scream.

Shrill. Uncontrolled. Terrified.

I look again toward the line of vehicles ahead of me in time to see a group of burly workmen—open beer cans in one hand, crowbars and tire irons in the other. They're sauntering past cars. Heading in our direction. Shattering mirrors and car windows and whatever else gets in their way. One of the men smashes his tire iron down onto the face of an middle-aged man who tries to stop them, and the man crumples to the ground. Another rips the purse from a mother guarding her children and throws it far down the hillside.

The assailants tread on. Laughing. Cursing. Jeering. Even from this distance, I can hear their drunken guffaws as clearly as if the men were standing at my side.

My blood chills.

Fortunately, our van is in the far-right lane. Driven by an urgent, ill-thought-out impulse, I spin the van to the right, onto the freeway's grassy side strip, and race back in the opposite direction. I recall that we just passed a freeway exit a few minutes ago, and my memory proves correct. A few hundred yards up, there's an offshoot. I head down it, scraping the bottom of the van as it bounds over the curb. I'm not really going that fast now, so the impact doesn't jar the van, and Darby remains asleep. Thank goodness.

Of all things, she doesn't need to see this.

I look in the rearview mirror as we drive slowly down the off-ramp. I can't see the shapes on the freeway clearly anymore. It looks as if the drunken men have stopped their march and a fight has broken out. I can't tell for sure.

But soon they are beyond my vision altogether. And, fortunately, beyond my concern.

In seconds, we emerge onto the wide and empty street that heads westward from the freeway. I stop the van then, allowing myself a couple of minutes to recompose myself. I look up at the street signs as we sit there, signs that mark the asphalt passage that has become our blessed escape route.

"Garden of the Gods Road," the signs read. And I'm thinking: we could surely use the gods' help right now.

I grimace at this thought, knowing that it is only by the grace of heaven's aid that we were able to leave the freeway when we did. I glance back one last time at the motionless cars sitting above and behind us, as the dancing flames reflect off random mirrors and windows.

It's time for us to go.

I turn back around, focusing again on what lies before us. Shift the van into gear. And press forward into our escape route's midnight darkness.

Headed—once again—to some place unknown.

CHAPTER 9

The Century City food-processing plant is a yawning warehouse of a building, a structure so vast that its outlines become clear long before we reach it. Squatting on the grounds of an abandoned movie studio, the building's bowed roof and wide open-air front calls to mind an old-fashioned airplane hangar. But no aircraft of any kind could pass here. The building's broad open face is lined with loading docks jammed together so tightly that they can't be used simultaneously. Even at this graveyard-shift hour several dozen trucks have pulled in, each bearing the Citizens Council seal, waiting to receive the food rations that they will transport to the government markets throughout the Los Angeles Basin.

The building's cavernous interior is lit with floodlights, a rare expenditure of energy in this era of legislated abstinence. The rear of the plant is given over to the sorting of foodstuffs into crates and boxes. At the building's front, these containers are routed on conveyor belts that crisscross at seemingly random angles, monitored by a battalion of workers who jump between platforms with such clockwork precision that their movements must have been choreographed.

But the plant's security preparations dominate all of these images. The facility is ringed by an eight-foot-high wall topped with electrified barbed wire, with red-lettered warning signs posted every few feet. Around this perimeter, armed guards patrol like sentries at an Army compound, keeping out the starving and seditious alike. In the skies overhead, Citizens Council drones fly low every few minutes, their electronic eyes watching more closely than any human could for night-dwellers intent on doing harm.

None of these security measure compare in their protective efficiency, however, to the main guard post that sits astride the facility's public entrance. Built of reinforced steel and occupied by at least half a dozen heavily armed Special Forces types, the guard post seems designed to deny passage even to those who are authorized to be here. Indeed, Mike and Alison and I must wait for almost an hour at three different military-class checkpoints before we are allowed to enter. *If our terrorists have managed to install a transmission box on this site,* I think as we stand here, *they must be either exceedingly clever or else very well-connected*—traits that describe few people in the city as well as they do James Alan Rooker.

I spend the long wasted minutes while we wait surveying the facility's grounds. At length, my eyes alight on a service road that extends through a double-gated opening in the security wall, off to side of the compound. A food truck is backed up there, and workers are tossing bags and boxes of random rations toward a mass of supplicants assembled before them. The crowd of lost souls—with its press of anarchy, it's hard to call it a line—stretches beyond sight down the hillside and spills out into the sepulchral nighttime streets surrounding the facility. In the haze of the light that escapes from inside the plant, I can make out the anxious, hardscrabble faces of the people waiting for handouts, hoping to collect for free what they must not have the ration cards to purchase. I'm surprised their numbers are so great.

"Spoilage," Mesoto remarks, following my eyes, as we are at last admitted onto the processing plant's grounds. I'm not sure whether he's referring to the people or the food. I decide on the latter, but still want to believe he's exaggerating, that these are only packages that may have been damaged or passed their recommended distribution dates. Then I remember the tainted wares of the merchants at the stadium, and I'm not so sure.

"Where's the control panel?" I ask Mike, forcing myself beyond these sights and onto our the business at hand as we quickly past the last guard post.

"It's in the back," he says. "We've kept the area clear of guards since midnight and turned off the electrified fence just to make sure our *traidores* weren't scared off. Hudson noticed someone milling around about two, but the control box is hidden behind the fuel tank, so he couldn't get a clear view.

"We didn't catch him?"

"We tried, but we had to hold back to keep from giving our position away. Unfortunately, there was a car waiting. He was gone before our men could close in."

I let out a grunt of irritation. That's a possibility they should have planned for. "No ID on the car either, I suppose?"

Mesoto looks across as if he couldn't care less. "You want this job back, *amigo*, you can have it. Any time."

I say nothing to this, knowing that he's only tired and frustrated, as I am. We pass the rest of the way in silence and eventually reach the rear of the plant. The control panel is hidden in a second-story alcove next to the fuel tank, a towering monster that serves the processing plant and several other facilities nearby. The tank looms above us, blocking out what little starlight there is, leaving us as wanderers through the darkness. Mike's high-beam flashlight provides our only illumination.

But it's enough to locate the metal stairs that lead up to the control panel. Mike heads up first, and Alison and I follow.

"Where'd you park?" he asks Alison as we reach the landing.

"At the back of the lot. By the storage shed."

Mesoto aims the flashlight over the fence behind us, down the steep grassy slope, and across a paved parking lot the size of a football field. The oval of light finally finds the van, standing alone in the distant emptiness, and then blinks away.

"Long walk," is all he says.

I'm sure Alison has an explanation for this, that she parked there to keep from calling attention to the van or some such. But she says nothing and gradually the tension of the past few minutes subsides. After scouting the area for watching eyes, Mike steps into the small alcove where the control panel is positioned, at eye level. He passes me the flashlight and extracts a screwdriver from his belt, wincing as he grips it in his thickly bandaged hand. I focus the light on the steel panel, and the evidence of intrusion is instantly apparent. There are fresh glove prints on the panel's weeks-old grime, the gray paint around the screws is badly scratched, and some of the screws are not even tightened. It's a second-rate job, or at least a quick one.

"Pretty obvious," I offer.

"Too obvious," says Mesoto. "Let's get it done. Camera ready, Alison?"

"Ready."

Mike steps away from the control panel just far enough to give Alison an angle so she can capture the photographic record. "Shoot me a Pulitzer," he tells her.

Alison hoists the camera and clicks. The flash that follows illuminates the entire landing, even the recesses that the flashlight left in the shadows. Before the glow vanishes, Mesoto has lifted his hand toward the control panel, the screwdriver poised again to do its work.

It's in the last afterimage of the flash that I see it. There, trailing beneath the panel. A short loop of wire, invisible in the next instant. Invisible, but no less deadly.

I reach out quickly and grab Mesoto's wrist. Freeze it in the fraction of a second before the screwdriver makes contact with the metal plate.

"What the—"

"Back up, Mike," I tell him. I aim the flashlight under the lip of the plate, and the thin silver glint of the wire comes into view. A stray loop, one of the hazards of a hasty exit.

An error that may have saved our lives.

"Is that the wire to the transmission box?" he asks.

But I'm already tracking the wire with the flashlight. Along the edge of the panel. Down to ground level. Across to a stack of old wooden crates stowed behind hillocks of trash bags in the corner.

"Not this one." I bend down below the control panel, pointing the light upward. The silver wire leads through a new drill hole, back inside the control panel's casing. "Know anything about electromagnetic triggers?"

"Nope."

"Touch that screwdriver to the plate and you'll find out in a hurry." I point the light back again toward the stack of crates, which no doubt contains enough explosives to turn the entire rear section of the plant into rubble. "We need to go."

We turn to head off, stepping quickly down the landing's stairs. But we've just reached ground level when the sharp ping of metal against metal reverberates all around us.

It doesn't take long to recognize the sound.

"Get down!" I call out.

All three of us hit the ground, then pull up behind a leg of the fuel tank. The shot has come from high above, beyond the other side of the tank, from somewhere off in the distant darkness. Immediately, Mike and I are back to our knees, quickly scanning the area, trying to locate the gunman. Our eyes go over the grounds. To the top of the security wall. To the darkened windows of the buildings across the street. But there's nothing.

And then I see him. A shadow crouching on the roof of a vacated office building, his head and shoulders just visible above a parapet. A high-powered rifle lies steadied across the parapet's surface, trained on us.

At this distance, there's no way Mike or I could take him out with our pistols.

As we're watching, the ping comes again. More faintly, on the far side of the tank. Nowhere close to us. I allow myself a fleeting gasp of relief. For a marksman, he's not a very good shot.

Then the relief explodes. The man isn't aiming for us. These shots must be his fallback, his insurance in case the explosives failed.

"He's trying to blow the tank!" I blurt out in an urgent whisper.

"The walls are too thick," snaps Mesoto. "He couldn't break through with a howitzer."

"Let's not bet on it." I'm up again, crouched low, grasping for Alison's hand. There's a section of the wall that gives way to a thick chain-link fence a few seconds to our right. Partly hidden by the curving wall, it's out of the line of fire. Our quickest escape.

"Come on, Mike! Over here!"

Mesoto gives the sniper a final angry glance, then joins in the dash behind us, pulling his radio from his belt as he runs. "Hudson! Do you read me?"

There's a crackle of a response, but I'm beyond it. Alison and I have reached the base of the fence. I quickly pile some nearby wooden pallets on top of one another to form a jury-rigged platform, the best I can do in fractions of a second. I help Alison step atop them, my hands pressed against her blue-jeaned thighs, and my mind flickers back to our already fading moments together only hours before. But I can't think about that now. Can't let it slow me down. Plenty of time for such thoughts later, once we're out of here.

I refocus, grasp her legs more firmly, and vault her upward.

Instantly she's up, almost over the top of the fence. I push again at her feet, giving her the last needed boost.

"Tell 'em to clear the area!" comes Mesoto's orders to Hudson over the radio as he rushes up beside me. "And shoot that imbecile on the roof!"

The instructions given, he slips the radio back into his belt just as Alison swings her last leg across the fence and drops to the moist hilly ground on the other side.

"Go!" I command her, taking Mike's keys and tossing them to her over the fence. "Get the van started! We'll be right behind you."

She looks up at me, catching my eyes with the same mix of love and concern that she greeted me with when we woke up this morning. Then she's up. Turning away. Running as fast as she can down the hill.

I look over at Mike, who motions me on. I'm up on the fence in the next second, struggling to climb over. My toes slip uneasily into the small openings made by the links, and for a moment my hands are all that hold me in place. But the months on the work crews pay off. I manage to keep from slipping, then pull myself to the top in one quick motion. My right leg is over, then the left. I feel the razor points of the barbed wire catch the cloth of my jacket and pinch into my arms. But somehow I break free and jump, landing on my feet and rolling a few yards before I get my balance back.

By now, Mike is halfway up the fence, his climb punctuated by two more pings against the fuel tank. *Hurry up, Mike,* I think, wishing him speed as I scramble down the slope.

A loud, muffled protest comes from behind me. I look back to see Mesoto hanging on this side of the fence. His bandaged hand is caught in the barbed wire as his free hand clutches at the links near the top to try to free himself. But his feet can't find purchase, and they flail beneath him as he struggles to pull the damaged hand from its trap.

I turn and dart back up the hill. Stumble once. Then dart forward, aiming to help him down and get out of here, madly glancing at the shooter as I go. I'm almost to the bottom of the fence when Mike's hand finally rips free from the barbed wire, leaving a banner of bandages waving in the night. He falls to the ground with a thud, landing on his back, losing his breath in the instant of the impact.

"You okay?"

He's holding his injured hand as his breath comes back to him. "No. But let's go."

We're down the hill and onto the parking lot in seconds. It's a prodigious expanse, endless in its emptiness, with the van at least a hundred yards ahead. Alison is already more than halfway there, running forward with quick short strides. Mesoto and I are sprinting along behind, Mike a few paces behind me but catching up.

A few yards more and we'll be out of the range of the fuel tank's wrath. Even if it *does* explode. *Some grace anyway.*

But we're not there yet. I run on, my eyes focused on Alison. She's getting closer to the van now, slowing down, fumbling for the right key. I don't even bother looking over my shoulder. Don't bother checking on the gunman. Even if we're not out of his view, we're beyond the range of his accuracy, fleeing toward safety.

In a minute, we'll be gone.

I glance beside me. Mike is running along, breathing the heavy breaths of a smoker. His staccato gasps beg me to slow down so he can keep up.

Come on, Mike, I think. *We're just about there.*

In the distance—thirty, forty yards ahead of us—Alison has reached the van. She swings open the door and climbs into the front seat. We're almost safe. Almost out of here.

I start to let up just a little, to allow Mike to stay even. We could walk from here and we'd still make it.

"Stupid thing probably won't even start," he mutters over his rasping breaths.

I grunt a response, but I'm not really listening. I'm watching Alison as she plunges the key toward the ignition. Can almost see the look of panicked determination on her face. Can hear the first rev of the engine as it catches. Seconds, and we'll be—

Gone. At first, I'm not sure what is happening. I'm looking ahead. I see Alison through the open door. Sitting in the van. Turning the key . . .

. . . and then I don't see Alison anymore. There is a streaking sulfur flash, and then I don't see the van either. I don't see anything. There is only an eruption of thunder that shatters my ears. A blaze of light that burns its way to the backs of my eyes. The blaze becomes a white-hot ball of fire, hanging motionless for an eternal instant and then bursting toward the sky. It billows upward and outward in one swift motion, lighting the parking lot like an exploding star.

"Oh no!"

I'm running forward now as fast as I can, propelled by some mad animal spirit that drives me beyond all restraint, with the frantic hope of saving Alison. I forget all about Mesoto then. About the gunman. About everything. My only thought is to save her. To pull her from this blaze before it takes her with it. I run on, ignorant even of my own footsteps, still looking ahead . . .

. . . but there is nothing to look at. Nothing left to save. There is no van. No Alison. Nothing at all. There is only fire.

And in the distance, in the space between Century's City's twin skyscrapers, something else. Heading away from us as rapidly as it must have approached. An aerial drone.

I have no doubt who gave the order.

But I don't have time to focus on it. The blast from the explosion reaches me then. Knocks me back like a barreling train. Sears me with its terrible heat. I stagger, buckle, collapse to my knees. Hit the pavement hard but don't even feel it. My hands lunge forward, asphalt scraping away skin. The heat envelops me, but I let it come, I let it bake me in its satanic flames, screaming out wild plangent sounds that I can't understand, can't even hear.

Then all at once the tears burst forth. Tears like hot rain flow down my cheeks, coursing in unbidden rivers, carrying with them these long months of pain. *Oh, dear God, no! No!*

I collapse in that moment, lurching forward in a penitent's bow, wailing violent lamentations at the fury before me. This can't be happening! *No! No! No!*

Then even my voice disappears, leaving me with silent cries. I must lose all consciousness in that instant, my senses completely closed down. I do not feel Mike step up behind me and lay his hand on my shoulder. I do not see the solitary tear slip down his cheek. I do not see the sullen and frightened supplicants from the food line assembling now at the hilltop, lit by the flickering fire, as they come to watch the conflagration below.

I do not feel, do not see, do not hear any of these. All I sense in that moment is the pain. The loss. The emptiness made new again.

And one thing more, something that even Denver, for all its horror, could not invoke.

I know the hatred of a thousand vengeant murders. It fills me. Pushes back the heat and the emptiness.

It is all that sustains me in this moment of pain.

For Denver, as catastrophic as it was, was an act of Nature. Alison's death was an act of Man. And one man in particular.

James Alan Rooker.

I can think only a single thought in that instant. I want to take a life for this one that has been taken from me. I want revenge. More than that, I want recompense, *justice.*

Through the tears and the hurt, I silently commit my soul to this course. Irredeemably. I owe it to Alison.

I owe her at least that much.

▼

It's two hours later, shortly before dawn. Mike and I have wandered to an old stone bridge somewhere in West Los Angeles. I don't know where exactly, but it doesn't make any difference. I'm not really here.

Mike stands behind the car that we commandeered from the processing plant's security detail, leaning over the wall, smoking. I'm pacing a few yards away, a grim shadow in the car's headlights, giving us both some room. In my aimless steps, I'm reaching for some undefined emotion. Or less, just a solemn thought to exorcise this newest loss. But it eludes me. All I can think is that it's so quick, this tragedy of life. Here and gone. People here and gone. Even my desire for vengeance, muted in the last hour but not yet discharged—even that is a false savior. It may punish those responsible, but it cannot bring Alison back to life. And that is all that matters.

But I know that these are sorrows for another time and I do not dwell on them. I can't mourn her now, as much as I want to. As much as I want to sink back into the mindlessness of the stadium that rescued me for those many dark months from the gutting loss of Jeannie. Of Cassie. Of Ray. And later, in a different way, of Darby. I must keep my senses. There is too much to do. And Mike can't do it alone.

Somewhere in the middle of this silent thrashing, I join Mike at the wall. We're looking over the empty water channel below. "Hundreds of people starve to death on the streets every night," I say in a harsh unforgiving tone. "Who cares if Rooker kills another one?"

Mesoto looks across at me. Blank-faced. Pained. He takes this personally, and I let him. Still, I know I shouldn't be so hard on him. This was his loss too.

"You're forgetting the bar, *novato*," he says quietly after a moment. "What Rooker did was unforgivable, but he's not the only one killing innocent people."

"I'm *not* forgetting the bar," I answer, my hatred hidden in the cold precision of my words. "The only two people who were supposed to die there *didn't*." At this, Mike's face registers a question. "You and me, buddy boy. Rooker knew we'd be in the bar, just like he knew—or guessed—we'd be at the processing plant tonight. We didn't have him fooled for a minute."

Mesoto takes a long drag on his cigarette, then flicks it over the wall. "That may be," he says, turning to look at me straight on. "I'm not saying you're right. But even if you are, there's still one thing missing."

"What?"

"Motivation."

"Screw motivation!" I storm. "He knew we were on to him. I don't know how, but he *knew*. We might as well have broadcast it on one of Amalfi's video screens."

"It wouldn't have given him reason to kill us."

"Oh, yeah? Maybe you haven't been hearing the same rumors I have. But if *I'd* just blown up five fuel tanks, I certainly wouldn't want to face a judge these days."

Mesoto considers this. He evidently sees the argument's merit but still isn't convinced. "Why would he have risked bombing the tanks in the first place then?"

My hands are pressed against the cold stone. Gripping it. I'm staring out over the bridge, searching for help that isn't there. My brief spurt of energy is gone.

"Money, power, glory," I say without spirit. "Who knows?"

"And Rooker already had all of those," Mesoto says. "Other than Amalfi, he was—he *is*—the most powerful person in the city." A beat, and then Mike goes on more firmly. "Think, *compadre*. We're back to the same question that we couldn't answer last night. What good did it do him to blow up the fuel tanks? It only made his job harder."

"*Not* necessarily." I draw the words out slowly, with dawning revelation. All at once, the possibilities come to me. Come to me as clearly as if Rooker had named them himself. "Now *you're* forgetting something, Kemo," I tell Mike. "The fuel that was supposed to be in the tanks didn't just disappear." I pause, staring at him. Probing. "Where do you suppose it went?"

Mesoto watches me, intrigued. I can see the same possibilities occurring to him as well. At last, I think, the pieces of this deadly puzzle are starting to fit together, their answer within our grasp.

"Your game, *amigo*," Mesoto says as he tosses me the car keys.

I catch them, but wait a moment before I move. Close my eyes in silent contemplation. Take a last few seconds to be alone with my grief before I have to set it aside.

"I want him, Mike," I tell Mesoto softly, after the moment has passed. "No way he lives."

▼ ▼ ▼

Darby and I are driving west along Garden of the Gods Road, headed toward the western edge of Colorado Springs, moments after having left the freeway behind us. I am surprised, given the explosion and the freeway's impassability, that no other vehicles followed us. But all I could see in the faces of the drivers we passed was confusion, even pity, as if we were the crazy ones. Perhaps they didn't see the drunken men headed our way. Or perhaps they were just too scared to move.

As Darby and I drive on, I am thinking that maybe they're right. Perhaps I am the crazy one. For while the wide road is bathed in the glow of sporadic streetlights, it's otherwise empty. There are no lights in the store windows. No people gathered anywhere. No other cars driving on side streets or idling in parking lots. And perhaps most importantly, no safety in numbers. I shouldn't be surprised—after all, it's almost 3:00 in the morning—but still the lack of any signs of life casts an eerie pall over the entire scene. The solitude itself is frightening. Were another mob to appear from somewhere along these empty streets, we would be easy and defenseless prey.

I don't know what I had hoped for, taking this detour. But just two days after the Catastrophe, in a city the size of Colorado Springs, I would have thought there might still be commercial activity of some sort at night. A convenience store. A bar. Something. At least an open gas station.

Especially an open gas station.

At this moment, that is what we need most. When we were at Ray's house, I had stocked what I thought was an adequate supply of gasoline to make up for the long empty stretches of road I knew we would face. But I had not expected to use a full tank of gas just to drive seventy miles. At this rate, unless we can purchase considerably more fuel along the way that I had anticipated, we'll never even reach Arizona, much less Los Angeles.

I look around more anxiously, but am met only with disappointment. The all-night grocery stores: closed. The twenty-four-hour pharmacies: closed. Even the 7-Elevens: closed. As is every gas station we pass. This road looks to be one of the major residential connectors through Colorado Springs. If there are no open service stations here, there may not be any in the entire city. I am beginning to wonder if we shouldn't pull over and wait until morning, in the hope that at least one or two of the gas stations will open their doors.

But even as I think it, I am not convinced they will.

And then, by the grace of God, I see it. Up ahead. On the right. A rim of bright lights surrounding a small white building. I can't make out the signage, can only pray that it's what I hope it is.

I close my eyes for a moment. Breathe deeply. Pray silently. And then press on.

In a few seconds, we are there. And it is what I had hoped: an open gas station. An off-brand, or at least one I've never heard of. I pull off the road and up to the pumps, peering inside the building. No lights. No activity. Maybe the station isn't open after all. Then I look back at the pumps, and I learn the reason for this absence of life. Each pump bears a hurriedly hand-scrawled sign: "No Fuel." I clench my jaw. The frail reed of the moment's optimism has been broken, the hope buried.

But then it strikes me: if the station's fuel supplies are gone, why are the outside lights still on? And why isn't there a "Closed" sign on the building's front door? The questions exhume a wisp of hope. Then I glance back at the signs on the gas pumps, and the hope escalates. The signs look fresh. Unmolested. As if they only recently had been put in place. Perhaps the proprietor had to run home for an errand or merely decided to call it a night and is planning to return in a few hours. Surely, we could wait that long.

Or maybe, I think, the signs mean exactly what they say. Maybe the station's owner really did run out of fuel.

I pull away from the pumps and park in front of the white brick building that looks out on the rows of pumps. Other than an adjoining arched-metal garage, it is the only structure on the property. I step out of the van and cup my hands against the building's front window, trying to see into the darkened main office. There's one flickering light that quickly reveals itself to be a dim neon sign. Then another—coming from the back—that looks like the glare of flickering light bulb, or maybe a small television set. Behind them, in the shadows of what may be product racks or furniture, I see what looks to be an open door, leading out the rear of the building.

And then comes the sound. I realize in that moment that a soft rhythmic thud has been echoing from the middle distance. Now I can tell that it's emanating from behind the building.

The open door, the rhythmic sound: there must be a connection.

I look back into the van, checking on Darby. She's still sleeping. The van is locked. The grounds are empty. She'll be fine, I tell myself. I'll be gone only a moment. Better not to wake her. So assured, I step around the building's right side, down a small walkway between the main office and the garage that leads into the back. I can see what looks like concrete or asphalt beyond the walkway's narrow path, where the sound is clearly coming from. As I step quietly forward, the sound grows louder. More distinct. I thought when

I first heard it that it might be a hammer at work, or a tarp flapping in the wind. But now the thud takes on a different quality. At times it's a rubbery slap. At others it's a metal clang. In another time and place, I would swear it was . . .

A basketball. I have approached the open area beyond the end of the path closely enough that an asphalt-covered courtyard has come into view. A single floodlight shines above a steel basketball stand, its metal backboard weathered, its net tattered and almost completely pulled from the rim. A middle-aged African American man stands at the courtyard's far edge, arcing the ball toward the basket. His coal-black arms are filled with indecipherable tattoos, and his shapeless Lakers jersey looks like it's ready for the rag pile. But the man's shot is sweet. Perfect. I've watched ten or a dozen jumpers while I've been standing there, and every one of them—even from the deepest parts of the court—has fallen flawlessly through the rim.

The man looks up then and sees me. "Care for a game?"

On this night, in the middle of some dark and unknown neighborhood, with all that we have suffered during the past two days, I cannot believe that I'm being asked to play a round of basketball.

"Actually," I tell the man, "I was just looking for some gasoline. But your signs say you're out."

The man cradles the basketball under his arm. Looking at him, I'm guessing he's at least fifty, maybe more. He's a big man, nearly seven feet, almost a foot taller than I am. And he's bulky, probably three hundred pounds or more. But it's a muscular bulk. All these years after whatever level of ball he played, he's obviously kept himself in shape.

"Oh, I've got fuel," he says. "At least a little. I just didn't want to be interrupted during my game." He flashes a smile, and I see a scar on his cheek that I didn't notice before. And on the other cheek, a bulge that's likely the remnant of a broken jaw.

"I'm sorry to bother you then," I tell him. "If we could just fill up, we'll be on our way." He looks doubtful and I quickly add: "We've got money. We'll pay you. Whatever you want."

"Oh, I don't need your money. I mean, I'll take it. But . . . where are you headed?"

I hesitate. Why does it matter? But I'm the beggar here, and so I can't be too particular about which questions I answer and which ones I don't. Besides, he's probably only making conversation.

"Los Angeles," I tell him. "We're going to LA."

He scratches his graying, closely cropped goatee as he considers this response. "I see," is all he says. Then he turns back toward the basket, ignoring me, and swishes a thirty-footer. I use the break to look back toward the back end of our van, visible beyond the walkway. It still sits there in silence, completely undisturbed.

I turn back, and the proprietor is stepping toward me. "'Daggers,' they used to call 'em. When I played. 'Darrell's daggers,' piercing the heart of the opposition. I shot fifty-six percent from beyond the arc one year. Can you believe it? Man, that felt good."

He retrieves a towel from a fence post and wipes his brow, then holds out his hand. "Darrell Santos," *he says.* "'Dagger' to my friends. So you need some fuel?"

"Martin Fall," *I reply, gripping the proffered hand.* "Yes, I could use a tankful. If you have it."

"You can have that and more." *We pass through the court's gate. He pulls it shut behind us and locks it, then stops before entering the rear of the building. The smile comes again, with just a hint of hardness this time.* "I'll give you the gas. No problem. But I need something from you too."

He pauses, his eyes watching me, and now I'm worried again. Worried what it is he might want and how brutal my choice will be this time. Giving nothing, he bores in on me, wearing a challenging expression that must be left over from his merciless days on the hardwood.

"Feel like makin' a deal?"

CHAPTER 10

The plaza outside the Citizens Council headquarters is jammed with people by the time Mike and I arrive. This must be the morning's inbound rush, the influx of the employed to their essentials jobs in the city's essential industries and agencies of government. As I have come to expect, hundreds of workers have gathered to watch the videoscreen high upon the Council building, attending to news of the city's concerns before heading to the jobs they've been told will solve them. For many of these people, I suspect, these minutes before the videoscreen must be a highlight of their day, their validation, the proof that what they are doing is the key to the city's salvation.

But this morning's presentation is no ordinary newscast. Fran Amalfi has chosen to speak to her constituents herself, and her image fills the three-story screen with the presence of a deity. She isn't a commanding speaker, but she's authoritative in her own way. The sharp lines of her face lend her a sternness that accentuates the gravity of her talk. She comes across as someone laboring against immense and powerful obstacles—which she no doubt is—and as someone whose sole aim lies in serving the people's best interests, which Mike says even some of her staunchest supporters have begun to question.

Today, however, she has good news with which to leaven the bad. The Council has thwarted an attempted bombing at the Century City food-processing plant. It's a victory, she says, "that will permit our limited food supplies to continue flowing to the people in greatest need." She can thank Mike for that. Because of his call, the bomb squad arrived in time to defuse the explosive device, saving the city a week's worth of food and dozens of people's lives. Of course, one life was still lost in the incident, in the destruction of the van. But that small casualty does not receive Amalfi's mention. Instead, she emphasizes only the triumph, telling her audience that they can take comfort in the fact that the long string of fuel-tank bombings at last may be coming to an end.

I don't really listen to her pronouncements as we pass through the crowd, although the loudspeakers are set on such a high volume that it's hard not to. In any event, her words help distract me from the memories of what occurred last night. Although Mike and I have managed to wash away most of the soot and grime and tears from the processing plant, the changes that we have made are only superficial. I am still vacillating in great thundering waves between eruption and collapse. And so I'm willing to take any island of stability—even the tendentious rhetoric of Fran Amalfi—as a life raft.

I suspect that Mike feels the same way.

It's not long, though, before Amalfi predictably moves from good news to bad, and that would draw my attention in any case. "As you know," she says, "this Council is obligated to hold our region's carbon emissions below the established national limits. And so we must continue to reduce the amount of energy that is produced and used throughout the Greater Los Angeles area. I realize that these restrictions have made it difficult for many of you to carry on with your lives in the ways in which you would like, and you have my deepest gratitude for the sacrifices you are making. But painful as these limits are, they are essential to our future, for they may be our only hope against the return of last year's devastating oxygen wipeouts. In return, I promise you this: I will do everything within my power to make sure that these tragic events do not happen again."

There is a smattering of applause at this line, and I stop to look over at the crowd. The faces are blank. Grave. Determined. They are the faces of workers gripped by the importance of their work, and the clapping of hands ends as automatically as it began. Yet there is also an edge of eagerness in their eyes—eagerness to embrace the challenges placed before them, as if more diligently exercising their duties is the way *they* stanch the guilt of privilege I pray that at least some of them feel.

"Unfortunately," Amalfi goes on, "there is much more to be done. We can do better. And we *must* do better. All of us. The National Energy Sustainability Board has just determined that carbon emission levels remain dangerously high in our country's southwestern quadrant. The Board has therefore ordered further reductions in energy usage, which means that we must continue to tighten our belts for just a while longer.

"As a result, until further notice, the Citizens' Council will reduce fuel allowances for all but the most critical industrial users, and will suspend electrical service to all other private businesses except for those that file an approved Certificate of Need. In addition, the Council will temporarily cut back electrical service for private apartment complexes to six hours per day, and will suspend until further notice all electrical service of any kind to multi-family dwelling units with a density of fewer than one person per two hundred square feet.

"By way of compensation," she finishes up, "I am ordering a small increase in fuel allocations for the Ventura County solar plant, and am authorizing the acceleration of construction on the Orange County and Riverside solar plants. These steps will greatly expand the amount of non-polluting power that will be available in the very near future to all of those living in our region.

"I will also be announcing, in the next few weeks, a new, area-wide allocation system to ensure that energy and food continue to go, not to those who already *have* the most—those who historically have consumed far more than their fair share—but to those who *need* it the most. By working together, we will not only survive this temporary crisis, but we will also be able to thrive in the sustainable tomorrows that our sacrifices of today make possible."

At this point, the applause returns. It's more enthusiastic than before, though still a bit muted, and once again ends as abruptly as it started. But Amalfi's mission has been accomplished. Even as their minds move onto other matters, the workers begin heading with renewed vigor toward their offices, striding forward with self-infused determination to take on the difficult tasks that lie before them.

Mesoto regards the fading videoscreen image of Amalfi with unaffected eyes. "Small-town girl makes good," he mutters as we near the Council's entrance, the thinning crowd vanishing behind us.

"Yeah," I say. "A year ago she was only human."

Mesoto just shrugs, and we press on. But it isn't long before we encounter someone who holds a more glowing opinion of Amalfi's ascent than we do. Standing in front of the glass doors that lead into the Council building—almost as if he were trying to block our way—is Barry Erthein, Amalfi's executive assistant. He wears a sick, self-congratulatory grin that tells me that he must have been responsible for this morning's masterpiece of persuasion.

"Went quite well, don't you think?" Erthein prods as we come within hearing.

But we just walk past him, through the doors and toward the elevators. He bounces along behind us like a guard puppy. "I understand you wanted to see us."

"Not you, *Barry*," I snap. "Amalfi. *Alone.*"

"What about?"

Neither of us bother to answer, which *is* our answer. But Erthein won't let it lie. "I'll find out anyway, you know."

"You do that," I tell him as I insert the white plastic keycard into the slot to call the elevator. Erthein just stands there, looking dyspeptic but having nothing more to say. Then he slumps away silently, back toward the building's entrance.

"Hey, Barry," I call after him. "Toss anyone else out of the hospital today?"

He turns sharply. "It's called 'triage,' as I'm sure you know. We help those we can help, and we don't waste resources on the rest." A scornful pause. "Besides, I only do what I'm told."

I look at him, a wave of affected pity mixed in with the disgust. "Yeah," I grunt. "You and Himmler."

▼

"Rooker's gone," Amalfi tells us when we reach her office, after the formalities and condolences have been dispensed with. "Cleared out this morning."

"You couldn't stop him?"

"We didn't *see* him. He was gone by the time we got here."

"Great."

"Along with all of our allocation files, I might add."

This last remark comes with a bitterness that goes beyond what Amalfi needs in order to position herself for our discussion. She is enraged—and obviously feels betrayed—by what Rooker has done. And she doesn't seem to mind showing it. But in a strange way, this spurt of honesty only diminishes her. Though we're seated again in the chairs with the too-short legs, she looks less imposing behind her huge desk than she did before—and not at all like her deified presence on the videoscreen outside. I recall my comment to Mike from a few minutes ago and think: maybe she *is* only human, after all.

But at the moment, she's also in command. That—and the fact that Rooker has now become our common enemy—has made us allies of necessity. My reasons may be personal and hers professional, but if my motives serve her cause, I'm sure she couldn't care less about their roots.

The same goes for me.

"He did *what?*" I ask her, after the import of her statement has settled in.

"Wiped out the allocation files for all four counties from our computers. And from the cloud too. All of the archives for the past six months are gone." A pause. "He even stole the physical backup drives and tapes. All of them"

I shake my head. "This just keeps getting better."

"We'll have to rebuild all of the files from scratch."

"For 80 million people?" I say, disbelieving. "That'll take months. *Years.*" She just nods at this. Slowly. Angrily. I don't even bother to calculate the chaos that this single act of sedition will cause. I'm sure that's all she's been thinking about, and her eyes sum up her conclusions as clearly as could any words. I press, "Why in heaven's name would he do that?"

"You tell me," she answers. "Why would he blow up five fuel tanks and run off with forty thousand barrels of oil?"

An issue, despite our insights on the bridge last night, that Mike and I still haven't been able to resolve. "To sell it to someone, I guess. That's the only logical answer."

She just scowls at this. Not in an unfriendly manner, merely anxious. "Say he did sell the fuel to someone. What could they do with it? They couldn't burn it. We've got people stationed in every factory in the Basin. They track production, labor costs, emissions, everything. All down to the decimal point. Anyone using that much extra fuel would have a tough time hiding it." She hesitates, considering this. "No, they *couldn't* hide it. It'd be impossible."

"Maybe they're storing it somewhere," Mesoto suggests. "We've got thousands of unused tanks in L.A. County alone. Maybe they're not planning on using it until later."

"Maybe so," Amalfi says. "But it still begs the question. Someone could store a *million* barrels of oil and they still couldn't burn it—now *or* later. Besides, the risk of stealing and storing it has to overwhelm any possible benefit. It just doesn't make sense."

"Unless . . . ," I say suddenly.

"Unless what?"

"Unless whoever he sold the fuel to was already using so much of it that burning a little more *might* escape notice. Especially if Rooker doctored the figures like he did with the reserve tanks."

"Forty thousand barrels is hardly 'a little more' oil."

"It is when you're already burning four *hundred* thousand barrels," I answer, and then bear in on her. I've just come to this conclusion, absurd as it might seem on the surface. Now I'm waiting for her to do the same.

She doesn't take long. "I know where you're headed, Martin. Except the reports from Golden West's factories go straight to the Feds. Rooker couldn't alter the numbers even if he wanted to." A beat, and she just shakes her head. "And he wouldn't do it anyway. Rooker hates Farraday's guts. He wouldn't give an inch on the extra fuel allocations for the solar plant until I forced him to."

I hold out my hands. "Then you explain it, Fran. I'm out of answers."

She leans back in her chair, her eyes peering aimlessly toward the ceiling. Even with the attention she pays to her appearance, she's beginning to look careworn, even haggard. *It's only going to get worse,* I think, recalling the reference in her speech to the new allocation system she plans to announce. Now the reason for that new initiative becomes clear. If the consequences of Rooker's having wiped out the allocation files weren't so catastrophic, it would be amusing watching Amalfi try to turn even this worst of disasters into a political triumph.

I'm considering the irony of all this when a thought occurs to me.

"Let me ask you a question," I cut in. "You said the Council has someone monitoring every factory in the region, right?"

"That's correct."

"Who assigns them?"

Her eyes go blank. Apparently, she hadn't thought that far. "Rooker, of course."

"Including the people at Golden West?"

"Yes."

I shrug. "Well, there's your answer. He didn't have to doctor the numbers. His people did it for him—on the spot—before the data ever got sent to the Feds."

"It's not as easy as it sounds," she says, shaking her head again.

"Look, if he can engineer a drone strike, he can put his people in play. It can't be that hard."

And now she's positively downcast. "I still can't believe it. Stuart Farraday may be self-righteous and belligerent and a thousand other things, but he's not stupid. Certainly not stupid enough to tamper with the Council like this. And Rooker's spent practically his whole career working for me. He's been more loyal than just about anyone I've ever worked with." A pause, followed by a grimace that's she's not quick enough to hide. "Well, at least I thought he'd been. But you're right. Whatever Rooker's reasons, whatever he's done, we can't ignore even the most implausible possibilities. Not at this stage."

She pauses again, grimly marshaling her choices. "All right, here's what we'll do. You gentlemen pay Mr. Farraday a visit this morning. See if he knows what Rooker's up to. Without giving him any idea that he might be under suspicion himself, of course. Farraday and I are meeting late this afternoon, and that will give me a chance to follow up on whatever you can find. If he's at all involved in this, I'll fry him." A discouraged sigh. "Figuratively speaking, of course."

She doesn't expect an answer to this, and we don't give her one. We simply wait long enough for her orders to settle into the dust of silence, nod our acquiescence, and then stand to leave.

She calls after me as we go. "Do you have a minute, Martin?" I turn to her questioningly, then look at Mike, who nods glumly and then proceeds out the door. When he's gone, Amalfi steps from behind her desk and comes up to me, the sullenness in her eyes replaced by compassion. "I meant what I said about Alison. I know you were friends. I'm so very sorry."

Her condolences at the beginning of the meeting come back to me now, but I don't say anything, I don't think I could bear to. And in a moment she goes on. "When I sent her for you a few days ago," she says, "I chose her because I knew the two of you were close. And because I knew you trusted her. I did it as much for you as I did it for myself. You had to get back here—back into some kind of life—and I needed you here as well. But now . . . now, it's just another terrible loss for you. I want you to know, if there's anything I can do to help, anything at all you need from me, just let me know."

I grunt. "There isn't. But thanks."

"I'm sorry, Martin. I really am."

I look at her long and hard, appreciating her sincerity, even if I don't show it. "Yeah," I tell her. "So am I."

▼ ▼ ▼

We are sitting in the living room of Dagger Santos's small apartment in the rear of the gas station. The old walnut clock on the end table tells us that it is after 4:00 a.m., although Santos apologizes that "the stubborn thing always seems to be ten minutes fast." Santos has brewed some herbal tea—"don't drink coffee, never have, can't stand it"—and he and I sit at what passes for a kitchen table, munching on strips of beef jerky. Santos has put a "Three Stooges" video in the DVD player for Darby, and she sits in front of the television, clutching her big stuffed penguin next to her, watching silently. Pepper alone seems excited by these new circumstances. Freed from the oppressive confines of the van, he darts around happily in Santos's fenced-in back courtyard, sniffing here and there at the unaccustomed smells.

"So what's the deal you mentioned?" I ask Santos, more anxious than concerned now, after taking another long swig of the tea. Having drunk metal-tasting caffeinated sodas most of the day to keep me awake, the tea's sweet savor is both odd and refreshing, and I relish its generic convenience-store taste as if it were a rare English blend.

Santos shakes his head. "In a moment," he says. "Let's talk about what you're doing, if you don't mind. You're actually gonna try to drive to LA by yourself? Just the two of you?"

"That's the plan," I answer hesitantly, not sure where this is leading. "We're going to rest in the van for a few hours and then head back to the freeway by no later than noon."

"You can't rest," Santos says, sipping his own tea. "Not for long. The roads are only gonna get worse." A pause. "And you can't take the freeway."

"Why not?"

"You haven't heard? Two oil rigs slammed into one another north of Pueblo a couple of hours ago. They're still burning. The whole freeway's shut down. Cars are driving through empty fields down there just trying to get through."

I sigh, not bothering to hide my despair. We're barely an hour outside of Denver, and already California is looking like an impossible dream.

"It's gonna be like that all the way to Albuquerque," Santos goes on. "One thing or another."

"We'll take the back roads, then," is all I can say.

A flicker of a smile. "Know the way?"

I shake my head. "But I can read a map."

"So can every other Tom, Dick, and Harry. You don't think all the state and county roads are gonna get jammed just as fast as the freeway? Probably already are." He takes another sip of his tea, and then leans back in the frayed blue armchair, steepling his fingers as he talks. "Here's the thing. Maps won't tell you the secret routes. The short cuts no one knows about. That's what you need"

"And you know 'em?"

"That I do." It's not a boast or challenge. Just a statement of fact. And then I realize. "You want to go with us, don't you?"

"It's not safe, with just the two of you. Who knows what'll happen once you get on the open road?" He finishes the last of the tea, then cleans out the remains with a napkin before setting the cup back down. "A man my size, my color. I scare a lot people. Especially at night." Another pause. "Might come in handy."

I glance over at Darby, considering this. I think back to the drunken workmen on the freeway. They were an isolated situation, of course. A group of work buddies who drank too much and had waited too long in the endless line of cars. Could it happen again? Maybe. Probably not. But what if we were alone on a back road somewhere and the van broke down? What if I had to go for help? What if I got injured? Incapacitated? Would Darby and I be safe if it were just the two of us alone on some dark back road?

And then there were the more practical concerns. What if we got lost trying to find another route to California? Santos was right. I didn't know much more than the freeways around here. Maybe he did know the back ways and maybe he didn't, but he certainly knew more than I did. And if it were true about what he had mentioned before—that we couldn't afford to stop and rest—then that was another argument in his favor. I could drive only so long by myself. And with less and less sleep, the chances of an accident or running off the road were that much greater.

With two of us, him and me, we could drive almost continuously.

I peer in at him. "So let's say I agree," I tell him. "What's your price?"

He shrugs, as if dismissing the importance of the thought even before he says it. "You got your papers?"

"Papers?" I ask, not understanding.

"Your government certificate? The chicken scrawls that say you're allowed to be on the roads?"

I pause at this, the awareness finally coming home. I had thought the Army man gave us the certificate in Denver only because I was driving a van I didn't own. But maybe not. "Yes, I have it."

"Well, I don't," Santos says blankly. "And I don't think it's a very good bet that I'd get one either."

Puzzled, I ask, "You're legal, aren't you?"

"Do I look Mexican?"

I just shake my head. "So what's the problem?"

He stands then, collecting the cups and spoons, and takes them to the sink. After a moment, he turns back. "Look at me." He lets the words linger for a moment, then mindlessly pulls a package of Oreos from a cupboard and offers me one. "You think," he says, munching on one of the cookies, "that those pale boys in their new Beemers and their thousand-dollar Armani suits want some low-class black dude breathing their air when there ain't enough to go around? Heck, one of the first things the government did when they started with all the new rules and stuff was cut off power to all the churches, synagogues, cathedrals. Who needs nonsense like religion when my golf cart's running low, you get what I mean? Well, if those government guys are willing to stand up to God, you think they would hesitate to squash a poor black boy like me if they had the chance?"

He sits down at the table again, staring at me. "Look, my friend. We can elect a black president and we can idolize black athletes and black rap stars and the black talk show hosts on TV. But if you think a bunch of frightened white guys are gonna voluntarily share their last breath of life with someone who looks like me, you've been watchin' MSNBC way too long. I don't care how progressive or open-minded those government types claim to be, when push comes to shove—when their own lives are in danger—they'll look out for themselves first. You hear what I'm sayin'?"

I don't answer right away. I hadn't thought of that point of view. And I expect he's just being paranoid.

But with the looks in the eyes of the people I saw on the road? Maybe not. I just don't know.

In the end, it doesn't really matter whether he's right or wrong. If he wants to get out of Colorado, he doesn't have many other choices.

And neither do we.

"I see your point," I tell him at last.

And he stands. "Good. I thought you might." He offers a smile of partnership. "So let's get busy. There's a lot to get done."

CHAPTER 11

The research wing of the Golden West solar plant is as devoid of activity this afternoon as the passageway beneath the solar panels was consumed by it when Mike and I last visited. We have been instructed to wait in a lounge area down from a computer lab where, we are told, Stuart Farraday will meet with us shortly. "Shortly" has turned into more than an hour, during which time neither Farraday nor anyone else has made an appearance. I'm beginning to think that the only research taking place here is of the somnambulant form.

Mike steps away to telephone Farraday's office to ask yet again when the chairman plans to present himself. As he does, I wander into the cafeteria behind the lounge. At first I see no surprises: folding tables, an industrial-green tile floor, windows that line one entire wall so that no artificial lighting is needed. Golden West certainly didn't break the bank here. Then I see the vending machines hidden in an side room near the cafeteria's entrance, and I think: *maybe they did*. The machines are filled with apples and sandwiches and gum and potato chips and—what's that?—geez, even candy bars. Milky Ways and Snickers and PayDays and several imported brands I've never heard of. A sign affixed to the machine's front panel reads: "Gold Ration Cards Only."

Instantly, my mind is drawn back to Alison's remark on my first night out of the stadium. *Not everyone suffers.*

And suddenly my thoughts aren't of ration cards and rare candies anymore. They are of Alison. *Sweet Alison.* The suffering she healed. The wounds she left behind.

Even in this world of selective privilege, gold ration cards can't buy everything.

Mike discovers me here a few moments later, his black mood a mirror to my own. He spies the vending machines, surveying their contents as if we actually had the means to purchase something. Then he slams the side of one of the machines with his broad open hand. Amazingly, a candy bar that had been dangling at the end of its row drops down into the dispensation slot. Mike reaches in, pulls it out, paws off the wrapper, and chomps down angrily.

"They teach you that in the Academy?" I ask him.

"Ten more minutes," he grumbles. "They told me ten minutes when we got here. *Incompetentes!*" He stews for a moment, takes another bite, then nods toward the machine. "You want one?"

But as he says it, there's a loud burst from the corridor, like a gunshot or a slamming door. We step back into the lounge and find the hallway as empty as it was before—although not for long. As we watch, the computer lab door flies open and a white-coated technician marches out. A woman. Someone, I realize, we've seen before. This is the same woman who interrupted our first meeting at the solar plant. Farraday's *chica latina,* as Mike Mesoto described her at the time. But while her expression that day was locked in neutral, her face now is fixed in a mask of rage.

The words she fires back into the lab are its equal. "And if you ever even *suggest* that again, I'll tell her more than you can imagine!"

"More problems in the lab, it looks like," I say to Mesoto.

The woman stands there for a few seconds, glaring back toward the laboratory. Then she sets off down the corridor in long vengeful strides, headed straight toward us, her white lab coat flowing behind her. She's wearing a shirt and wool slacks underneath, loose in places and tight where it counts, revealing an athletic frame that would be inviting if I were in a different state of mind. But it would be an invitation to self-destruction, I suspect, given this display we've just witnessed.

She walks by us in the next moment and her eyes briefly catch mine. She flashes a hard and unforgiving look that says: *you wanna be next?*

No thanks, lady, I think, as she storms past. I watch her until she disappears around a corner, and then I turn back toward the lab to see that a man has stepped into the hallway, looking after her. Tall and silver-haired, still dressed in dignity despite the woman's lambaste.

Stuart Farraday.

We didn't have to wait even ten minutes.

Mike and I walk toward him, and Farraday doesn't focus on us until we're a few feet away. In that instant his outrage fades, replaced by the corporate, busier-than-thou expression that I know so well from years past. No more kindly museum docent, I guess.

"Unhappy customer?" I say coldly, nodding toward the other end of the hallway.

He hesitates, evidently choosing whether to respond in kind, but must decide against it. "What can I do for you, gentlemen?"

Mike and I had already agreed that there was no point in dancing. "We'd like to talk with you about James Alan Rooker," Mike says. "Perhaps you heard that he destroyed the city's allocation files this morning."

"Yes, I've heard."

"And did you also hear," Mesoto goes on, "that's he's been diverting fuel for the last three months? Some forty thousand barrels, to be exact."

Suddenly, Farraday bristles, as if Mike has accused him. "What is *that* supposed to mean, Mr. Mesoto?"

"That's what we're trying to find out. Maybe you could give us some idea where he has been sending it?"

"I know nothing of Mr. Rooker's business," Farraday replies, "except that he's sat on our allocation enhancements for the past three months. If he's been diverting fuel to anyone, it certainly hasn't been to me." A pause, rimmed with disgust. "Is that what you wanted to know?"

Mike is stopped short by this response, and so am I. I would have expected Farraday to deny the charge if asked, but not to raise the issue so bluntly on his own.

"No, Mr. Farraday," I reply as diplomatically as possible. "That isn't what we were asking. We know Rooker wasn't shipping the fuel to you. But we wanted to see if you had any idea where he *might* have been sending it. And why."

Farraday relaxes at this, his busier-than-thou expression back in control. "Perhaps I *can* help you, after all," he says in a slow, assessing tone. "But you'll have to come with me. I have a meeting out of the office, and I'm afraid I'm already late."

▼

Within half an hour we're riding in a hydrogen-powered limousine along the Pacific Coast Highway north of Ventura, being driven by Farraday's aide, Luis Rojo. Farraday and Rojo are seated in the front of the limo and Mike and I are in the back, but my attention for the moment is directed outside, through the limo's smoke-tinted windows. The noontime sun has illuminated the ocean's succession of rolling whitecaps, waves so full of light that I think they must be bearing diamonds to the shore. I imagine the beach itself would be just as resplendent—if we could see it.

But the beach is covered with people, almost lying on top of each other. These are not sunbathers, not this late in the year. Instead there are tents, cook stoves, sleeping bags, children dressed in parkas and parents draped in blankets. These are the new ornaments of the shore, and they are spread out for miles along the coastline. Yet even this far from the city the arms of the Los Angeles Citizens Council reach. The once-pristine sands are now dotted with Council food wagons and Medivac trucks, dispensing their rations and ointments as matter-of-factly as if they were seaside burger shacks.

Farraday, who has been talking on his cell phone the entire trip, turns to catch me watching this scene, then gives the order to Rojo to pull over. In minutes, the car stops and we climb out of the vehicle. Farraday leads Mike and me onto an outcropping of rocks that juts out over the beach, a vantage point from which we can easily take in the thousands down below. Rojo stays behind, leaning possessively against the limousine, pulling his pearl-handled pocketknife from his pocket and performing his meticulous surgery on the bright red skin of another apple.

"Would you really choose to live like this?" Farraday asks us, drawing us back to the scene below. "Give up everything you've ever owned just to make sure you had enough air to breathe?"

I look across at him, already tired of his self-serving lectures. "I *have* lived like this, Mr. Farraday. Except I didn't have the view."

"No, you didn't," he replies. "And neither do ninety-nine percent of the rest of what remains of this so-called country. People here used to bleat about liberty, justice, economic progress—all those happy history-book bromides. But when they didn't have the air to breathe, none of it counted for one fine farewell."

He stands there quietly for a moment, then gestures toward the ocean, as if we could see the shores on the other side. "Do you know how China and Korea and the rest of the Pacific Rim have responded to the Catastrophe? And South America and Africa, and Russia and Eastern Europe, for that matter? They're *increasing* production. Did you know that? Burning more coal and fossil fuels than ever before. Doing all they can to raise their standard of living and boost their exports. Trying to eke out whatever advantage they can over us, as if nothing ever happened. And do you know what they're telling us, China and Brazil and all the rest?"

He looks away from the ocean then and turns to face us head-on. "They're telling us, 'We're not paying for your sins. *You* did this to the air—you in the West with your capitalistic greed and waste and mindless consumption. *You* did this, not us. You had your time at the top, and you blew it. Now it's our turn to thrive.'

"Sure, most of these other places have had their own air shortages, and some of their cities and towns have been just as devastated as ours. Iran and Afghanistan and the mountainous regions of India and Pakistan have lost more than half their population. But when millions of their people are already dying from starvation and malaria and TB and diarrhea, for heaven's sake, who cares if a few million more die because they can't breathe? So what do they do? They turn their factories up to full power and try to capture every niche in the marketplace that we once had. And when we insist that they stop, for the good of the rest of the world, when we insist they shut down their countries like we have—all so we can move back into our million-dollar hillside homes and start driving our Porsches and minivans again—they don't even give us the respect to listen. They just laugh in our faces."

Farraday folds his arms and stares at us. Though the wind is whipping through his hair and droplets of the ocean's salt water must be spraying against his face, he stands as calmly as if he were addressing us in a climate-controlled assembly hall.

"And do you know what I think, gentlemen?" he sums up. "I think they're absolutely right."

At this, he relaxes, and the didactic air slips from his voice. "Come, Mr. Mesoto, Mr. Fall," he says, motioning toward Rojo and the limousine. "I have something to show you."

▼

If the solar plant looked like the stuff of fantasy on first sight, what we are watching now is direct from dreamland. A world wholly disconnected from reality. Magritte in silver and gold.

We are standing on a hillside high up in the Sierra Madres, looking out onto a high plateau no more than three or four miles wide. We crossed into Santa Barbara County on our journey here, and so have left the jurisdiction of the Los Angeles Citizens Council. But I feel more like we have escaped the authority of any earthly force whatsoever. If anyone lives in this city below us, it must be men and women from the future, or denizens of another dimension.

Arrayed before us, covering almost all of the small plateau, is a matrix of tiny matchbox houses. Each is adorned with reflecting roofs, reflecting yards, and reflecting sidewalks—all solar collectors. Running through this matrix are two broad, intersecting lines of low-level buildings, presumably offices and shops, each covered with the same silver plates. Higher up, lining the edge of the plateau, are rows upon rows of three- or four-story-high solar panels, cousins of the billboard-size monoliths that we saw at the solar plant, each tilting in slow arcs to track the sun. In the middle of this tableau stands an imposing octagonal glass dome, at least four stories high and two or three hundred feet across, a spectacular and fitting centerpiece for this glass-and-metallic wonderland. Yet despite this mass of structures, there are no cars, no vehicles of any kind. And, for now, no people. There are only slowly moving sidewalks and cable car–shaped golden trams suspended by wire.

It's easy to see where the government's grants to Golden West have gone. If this is a demonstration project, it's a very convincing one. Mike and I are both so stunned that it takes some time before either of us can speak.

"Farraday City, I suppose," I say at length, although I don't mean it disparagingly.

When Farraday looks at me, he can't mask a builder's pride, in spite of my ill humor. "'Skylight,' Mr. Fall. I'm not that vain." He joins us in our gaze, and for a moment he's the benevolent museum guide again. "One day, with adequate government funding, communities like this will house a quarter million people—with no outside energy requirements whatsoever. No carbon footprint. No greenhouse gases. No pollution of any kind."

"Close quarters, though," I say.

"Not at all," replies Farraday. "Almost everything is underground. Come, I'll give you the king's tour."

And in minutes we're there, stepping inside a world that's even more removed from reality than the one we saw outside. The service entrance we take opens onto a tram station filled with van-sized, pilotless trams. Farraday leads us into one, and the vehicle slowly takes off, heading a couple hundreds yards down a sloping parkway. Up ahead, we see the lights and signage that mark the portal to what Farraday tells us is one of sixteen stacked residential spokes that comprise the wheel of the subterranean city called Skylight.

When it arrives at our destination, we exit the tram and begin walking down the spoke's simulated street—a large tunnel, really—whose cobblestone path runs for a few hundred yards more toward the city's hub. Above us, randomly shifting blue-and-white images project on the twenty-foot-high ceiling, yielding a remarkable likeness of a midday sky. Man-made breezes blow down the street, warm and fragrant like the gentle winds of spring. In their midst, audio-animatronic birds flit about, singing and cawing and warbling with such verisimilitude that it would be hard to contend that they weren't the real thing. On either side of the street are moving sidewalks similar to those on the surface—and behind these, tiny half-finished houses that look like something out of Norman Rockwell, complete with shutters and screen doors and shingled roofs slanting up toward the ceiling. Within these houses, carpenters and electricians climb through windows and doors, applying paint, laying carpet, and wiring for power. There must be scores of workers on this street alone.

Whatever else he has done, I decide, Stuart Farraday has solved the region's unemployment problem.

"Notice the temperature, gentlemen," he says, after we've passed a cross street that circles around to connect with the other residential spokes on this level. "The atmospheric seals, combined with the natural cooling power of the earth, keep the city at a constant seventy-five degrees."

"Seems pretty claustrophobic," I remark.

"And not being able to breathe isn't?" he asks with a sudden sharpness. Then he must remember what I've gone through. Either that or he realizes that he is doing his own cause no good, and he lets the irritation drain away. "'Oxygen breakdown,' 'carbonization,' 'chemical deconstruction,' 'O2D2'—I presume you've heard the terms?"

And who hasn't? All of these—and more—had become universal buzzwords in the months following the Catastrophe, after scientists claimed to have discovered the cause of that cataclysmic event. Atmospheric carbon and greenhouse gas levels had reached critical mass, they argued, prompting the breakdown of oxygen molecules into novel, unbreathable compounds. It was a form of molecular cannibalism that accelerated to the point that, in many moderate- and high-altitude places, the oxygen briefly but selectively became so depleted that there simply wasn't enough air left to breathe.

But the buzzwords were just that—handy catchphrases for describing a phenomenon that, later research showed, might or might not have even occurred, at least at a sufficient rate to explain what had actually happened. As a result, the great body of newly ordained public knowledge became little more than mass theorization. Floating on this sea of ignorance, scientists had understandably grasped for every superficially reasonable explanation they could, flailing with the desperation of a drowning man lunging for a passing log.

A point that Farraday is quick to make. "For decades," he goes on, "we've heard constant warnings about the environment. Global warming. The destruction of the ozone layer. Rampant greenhouse gases They were all slow cancers we knew we'd have to deal with someday. *Someday*. But no one predicted *this*—this atmospheric heart attack. So now we're faced with the kind of ecological disaster that even the most wild-eyed pessimists didn't dare forecast, and all of the terrible consequences that go with it. We know—we *think* we know—that it has something to do with carbon levels and greenhouse gas emissions. But the 'how,' the 'why,' and the 'how much,' we still aren't sure. No one is."

"And whose fault is it that we're in this predicament?" Mesoto asks. It's more of an accusation than a question, as if challenging Farraday for excluding himself from blame.

But the Golden West chairman doesn't take the bait. "Whose fault is it?" Farraday responds calmly. "The scientists who didn't want to make predictions without hard data? The capitalists who never met a tree they didn't want to chop down? The politicians who always kept one eye on the next election? Consumers with their mindless obsession for every new product that came on the market? Pick any devil you want—we *all* played a part. We all looked after our own interests and desires. We all put ourselves first—before anything else—including humanity itself.

"And do you want to know something?" he bores in. "With only a few exceptions, people have been doing the same thing ever since they started walking on the savannahs."

He stops for a moment, watching for our reaction, ready to defend against any objection. When we say nothing to this, he simply turns and silently leads us on. We've arrived at a bank of escalators arrayed in front of us that descend, in stages, several more stories deeper into the earth. Flanking the phalanx of elevators are sheer silver walls that rise almost to the surface, great metallic sheets broken only by rectangular openings that I take to be windows. *Commercial offices*, I slowly realize. *Underground skyscrapers. The business centers of the future.*

We mount the escalators as we look over this scene, taking the slow ride down, and Farraday resumes. "*That*," he says, returning to his earlier thread, "is what almost everyone who was concerned about the future of our planet seemed to forget. People are going to act like *people*, not like some textbook model of Altruistic Man. Look at what the experts said were the answers to our environmental crisis. Some of them told us to start using renewable energy sources, like windmills and grain alcohol and cow manure, so-called solutions that were so inefficient that some of them would have cost a hundred times as much as good old fossil fuels. And they said it with a straight face, as if the price of energy didn't matter to anyone but Pecksniff accountants with big black hearts and shiny green eyeshades. Either that, or they put together nice little booklets with a hundred-and-one things people could do to save the environment, good ideas like recycling and turning down thermostats and turning off lights in empty rooms. Wonderful ideas. But add them all up and they wouldn't have made a dime's worth of difference in our problems with the atmosphere."

"There was a lot more talked about than that," I interject. But I say it without much force, long ago tiring of his black-and-white logic.

"Of course there was," Farraday goes on, undeterred. "Let's definitely not forget the eco freaks, the ones who said the only way we could save the planet was to eliminate population growth, shut down our industries, and move back to some agrarian Stone Age. They seemed to think that middle-class families would willingly give up their homes and their cars and their jobs and all the conveniences of life if only they knew how much harm they were doing. Those folks' hearts may have been in the right place, but their policies were a joke. Any concept that can never be implemented is as useless as no concept at all.

"But even the more thoughtful environmentalists weren't any more realistic. Their great idea was for all the people of the world to band together to create global carbon budgets, enforced by mechanisms like cap-and-trade and carbon taxes that would tell each country how much they could produce and how they could produce it. Just tax carbon use and greenhouse gases out of existence, and voilà—no more environmental problems. A great idea. In theory. But do you know how many countries actually passed provisions like that? Keep your hands in your pockets, gentlemen, because you're only going to need four fingers. Us, Great Britain, Canada, and Australia. That's it.

"Now if the rest of the world was just as concerned about the environment as we were, why didn't they go along? Well, just think about it: many of these countries are the same ones that have spent centuries building bigger and better military forces to kill off their neighboring tribes and religious sects. Most of them won't even let peacekeepers inside their borders to put an end to genocide. But now they're supposed to turn their sovereignty and resources and hope for the future over to some new-and-improved United Nations that tells them what they can and can't do economically—without even a whisper of protest? Think that'll happen in *your* lifetime?"

We step off the escalator, and Farraday just stands there, waiting to deliver the final stroke. "That, gentlemen, is two generations' collected wisdom on how to save the planet. It's as well-intentioned as it can be. But if you want to see how it's worked—well, just look outside."

I watch him for a moment, but choose not to respond, not to engage in an argument that—even if I cared about it—I doubt I could win. At least not against a man with such blind self-righteousness as Stuart Farraday. And so I turn instead to inspect the area of the city that we 've come to, and I'm once more amazed at what I see. Spread out before us must be the core of Skylight. It's a broad circular plaza, several hundred feet across, covered in expensive earth-colored tiles. At ground level, the plaza is ringed by façades boasting the marquees of stores to come—clothing shops, gift stores, bookstores, restaurants. Each of the eight rings above the ground level is fronted by a walkway and railing that overlook the plaza. And, behind them, more façades—many still under construction—that must be either apartments or offices.

Across the plaza, at about two o'clock from our entry point, stand two seven-story oxygen tanks—air reserves that must feed the whole complex. A team of workmen labor there, pouring concrete and erecting steel barricades to harden these structures, I presume, against earthquakes, outside assaults, and other destructive forces of nature and man.

To our left, opposite these tanks, sits a construction crane lifting steel girders up to one of the higher levels. My eyes follow it up to a roof that's at least a hundred feet above. I find that I am looking at an arched glass ceiling—octagonal and transparent, with the thick panes held in place by a spiderweb of black iron beams. The sun streams in through these panes, muted to a soft glow, lighting up the entire plaza with a spectral golden tint. It takes me a moment to realize that we are standing beneath the dome—the city's centerpiece—that we had seen from the hill outside.

Farraday lets us absorb this panorama, in all of its intricate and unexpected detail. Then he proudly sweeps out his hand to encompass the setting.

"Look around you," he says. "Not one of the great defenders of the planet ever did *this*—*proved* it was possible for people to have both a pristine environment and a plentiful life. You can wish until doomsday that human beings were less self-centered. That they were more concerned about the future or saving some nameless civilization halfway around the globe. That they were more satisfied with having only the barest necessities of life rather than spacious homes and fast cars and filet mignon. Wish whatever you want, and if those wishes were gold, we'd end our environmental crisis tomorrow. In fact, give me the power to change human nature to my liking, and I'll solve every problem you can imagine—crime, ignorance, world hunger, cheating on your income taxes. Every one of them.

"But the truth is, human nature is what it is. And that being the case, if people have to choose between protecting the environment and having a prosperous and abundant life, they'll take prosperous lives—every time. You don't believe me, just ask the Chinese. Or the Brazilians. Or the millions of kamikazes who are flocking to the factories in our own danger zones right now so they can earn a better wage doing what everyone else is afraid to do. For that matter, ask the people who line up every day at your own food wagons. Even with all they've been through—even though they've *seen* the horrors of an atmosphere gone out of control—do you think for one minute they'd say no to a job and a car and a big, warm house if Fran Amalfi would let them have it?"

He leads us to an elevator, just down the wall from the massive oxygen tanks. "You look at all I've shown you, gentlemen, then look at the people camped out on your streets or those helpless fools packed like sardines along the shore. Look at all of that and tell me I'm not doing the right thing." A pause, and he stares in. "*That's* my message for you and Ms. Amalfi and all the rest of you who think I'm wasting this city's precious fuel. Take *that* back to your Palace and smoke it."

I look back at him, as infuriated by his arrogance and evasiveness as I am impressed by his architectural skills. "You still haven't told us about Rooker."

"I'm afraid there's nothing to tell," Farraday answers, calm and businesslike again. "I've had no dealings with the man other than my formal appeals to the Council, which you can look up any time you choose. Beyond that, whoever he's been shipping fuel to, I have no idea. But it wasn't me."

▼ ▼ ▼

"We'll have to take your van," Dagger Santos announced six hours ago. "It's a bit small, but it's the only one listed on your certificate. I'm not sure what would happen if we took mine."

With that judgment issued, Santos ordered me to sleep. When I resisted, he reminded me that I couldn't drive if I couldn't stay awake. "Anyway, I don't need you now. You'd just be in the way."

I didn't like the idea of leaving our only mode of transportation in the hands of someone I had just met. And someone, frankly, I had no reason to trust. But I rationalized the decision by telling myself that I would have been doing the same thing, in what used to pass for normal circumstances, if I had brought the van to any anonymous mechanic in an unknown town. Of course, current circumstances were a bit more urgent than an ordinary car repair, but perhaps that made trust even more necessary. I had been in war. I knew all too well the extraordinary and unexpected logic of battlefield decisions, the unpleasant choices and unaccustomed alliances that such times often imposed. This was one case, I concluded, where the risk of trusting a stranger was probably far less than the risk of doing nothing.

Besides, I had to admit, if Santos were right about our chances of reaching California, this was the only real choice I had.

The decision made, I handed Santos the keys and returned to his apartment behind the gas station, where Darby had fallen asleep in front of the TV. I turned the television off and lay back in our host's worn and uncomfortable recliner, just as I had at Ray's house only the day before. Sleep came quickly, enveloping me. And soon, following behind, came dreams. Pleasant at first and then growing nightmarish, dominated by loss and suffocation. I was looking for Darby on some forested mountaintop, the surrounding air thin, almost unbreathable. I kept thinking that I saw her up ahead, darting behind some tree or boulder. But when I approached, the motion proved only to be that of some small animal looking for food. Gradually my search became more desperate. I started racing through the forest, looking in every direction I could. Nothing.

Darby was nowhere to be found.

I raced on, calling out for her, until I slammed to a halt. I had reached the edge of a cliff, perched hundreds of feet above the wooded valley floor below. And there, at the edge of the precipice, I saw something that made my heart sink: several footsteps amid the leaves and dirt. Footsteps the size of a child's. I knelt down, looking over the cliff's edge, hoping against reason that Darby somehow would be there. Hanging on . . .

. . . when suddenly the rock beneath me broke off and plunged toward the *valley floor. I reached back for a tree root. Grasped it. Then lost my grip and began to follow after—*

And awoke with a start. I looked around anxiously, in near panic, toward the beanbag against which Darby had been leaning while she slept. Gone! I leapt up, stepped quickly to the bathroom, thinking she might be there. But it was empty as well. My heart started pounding.

Could Santos have taken her? Where was she?

I was just about to convict the man in my mind when, finally, I saw Darby through the window of the apartment's tiny kitchen. The terror caught in my throat like a sour swallow, so foul that I had to close my eyes to keep from choking. When I opened them again, she was still there in the back courtyard, playing ball with Pepper.

It was the first real sign of life I had seen in her in the past two days.

I have to stop dreaming, *I told myself, as I watched her silently for a moment. I could not continue waking up like this every time.*

It took several minutes before I felt like talking with Dagger Santos. But eventually I recovered from the nightmare's cruel taunts. Now I am there, standing inside Santos's cavernous garage, the sun's mid-morning rays streaming in. The building, I decide, looks more like a barn than a repair shop. Tools are suspended from the ceiling on long chains, and bulging shelves are stocked with bags and cartons of supplies. In the rear of the structure sit an old twelve-seat van, a broken down Jeep, a pair of ATVs, a line of snowmobiles. An entire wall is devoted to weapons of every kind— handguns and rifles and military overstock. Boxes of ammunition and military rations are stacked to the ceiling on wide metal shelving, clearly labeled with dates and content.

This is a man, I conclude, who is prepared for anything.

But what interests me most in this survivalist setting is the vehicle that once was Ray's van. It has been transformed in ways I could not have foreseen. Santos has welded a large steel luggage carrier to the van's roof that is at least two feet high and runs the full length and breadth of the vehicle's top. The metal contraption doesn't look to be terribly aerodynamic, but if yesterday's travel was any indication, I doubt if we will be moving fast enough for physics to matter. The sides of the luggage carrier fold down, and I can see that Santos has placed all of our luggage and food in the metal bin, along with several boxes of his own food, clothing, and medical supplies.

We have become, I realize, a traveling supermarket.

The rear of the van has been similarly transfigured. The two back seats have been removed along with all that I had originally stored there. A pair of steel fuel drums have been mounted in their place, and Santos is filling one of them with fuel from his gasoline reserves. Atop the fuel drums sits a pair of jury-rigged gun racks with at least a dozen firearms from Santos's collection. Interspersed among these storage devices are camping, climbing, and safety gear along with an array of tools and electronics whose purpose I cannot surmise. All in all, it's an impressive job. In fact, all I find amiss is that the guns I brought from Ray's house are scattered on the garage floor, pushed out of the way.

"What about mine?" I ask, nodding toward them.

"No can do," says Santos. "They've been illegally modified, for one thing. And I'm assuming you don't have the permits with you."

I shake my head. "No, they were my friend's. The one who died. I just brought the guns."

"And no government authorization for the ammo, I'm guessing?"

Another shake of the head.

"You're a lucky man, Mr. Fall," he says, "If those soldier boys who stopped you had seen these, you'd be wearing a nice little orange jumpsuit by now."

I pause at this, realizing that Santos is no doubt right. I hadn't thought about it. Carrying an unregistered automatic weapon was a crime in Colorado even before the Catastrophe. Now, it's a misstep that could have cost me my freedom—and Darby any chance of returning home. And if we had crossed state lines? I choose not to even think about it.

"I'm assuming your guns are registered?"

"Every one of 'em," says Santos. "I used to own a gun shop, back before the laws got so strict. Decided it wouldn't hurt to keep a few for myself." He finishes filling the fuel tank and caps it off. "Now I'm glad I did."

"You think we'll need that many?"

"I hope we don't need any of 'em," says Santos. "But play it safe, that's what I always say. Besides, I hear rumors. Whispers in the night. Maybe none of it's true. Lot of crazy people out there just makin' things up." He slams the back door of the van shut and towels off his hands. "Still, I don't like what I hear."

He pauses to kick a few of Ray's guns further into a corner and then looks at me. "Time to go, my friend. You ready?"

"Sure."

"Good. Get your girl and your canine and let's get going. I wanna hit Durango by midnight."

"And then what?"

"And then, who knows?"

CHAPTER 12

"You know he's lying."
"He's also got the city by the cajones," Mesoto tells me. "You'd have to prove it."
"Yeah, well, I'm working on it."

It's early evening, a few hours after our return from Skylight. We have tried several times to reach Amalfi, to report back to her before her meeting with Farraday. But she has been indisposed. Out of the office. Taken away by one problem or another. Even the normally omnipresent Erthein was not available. We camped for a while in Fran's reception area on the promise of her return, and then in Mesoto's office two floors below, but eventually darkness began to set in. And so we retreated to my apartment, leaving the appropriate messages, to await her call. Without luck, as it turns out. By now, it looks like we'll have to wait until morning.

Not that it matters. There isn't much we can tell her.

"Did we learn *anything*?" Mesoto asks. He sits on the sofa, smoking. I pace the room, sipping the black-market scotch Mike brought with him, but I don't really taste it. My mouth is filled with anger and frustration and the sorrow of Alison's loss. Set against the cruel backdrop of all that I lost before, they overwhelm any more comforting flavors. The drink might as well be dishwater.

"Well, we learned that Farraday builds a heckuva lot more than solar plants," I say at last.

"And that he's not shy about complaining when he doesn't get his way."

"True." We checked the files that Farraday had mentioned—the records of Golden West's formal protests against Rooker's allocation decisions. They were there. All fifty-seven of them. All unremittingly hostile. If Rooker were diverting fuel to Farraday, it probably wasn't as a payback for the man's kindness. "And we learned that Farraday's girlfriend has one nasty little temper," I finish. "None of which tells us anything."

I drain the scotch, then pull a chair from the seventies-vintage dinette set and sit on it backwards, facing Mesoto. "Look at what we've got, Mike. Let's assume that every one of our suspicions is right. Farraday pays Rooker to blow up empty fuel tanks. Rooker ships the fuel that should have been in those tanks to Farraday. Then Rooker puts his own people in as monitors in Farraday's plants, to make sure the Feds have no idea what's really going on."

"Okay, assume it," says Mesoto. "Then what?"

"Exactly. Then what? What's Farraday going to do with the extra fuel, even if he did find a way to burn it? An extra 40K isn't going to be that big of a shot for an operation the size of his."

"It's enough to run his factories for a couple of months."

"But what does that buy him? If Rooker's right, even when the plants are completed, they won't be much more efficient than the current one is. So what does he gain?"

A grunt. "The Feds are coming in for an inspection of the Ventura solar plant next month. Maybe he thinks, if he gets it finished, they'll give him more money."

"Yeah, maybe. He's done pretty well in that department up till now." A loud sigh, and I stand, dragging the chair back to the table, then pour myself another drink. "But why would Rooker want to help him do that? What does it buy *him*?"

"Make his job easier, I guess. Like you said before."

"A job he just walked away from." I shake my head, then hand Mike back the bottle of scotch. None of this is making any sense. "Look, we're talking in circles, Kemo. Even if we're right on everything else, we're back to square one. The files in Rooker's office were stripped clean. Nothing. *Nada*. So we can't prove a thing. And we interviewed all of Rooker's people at the solar plant, grilled them really hard. I've broken a few gang members and even a couple of Mob guys back in the day, and these pantywaists aren't anywhere near that tough. If they knew anything, they would've told me. And they didn't."

This time, it's Mesoto glumly shaking his head. "It's hard to believe they'd miss that much fuel. These guys are trained—a lot of 'em by me. Some of 'em have been in the field for twenty years. If there was something to see—"

"Wait, Mike! Hold on." My body suddenly fills with electricity. I freeze in place, my mind racing. *That's* the answer.

It *has* to be.

"Maybe that's why they didn't see the extra fuel at the solar plant or the factories . . . ," I begin slowly, then let the thought form full-blown. "Maybe they didn't see it because it was never there in the first place."

"Then where—"

"Tell me this: who appointed the fuel monitors at Farraday's little city in the mountains?"

He shrugs. "I don't know. Rooker never mentioned it."

"Of course he didn't. Because there *are* no monitors at Skylight. That's where the fuel was going, Kemo. *Has to be.* Rooker was sending it to Farraday's little architectural wonder—and he didn't want either Amalfi *or* the Feds to know. He didn't want *anyone* to know. Destroy the Council's allocation files, and cities like Skylight are the *only* place people will be able to live. Farraday's rules. His rents. And his power over every government agency in the country. In the world eventually. Farraday and Rooker will get a whole lot more out of the deal than just money, that's for sure."

Mesoto pauses for a moment, considering what I have just told him. "It's nice speculation, my friend," he finally says. "But if what they're doing is supposed to be so secretive, why would Farraday take us there?"

"What better way to throw us off? Throw off the whole investigation? Put the secret in plain sight and no one will question it."

"*Tal vez.*" Mesoto shrugs. "But again, you'll have to prove it, or Amalfi won't budge. You need to find the records. The memos. The emails—"

"Of course we do!" I tell him, the emphasis overcoming me with a certainty I haven't felt since returning to this job. "And that's just what we'll get."

"What?"

"The *records*. I already checked with the guard at his apartment. Rooker never went home last night."

"Meaning?"

"Meaning, my friend, that there's probably an entire Library of Congress waiting for us there. Everything Rooker ever wrote." A beat, and the certainty holds. "If there's an evidence trail of any kind, Mike, that's exactly where we'll find it."

▼

Rooker, like Mesoto, chose to live somewhere other than the apartment complex that Amalfi had commandeered for use by the Citizens Council staff. Mike moved to a cooperative a few blocks from the Council headquarters, a spartan prefab structure erected shortly after the Catastrophe that I know of only by Mike's description. Rooker, however, selected for himself the top floor of what used to be a small luxury hotel, one of the early victims of Amalfi's business-termination orders. I have never seen Rooker's residence either, but I'm about to.

Mike and I pull up in front of the hotel, wary of leaving the Council car unattended but having no other option, and we stroll into the hotel's foyer. It's quiet, almost deathly so, and empty except for the single guard at the registration desk. This is the same man whom I spoke with earlier in the evening, and Mike and I only have to flash our Council identity cards to gain admission.

"Long day," I say to the guard, making small talk.

"Five minutes and I'm off, thank goodness."

"No sign of Rooker?"

"No, sir. Not yet."

I nod my thanks, and Mike and I leave the guard to his clock-watching and walk to the elevators. I'm not surprised to find them working.

"Anyone else live here?" Mesoto asks.

"No, just Rooker."

"*Imbécil.*"

"Good for privacy though," I say, as the elevator opens and we step inside. "And for those loud, raucous parties I know our boy loves to throw."

Mesoto just shakes his head at this. The reclusive Rooker probably would implode if he had to be in a room with more than three or four people, I suspect.

We ride to the hotel's fifth floor in silence. It's a quick trip, and when we step out of the elevator, we find ourselves in total darkness. It's a few seconds before I see the softly glowing switch plate to my right. I tap it and the hall lights flash on, up and down the length of the corridor. For an instant, I'm almost blinded, having grown accustomed to the single dim bulb in the hallway at my apartment complex. I have to rub my eyes for a moment before I can see clearly.

"Rooker certainly wasn't too worried about his own allocations."

And then, a few seconds later, the lights blink off. "Maybe he was," Mesoto says mordantly, and hits the switch again.

We make it halfway down the corridor before the lights go out again, and this time Mike is ready with the flashlight. He runs its light over the doors until we find Rooker's room. *The Presidential Suite.* It figures.

Mesoto hands me the flashlight and brandishes a white keycard programmed before we left the Council headquarters this evening. He slips it into the slot in Rooker's door plate, turns the handle, and the door clicks open.

"That was easy," I tell him.

"Like you say, white gold."

He edges open the door to Rooker's suite, both of us with our guns drawn and ready. There's no sound. No motion. No sign of any life whatsoever. We cautiously step inside, and Mesoto sweeps the flashlight over the entryway. There's a kitchen off to the side, a living area with a curved picture window directly in front of us, and hallways stretching out for a couple dozen yards or so in both directions.

"Let's go," he says.

We head first for the kitchen. The room is sparsely appointed. There's a scattering of tableware, a few pots and pans, a toaster, and little else. But there's plenty of food, and not the Council's tasteless rations. All imported stuff, coffee and fruit and bread and packaged cereals. And a refrigerator with milk and wine, even eggs and butter. Rooker hasn't gone mad from starvation, I'll give him that much.

We move next into the living room, also sparsely furnished. Sofas. Tables. Shelves with bargain-table display books. A few generic mass-produced prints on the walls. Exactly what you would expect to find in a hotel. But the tables are thick with dust, and everything is in such perfect order, that it hardly looks like the room has been entered in months.

We split up now. Mike takes the hallway to the left of the entrance and I take the one to the right. I open the doors, one-by-one, peering in first with the gun and then with Mike's spare flashlight. They're all bedrooms, all neatly made up. And all empty.

"*Madre mía . . . !*" I hear Mesoto exclaim from the end of the other hallway.

I'm out of the last bedroom in an instant, back into Mike's hallway, my gun held out and ready to fire. But Mike is just standing there, looking into an open room.

"What is it?"

He waves me closer. "You've got to see this, *amigo*."

I step up behind him, then look over his shoulder. The room is large, maybe twenty feet square. Definitely not a bedroom. Maybe it was a study at one time, or an office. But it has been transformed during Rooker's tenure into a high-tech wasteland, full of computers and monitors and electronic maps. One whole wall is given up to bookshelves, spilling over with technical studies, meteorology textbooks, government reports. There's a bank of telephones on one table. A printer. A graphics pad. And jammed in what used to be the closet: a row of file cabinets.

It's not easy making our way to any of these treasures, however. Most of the floor is overflowing with computer printouts, stacked three and four feet high.

"You are one messy housekeeper, Mr. Rooker," I say, exulting in this discovery. But it's almost too much, this mass of material before us. And we don't even know what we're looking for.

"See what you can find in the file cabinets," I tell Mike. "I'll take the computer."

I wend my way to the terminal, stationed on a desk along the far wall. I flip the switch and it's on, whirring and then offering a greeting. "Good evening, Mr. Rooker," the screen reads. "Please enter today's password."

"Great."

"What?"

"I should have known. We need a password."

Mesoto pulls a crumpled sheet of paper from his pocket and hands it to me. "I figured you would. Try this. I found it in his desk downtown."

It's a list of women's names, organized alphabetically from A to Z. "What's this?"

"Either Rooker's signed up as a lifetime member of eHarmony or else it's a list of his passwords."

A good guess, I see as I look more closely. Every name has precisely eight letters and three trailing numbers.

I set to work, entering the names in order, listening to Mike behind me trying to jimmy the file cabinets open. I'm up to G, with no success, when I hear Mike snap, "Forget *this*. Hold your ears."

I turn in time to see him pressing a seat cushion to his gun, which he is now pointing at one of the locked file cabinets. A silenced shot, and the lock is obliterated. Three more shots, three more dead locks.

"You'd make a heckuva locksmith," I tell him, my ears still ringing.

He grunts a response, then pulls open the drawers. While he's skimming the file folders, I swivel back to the computer, entering more names. But the response is always the same: "INVALID PASSWORD." Even the last hope, some exotic siren named Zhyphora927, is no help. The computer rejects her without a second thought.

"Worthless," Mesoto growls from behind me. "Old fuel use reports. Satellite tracking data. Weather reports. Nothing we don't already know."

"I'm not doing any better," I tell him. "None of the passwords work." A pause, and the frustration builds up inside of me. "Alison, why aren't *you* doing this?"

And then, in the moment the words come out, I realize what I've said. The tension culminates again a year of baneful memories, a dark foul eruption filled with the anger and hatred and loss that I'm holding back worse now than I was when I was in the stadium. Suddenly I know I'm on the verge of losing it. If Rooker were standing before me, I wouldn't need a weapon. My hands would be around his throat so fast he wouldn't even have time for a final breath.

I discharge the anguish with sound, wailing some incomprehensible animal cry that emanates deep from within me. Then I shove the recalcitrant computer's monitor so hard that it carves a long gouge in the paneled wall behind it before slamming to the ground, then hissing to a silent death.

"Lot of good that did," Mesoto says, after a moment.

The tension finally slakes enough that I can speak. I look back at him, vaguely embarrassed. "We weren't getting squat anyway."

"It's probably networked downtown. Even if you'd found the local password, you'd still have to know all of the other codes. Alison herself couldn't have done anything with it." He hands me a screwdriver. "Here, pull the hard drive. I'll have one of the guys I trust look at it tomorrow."

I'm not even thinking. "The what?"

"The local drive. It's probably bolted in back. It'll have the files he *didn't* want sent down—"

We freeze. All at once, the silence outside the room is disturbed by a distant ping. Quick. High-pitched. Unmistakable. The sound of the elevator door announcing its arrival on the fifth floor.

"Shhh!" I whisper, and Mike is instantly quiet. We're both locked in place. One part of me is thinking that it's probably just the security guard, coming to check up on us.

The other part knows that it isn't.

"Here, get the drive," I say to Mike. I pass him the screwdriver, switch off the light, and shut the door into the hallway. Dropping to my knees, I edge the room's door open half an inch so that I can see out, holding my pistol at eye level. Kneeling. Waiting. Listening.

The expected sound comes. There's the wisp of the keycard being inserted into the suite's main door, then the soft click as the handle pivots and the door swings open. And then footsteps. Hurried. On a mission. As unhesitant as if their owner lived here.

This isn't the security guard, I'm thinking.

"Come on, Rooker," I whisper. "Gimme some target practice."

There are sounds from the kitchen now, a rummaging of some sort. Then more footsteps. They stop. Perhaps he's looking into the living area, though he won't see anything amiss. We didn't touch anything there. But it's evidently only a pause to find the light switch, for suddenly there's a spill of light flooding the hallway. Followed by more footsteps. More insistently now.

Headed this way.

I soundlessly push the door shut and pull up closer to it so that I have a clean aim when he opens the door, ready in case he's armed. But as I shift, my shoe catches on an electric cord, sending a desk lamp tumbling to the floor. In the nervous silence, the crash ricochets through the apartment like a cannon shot.

And instantly the footsteps come again. But this time, they aren't the careful steps of entrance, walking toward us. They're running in the opposite direction, as quickly as their owner can move. And at once, they're joined by the sound of the front door, quickly being opened and then slamming shut.

I rip the electric cord from my foot, fuming. "Stay here!" I command Mike in a harsh whisper.

I'm up in that moment, hurtling into the apartment's hallway, toward the living area. My gun up, and I'm thinking this escape that we've just heard might be a ruse. Maybe Rooker is hiding in the kitchen, waiting to fire on these unknown intruders. But no. I scan quickly, anxiously. The rest of the apartment is empty, as lifeless as when we entered.

Rooker is gone.

I rush to the front door. Swing it wide. Then peer urgently into the fifth floor corridor, looking both ways. *Where did he*— There, to the right! I hear footsteps. Rapid breathing. The quick drumbeat of exertion echoing off the walls. But in the funereal darkness I can see only the barest outlines of a shape, only enough to make out the image of Rooker's trench coat billowing behind him as he runs.

I'm searching desperately for a light switch now, for some way to confirm this vision. And more, to aim my shot, so that I hit him in the arm or the shoulder and not in the head. I don't want him to die. Not yet. Not until I've had the chance to face him. But I can't find the switch plates. *Where are the light switches?* And then I see one. *There!* Up to the left. I dart toward it, stabbing my hand against it so hard that my palm explodes in pain, and the corridor comes alive with light . . .

. . . just as the door to the stairwell at the corridor's far end is falling shut.

I race to the closing door and have to tug on it twice to pull it open. Then I bolt into the stairwell, craning ahead, searching for some image below. But the flights of stairs are pressed so closely together that there's no line of sight down the center. I couldn't see much anyway, not in the faint light of the bulbs on alternate landings. I can only hear. And what I hear is the receding thud of leather on cement. Two, maybe three flights ahead of me.

I don't even take time to think. I whip around the stairway's steel posts. Bound down the stairs in twos. Listen over my own acrid breaths for the footsteps ahead of me. They're still there. Racing on. Almost to the bottom. But Rooker is slower than I am, and by the time I'm halfway down, I can make out the flash of a shadow on the stairwell wall. A phantom rousted from his lair.

"You're mine, Rooker!" I call out.

And then I stumble. My body lurches forward, and I barely catch the railing with my free hand. I spin around, almost a full three-sixty. My back slams against the stairwell wall, and my arm arcs with fire as its muscles are stretched beyond their limits. For an instant I lose my breath, and the gun spits out from my hand, clattering down a half-dozen stairs. My head is pounding. *No time to rest!*

Just then, two floors below, the door to the street pivots open. A bath of moonlight fills the stairwell below me, calling me back to the chase. Yet before I'm even moving, the outside door has slammed shut again with a blast of metal on metal. The light is gone. *Too late!*

But I can't quit now. Not when I'm this close. I push myself up from the wall and nearly leap down the next flight of stairs. Locate my gun and haul it into my hand. Then spring onto the next-to-the-last landing, and then onto the last. Three quick steps more. The ground floor lies just ahead. I bound forward, barreling into the wall beside the exit door. Then, just as quickly, I reach out and grab the doorknob.

A pull, and it's open. And in seconds, I'm outside . . .

. . . standing on the sidewalk beside the hotel. In front of me, fifty or sixty feet ahead, the form with the billowing trench coat races on, toward a parked car. I level my gun, preparing to shout a warning. Preparing to shoot if I'm ignored. But I can't find the aim. My quarry sprints on, throwing open the driver's-side door and leaping inside. I rush toward the car . . .

. . . as it revs to ignition. Lurches ahead. And then spins away. It races up a few yards, then angles left, toward a side street, before I have a chance to call out or even fire. So quick and flawless is Rooker's escape that I've had time to take only a few useless strides in pursuit.

But the chase isn't completely in vain. The half-masked moon moves fully out from the clouds at that moment. In its rich reflected light, I can clearly make out the symbol on the side of the car as it's speeding away. It's not the Council symbol, as I would have thought. Instead, it's the golden sun rising over craggy blue mountains. A revelation in itself.

The emblem of Golden West Power.

And one thing more. In the last second before the car disappears from sight, the light hits just the right angle. I have a clear view of the driver then, a sight of the desperate and startled expression that fills its bearer's face. It is a face, by now, that I have come to know well.

But it isn't Rooker, this visitor who interrupted us tonight. It's someone else, someone whom I had not expected.

The woman from Farraday's lab.

▼ ▼ ▼

In an effort to reduce the gridlock of eco-refugees on freeways and highways in the Western United States, the President today announced that most of the on-ramps to these thoroughfares will be closed until further notice. Military personnel from Camp Pendleton in San Diego and the US Air Force Academy in Colorado Springs will be deployed via helicopter to these sites within the next twenty-four hours.

"In addition, under the authority of the Emergency Environmental Response Act, signed into law by the President yesterday, the White House has ordered the temporary nationalization of the country's major bus lines, and will use these vehicles to ferry stranded travelers to their destinations. An estimated seventy-five people died on Western freeways yesterday, mostly from traffic accidents, untreated medical conditions, and the growing incidence of violence. Henceforth, therefore, military personnel also will be stationed at random intervals along these routes. The President is determined to end this unnecessary loss of life.

"In other news, the US Supreme Court today struck down California's recently passed 'Border Security Law,' which would have banned all migration into the state. The Court did rule, however, that the state could exclude foreign nationals, illegal immigrants, and individuals without proper documentation—"

I reach over and turn the radio off. We've been listening to it for hours, and the news is all starting to sound the same. "Looks like you were right," I tell Santos.

"You're surprised? I'm just hoping we get there before they start shutting down the side roads. It's a mighty long trip if we have to walk."

I nod in agreement, and breathe a silent sigh of relief. Our prospects of arriving in California within a couple of days are actually looking better than when we started. Santos's trip-routing abilities have proven to be as skillful as advertised. Not only did we reach Durango before midnight, but most of the side roads were moving at posted speeds. Although traffic was heavier than usual, it probably wasn't that much worse than it would have been at the height of tourist season.

Still, I hardly feel like a tourist. I always drove the entire way on our family vacations, and so I am unaccustomed to riding in the passenger seat, as I have for most of our journey from the Springs. I don't like being out of control, but I have had no choice but to turn most of the driving responsibilities over to Santos. He seems to know the way by instinct, and makes spur-of-the-moment decisions that would have been impossible to map out ahead of time.

Eventually, I was able to cast aside enough of this discomfort that I could sit in the backseat with Darby for an hour or two. It was the first time I had tried to communicate with her for any length of time since we arrived at her parents' house. I read her a story and we played cards for a while, but I could tell her heart wasn't in it. I asked a couple of times how she was doing, and her only response was a tepid "Okay." I knew that she needed to talk, that she needed to give voice to whatever painful feelings she was holding inside her. But I also knew that this catharsis would have to come on her own schedule and not mine.

I left her to herself at our last stop and am now in the front seat again, glancing back at her while she silently plays with some plastic horses. It amazes me that she has not cried since the first day. Cassie was a studious girl, but she was also emotional, and hardly a week passed without one or two end-of-the-world crying spells. Although I never saw Darby cry during the many times she stayed at our house, I can't imagine she would be that much different than my own daughter. I wonder if what happened— to her parents, to our lives—has fully registered with her.

I am thinking about this possibility when my phone rings. It's a number from the Los Angeles Energy Office, where I work, and I'm assuming that it must be Alison Leary again. Cell service returned a few hours ago, somewhere south of Crede, and Alison had called then to resume our previous conversation. I told her that we were driving back to California and expected to be there in two or three days. She asked after Jeannie and Cassie, and I was forced to tell her then that they had died in Denver. Alison was clearly shocked by this news, but she said just the right things on hearing it, as she always does, and her sympathy and compassion were as genuine as I could have hoped for. Still, I quickly moved on to other matters, and ended the call with as much haste as I could. It was best that I didn't think about Jeannie and Cassie for the time being, and Alison's call—heartfelt as it was—was more of a distraction than a comfort.

Now, with the phone ringing again, my first thought is to hope it isn't Alison. I could handle a call from Mike Mesoto, who holds back his emotions as much as I do, or even from Barry Erthein, who has no emotions at all and is therefore a perfect antiseptic for times like these. But speaking with Alison again would be too much of a strain, especially right now, amid the deepest and most starlit part of the night when the sky and all its portent envelops us.

Knowing this, I am tempted just to let the phone ring. But the call could be important, and I reluctantly answer it. To my surprise, it isn't Alison or Mesoto or even Erthein.

It is Fran Amalfi herself.

"Martin," she says in her habitually clipped speech, "Alison tells me you're headed back to LA."

As Fran speaks, I'm thinking that it's as if we had last talked only this afternoon and not more than a week ago. No greeting. No introductions. Just business. Vintage Fran Amalfi.

"Yes, we're in southwest Colorado now," I tell her, repaying her formality with my own. "I expect to be back in the city in two or three days."

"Good, good. Hurry then," she says. "We really need you here. I'm flying to D.C. for some meetings tomorrow. So if I'm not back when you arrive, just check in with Barry. He'll have the assignments."

I can't resist asking. "You're flying? I thought the government had banned all flights."

"They have. It's a government charter. DOD, I think. Some urgent meeting the President wants me there for. I shouldn't be long."

And with that, she rings off. No further explanations. No small talk. It's so like Fran—the consummate executive—but still it rankles me every time I speak with her. She may be a small fish, but whatever pond she swims in, she makes sure everyone knows that she's the highest fish on the food chain.

I click the phone off and cradle it in my hands, turning to stare out blankly at the night sky. And that's when I realize. Amid all that Fran did not say, one omission stands out. There were no condolences, not even the smallest expressions of sympathy. Could she really be that cold?

Or perhaps, I hope, she had simply not yet been informed.

CHAPTER 13

The sights that appear before me make me feel as if I am walking into a prison. The central corridor that leads away from the building's main entrance is bare concrete, no more than ten feet wide and stretches out for half a city block. On either side of this cracked and stained walkway, walls made of thick wire mesh rise toward a corrugated metal roof a dozen stories above. The walls are marked off into cramped little boxes the size of a small jail cell, and each row of boxes is fronted by a metal catwalk. Open metal stairwells complete the assembly, connecting the structure's rising levels to one another with proletarian efficiency. As I pass through this scene, ill-shaven men in old plaid shirts and gray Council-issue work pants climb up and down the stairs, traverse the catwalks, and enter and leave the boxes, meandering in aimless formation like the ink-sketched men from an infinite Escher loop.

Though it looks like some surreal prison, I know it isn't. These boxes are tiny apartments—emergency housing units constructed by the Council in the months following the Catastrophe. They're not much to call home, perhaps, but they're better than living on the streets. And for most of the occupants, that may be their only other choice.

For most, but not all. Certainly not for the man I'm visiting tonight. A man who moved here, he says, because of the building's proximity to his work and the simplicity of his needs.

Mike Mesoto.

I head down the facility's main corridor, moving past two intersecting passageways before I reach a third—the corridor where Mike lives. I turn to the left and walk a few feet to dimpled metal stairs that are barely wide enough for two men to pass, then start the long and arduous journey to the seventh level. I think as I head up: *If Mike has to make this journey every day, I'm surprised he isn't in better shape.*

At length, I reach the seventh level, and chance to look out over the waist-high railing. I'm not really afraid of heights, but it's still a long, straight drop to the hard concrete below, and so I quickly turn away, not wanting to invite nausea to join the anger and uncertainty I already feel. Instead, I look toward the sleeping units that front the walkway, taking in the hand-lettered nameplates on each of the doors and the colorless canvas sheets draped behind the wire mesh walls that afford some small measure of privacy. The apartment I'm looking for is just a few yards down, marked by hurried lettering that reads: "Migués Mesoto." I had forgotten this was Mike's given name.

I rap on the door, the metal stinging my knuckles but yielding only a dull hollow thud. "Mike, it's Martin." I doubt that Mike even hears me, but he must. The door swings open, and I'm peering for the first time into the room that Mike Mesoto has made his home.

At once I notice: he actually has less space than I did at the stadium. There's a metal bed with a fist-thick mattress jammed against the side wall, looking like something out of an Army MASH unit. An off-balance chair with one leg shorter than the others. A narrow unpainted fiberboard structure that passes for a desk. A telephone. A naked sink and counter, with a hot plate and a smattering of Council food rations. Stark metal shelves along one wall, weighed down with Council reports and a few old murder mysteries. An open metal toilet. A collection of candles, for the times when the electricity is off. And a single light bulb, screwed into an incongruously decorative light fixture hanging from the ceiling.

In all, a self-imposed penitence for his imagined sins of privilege.

With only a nod as a greeting, Mike returns to work on the light fixture, opening the false side panel and storing the hard drive from Rooker's computer inside. A few twists of the screwdriver and the job is done. He steps away and slumps into the chair, his shoulders sagging, as I sit on the bed across from him.

"There's a gold mine buried in that drive, *amigo*," he says. "That's what Enrique tells me."

"Yeah?"

"But it does us no good. The files are encrypted with a 128-bit key. With the resources we have, there's no way we can break it."

"Ah, great."

He merely nods his displeasure. "And there's more. It won't make you feel any better, I assure you." I wait for him to explain, but he says nothing for the moment. He only pauses to light a cigarette and then exhales deeply, the smoke swirling around him like a hangman's noose. "I spent the entire day seeing what I could turn up on Farraday and Rooker," he resumes. "Even dragged myself back out to the solar plant. And then, just when I thought I was getting somewhere, Amalfi called me in." A beat. "Called me in and told me to give it up."

"She did *what*?" I'm sure I've misheard him.

"Told me—ordered me, really—to leave it alone. Farraday. The investigation. Everything. Said she read him the riot act last night, and he promised to stop badgering the Council if she kept *her* promise to fast-track the allocations and permits he needed."

"And what about Rooker?"

"She thinks he probably *was* behind the bombings. But now that he's gone, she just wants to get on with the cleanup."

"And that's it?" I say, refusing to believe it. "Business as usual? Are you serious?" Mesoto nods, but it still feels wrong. Even in the midst of a crisis, Fran Amalfi is not the kind of person to let betrayal go unpunished—especially with such obvious suspects. Or to let questions go unanswered either.

Then I think: *Maybe she's more desperate than she lets on.* Maybe she *doesn't* want to take this any further than she needs to. "She didn't even want to pin down Rooker's connection to Farraday?" I ask Mike at last.

A derisive snort. "She doesn't think Farraday's involved."

I just shake my head at this, not even willing to dignify that nonsense with a response. "She's just afraid he'll try to get her tossed out of the Council so he can put his own man in her place. Pure self-preservation on her part—that's all it is."

"Maybe," says Mesoto. "But you're right, what you said before. Amalfi definitely won't move against him without proof."

"Which we still don't have."

"No, we don't. And our chances of getting any with her blessing and support just flew out the window."

I let out a frustrated sigh. "Any suggestions?"

"We get it on our own," Mike says, more firmly than I would have expected. He stabs out his cigarette, then hands me a folder full of notes, photographs, journal articles, employee records. "And here's where we start."

A glance immediately tells me what he has collected: the particulars on the woman from Farraday's lab.

"But you said Amalfi—"

"Forget her. She doesn't need to know. Not yet anyway."

I only shrug, but I'm thinking: *This isn't the Mike Mesoto I used to work with.* He never would have stepped outside protocol in times past. Maybe Alison's loss got to him more than he's letting on.

Or maybe he just doesn't care anymore.

I nod toward his cache of documents. "So what do you have?"

"A few things," he answers. "The woman's name is Maria Maas. She used to work in Rooker's shop, back when he ran the policy office."

I'm skimming the materials in the folder. "Yeah, that would explain a lot."

"Well, get this," Mesoto says. "She transferred to Golden West exactly one month after the Catastrophe. Went to work for her father."

I'm only half-listening while I scan the papers, but that comment jars me. I look up. "Her father? Who's her dad?"

"His name is Alejandro Maas. He has a lot of solar patents, fuel cell patents, thirty years in the industry." A pause. "And you'll like this. He used to be Farraday's top scientist."

"Used to be?"

"Yep. He vanished about eight months ago. Disappeared. Dropped off the face of the Earth." Another pause, as Mike lights a new smoke. "Word is, he went insane."

Not surprising, I think, *if he worked for Farraday*. But I don't say anything. Mike clearly has more to tell me, so I let him continue.

"Farraday supposedly kept Maas on as a favor to the old man. The guy had been with him for decades, you know. But Maas got to be such a raving lunatic that Farraday finally had to let him go."

"Really? What was he raving about?"

Mike frowns at this, confusion taking over his face. "That's the kicker, *amigo*," he answers with a slow, uncertain turn. "This guy Maas? He wanted the solar plant shut down."

SKYLIGHT

▼

Despite our renewed determination from the night before, the day has proven as fruitless as I feared it might be. Even our most creative efforts to gather the proof we needed for Fran were blocked at every turn by random combinations of bureaucracy and bad luck. Mike had returned early in the morning to Golden West, to try to pry loose additional clues about Alejandro Maas and his daughter from his contacts there. But by the last time I had spoken with him, just after noon, he was coming up empty. No one knew anything, or wouldn't talk about it if they did.

At the same time, I agreed to take on the task of tracking our elusive lady scientist, to see if I could speak to her without the interference of guns or midnight chases on the stairwell. But first I closeted myself in the Council's records library, searching for some further link between Rooker and Farraday. I didn't find anything new, although the time wasn't entirely wasted. I was able to hide from Amalfi, who had summoned me for what I presumed was the same lecture she had given Mike. It could wait, I decided.

When I had the information I needed to convict both Rooker and Farraday, then we could talk.

Now, my hours of seclusion are behind me. I'm crouched on top of a small apartment complex near Golden West's Santa Monica research laboratory, where Maria Maas has passed the day, according to a cooperative receptionist. The laboratory—the old RAND Corporation headquarters that sits across Ocean Avenue from the Pacific Ocean—is an arc-shaped building that's several hundred feet in length, but that for security's sake boasts only a single entrance. It is on that set of doors that I have my binoculars trained, waiting for the mysterious Dr. Maria Maas to appear.

She does so, a few minutes after seven, walking out of the building under the protective anonymity of the crowd. It's difficult to miss her though. The white lab coat. The dark, nearly black hair falling in loose curls to her shoulders. The hard chiseled features that are visible even from a distance. These are all familiar images from before, and they help me quickly lock in on her. But even if I hadn't known what she looked like, I would have recognized her from her gait. She walks along quickly, like a person with a purpose. Her eyes move warily over the scene, and she turns her head as inconspicuously as possible every few seconds to look behind her. No doubt, after last night, she suspects that someone must be following her. Tracking her.

I wonder who she thinks it is.

Once outside the barrier of the lab's security fence, she strides the two blocks to the elevated tram stop and heads up the stairs to board. I've climbed down from my perch and am behind her now, thirty feet or so, but she's tall enough that I can easily keep her in view. She runs her identity card through the slot at the tram's turnstile and is allowed to pass, then moves quickly to the nearest car. I push ahead, stepping on toes and ramming elbows but not bothering to excuse myself, and make it through the gate just as the station's automated voice is commanding passengers to step away from the sliding doors. As the tram's doors are about to lock me out, I slip inside the car, and the tram begins its northeastward journey.

Unfortunately, the trip is a wash. Worthless. I press against the tram's back wall the whole time, crammed in among the working masses like a commuter on the old New York subways. Maria Maas stands halfway toward the front, holding onto the center pole, looking around furtively for suspicious faces. Apparently finding none, she settles into a motionless pose for the remainder of the ride. But each time new passengers step on board, she is wary again, looking around with the caution of a fugitive, no doubt knowing by now that her life may depend on her vigilance.

Nearly an hour passes until we reach her stop. She's off the tram as quickly as possible without drawing attention to herself, filled again with a purpose. We're somewhere in the southern end of the San Fernando Valley, well outside the protected perimeter of downtown but also beyond the borders of mid-town's most dangerous zones. I don't know whose apartment she is headed toward, but it certainly isn't Rooker's. Not this time.

Shortly, I'm off the tram and on the sidewalk as well, half a block behind her. I have to dodge overturned trash cans and mounds of trash bags clawed open by raccoons and scavengers just to keep up, and yet maintain a safe distance between us so that I'm not seen. All around us, the streets are lined with beggars. Penitents. Those long since cast out of their former homes or never able to find one. Maria walks by them as quickly as she can. Many of the vagrants reach out to touch her as she goes, perhaps taking her white coat to mean that she's a medical doctor. They offer frail and quivering hands in exchange for her assistance, but she only brushes past them and heads on, bundling her lab coat more tightly around her.

Another block, and she's turning the corner, hidden for a moment by the brick wall that surrounds the four-story apartment building to our right. I give her a few seconds to gain some separation, then rush to the same corner she just turned, peering around the edge of the wall. I'm there just in time to see her step up to a guard post, where she trades a few words with a heavyset, coal-black Jamaican guard who carefully checks her identification. I move in closer, trying to hear what they're saying. But just then a fire engine rushes up the street from behind me, its siren blasting at the moment it speeds past. Maria looks after the fire truck as it goes by, holding her gaze until it is out of sight. Then she steps away from the guard post, toward the apartment building's entrance and out of my view.

I reach the guard post a few seconds later, watching as Maria makes the long walk to the building's security-guarded entrance. The guard at the post immediately eyes me with distrust, then—when he sees I'm not stopping—steps out to block my way. A rifle is strapped across his shoulder, and there's a pistol in the holster at his waist. But his hostile glare, if anything, is more of a warning than his weapons.

"What d'ya want?" he demands.

I hold out my Council identity card, mutter a response about having business inside, and attempt to pass.

The rifle is off the man's shoulder in an instant, its muzzle held inches from my chest. "That card don't mean nuthin' here, Mister. And if I were you, I'd keep it hid. 'Cause you Council boys ain't real popular with the street folk, if you get my meanin'."

I get his meaning all right, and I know he's just doing the job that the residents here hired him to do. But while he's standing here playing rent-a-cop, Maria is walking into the apartment building. Once she's inside, there's no way I'll be able to find her. If Rifle Boy wants it official, I'll make it official.

And so I reach inside my jacket for the papers that Mike had prepared for me, granting me the power to act with the full authority of his office. But no sooner do my fingers touch my inside pocket than the barrel of the guard's rifle lurches ahead, pressed tightly now against my chest.

"I ain't sayin' it again, Whiteface," the guard spits. "Get your fat butt outta here before you gets to be a *dead* Council boy. *¿Comprende?*"

I say nothing to this. I just slowly withdraw my hand from my inside pocket, deciding that I no longer like the odds. He might shoot. He might not. But Dr. Maria Maas, whoever she is, isn't worth the risk. Besides, in the moment of the guard's challenge, she has slipped inside the apartment building, out of view and beyond my reach. I couldn't follow her now even if I were offered the chance.

It's time to call it a night.

I give the guard a final vengeful stare—my last and only defense—and then turn lamely away. Even without looking back, I'm sure that his rifle is still held ready, threatening me with instant extinction, until I have rounded the corner and disappeared at last from his sight.

▼

I retrace my path to Santa Monica, to the block down from the Golden West building where I left the Council car that Mike had procured for me earlier in the day. It's still hidden there, intact and undamaged, in the alley between two aging office buildings that are no longer in use. *A lot of good my secrecy did me tonight*, I think. But at least there's one small blessing: I won't have to walk the several miles back to my apartment building, or else chance finding a bus or tram that's still running at this hour.

I opt to take Wilshire, or what's left of it. The boulevard—once the prestigious east-west passage through Los Angeles—has become an open landfill, testament to a city that long ago toppled over the edge. In the early months following the Catastrophe, the Citizens Council tried to maintain regular trash collection services. But with the press of migrants and more urgent tasks, the garbage accumulated faster than the city's sanitation teams could remove it. Soon, the best the city could do was plow one lane clear in each direction, leaving people's foul discards piled up along the sides.

They still sit here, these rivers of refuse, ignored like an unpleasant fact. In several places, fires have spontaneously ignited or have been intentionally set. Flames dance atop these mounds, burning or smoldering, sending waves of dark smoke skyward to line this forbidding corridor. Their stench fills the car, burning my nose and eyes, even with the windows tightly shut. And so I abandon Wilshire as soon as I can, turning off to the northeast and toward my apartment. The time that I squandered trailing Maria and the encounter with the guard have started to weigh down on me, leaving me spent and defeated.

It is time to sleep, and to pray for a better day tomorrow.

But first, before I'm too tired to think, I decide to check in with Mike, guessing that he should be back from the solar plant by now. I punch his number into the car's built-in cell phone. When his line begins ringing, I expect him to answer right away. But he doesn't. All I hear is the coarse, clanging echo of the signal from his end, ringing on and on. Maybe he's in a dead sleep, I think. Or maybe he's playing cards in one of the other cubicles and left his phone behind.

Or maybe, more likely, he just doesn't want to be disturbed.

"Hope you had better luck tonight than I did, Kemo," I say to the air, switching off the phone and deciding to call again once I'm inside my apartment. The drive from that point proceeds mindlessly as I try to purge myself of the day's remains, and so quick is the journey that I'm almost surprised when I arrive at my complex. The building looms ahead of me in the darkness like a sanctuary. It's good to be back, I think, for a few hours at least.

I round the corner toward the building's main gate without really looking, and I'm almost upon it before I notice the swarm of activity that has taken over. A group of street people have clustered around a car that has pulled up to the entrance. Some of them look on curiously, while others crowd in more aggressively, trying to pry open the doors or the trunk. The car's uniformed driver is outside, attempting without success to push them away.

I slow down as I get closer, wondering at the source of this spectacle. My eyes go to the partially visible car door and I receive half an answer. Painted there, in luminous blue and gold, is the logo of the Golden West Power Company. Apparently, they are no more popular on the streets than the Council is.

But then the other half of the answer comes, and I'm not worried any longer about the opinions of the street. Standing at the guard booth, protesting in loud and vindictive phrases to an unyielding guard, is the car's passenger. This is a man who has no business at this apartment complex, at this time of night, unless it's with me.

Farraday's assistant, Luis Rojo.

I stop my car then, preparing to confront him to see what he wants. I have just stepped outside when he looks over, noticing me. The expression that comes to his face in that instant of recognition is not the passive, almost saintly look that he wore in our previous meetings, nor even a cast of anger. It is hatred. It is rage. It is a desire to kill.

And it is directed at me.

The sweep of his hand toward the gun holstered under his jacket explains everything and yet nothing all at once. Whatever I need to know, I won't learn it here.

I shoulder my way back into the car and slam down the accelerator all in one fluid motion, then spin the car around so that I'm headed in the opposite direction. The vehicle spurts away after a second's grudging hesitation, racing toward the end of the street. I glance in the rearview mirror and see Rojo rushing toward the passenger side of his own car, mouthing useless commands to the street people who have gathered around. The driver is still trying vainly to chase them away, with little success. By the time I round the corner, Rojo's car remains stalled at the guard post, blocked in its exit by this human wall.

My mind races. *What is going on?*

I'm spinning the car around another corner now, bringing the vehicle up to forty, then fifty miles per hour, not caring to find out firsthand. Here, the streets are more crowded than in front of the apartment complex, and I have to swerve to avoid hitting a burnt-out police car, tents spilling into the roadway, night children darting across my path. For a moment, my mind is back in Ray's van, almost a year ago, hurtling along a Denver parkway, dodging obstacles of a darker kind.

But only for a moment. Because my mind leaps in the next instant to Mike, and the images of Denver are gone. I'm back in the present, thinking that Mike may be next on Rojo's dance card.

I reach out to the car's phone again, aiming for the redial button. But before I can hit it, I have to slam on the brakes. A fire truck is charging through the intersection in front of me, its siren silent, its driver oblivious to the accident he almost caused. *Idiot!*

And then the fire truck is past. I press the accelerator again and shoot forward, checking the rearview mirror. No sign of Rojo. Faint solace. If he's not following me, he must be headed toward Mike's.

If, I think sourly, *he hasn't already been there.*

I grow anxious at the thought. Stab at the redial button again. Hit it this time. But I'm rewarded with only the same endless ringing as before.

"Answer the phone, Mike," I say, almost a prayer.

But there's no answer. The phone just rings on.

I hang up, slamming down on the accelerator as far as it will go. I'm focused single-mindedly now on a new destination: Mike's apartment complex. Compelled by urgency and, worse, by fear. A cloud of dread swirls around me, like the forewarning of a dangerous storm.

I try to wish the feeling away, but it stays. Persistently. Tenaciously. Refusing to leave. In that moment, all I can think about is Mike, and the hope that he had sense enough not to be home if Rojo came to call.

Get your butt out of there, Kemo, I think, gunning the car along the littered side streets. In minutes, vaguely remembered neighborhoods begin coming back to me, and I'm spinning the car around the final corner and onto the street that runs past Mike's cooperative. The engine is a demon now, wailing its harsh metallic curses into the darkness, while people scatter before me, rushing from its path in fright. I don't pay attention to them, don't really even see them, my mind is so focused on the building up ahead. Hulking. Shadowed. Lurching up into the nighttime sky like a prison complex on an empty plain.

Mesoto's home.

I race the car forward, drawing the last rush of strength from the engine, then swing wide as I brake at the entrance and barrel through the gate. There are no guards here to block my way—and no crowds or Golden West cars, thank goodness—allowing me to whip the car around to the front door of the building undeterred. I brake and turn the vehicle off and then leap out before the motor has ceased its chatter. The cooperative's main door—metal, glass broken glass, unsecured—is straight ahead.

I swing it open, and I'm inside.

And all at once I'm overwhelmed by the silence. There are men on the metal walkways overhead. Men peering out the doors of their cubicles. Men looking out into the concrete corridor. All wearing blank faces and empty stares. No one is talking, no one is even moving. In the dim rays of the ceiling's naked lights I think I'm watching the shadows of human statues. There isn't even any background noises. All I can hear is the slapping of my shoes on the concrete and the squalling bellows of my own anxious breaths.

I head on, running now, past one cross-corridor and then another, and finally reach the cross-corridor where Mike's unit is located. There's a police officer standing at the intersection, a young Hispanic cop talking in hushed tones to an old gray man in tattered work clothes, holding out his pen and notepad as if expecting some great revelation to pour forth from the old man's lips. The officer idly looks toward me as I near, then turns away, facing back to his witness. The older man doesn't even glance up, doesn't acknowledge this strange intrusion.

I ignore both of them too. Just turn the corner. Run on.

And now I'm in Mike's corridor. Here, more men line the catwalks—singles and groups of twos and threes. They stare down from their elevated vantage points, their eyes focused ahead of me. They still aren't moving, are merely standing fixed in place—whether immobilized by shock or curiosity, I don't know. But now their silence is replaced by sound. For rising from among them is a soft chatter, dark and ragged, like the whispered screams of tortured souls. I follow their eyes and see that their collective gaze is directed toward a knot of cops up ahead, five or six men gathered around a rope suspended from a pipe that spans the upper railings.

I run on now, all too certain of what I'm about to find, certain of this horror that waits before me. As if bidden, one of the cops obliges my fears and steps away from the circle to speak with a colleague. In the opening that he vacates, I see the weight that's tied to the end of the rope, the anchor that pulls it earthward. A body, a human form, spins slowly like an ornament left in the wind, circled around to face me.

At first, I see only the eyes, the anguish of their death. Then the neck, red, swollen, bulging over the noose. One arm is turned back at the elbow, sickeningly reversed, the fingers straight and stiff. But it is the eyes that hold me. Black. Dead. Beseeching.

Mike's eyes.

And I realize: I am completely alone again.

I can say nothing, can't even mouth the words. My body begins to shake uncontrollably. I race toward him, pull him toward me, embrace him as if I could impart some breath of life. My heart, my head are thundering. But there's no breath of life, nothing I can give. I'm holding a dead man. A corpse.

"It looks like a suicide," one of the cops says as he edges in front of me to cut down the body, as others snap photographs for the official records.

But I don't stay to listen. All at once, I'm darting toward the steps, charging up them like a man running from the devil himself. I take them two and three at a time. My shoes clang against the metal, sending their death knells echoing throughout the corridor. Mike's 21-gun salute.

I'm on the seventh level in seconds, racing to his unit. The rope is off to the right, tied to the pipe that spans the chasm below, knotted tightly and expertly so that it wouldn't slip. To the left is the door to his unit, swung open but crossed with yellow tape, the barrier blocking off the crime scene. I burst through, snapping the tape like a finish line, tearing my way into the apartment.

The room is a disaster. The desk and chair lie splintered in the corner. The sink is ripped from the wall. The bed's thin mattress is sliced with a massive X, its thin filling pouring out. And in the middle of the floor sits the decorative light fixture, bent and broken, fragments of metal and glass splayed around the battered center. The remains of a vicious struggle.

Mike didn't give up without a fight. I reach for the light fixture. Pull it toward me. See that the side panel is still intact. The metal has been crimped, and I slip my fingers into the opening, not even bothering with a screwdriver, pulling with such desperate force that the tiny screws snap like toothpicks. Rooker's hard drive is still there. It tumbles out as I rip the panel away, clattering to the metal floor, emitting a quick bloody screech that fills the emptiness, and then ends in silence. Quickly, I retrieve the hard drive from the floor and drop it into my pants pocket.

It's then, as I'm kneeling there on the unit's floor, that I see it. A shot of light from one of the bulbs outside makes its way into the cubicle, slanting toward the shattered sink, and then beneath it. I notice the reflection first as just a glint of silver, and then I see it full. A pocketknife, rope fibers pressed across the blade. Drops of sweat still glistening on the pearl handle.

Rojo's knife.

The police, in their rush to close a case they'll never solve, must have missed it.

In that instant the knife is in my hand. I scream, a wild predatory roar that must shake the entire complex, then ram the blade into the fractured sideboard that was once a desk. The knife snaps in half on impact, the handle breaks apart, and the wood of the desk erupts into an explosion of fiberboard debris.

But I'm not seeing a demolished piece of wood before me. I'm seeing the face of Luis Rojo, and the favor I intend to repay him. A favor for the one he has just rendered Mike, my last and only friend.

▼ ▼ ▼

By midmorning, Santos, Darby, and I have crossed into Arizona, and are nearing a town with the unpronounceable name of Kykotsmovi, somewhere northeast of Flagstaff. The President's edict to close the most of the freeway on-ramps may have lessened traffic on the interstates, but the action's collateral effect has been to transfer that congestion to the state highways and county roads. These passageways are jammed almost as badly as I-25 was south of Denver. To make matters worse, now that we are out of Colorado, Santos's familiarity with the byways and side paths has diminished considerably.

Most of the time, we are left only with an old Thomas Guide as our compass. Wireless service once again has turned sporadic, and so even the van's GPS system works only intermittently. For the moment, we are given little choice but to blindly rejoin the great mass of migrants in their anxious journey toward the coast. But Santos says that he knows a man in Flagstaff who can help us navigate the parking lot that Arizona's state highway system has become, that this will greatly speed our travels.

And so we wait, girded by that expectation, for the hours that must pass as we crawl along to reach him.

After driving most of the night, Santos is reclining in the backseat of the van, snoring so deeply that it sounds like a semi roaring past every time he breathes. I don't think I've ever heard anyone snore that loudly. But our passenger's nocturnal rumblings are therapeutic for Darby, who sits with me in the front seat, as Pepper curls around her feet, lost in his own canine dreams. Once or twice, Darby even snickers at a particularly loud outpouring from Santos, and I make a joke of it. She giggles then, and I am reminded of the taunting conversation that she and Cassie had had about the boy and the dead bird when we were driving to the soccer game so many eons ago.

I am also thinking about how good it is to see even a flicker of pre-Catastrophic life in my young companion again.

We plod on down the road, at some times able to accelerate to twenty or thirty miles per hour, at other times having to brake to one sharp halt after another. Darby alternates between the aimless reading of her *Tiger Beats* and the mindless consumption of Twinkies and Doritos. The giggling subsided, she is mostly quiet now but not uncommunicative, and in idle moments we talk about the music stars she likes. The clothes she hopes to buy for winter. The stories her friends have told her.

There isn't any mention of soccer, which doesn't completely surprise me, *but which I still find a little unsettling. Before last week, it was all she could talk about. Nor is there any mention of Cassandra Fall, who used to be her best friend and who likewise dominated her conversations. But this latter omission I do not question. It is one small blessing for which I am grateful.*

It strikes me now as I watch her how much I cherish this time alone with Darby—the interdependence that it signifies, the opportunity that it affords me to connect on something more than a survival level with another human being. And so I become an active participant in the conversation as well. I tell her about my work in Los Angeles, about the theater room I added this summer to our home, about how much the city has changed since she and her family moved away. She asks if I like to surf, and I tell her that that's a talent I never acquired. She wonders how frequently I go to Disneyland, and I reply that I haven't been for many years.

I realize then that this is all she remembers about that great seaside metropolis called Los Angeles: beaches and Mickey Mouse. I envy this power of selective recall and the innocence and forgetfulness of youth that drives it, and I wish I had a little more of that quality myself. "You need to go to Disneyland more often," she interjects. I tell her that I probably should, and say that perhaps we can go together sometime. She smiles briefly at this remark, and then falls to silence for several minutes.

Our exchanges continue like this, in brief and unexpected spurts, but the principal connection that binds us is left unspoken. Not once does she mention her parents. In fact, she hasn't asked about them at all since that first night, when she wondered aloud if I saw them die.

"No, honey," I told her. "I did not."

During the times Darby is engrossed in her magazines, I listen to the radio, losing myself in the mundane and often heated discussions of the crisis that have come to replace the continuous stream of reports of deaths and declarations rendered by one government agency after another that had filled the radio in the days before. Yet even as I listen, I feel as though I am attending an argument about the demise of the dinosaurs or the fall of the Roman Empire. The commentators seem detached, almost clinical, in propounding their many theories, as if winning academic plaudits were their sole concern. The callers themselves are little different, seeming to be engaged in more of an intellectual exercise than an emotional expurgation.

That's only to be expected, I suppose. Emotions do not mix well with understanding, and in the aftermath of what transpired, understanding is what we need the most.

Fortunately, the few scraps of knowledge that have been gathered are starting to coalesce into some skeletal form of meaning. Although even the government's own scientists do not know precisely what happened or why, a consensus seems to be emerging that the Catastrophe was an isolated occurrence. A fluke. A one-time warning. In this confident judgment, I allow myself a mite of comfort. For I am not sure that I could survive the events of this past week were they to be replayed again.

Still, I can't help recalling a small artifact of history, that the world war that raged in the 1910s was referred to afterward—with assurance and simplicity—as "The Great War," until a second global conflict came along to numeralize it.

But those are worries for another time. For now—despite the traffic and the deadening, nonstop driving—there is much to be thankful for. For the afternoon sun is shining with eternal desert brightness. We have safety and a sense of normalcy. And Darby and I have the presence of each other.

It is enough to lighten our ever-present worries, and to steel us both as we move on down this long and uncertain road.

CHAPTER 14

Midnight. I can't stay here any longer, not in this prison of death that was once Mike Mesoto's home. And I can't return to my apartment, where my own demise almost certainly awaits. I have nowhere else to go. Nowhere but Fran Amalfi's. And so that is where I head.

I know where Amalfi lives because Alison took me past the property's entrance a day or two after my return, and I now follow the route from memory. I drive through three neighborhood checkpoints along the way, using my Council identity card to pass each time. These are Amalfi's people and they wave me through, not having the slightest idea that they would have to kill me if they wanted to block my passage. I am so overwhelmed now, pushed so far beyond pain and sorrow, that even my own death would be a blessing.

But I can't let it come. Not yet. I have too many debts to repay.

I finally reach the main entrance to Amalfi's house a little before one in the morning. The property looks like the embassy of a small country. Floodlit grounds. Security patrols. Guard dogs. Electric fences. Bowing to protocol, I pull up to the main gate so that I may be announced. I am then escorted to the front door, which opens as I step onto the porch. Amalfi is standing there, hair down and disheveled, wearing a white silk robe, winter slippers, and an expression that invites bad news.

I don't disappoint her.

"Mike's dead," I tell her.

In that instant, she loses what little color she had. "Mesoto!" she stammers, searching for a response. "When? How?"

She's doing her best to balance a glass of wine in her hand, but her fingers tremble and the glass tilts, sending the golden liquid dripping over the rim and onto the cuff of her robe.

"Are you coming out or am I coming in?" I ask.

A beat, and she shakes her head, clearing her thoughts. "Yes, come in, please. I'm sorry."

She turns then and heads toward a sitting room just off the foyer. I follow her, closing the front door behind me. *It's time travel time again*, I think as I take in the trappings of her privileged status. Cathedral ceilings. Pale rose walls. A balcony that hangs over the entryway. Polished redwood banisters and flooring. A sweeping petaled chandelier softly lighting the artwork, all classical paintings and sculptures, that tastefully warm the room. The sitting area, which we presently enter, is the foyer's equal: richly carpeted, lined with book-filled shelves, crowded with lush seats and small tables and reading lamps. The décor of a person of power.

But tonight, the trappings mean nothing. For all my rage and desperation, the room might as well be a dungeon.

Fran indicates a sofa, which I take, and then she slumps into one of the armchairs. Worried. Anxious. Unsettled. "What happened, Martin?"

I tell her.

"You're sure it was Farraday's man?" she presses, after I've finished.

"It was *his* knife," I answer harshly, not caring if I offend her. Not caring about anything now. "I already told you. He left it there on the floor, where he knew I would find it. And by now he knows I've seen it. So there you go."

She pauses, absorbing this. "You're probably right. It had to be Rojo. No one else would have the resources. Or the stupidity." A frown as she presses for some sign of hope. "Did anyone in the complex see him?"

"You figure these people don't have enough to worry about already? They're so afraid they'll lose what little they have left, most of them wouldn't talk even if they *did* see something." I pause, watching her. Making sure she understands. "This is *our* problem, Fran. We have to solve it—no one else."

She considers this, then shakes her head. "I just don't understand why Farraday would do it. He knows I told Mike to back off."

"Yeah, well, he didn't."

"He didn't *what?*"

"Back off. Mike was out at Golden West again all day today."

She closes her eyes at this, jaws clenched, looking sullen. The audacity of her orders being disobeyed. "Why did he do *that?*"

"You know perfectly well why he did it. Farraday was involved with Rooker up to his eyeballs in these bombings. But you wouldn't listen. And so Mike was trying to find some evidence you *couldn't* ignore." A pause. "He told you about the woman, right? Maria Maas?"

"Yes, yes, he told me."

"Well?"

"I looked into it. She used to work for Rooker."

"I know."

"But that doesn't mean Farraday was involved."

I'm wondering: is she still half-asleep, or is she being this dense on purpose? This isn't like Fran. "Look," I tell her, "I'll say it one more time, and you can either start putting two and two together or you can say good-bye to this house and the Council and all the rest. Farraday needed the extra fuel to finish either the solar plant or that emerald city of his up in the mountains. Or both of them. I don't know which, but it doesn't matter. Neither you nor Rooker would give him the allocations he wanted, and so he paid Rooker some huge sum of money to divert the fuel to him. And then to blow up fuel tanks to cover it all up. Mike and I found out what was going on, and now Farraday's getting rid of the evidence. One piece at a time." I pause again, trying to make her see reason. "You've already lost Mike and Alison. Isn't that enough?"

She just stares at me, and I can't read her expression. It isn't really disbelief, but it's not the pain and shock that I would have expected either. Maybe it's only numbness, the anesthesia of tragedy, like the kind that has enveloped me over the past few hours.

Even Fran, for all her hardness, can't be that unmoved.

And then the expression breaks, and I see that she isn't. There's only a sadness in her eyes, a recognition of what this loss will mean. "Poor Mike," is all she says.

"Yeah, and poor Fran," I tell her. "Don't think you're safe just because you've got a small army outside. You stand in Farraday's way more than anyone."

She takes a final sip of her wine, then wearily sets it aside. "I don't know, Martin. If he did anything to me, this whole operation would become a Federal matter—no local discretion whatsoever—and Farraday can't want that. Especially if he's involved in the way you think he is. But you don't have anything left to lose. Which means you would do whatever you could to bring him down, no matter what the consequences. And that must terrify him."

She looks at me again, almost with sympathy, and then stands. "We'll have to talk this through in the morning. We can't do anything about it now." She pulls her robe more tightly around her and stands. "I want you to stay the night. Keep out of sight and keep safe. There's a guest bedroom on the second floor—"

I'm already starting to tell her no.

"No, I mean it," she cuts in. "And not just for your own well-being. If I lose you, there's no one left I can trust." A pause, and then a morbid half-smile. "My little army may not be invincible, but at least they'll give us a good night's sleep."

My eyes hold on hers, wondering. "What's he after, Fran?" I ask her after a moment. "A couple of months' faster production can't mean that much to his pocketbook. Not enough to justify the bombings and the cover-up. What does he really want?"

She just shakes her head. "I wish I knew, Martin. I wish I knew."

▼

I accept Fran's hospitality—I feel almost forced to do so, although I really wouldn't have had any better options if I had turned her down. Eventually, I find myself upstairs in a second-story bedroom that's almost forbidding in its elegance. A king-sized bed with silk coverings and coordinated silk pillows. Side chairs and a love seat and ottomans, all in expensive imported fabrics. A vaguely oriental dresser and chests and tables, hand-painted with gold-thread designs. Floor-length draperies covering the two sets of windows. A pair of glass doors that open onto a balcony on the home's western face, just around the corner from the main entrance. A paradise, if it mattered. But I am too numb, too angry, too exhausted and hopeless to care.

I lay my clothes across an antique Chinese foot locker that sits at the end of the bed and hang my jacket over the back of a chair, checking to make sure that my revolver is still safely lodged in its right pocket. Then I slip Rooker's hard drive, retrieved from Mike's apartment unit, into the jacket's other pocket. I gulp down the last of the scotch Fran offered me when we reached the room, and then I lie back, eyes wide open, wishing to lose myself in sleep.

But I don't. I am surrounded instead by a fear that comes to me in suffocating fullness. All at once, I feel alone and vulnerable again, more so than I ever felt at the stadium. It does not take me long to understand why. There, I was a random victim, anonymously recomposing the fragments of a life, of personal interest to no one who could do me harm. Here, I am a target, closing in on some perilous truth. That quest already has cost Alison and Mike their lives, and soon might cost me my own.

By logic and sensibility, I should quit now. Just walk away, save what's left of myself and move on. But I know I have no choice but to press ahead. Know it because, even in my hopelessness, I realize that I am again the survivor. And this time there are thinking, breathing agents of my suffering who must be brought to account. This time, I can exact retribution.

And I will.

Was there a moment when I grappled with the larger significance of this situation, when I started to think and act with a dominating sense of professionalism? When I was impelled by a recognition that survival brings obligations of its own—not just to myself but to those nameless millions around me?

If I once thought that way, in the torment of recent days, the memory is gone. I find myself vowing to stay the course now in order to satisfy needs that are purely personal—needs that, in this sense, are as selfish as any that Amalfi or Farraday might possess. But selfishness in the pursuit of one's own desires always seems more noble than someone else's selfish aims, and I draw strength and justification from that fact.

So sure am I of this path that, when sleep finally nears, my mind is still groping for a means to my vengeant ends, and I find myself silently trying to choreograph the fates of Rojo and Rooker.

And yet as my eyes close, my thoughts begin alighting elsewhere. On the image of the woman from Farraday's lab as she stormed out of Farraday's office. As I chased her from Rooker's hotel. As she looked back at me with surprise and desperation while she raced away in the car. It is an odd recollection, coming after what happened tonight, and I fall to a nervous sleep wondering what it means.

Or, more to the point, if it means anything at all.

▼

Neither my exhaustion nor the alcohol impair my alertness, and I wake after only an hour's sleep to footsteps and deep whispering voices in the hallway outside my door. Reflexively, I reach under the bed for a weapon. Then, finding nothing there, I start to grow anxious until I realize where I am. Then I step to the chair where I hung my jacket and probe the inner pocket for my revolver. It's still there.

I take it in hand and stand there. *Waiting. Listening.*

The footsteps come again. Moving down the hall, away from my door, and then stopping. More whispers. I can hear two distinct voices. *Men's voices.* But I can't make out what's being said. I quickly pull on my clothes, then step to the hallway door, my gun still in my hand, ready to fire. But it's quiet again.

Amalfi's security men? I wonder, relaxing my grip on the trigger. If they had come for me with intent to do me harm, I'd already be dead. Simply open the door and shoot me while I sleep. So that can't be it. What then? Maybe this is standard. They walk the floors, post a man near Amalfi's bedroom at the other end of the hall, guard her around the clock. Maybe this is just a shift change. *Maybe.*

But I still don't like the way it feels.

I stand by the hallway door, my back pressed against the wall, trying to place my paranoia. And then, as if it were summoned, I hear a sound. A whirring sound, very faint at first, that gives my paranoia substance. A generator kicking on somewhere, or a truck rumbling by? *Perhaps.* But the sound isn't on the ground. It's coming from the air. From somewhere above me.

A helicopter.

For an instant, the thought chills me. And then I come to my senses. Such worries are stupid. There are police helicopters, Council helicopters, FBI helicopters in the skies all the time these days. That's surely what it is.

Nevertheless, I quietly wedge a chair beneath the handle of hallway door.

Just in case.

As I stand there, the sound begins coming closer, growing more defined. The chills return, despite my dismissing them. I have to know what is happening.

I slip on my jacket and move to the glass doors that lead out onto the balcony. Unlock one of the doors. Slide it back just far enough that I can slip through. Then I edge out onto the balcony, closing the door softly behind me.

Crouched low, I move to the front-facing railing, hiding behind a small potted tree, peering toward the sky. The whirring is louder now. And as I look out, the sound takes form. A small speck in the star-filled panorama. Nearing us. Growing larger.

All of a sudden, I feel trapped, claustrophobic again. Just like in the bar. I want out. Out of this house. Away from these grounds. It's only a fifteen-foot drop to the lawn below me, a quick escape route. But I can't risk it. Not now. There is a guard walking directly below the balcony, strolling in slow mechanical paces, carrying out his watch. If he saw me . . .

And then, suddenly, he's not moving anymore. A small Council car has pulled into the home's circular driveway, off to my left, and the guard has taken notice. The car stops, and its occupant steps out, striding in great fury toward the home's entrance.

Barry Erthein.

As he heads on, I hear the front door of the house open. A canopy of light spills out onto the porch. A voice comes, one that I immediately recognize. *Amalfi.*

"Barry, what are you—"

"I *said* I'll get the girl!" Erthein fumes, his usually firm and self-important voice now reduced to petulant self-defense.

"Will you now?" Amalfi spits back, just beyond my vision, in a hard mocking tone. "Just like you did with Mesoto?"

And now she enters my line of sight. Dressed in a jacket and slacks, she leaves the porch and head toward the broad lawn beneath me, with Erthein trailing fecklessly behind her.

Above them, the helicopter comes into full view, descending slowly. Its destination is clear.

"It *wasn't* my fault," Erthein protests, stabbing his arm toward the chopper. "*He* screwed up. Not me. I told him exactly, precisely what to—"

But I can't hear anything else. The helicopter has reached within a couple of hundred feet of the property. It slowly maneuvers in, hovers over the expansive lawn, then sets down on the grass. The sound is deafening, and I have to cover my ears until the motor is turned off.

Standing in the craft's shadows, Erthein gesticulates wildly, his fulminations punctuated by biting glances from Amalfi. I can't hear a word they're speaking, can't even read their lips. But I don't need to. I can imagine what they're saying.

The chopper's rotors spin to a stop. Amalfi gives Erthein a parting, acid glance and then steps over toward the aircraft. The helicopter's door opens, a metal stairway clangs into position, and two men climb out. The first, despite the early hour, is calm and dignified, as he always is. *Stuart Farraday.* And behind him, comes the second man, another familiar face, this one from only hours before. *Luis Rojo.* It's then I notice the Golden West insignia on the helicopter's side.

I should have expected this.

The two men move toward Amalfi, and she extends her hand in greeting, just as if she were waiting for them. Erthein angrily watches this display from the edge of the circular drive. I do not hear the words that Amalfi exchanges with her nearly arrived visitors, but I catch a glimpse of her face as she turns back toward the house with the men at her side. There is concern, worry, maybe even unease. But nothing like fear. Nothing approaching animosity. If anything, there is the slightest hint of relief, as if an important problem were on the way to being solved.

At last, I understand the reason for my ease of entry into Fran's complex. For her invitation to spend the night at her house. For her decision earlier in the day to pull Mike and me from the case. Whatever Farraday told her—or threatened her with or promised her—two nights ago, it must have been enough. What was it specifically? I don't need to know. I don't think I want to know. I already know enough.

And now I have no other options and no time to waste. I am the quarry now, and the quarry has been cornered.

I wait until I hear the front door of the house close, and then a few seconds more, until the guard below me has resumed his patrol. He's a young man. Thin, sallow-faced, a little nervous. Perhaps this is his first important assignment. *Too bad.* He's just about to fail.

I watch him pace beneath me, back and forth, with military

precision. I move silently to the balcony's rear-facing edge, protected by the shadows of the home's eaves, and am in position at just the right moment to see him step into view below me, heading toward the back of the house.

I do not have time to calculate the jump. I just do it and land squarely on his shoulders, knocking him out with a quick slap of my gun to his temple. He crumples to the cold ground without a sound.

I roll off him. Then, in an instant, I'm on my feet again, crouched in the darkness. I strip the guard of his rifle. His pistol. His radio. Then I drag him behind the hedges, hiding him from casual inspection. I'll have maybe ten minutes, fifteen at the outside, before the other guards notice he's missing. Not much time. But if I'm not off the grounds by then, I'm a dead man anyway. So I don't worry about it.

I need a car. *My car.* But one of the guards must have moved it to the small lot on the other side of the house, far beyond my reach. Either that or confiscated it. But it hardly matters. Even if I could reach the car, I wouldn't be allowed through the front gate. By now, the men at the guard post surely have been instructed not to let me leave.

And then there are the guards' omnipresent dogs, a threat wherever I am. I crane my head, listening for the sounds of their presence, but hear nothing. Not yet, anyway. But they could be here in a minute, surrounding me. I can't take that chance. I'll have to take another car. Find another way out. *Quickly.*

There are two vehicles parked in the spaces on this side of the entry gate, next to the row of hedges that runs part way around the circular drive. One is a Cubic, probably the head guard's. He won't be leaving anytime soon. *Useless.* But the other car may be just what I need. A tiny Prius with the Citizens Council seal printed on the door. A customized license plate that reads: *LACC-2.* The car that I watched drive in earlier. It can belong to only one man.

Barry Erthein.

I bolt across the five or six yards of open space toward the driveway's main entrance. Keep low. Reach the hedges and edge along them until I find an opening wide enough for me to crawl through. As I'm moving, from somewhere on the other side of the house I hear a muffled howl. One of the dogs. Alerted? Or just baying at the moon?

Whatever the cause, it's enough of a warning.

I have to get out.

The car. It's directly in front of me now. I shoulder my way through the hedges as quietly as I can. The rifle catches once, breaking a tiny branch with a snap. I freeze, listening. But there's no movement. No sound. *All clear.* I wait. Take a breath. Then climb the rest of the way through the hedges, scratching my face and hands as I move through but not letting it slow me.

I'm on the passenger's side of Erthein's car in that moment, right by the rear door. I reach up: it's unlocked. Slowly, I pull the handle and the door pops open with a deep metallic creak. It sounds like an explosion to my ears, but it fails to draw the attention of the guard at the guard post. And apparently fails to alert the dogs. Another small blessing.

And then in an instant I'm inside the car. Crawling into the back. Ducking low in the cramped space behind the driver's seat. I close the door as silently as I can and huddle there, my shadowed gun pointed toward the window, waiting for the driver to return.

It happens within minutes. From behind me comes the sound of the front door of the house opening again. And then slamming. Footsteps follow next, growing louder, nearing the car. Close, almost upon it. The car's front door swings open then. Violently. Hard enough to rip out the springs. *Erthein.*

He doesn't see me, doesn't even look back. In the state he's in, I don't think he'd see an elephant. He just throws himself into the driver's seat, shutting the door so hard it makes my ears pound. A second or two and the car starts. The engine revs harshly, then grinds into gear, and the car jerks away. Fast. Too fast for the driveway.

"*Idiot!*" Erthein rails. "Who does she think she is! She wouldn't last a week without me!"

Each word comes more harshly, laced with acid, a worthy complement to the still-grinding engine. In the midst of these sounds, the car brakes abruptly at the guard post, and I have to brace myself to keep from being thrown up against the back of the front seat.

Erthein rolls down the window, just long enough to snap to the guard, "I'll be downtown." Then the car squeals away, out into the street, outside the perimeter of Amalfi's army.

I wait a few minutes before letting Barry know he has company.

We've gone three or four blocks and are just exiting Amalfi's fortified subdivision, moving into the city's unprotected zones. A couple of more blocks, and it's time.

Slowly, I lift myself from the car's rear floor, raising the gun in the same motion. I don't know whether he first sees my reflection in the mirror or feels the barrel of the gun against his skull. But he acknowledges this bad news by inhaling so quickly that the breath catches in his throat. And then by jamming his foot on the brake.

"Keep driving!" I order.

But he doesn't react. Doesn't say anything in response.

"Keep driving, Erthein!" I repeat, in a hard unbending tone that lets him know we aren't playing office politics tonight.

In that moment, still without a word an untoward gesture, he starts the car down the street again. Only his irregular breathing, which has taken on the quality of an old man's wheeze, lets me know that he understands his predicament.

"I'm going to ask you some questions, Barry," I say as I bend closer to him. "Easy questions. Are you ready?" I press the pistol harder against the side of his head, drawing a low moan and then a slow, prayerful nod.

"Good." I let him wait, let him imagine the consequences for a moment. Just like Amalfi would do. "Let's start with Farraday and Rojo," I demand, after several seconds. "What are they doing at Amalfi's?"

He hesitates, and in the silence I can hear him clearing his throat, trying to talk over a desiccated palate.

"Farraday and Rojo. What are they doing there?"

"I— I don't know." He stops, clearing his throat again. "She told me to leave. I asked—"

I cock the pistol. "Wrong answer, Barry," I tell him calmly. "I know how to use this thing. Don't think I won't."

"I don't *know!*" he bursts out. Then a pause, gathering some strength. "Please, Fall, I swear. It's true. She made me leave. She wouldn't tell me. Please, put the gun down! Come on!"

I let him babble for a few seconds, watching the sweat bead on the side of his head and drip down onto the gun barrel. This is foreign territory for Erthein. He isn't that brave, and his loyalty to Amalfi is self-serving. If he could tell me the answer, he would.

"Doesn't feel so good being on the other end, does it, Barry?"

He doesn't say anything to this. I didn't expect him to.

"Next question," I say. "Who's the girl?"

Sharply. Defensively. "What girl?"

"The one you and Amalfi were talking about right before your friends arrived." A pause. Then coldly: "The one you said you'd 'get.'"

"I don't know," he says. "Some woman who works for Farraday."

I run the pistol softly in a circle around his temple. "You can do better than that, I think. Who is she, Barry? I need a name."

He hesitates again. I can see him clenching, then unclenching his teeth. "Maas . . . Maria Maas, I think. Look, I really don't know her."

"Uh-huh. And what were you going to do with her? Kill her like you did Mike?"

The image of Mike's dangling body flashes in my mind. It's all I can do to keep from pulling the trigger right then.

"I didn't kill him!" Erthein stammers back. "It wasn't supposed to happen that way."

"And just how was it *supposed* to happen?"

"I—" He's nervous again, more so than before, his hands shaking. "Come on, put the gun down! I'll tell you whatever you want to know. Just put the gun away!"

I don't say anything, which tells him the gun stays. After a moment, he's stopped shaking enough to answer.

"I was following up," he says. "Amalfi told Mesoto to lay off Farraday, and I was— I was making sure he understood. And I talked to Rojo, just asked him to let me know if Mesoto—"

"You worthless little fool!" I spit. "No wonder he knew!" And then I fall to silence, not trusting myself to say anything more.

"Stop the car!" I tell him at length. This time, amazingly, he complies. He must know that I'm beyond the point of caring, that I would end his life on a whim if that's what it took. "Hands off the wheel." Again, he follows the command and just sits there, his hands lying limply at his side.

I climb over the seat then and into front, sitting next to Erthein. I keep the gun trained on him, as I try to force myself to some semblance of calm. The rage just stays there, like a putrid taste in my mouth, undiminished. But I have to move on.

"Let's go," I say evenly.

Like an obedient robot, his hands are on the wheel again and the car is moving. *Good.*

"When were you supposed to get the girl?" I ask him.

No answer.

"*When*, Barry?"

"Tonight," he mutters. "Sometime tonight. About now, I guess."

"That's why Rojo was at Amalfi's, wasn't it?"

I've asked it almost to myself, but Erthein answers. "Yeah, maybe. I guess so. I don't know for sure—"

But I've already shut him out, the implications coming to me in a rush. I'm looking outside now, moved again to urgency, trying to get my bearings. *About now.* If that's true, Rojo is no doubt already on his way.

I look back across at Erthein, suddenly anxious. "Turn left!"

Once more, there's no response. The robotic obedience is gone, or maybe he's just stopped paying attention. I jam the gun into his side. "I said *turn left!* Do it!"

"Okay!" he snaps, then spins the wheel so sharply that the car skids halfway across the intersection.

I'm looking outside again, figuring the time. *Where was it she lived?* I was there just the night before, but I came and left by tram, hardly paying attention to the street signs. That information seemed irrelevant at the time, and so I didn't make a point of remembering. Now, it couldn't be more urgent.

But there was a sign on the front of the building. I was looking right at it while I was being interrogated at the guard post. *What was it?* Macco? Makkadoo? *Mikkaido!* That was it.

"Mikkaido Towers?" I ask Erthein. "Do you know where they are?"

He just nods.

"Then get us there! *Now!*"

And the car speeds up. I reach for the phone, the same model that was installed in my car. But I have no idea how to contact Maria Maas. "What's her phone number?"

"I don't know."

"How do I get it?"

A beat. "Try Rooker's directory. Maybe he called her. I don't know"

I take the suggestion. Punch in the appropriate codes. And then wait.

And wait.

Finally, Maria Maas's name flashes onto the screen next to several phone numbers. Home. Cell. Her office at Golden West. I choose "Home," the likeliest to reach her at this time of night.

The call initiates. There's a ring. And then nothing but dead silence. I think I've must have lost the connection and hurriedly reach for the phone to try again when the rings resume. Once. Then twice. Then: *nothing*.

But only for a moment. There's a curt, sleepy voice on the other end. "Hello?"

"Maria?"

"Who is this?"

"You need to listen to me very carefully. Get out of your apartment. *Now*. You're not safe."

At once, the sleepiness is gone from her words. "I said, who *is* this?"

"Someone who's trying to save your life. Listen, I need you to go to the corner of—" I pause, studying the GPS map on the screen, right below her name. "To the corner of Dickens and Coldwater. We'll be—"

"Who *are* you? And what are you talking about? Who told you to call?"

"Who I *am* doesn't matter. What does is that your buddy Rojo just canceled my friend Mesoto. Now he's on his way to do the same to you." I pause, letting the message sink in. "Or didn't Farraday tell you about that one?"

There's only silence from the other end.

"Twenty minutes. We'll be in a Council car, a white Prius. Be there."

I hang up, not waiting for her to answer. I turn to Erthein. "Step on it."

He does, blindly obedient again. In minutes we're on Coldwater Canyon, roaring up the hills and through the switchback curves that lead into the San Fernando Valley. I'm hoping that, if Rojo *is* going after Maria, he's doing it by car. If they're taking the helicopter, we won't have a chance.

The only saving grace: Rojo has no idea *I'm* headed there as well. No idea Maria's already been alerted. No idea of the deadline he's under. And so no reason to hurry. Until he discovers I've escaped, he'll probably drive at normal speeds while we race on.

It's not much to count on—and the advantage won't last long—but it will have to do.

I glance feverishly at phone's clock, for the tenth time in the last minute or so, and I imagine how Maria Maas must be reacting to this call from the darkness. Surely she pauses for a few seconds to take in my words, a few more to let the disbelief drain away. If she's that close to Farraday, she'll know exactly what Rojo can do. And if she's smart—which she no doubt is—she'll be up and hurriedly dressing. Dumping whatever tokens and secrets she can fit into a shoulder bag. Off-loading as many files from her computer as she has time.

And then, within the time I've told her, she'll be on the street.

Either that or—if she decides not to believe me, or if Rojo gets there first—none of it will matter. She'll be dead or in custody. Beyond hope in either case.

I don't take the time now to weigh the chances. Instead, I watch the road, keeping one eye on Erthein, taking what perverse pleasure I can from his discomfort. It won't last long. Once we get Maria and reach safety, Erthein can go, unharmed but for his shredded dignity. But he goes nowhere until then.

Until then, he's mine.

We're up over the hill now, heading downward into the valley. It spreads out before us in the darkness, silent and brooding. The shadows of spacious and expensive homes lurk in the foreground, surrounded by the charred remains from the Sherman Oaks riots. Beyond them, squat rectangular apartment units and office buildings line the distant background.

When Jeannie and I used to live in the San Fernando Valley, in the proletarian sectors, we would occasionally drive these paths of luxury as we were headed home from downtown. We would marvel in those times at how the Valley glowed with its sea of lights spread out before us, like some giant electric welcome mat. Now, the only break in the darkness comes from our car's headlights and the scattered fires in the Valley down below. In the car's tepid beams, hillside neighborhood after neighborhood look dead, deserted, as if they had been abandoned for years.

But that's not my concern now. My world of interest is confined within the radius of a few blocks. I follow the headlights' weak rays, searching for street signs, trying to place us. Another mile or two and, finally, I see a street name that's familiar. If I remember right, Dickens is just three blocks ahead.

The GPS confirms it. We're almost there.

And then, in the distance, cutting across an intersection, I see something else. Another car, racing toward the Mikkaido Towers' main entrance. Its blue-and-gold emblem fluoresces in our headlights. *Our competition.* Here much sooner than I had expected.

"Floor it!" I tell Erthein.

And the car spurts forward. We're closer now, and I can see the front of the apartment building. The Golden West car has shot through the building's entry gate, into the parking lot, unhindered by whatever guards or weaponry must be stationed there at this time of morning. I roll down my window and can hear the opening and slamming of four car doors, all at once. The slapping of footsteps. The swinging open of the apartment building's front door.

At the same time, up ahead, on the third floor of the apartment building, I see a front-facing curtain drawn back in the corner unit. A face peers out, looking down on these sudden sounds. Taking them in with shock. *Maria.*

Get out of there! Now!

As if she could hear me, she lets the curtain fall away, and I can see the shadow of a form racing to the rear of the apartment. Then, a moment later, a form appears at another window, on the side of the building where we're headed. The shade is lifted, the window raised. Legs come out onto the landing, then the whole person. Maria Maas, a canvas bag hoisted over one shoulder, climbs onto the fire escape. She looks out, sees our car, and begins racing down.

"There she is!" I shout at Erthein. "Pull up!"

Our car shoots ahead, slams against curb adjoining the sidewalk, then halts with a jar. Before the car's even stopped, I have the door open and am barreling out the passenger's side. "Don't move," I tell him, "or I'll blow your head off!"

He sits stubbornly still, more intensely angry than I've even seen him before. But at least he's compliant. In seconds I'm around the car, moving toward the back, coming up around the driver's side. Maria has made it to the base of the fire escape by now, and is scrambling across the building's narrow lawn. Up a dead tree. Then climbing over the concrete wall that surrounds the complex. A push from her trailing foot and she's over the wall, dropping to the ground, mere feet ahead of us.

And in that instant, I'm beside her, taking her hand, leading her to the car. We haven't gone more than a step or two when there's a clatter of sounds from behind us. An explosion of metal against metal reverberates all around us, and the side panel of the car becomes a sheet of burnt-out perforations.

"Get down!" I command, pulling her toward the rear of the vehicle. "This way. Come on!"

I don't need to look back toward the apartment. I know what must be happening: Rojo and his men have burst through the same window that Maria exited only seconds before and are now moving onto the fire escape, full firepower in hand.

Their barrage goes on. But somehow, miraculously, we make it to the back of the car and then are moving up along the far side. The gunfire stops for a moment as the men vault down the stairs, giving me a brief space of safety to rip open the car's back door. I press Maria inside, then climb in behind her. Slam the door. Command Erthein.

"Hit it, Barry! *Now!*"

But the car doesn't move. What's he doing? *Sleeping?* "Barry, I said—" I start. I look frantically over the seat, and I see in that baneful moment that we won't be going anywhere. The image comes to me, all at once. The driver's-side window has been shattered, the fractured glass strewn across Erthein's shoulders, his bloodied head slumped against the steering wheel. *Dead.*

I almost retch but hold back and hurtle over the seat. In the side mirror, I see Rojo's men just mounting the concrete wall, their guns being raised into position. We have seconds, if that.

I'm in the front seat now, beside Erthein's lifeless body. I climb over him. Shove his body toward the passenger's side of the car. Pull myself behind the wheel.

You were a nasty little man, Barry, I think, *but you didn't deserve this.*

And then, just as quickly, my mind's focused on the task at hand. I see the car's still running, our only salvation. I slump down in the seat, hoping that Maria is already doing the same in the back, and jam the vehicle into reverse, pressing down on the accelerator as hard as I can. Rojo and his men didn't expect this move and have to scramble to avoid getting hit. When their gunfire comes again, it is random, delivered without aim. It sprays across the car's hood. Shatters the windshield. Sends shards of glass skimming across our heads. But all I'm thinking is: *I hope they don't hit the tires.*

They do that, and we're dead.

But they miss, or don't try. There's no time to turn around, so we just continue racing backward for thirty, maybe forty, yards, weaving wildly along the narrow street, fishtailing all the way back to the intersection. We spin backward around the corner, and I ram the car into drive. Push down on the accelerator again. Send the tiny vehicle lurching in a jagged arc away from our pursuers. Then spurt off down a darkened side street, the quickest route away from them.

Rojo's squadron chases after us, following the roar of the engine. But they're on foot, and the most they can do is turn the car's rear window into fragments of dust. I don't have time to look back at Maria. Don't have time to check on her safety. Don't even have time to ask. I just race the car down the street, peering over the dashboard, and then up at the rearview mirror.

They're still running, Rojo and his men. But we've put enough space behind us that they're quickly insects in the distance, out of range. I can just make out Rojo's tall, angry frame in the bright moonlight. He pulls up a few feet in front of the others, his long dark hair falling around his reddened face, his machine gun raised vengefully toward the sky. It's almost as if I could hear his curse.

Next time, he must be swearing to gods unknown, *I won't miss.*

▼

A few minutes later, we're driving northward. We stopped long enough to stow Barry Erthein's body in the trunk, wipe down the seats, and cover the bloodstains with a blanket. Maria has moved into the front seat now, and I glance over at her, the first moment of reflection I've had since arriving at her apartment. Her hair is damp, the large black curls matted to her forehead, streaks of blood and sweat painting her olive skin. But she sits there nearly composed, breathing hard angry breaths without a hint of terror, as if infuriated only that her plans, whatever they were, have been thrown awry. She's as tough as I thought she'd be.

"Are you all right?" I ask her.

"I'll live," is her blunt answer. A pause, and then she's glaring at me. "Now, suppose you tell me who *you* are."

Your savior, lady, I think, but don't say it. I'm not offended, even though I should be. It's exactly how I expected she'd react.

"Martin Fall," I tell her instead. "Council Operations. I'm the one who ran you out of Rooker's place."

She returns this comment with a derisive laugh. "So you're the *imbécil* who almost got me killed."

"Doesn't look like I'm alone in that distinction, does it?"

She just continues to glare at me. Then the wall breaks, only slightly. "I guess not."

"Apology accepted. So now I need you to tell *me* something, Doctor. What *were* you doing in Rooker's apartment? And why is Pancho Villa back there so anxious to put you away?"

A beat. "It's a long story."

"We have time."

Another beat, and the mask of hostility crumbles further. She looks over at me, if not with trust, at least with acceptance. "We can't talk about it now," she says. "We've got to ditch the car. They get a drone in the air and they'll find us in a second."

I nod toward the chrome bracelet on her wrist. "Can't they already?"

She shakes her head. "It's been reprogrammed. By some friends. The Council knows where I am only when I want them to."

"Then where do we you suggest we go? There aren't many all-night diners open these days."

She's already looking around outside. Her eyes dart from one side of the street to another and finally alight on an alleyway half a block ahead. "Up there," she says, pointing. "Pull in and park."

"And then what?" I ask doubtfully.

"And then, Mr. Fall," she says, "we walk."

▼ ▼ ▼

We arrive at the outskirts of Flagstaff, Arizona, by nightfall. The trip has been tense and grueling, and for the last fifty miles, as Santos drove, the speedometer barely crawled out of single digits. But then I recall the freeways south of Denver, and I am grateful for one thing. At least we were moving.

Once cell service resumed during our drive, Santos phoned his contact in Flagstaff—a Native American named Echeverria—who agreed to meet us at a truck stop just off the state highway. We have pulled into that location well ahead of the scheduled time, and since we have to wait, I propose to treat Darby to a hot meal and an ice cream.

She asks if Pepper can join us, and I tell her that dogs are not allowed in the diner, that he will have to wait in the van. She seems to find something amusing in this edict, that—despite the chaotic events of recent days—at least the important social distinctions have remained. And so she gives Pepper a good-bye stroke and tells him to guard the van for us while we are away. Then she jumps down from her seat and paces beside me. As we near the diner's entry, she silently takes my hand, squeezing it softly. I squeeze hers in return, remembering the soft feel of Cassie's hand the last time I held hers. But the thought brings back memories that I don't want to recall at the moment, and I let my hand relax, wiping away a stray tear before Darby can see.

Santos has decided to wait for us in the van. I urged him to come inside as well, but he declined, saying that he preferred the solitude of the night sky—and, besides, remaining outside was the only way for his friend to find him. I accepted his choice, but was startled, as Darby and I stepped away, that he called after me. And was even more surprised when he tossed me the keys to the van. When I asked why, he said simply, "I don't want you to worry about it." I told him that wasn't necessary, not after all we'd been through. But I still kept the keys.

Now that Darby and I have reached the diner's entrance, it's clear that our wait will be a long one. Customers are queued up halfway around the building, and the line is not moving. While we stand there, I pass the time by observing those around us, and am struck by their pedestrian qualities. Families, couples, individuals of all ages and races. And nothing exceptional about a one of them. An African-American family with five hyperactive kids running around near the entrance. A tiny gray-haired woman directly in front of us, resting her head on her elderly husband's shoulder. A goth girl and a pair of punk teen boys moving in behind us, speaking in a slang *dialect I don't even try to understand. And mixed in among them, the inhabitants one would expect in this desert town: truck drivers and night shifters, Native American workmen and rough-hewn tradesmen from the nearby construction projects.*

In all, a portrait in plainness.

So ordinary is the scene, in fact, that if I block out everything but the people, I have the feeling that I'm waiting in a concession line at Dodgers stadium rather than queuing up outside a truck stop in the middle of nowhere. I have stood in such stadium lines more times than I can count, and nothing could be more commonplace. Indeed, if it weren't for the look of concern that shadows every face around me, I could swear that this was a week like any other.

Amid these idle thoughts, a half hour passes, and soon we're near enough to the doorway that I can see through the diner's plate glass windows and into its interior. An older couple—the owners?—are there, working furiously behind the counter. Busboys and waitresses scuttle about, clearing tables and serving meals so fast they look like characters in a time-lapse movie. To a person, they appear perversely happy within this atmosphere of unease. And little wonder: this must be more business than this small diner has had in years.

Finally, our turn to enter has come. We press our way through the crush of bodies to a table in the middle of the room, following a young Native American waitress with eyes that sparkle like sunshine. Despite the rush all around us, she takes a moment to engage Darby, complimenting her on the pink ribbon she's wearing in her hair and asking about the teen heartthrob featured on her sequined T-shirt. As they talk, I am transported to a long-ago evening in Monterey, when Jeannie and Cassie and I sat at an outdoor restaurant overlooking the ocean, being beguiled by a similarly charming young waitress. It was one of the most perfect moments in my life, watching the two ladies I loved the most absorb the compliments and conversation. And now, even with the chaos that surrounds us, I experience a hint of that perfection again, like a distant fragrant scent or a sweet melody playing from afar.

Life with such moments, I tell myself, cannot be that bad.

And then a moment later the moment fades to a memory, as the waitress with the sparkling eyes is all business again. She asks for our orders, encouraging us to select quickly so that we don't have to wait any longer than we already have. I decide on a hamburger and fries, thinking it won't take long to prepare, and order the same to take out to Santos. Darby chooses the Tex-Mex chicken strips with a side of guacamole—a meal I suspect appeals to her more because of the colorful picture on the menu than because of any calculation of her tastes. But at least she's eating something more nutritious than the snack food she's been munching on for the entire trip. It's a good thing: she'll need the strength to sustain her on the long ride to come.

Darby and I don't speak while we wait for our food, but instead build fragile castles out of the white and pink sugar packets stacked in the condiments stand. The table is slick and the castles don't last, but at least the construction work occupies our minds. At last—as one of our most spectacular creations collapses—our food arrives. The meals are hot, which is all that matters, and we both dig in, relishing their unaccustomed warmth and textures after days of cold sandwiches and sugary carbs. As she eats, Darby even begins to talk again with some of the animation and energy I'm used to, waxing about ice cream and chocolate sundaes, and I tell her we'll order dessert as soon as the waitress returns. At this, she offers the hint of a smile.

It's a moment as close to normal as any I've experienced in these past few days.

And then, with the suddenness of death, it ends. As I reach for a fry and Darby for a chicken strip, an ashen-faced truck driver bursts in through the front of the diner, and all thoughts of normalcy go rushing past him, slipping out the open door like a foul wind.

"It's happened again!" the driver bellows, his words aimed at no one and everyone. "The thing came back! It's killin' everyone!" As if, *I think*, it had intelligence and intent.

But I can't dwell on these thoughts. There is a scream from behind me, and I turn to see a white-haired woman clutching her table, oblivious to the scalding coffee spilling into her lap. Her screams go on and on—*piercing and hysterical*—and her husband's efforts to pull her from the table have no effect on her now rigid body.

I look around frantically then as other diners begin standing. Yelling. Shoving their way out of the restaurant. Our table is jarred, and in that moment I glance across at Darby. Her chicken strip has dropped to the floor, and a dollop of guacamole falls onto her shirt. She sits there, her eyes glazed, her mouth flexed open. And then she starts to shake. Even as I leap beside her, wrapping my arms around her and telling her we'll be all right, even then she continues to shudder, like a tiny plastic doll whose spring has been spun too tight.

And then my breath catches, and I remember: Flagstaff sits on the side of a mountain. We're thousands of feet above sea level. And while the Catastrophe somehow missed the city before—

I don't finish the thought. We have to get out of here! But the doorway is jammed, impassable. I look around, panicked, and reach for the leg of the metal table near the front window. I pick the table up in both hands, its plates and glasses crashing to the floor, and hurl it toward the plate glass window. The glass explodes into hundreds of fragments that spray to the ground like a waterfall. I fold Darby into my arms and carry her toward the broken window, then knock out the rest of the shattered glass with a nearby chair and rush through, followed by dozens of others who take advantage of the same escape.

Santos is standing directly outside, waiting for us, a small oxygen tank strapped to his back. Two other oxygen tanks dangle from his hands, as curtains of red and yellow cascade ominously in the sky, washing over the scene all around us. I take the two spare tanks from him and hand him the van keys in return. As he sprints off, I quickly fix the mask from one of the oxygen tanks over Darby's mouth, then place the mask of the other over my own.

In seconds, Santos pulls the van up to the front of the diner, and we barrel in through the vehicle's side door. Santos crushes the gas pedal and the van spurts off through the parking lot, maneuvering past darting pedestrians and parked cars, until we reach the road. It's already jammed, unmoving in both directions. Ignoring the blockage, other cars press on, crashing into one another, trying to open a pathway where there is none.

Wordlessly, Santos guides our van off the roadway and onto the desert scrub. He races the vehicle along the sandy terrain that parallels the northbound highway until at last an opening appears on the road above us. Then he roars up a small embankment and onto the asphalt again, the tires screeching.

My mind is catapulted in that moment back into the diner, only minutes before. The terror. The chaos. And yet also the uninvited knowledge. For in this calamity, we have been granted a new awareness. The comforting assurances we have been hearing from the government and scientists alike these past few days are nothing but lies. All of them.

Abject, ignorant lies.

For the crisis wasn't over, at the end of that long dark night in Denver, like they said it was. It had only made its first appearance.

And now, set to the score of an old woman's screams and the termagant squeal of tires pressed beyond their limits, it has deigned to make its second.

CHAPTER 15

Having hidden our escape vehicle in the dark and narrow alleyway Maria Maas had chosen, I now walk along beside her in silence. We are headed northward out of Sherman Oaks toward the heart of the San Fernando Valley, our pace a combination of prudence and haste. We do not want to attract attention to ourselves by running or even walking too fast, and yet we must quickly put as much distance between us and her apartment as we can in order to keep Rojo and his men off our trail. I remain quiet during this time, not because my questions have become any less urgent, but because our surroundings command it. To talk, other than in the hushed and hurried tones of the trespasser, would be to recognize our presence in this hell.

It is an admission I do not want to make.

We have progressed in the span of a few blocks from empty streets to passageways that no longer warrant that name. These are waste channels, man-made sloughs, broken asphalt paths through a dark and forbidding human jungle. There used to be decorative concrete dividers down these streets, adorned with shrubs and flowers and colorful inlaid tiles. Stoplights, streetlights, road signs, sidewalks. There were quaint little shops with too-cute names like "Moonstone Jewelry" and "A Change of Hobbit" and "Saks Fish Avenue." And there were people, glorious in their diversity. Teenagers in spiked hair and Metal Mulisha tees. Middle-class matrons in flowered kimonos. Young upwardly mobile couples with his-and-her laptop bags bundled along like children.

There used to be all of these things, and now they are gone. In their place, the streets have become muddy tributaries of sewage and sludge, narrow lanes that wind through rows upon rows of the crude little shacks that line these human corridors. The walls of these shacks are made of decaying two-by-twelves, tin sheets, paper, burlap, plastic, cardboard—whatever their owners can find—all tumbledown and dirty and ready to collapse. Inside are rickety tables filled with the jetsam of once prosperous lives. Produce and shoes. Bits of apparel. Useless medicines. Knives and other implements of protection. All aligned in such disorder that they make the booths at the stadium look like Bloomingdales.

Behind these ramshackle structures stand the real engines of local commerce. Crowded in the doorways of burnt-out buildings—looted and blackened shells whose once pristine floors are now covered with urine and syringes and blood and vomit—black-clothed peddlers hawk tobacco and hookahs, marijuana and harder drugs, needles and powdery white rocks in filthy vials, all in pursuit of a meager day's profit so that they too can lose themselves in the dissolution of their own oblivion.

As we head on through these dark channels, bicycles and skateboards pass by at unpredictable intervals—only human-powered transports like these—because there would be no room for cars even if there were fuel. Their owners splash us with mud and filthy water, not even turning to view the damage they wreak, and after a while I give up trying to wipe the soilage from my clothes. All around us, a vile olio of smells assaults us—suffocates us, really—but all we can do is try to ward it off with broad sweeps of the hand or long exhalations of their fumes, as we do our best to keep from gagging.

And then there are the people. People are everywhere, carrying baskets of food perched on their heads, pushing wheelbarrows filled with trash and purchases, items so intermixed that it's hard to tell the difference between them. These people walk, most of them anyway, with no direction or purpose other than to keep moving, as if the pretense of motion were enough to keep them alive. Others stand half-clothed around small bonfires lit in the overturned remains of automobiles, trying to draw some warmth against the chill of the early morning, or else sit isolated against fractured wooden fences, smoking stale cigarettes and staring up vacantly at the sky.

Nobody sleeps as we make our way past, nobody except the very young and very old. Everyone else watches us with wary and hopeless eyes. The light from the fires catches these faces, casting smoke-veiled shadows that paint their empty expressions with mocking, malign intent. Maria is no stranger to this area, and every so often she exchanges silent greetings with one of the residents, people who reply with a quick nod before looking back at their feet. Once, she even stops and asks me to stand back while she engages one of the merchants, an old black man with one good eye and rotted teeth. She trades a bottle of perfume for the man's two small bags of rice, and then we move back into the flow of humanity, headed on toward our uncertain goal.

Before today, I had known districts like these only secondhand. I had heard the stories from Mike, had read the reports that the regional supervisors filed, had even looked out over the area from the helicopter the morning we flew to the solar plant. But these were expurgated versions of the truth. Images sanitized by time and distance. Visions devoid of the stench of sulfur, of the pulsing red strobes of the bonfires, of the anarchy of lost and wandering souls that the city of North Hollywood has become. Now I see these elements in full, spread out endlessly before me in the dim crimson light, and I cannot imagine that life can descend any lower.

Then we turn the corner, and I find that I am wrong. We are suddenly awash in a fluorescent brightness that rivals the Pigalle or the St. Pauli district or Times Square before the Puritans moved in. Around us, the bonfires line the street like neon marquees, their flames arching twenty feet or more into the air, flickering off the second and third levels of battered townhomes crammed in along either side. Carelessly lettered plywood signs sit in front of these houses, advertising with unmistakable clarity the services offered within. Gold-chained barkers shout out at passersby—men, women, those of indistinguishable gender, it makes no difference. They point with proprietary insistence toward the upper levels, where the shattered glass of windows has been replaced by torn and gauzy curtains, greased-stained plastic drapings, or—more often—nothing at all.

I follow the salesmen's gestures, and see the wares displayed there, in the instant before I look away. Young anorexic girls—limbs scarred with dirt and bruises—sit in torn smocks that barely cover their bodies, their arms folded nervously across their hollow chests.

Women well into their twenties sway insensate to imagined rhythms, lifeless dances offered for the promise of equally lifeless liaisons. The middle-aged, more practiced in their professions, stroke their barely hidden pancake breasts and varicose thighs in resistible invitation. There are men too among them, and couples, simulating affection with feints and touches. And then below them, at street-level, steal the furtive customers, an occasional old man or sometimes a group of teenagers, the deluded and desperate, trading cigarettes or dope or their last ration card for a sham fantasy and a chance to forget.

"Are we almost there?" I finally ask Maria, although I still don't know where we're headed.

She looks straight ahead. "Almost."

And so we walk on, street after street, filled with more of the same. Finally, we approach and then turn into an old complex of garden apartments, long since overrun by vandals and now left for ruin. A group of boys, not yet adolescents, patrol the entrance. They wield long knives and chains while their elder brothers stand just inside the ramshackle gates—citizen-soldiers on alert—their rifles and AK-47s held ready to fire on unwanted intruders. Beyond this ring of defense, a cluster of ancient Hispanics sit around an oil-drum fire in what used to be a courtyard, obliviously playing cards and muttering about the past.

Maria takes my arm and nods to the young guards, and we pass through uncontested.

"What do you think?" she asks without expression, after we're past the gates and are inside the courtyard, headed toward the rear of the complex.

At that moment, a small furry creature—a raccoon, maybe, or a large rat—scampers across my feet, pursued by a young boy with a stick.

"There goes breakfast," I say in a dead tone.

"Dinner, if he catches it." I turn to her, disbelieving. She only shrugs. "It beats starving."

I look around me then. At the collapsed porches and punctured walls of the units. At the long-haired Hispanic youths standing guard at each apartment. At the decay and desolation that lurks behind each of these walls. And I realize: our surroundings have hardly improved from the streets we have just left. We have only entered into a more compact and self-contained version of that world, and its promise is as thin as what's outside.

"Why are we here?" I ask Maria at last.

She frowns at this, betraying the first hint of reticence since she came into my company. "This," she says slowly, "used to be my home."

▼

We step inside one of the units at the rear of the complex, making our way in the pre-dawn darkness by the frail light of scattered, dying candles. The apartment has been vandalized inside as well as out, I see, as the pale orange light plays off the unit's framing walls. They are all that remains of what once were the living room, dining room, and kitchen. Spiderweb cracks decorate these walls, and large chunks of plaster have been hammered or blown away, exposing the damp wood understructure and the frayed remains of the insulation and wiring. Some areas of the floor are still covered with threadbare industrial carpet, but it's no longer possible to tell what the original color might have been. The rest of the floor is stripped bare to the concrete, stained with the leakage of rain or broken plumbing. The sofa and chairs are covered with ragged hand-sewn blankets—the only real color I see—and the rest of the furniture is skeletal, plain, and barely functional.

But at least it's the vision of a home. And compared with what exists beyond these guarded walls, it must be a sanctuary for these people. By rough count, there are a dozen souls crowded into this small room, all Latinos. Four teenage males, sitting in the corner, smoking and trading stories in quiet voices. A young couple wrapped in each other's arms, lying on the sofa, trying to sleep. An old man seated next to them, watching them with worried and melancholy eyes. A squat and wizened old woman in what must have been the kitchen, minding a pot that boils above a pile of wood chips and dead branches. A crying newborn held by a somber waif-like girl just past puberty herself. An infant—quiet, smiling, nibbling on a cracker—being fed by a wide-eyed four-year-old boy. Others I can't quite make out.

I draw some anxious stares from these people at first, especially from the teenage boys. But Maria puts them at ease with a few quick words that are well beyond the grasp of my rudimentary street Spanish. She leans over the smiling infant, then whispers something to the four-year-old boy, who breaks the cracker into smaller pieces before offering it to the baby again. Then we step toward the old woman at the pot, and Maria greets her with a kiss on the cheek. She hands the woman the two bags of rice, and is given the ladle and two clay bowls in return. After stirring the contents of the pot for a few seconds, Maria scoops out small portions of the yellowish broth bubbling inside, a bowl for each of us.

In a moment, we're seated on a storage chest at the edge of the living area, drinking the wan Spanish soup, taking in its nourishment like a blessing from the gods. I realize then that I have not eaten since the solitary orange that I had yesterday for lunch, and I barely notice the soup's strange and vaguely unpleasant mixture of flavors. I am surprised, in fact, that I haven't already collapsed from the lack of food. I must be running on nervous energy. On hatred. And on fear. They alone must have sustained me.

Maria finishes her soup, then looks toward the young boy and the baby. "See the little one?" she asks. I nod. "It's my sister's. He was born just a week before the Catastrophe."

Now it's my turn to frown. "That must be hard for your sister."

"She makes do," Maria says. "Actually it's best for her, having the baby. Sometimes, he's all that keeps her going."

I nod again, acknowledging the feeling. "What about the little boy? Is he hers too?"

"Eduardo?" Maria hesitates, a long reflective pause. "No," she answers at last. "Eduardo is mine."

I look at her, surprised. I wouldn't have guessed.

"Sometimes he's all that keeps *me* going," she says, before turning away.

I shift my gaze from Maria to the boy and the baby again, child tending child, as the feeding ritual goes on. But my mind is elsewhere. On the dangers in the streets outside. On the horrors that we passed on the way. On the fact that Maria must have to spend so much time away from her son. "Is it safe for him here?" I ask her. "Without his mother?"

And in the moment I say it, I know what a stupid and inappropriate question it is. Stupid because the little I have learned about Maria makes it clear that she wouldn't accept such a tenuous situation as this if there were any alternative. Stupid because she has just finished telling me what Eduardo means to her. And most stupid of all because it's really none of my business.

Then I realize that my judgment wasn't directed toward her anyway. I was thinking not of Maria and Eduardo but of myself. And of Darby. My question arose from the volcanic vestiges of guilt still buried within me after the Children's Bureau deemed me unfit to keep her. And the question came at least partly—and despicably—from my sudden envy. For these might be only the tattered remnants of a family, what I see before me, but they are more than I myself have had for nearly a year.

But before I can withdraw the question and make amends, Maria answers me. Sharply. Bitterly. In the way I deserve. "You think maybe he would have been safer in my apartment last night?" she asks. She watches me for a response, the reflectiveness of moments ago turned now to a challenge. But after a few seconds, she softens, perhaps seeing some of her own anguish and frustration in my eyes.

"Look," she says, "I'm sorry I've been so hard on you. Thank you for saving my life. It's just that we don't have much time."

And suddenly I'm lost again. "Time for what?"

A beat. "To get the data my father needs."

"Your father?" I say it like a simpleton, startled by this reply. "You know where he is?" All I can remember is Mike telling me that Alejandro Maas had dropped off the face of the earth.

"Of course I know where he is," Maria answers. "That's why I went to Rooker's apartment. To get his computer files. Unfortunately, when I went back, I saw that someone had beaten me to them." A pause. "I'm guessing it was you."

"It was."

"The files are worthless to you, Mr. Fall. Please. Can you get them for me? My father needs them."

I study her as she talks, trying to spy the source of the sudden interest, even desperation, that now fills her eyes. And then I remember where I am, remember all that has taken place in the last twenty-four hours, and what happened the last time somebody told me she needed my help. My voice and my expression harden in the moment that these thoughts take over. And as Maria watches me, her interest transforms into doubt. And then to worry.

"I need to know some things first," I tell her.

"Like what?"

"Like why I should trust you enough to give you the files. Like why your father needs them so badly. And where I can find Rooker." I set the empty soup bowl on the table beside me and look directly at her. "When you've answered *my* questions, Doctor, then you can have your files."

She pauses again, and her eyes glance over me, perhaps evaluating my determination or my susceptibility to persuasion. Gradually, a look of resigned agreement comes to her eyes. She stands, collecting our soup bowls. "*De acuerdo*," she says, defeated. "But let's rest for a bit first. I want to be awake when I tell you."

▼

When my restless sleep ends, two or three hours later, I find that I'm lying along a wall near the apartment's entrance, facedown on a prickly straw mat, with a blanket draped over me to ward off the cold. I barely remember lying down.

I look around, taking a moment to focus. The midmorning sun is streaming in through the apartment's only uncovered window—a tiny porthole above the useless kitchen sink—and I see that the crowd of inhabitants from the early morning hours has thinned to a mere handful. The old man and woman, sleeping against each other on the sofa. The infants. A young paraplegic woman I had not seen last night. Eduardo, lying next to the storage chest, dozing. And that's it.

I get up slowly, yawning myself awake. My back and all of my muscles hurt, as if I had just passed through some malefic endurance contest. I reach across to massage a scratch on my arm where the sharp points of the hedges must have torn through my jacket last night. As I do, my revolver falls from my pocket and clatters to the floor. This sound instantly awakens Eduardo from his sleep, and after taking a moment to orient himself, he looks toward me with his wide brown eyes. Then he darts over, taking my hand in his, as if to pull me from my own torpor.

"*¡Señor Fall!*" he says urgently. "*¡Ven acá! ¡Ven acá!*"

I offer him a smile as I surreptitiously return the gun to its hiding place. Then, as an afterthought, I check the jacket's other pocket for Rooker's hard drive.

It isn't there.

It takes only a few seconds before I begin to panic. I recheck the pockets. Then my pants. And then I'm on my knees, searching the floor. Beneath the blanket. Under the sofa. *Nothing.* But I looked a few hours ago, before I let myself fall asleep: I know it was there.

Then all at once I know where it must have gone.

And now Eduardo is tugging harder on my hand. "*¡Ven acá!*"

"Yeah, *ven acá!*" I say, the rage building. "Like *now. ¡Ándale!*"

I let him lead me out of the living area and down a short hallway whose only outlet—what once must have been a bedroom—is now boarded up and impassable. But he pulls me forward anyway, toward a closet whose door hangs halfway off its hinges. He swings it open, revealing a metal ladder leaning up against its rear wall.

"*¡Vamanos!*" he urges, and then ducks into the closet, scampering up the ladder. I look in just in time to see him push open a panel at the top of the closet that leads out onto the roof. And then he disappears beyond it. After a moment, I follow.

Almost instantly, I'm up the ladder, pulling myself through the small opening above, scanning these new surroundings. I feel as though I'm peering into an army tent, or the back room in a warehouse. The walls of this jury-rigged second level, such as they are, are made of a thin wire mesh, covered by a black tarp that is flapping in the morning's wind. The interior of the room is a diffuse salt-and-pepper gray, darkened to translucence by the black covering and brightened only here and there by the slivers of light that slip in through the rents in the tarp. One opening in the far corner, a little bigger than the rest, gives a partial view of the apartment's roof, and I can see the edges of a solar collector installed outside, its thick silver cable winding back into the small rooftop cubicle.

But none of this interests me as much as what I see before me. Maria is sitting along the far wall, working at a computer, the monitor's soft glow creating a blue-green nimbus around her head. Off to the side, plugged into the computer's external docking bay, is what I'm looking for. Rooker's hard drive.

In this second of recognition, my body tenses, and I stand stock-still a few yards behind Maria. Eduardo steps back, out of our way.

"I'll fry you for this," I say in a cold unrelenting tone.

Finally, she looks around. "I told you, I needed the files."

"That wasn't the deal."

Her eyes go to Eduardo, stationed behind me like a soldier at attention. "Go back down, son."

He nods, then scampers down the ladder, closing the floor panel after him. When he's gone, Maria turns all the way around in her chair to face me.

"I'll give you the hard drive back, if that's what you're worried about. But this comes first. I've got to get these files to my father. They're transmitting to him now."

"Look, lady," I say. "I don't care what you do with the computer files. Burn 'em. Sell 'em. Broadcast 'em on the Council plaza. I don't care. All I know is that two of my friends are dead, and now Fran Amalfi's apparently put a price on *my* head too. And I want to know *why*."

A beat. "So do I."

I stop at this, just staring at her. I know she must be lying. Know that this profession of ignorance has to be false. *It has to be.*

And then she breaks the gaze, her defeated expression taking over again. "Obviously, I know something of what's going on," she says. "The fuel-tank bombings. The cover-up. The fact that you and Mr. Mesoto were getting a little too close to the truth. And the fact that *I* was becoming too much of a liability as well. I know about all of that. And I think you do too." She pauses, then offers a look of frustration whose sincerity is impossible to gauge. "What I don't know," she says, "is *why* it's happening. And why *now*."

"Well, if you don't know, I don't know who would." I shake my head, trying to hold my anger in check. "Maybe you should have asked your pal Farraday before he put you on the chopping block."

"I've always been there, Mr. Fall. The only reason he didn't come after me sooner was that he thought he could use me as a bargaining chip if he ever found my father."

Now I'm more perplexed than when we started. "Farraday *fired* your father," I say. "And now he wants to *bargain* with him? That makes no sense at all." Another pause as I search for some clue in her eyes. There's nothing. No hint. Not even a suggestion. "Besides," I go on, sickening of the entire game, "how could your father bargain with *anybody*? They said he went insane."

She responds to this with a sudden resentful glare. "My father, Mr. Fall, is the sanest man I know."

I can't even muster the words to express the contorted jumble this discussion has become. Maria must notice because she quickly continues. "Yes, Farraday said my father went insane. He had to discredit him. To justify his firing. And to make it difficult for my father if he ever tried to do something on his own. But insane? No, not at all. Not a shred of truth to it."

She holds the look for a moment, and then there's a beep from behind her, the computer signaling that another part of the transmission is completed.

"I have to get back to work," she says.

I don't move. "You still haven't given me any answers."

"You'll have all the answers you want. Very soon. All that I can give you anyway. I promise."

"Yeah, like you promised with the hard drive."

A frown, almost apologetic. "I'm sorry, I couldn't wait. But no tricks this time. Okay?"

I shrug, and my anger completes its collapse. My silence is my assent.

As if, I think, *I had any other choice.*

"Now please, let me finish," she goes on, anxious to turn back to the computer. "There's a vehicle meeting us on Van Nuys in exactly two hours, and I have a lot to do before we go."

I stare at her, trying to summon an emotion. Some form of protest against this delay. But I don't find any. There's no feeling. Nothing.

This time, I'm the one wearing the look of defeat.

I just step away and climb back down the ladder, without saying another word.

▼ ▼ ▼

arby's seizure in the Flagstaff diner, if that's what it was, lasted for only a few minutes. She did not lose consciousness, and by the time the van pulled back onto the main road, her shaking had subsided to the point that I could loosen my hold on her. We were able to remove the oxygen masks by then—the air shortage had lasted only about ten minutes—and I tried to speak to her, to ask if she were all right. She said nothing, but only nodded, and I took that as a good sign.

At least she could understand and respond.

Nevertheless, even hours later, I fear for her safety. She needs to see a doctor. To be examined by someone far more experienced in these matters than I am. But doctors and hospitals are no longer an option. The roads into and out of Flagstaff were jammed even before this latest calamity. And within minutes after the air shortage had started, the highways were completely blocked as well.

And even if we could manage to find a way into the city, I wonder morbidly, would there be any doctors left alive to see her?

It is an idle speculation, and one that I have long since abandoned. We are now in the middle of the desert, where there are neither doctors nor hospitals of any kind. We have been traveling northward for the last several hours, traversing county byways and government maintenance roads far from the main highways. The middle-of-the-night sky is clear and cloudless, but even with the starlight and nearly full moon, I am unable to distinguish our surroundings, and have no idea where we are. The terrain is beautiful but undifferentiated. In the dark, the mountains and rugged cliffs lose all shape and form, becoming little more than imposing shadows, lining our way like silent guardians.

Santos drives while I sit in back with Darby, cradling her on my lap as she sleeps. Pepper, who was able to survive thanks to periodic dollops of air from my own oxygen mask, lies curled around my feet in a recuperative sleep of his own. Darby is an athletic girl with strong muscles and a solid frame, but she feels almost weightless in my arms, as if her spirit had departed for calmer venues. Her breaths are soft and steady, a rhythm of assurance, and they provide some small sense of hope as I stare out into the merciless sky. But even as I fear for her, I find once again that I embrace her dependence on me. She keeps my mind from its own dark memories. Keeps me from giving up. Gives me a reason that I otherwise might not have, in these lost and desperate times, for staying sane.

In fact, for the first time in my life, I feel as if I have become wholly *reliant on others for my survival. Immediately after the Catastrophe, it was Darby who was my anchor and savior. Then it was Dagger Santos. And now it is the small reed-thin Native American whom I know only as Echeverria, whom we picked up just north of the diner about an hour after the air shortage, and who now rides along in the front seat beside Santos.*

How Santos and this man could have become friends—what they even have in common—is beyond my speculation. But it's an association whose origins I do not question. I worry only for our future, and so I strain to hear their conversation over the van's clattering engine for some fragment of understanding of where we are going and why. But few words pass between them, rarely more than the curt and cryptic instructions that Echeverria gives to Santos when we reach an intersection or turn-off.

Still, I have learned this much. Echeverria is of the Havasupai Tribe, a small aboriginal band of Native Americans who occupy a reservation that spans a few hundred acres on the south rim of the Grand Canyon. As their domicile uniquely permits—and because so much of their land was taken away from them by the government more than a century before—the Havasupai have turned to tourism to sustain their community and their way of life.

Although Echeverria works in Flagstaff in some unnamed profession during the fall and winter months, he serves as a helicopter pilot and tour guide on the Havasupai Reservation during the summers. He boasts proudly of the region's red-rock beauty and its rushing waterfalls—a travelogue that might be of interest in other times, but that I now consider to be only a sad reminder of all that we have lost. But as he recounts the story—for my benefit, or for Santos's, I don't know—he eventually reaches the punch line, and I am finally allowed the reason for our coming this far north. Echeverria says that he has access to the Havasupai Tribe's sole sightseeing helicopter, and promises to use it to ferry us out of the state and to our desired destination. All for a fee no greater than that of Santos's friendship.

I think, upon hearing this news, that perhaps there still may be a cause for hope. A hope that, by sometime tomorrow, we may actually be in California. And that Darby may be in a doctor's office, beginning her long path to recovery.

Santos drives on as I reflect on this possibility, and at length we reach the Havasupai Reservation's entrance. Dawn breaks then, the hazy morning sunlight casting the nighttime's gloom into shrinking shadows. I see at once that Echeverria's proud descriptions were an understatement.

The land is stark and beautiful, its red rocks even more vivid and otherworldly than those of Flagstaff. Still, it is the barrenness and not the beauty that stands out to me. As we journey onto the reservation, there is hardly any plant life—not even a cactus—and I wonder how these people could have subsisted in this stunning but forbidding terrain for so many hundreds of years. I start to ask Echeverria that question, but think better of it. This is a moment of resplendent and unexpected grace, and it is best enjoyed in silence.

Then I hear a timorous gasp from Echeverria, and I realize that something must be awry in this red-desert refuge. My eyes follow his, and I see what looks like a large black rock some distance from the road. In the next instant, though, the image of the rock is replaced by a more ominous one. The black form is the body of a horse, lying dead on the ground. Its rider is splayed in similar repose a few yards away. It does not take long to decipher the source of this saddening circumstance. Lacking a precautionary cache of emergency oxygen, as we had last night, this poor man of the earth never had a chance when the air shortage struck.

I find myself hoping that the duo's fate was a mere consequence of personal misfortune, that man and horse suffered this untoward end only because they had strayed too far from the tribe and were simply in the wrong place at the wrong time.

But as we press on, we quickly discover that this lone rider and his prostrate mare were not the second Catastrophe's only local casualties. Every few hundred yards along the side of the road, the body of another horse and rider materialize into view. Were they felled by the oxygen shortage as they went about their evening rounds? Were they trying to escape a breathlessness that they could scarcely understand? What must have been going on in their minds when this inexplicable and deadly turn of events transpired? How sad, I realize then, was their folly of trying to outrun the atmosphere. How naïve was their ignorance in thinking they could escape the end of their world by racing away from the invisible storm.

And then I look around inside the van at our own tiny crew and I wonder: are we not doing the same thing? Are we also not victims of the same foolish hope of escape?

But I have no time to consider the thought. We have reached the tribe's main settlement, a mixture of adobe homes and low brick buildings and hand-lettered signage. It is then that the vision comes to us in full. This could be a struggling small town anywhere in the Southwest except for one tragic difference. Lying everywhere within our view are the silent and lifeless bodies of Echeverria's fellow tribesmen and their families.

Dead. All of them dead.

These hundreds of brave souls—whose ancestors survived the mindless butchery of the Western settlers and the bullish arrogance of a young national government—lie decimated by the momentary insanity of the natural environment. An environment that they faithfully embraced as their friend and protector. Except for random remnants like Echeverria, their tribe is gone forever. Their rare and rich heritage. Their irreplaceable stories and trials and triumphs. Their vibrant culture so meticulously tended over the centuries. Thanks to the callousness of forces beyond anyone's imagination or control, their very existence has now become nothing more than a memory.

We are witnesses to extinction, as sure and unavoidable as death itself.

With the scene laid out before us, Echeverria's frail prayer for an imagined miracle has turned into soft rolling sobs. Santos and I sit with him, in stunned silence. I am thankful Darby is still asleep.

At last I avert my eyes, unable to absorb any more of this scene's pedestrian horror and am greeted with an image of destruction that is at once more banal and yet far more personally catastrophic than what we have already seen. Sprawling in a twisted metallic heap beyond what looks like a small gift shop lies the tribe's sightseeing helicopter—our intended ferry of salvation—now broken into a mountain of useless debris. I can only surmise that it too was the victim of one last desperate flight toward safety. That it fell from the sky like a bird with fractured and fruitless wings as its pilot lost, for those few fateful final moments, the ability to breathe.

This time, in the isolation of my mind, I am the one who must choke back tears. For it appears that the three of us will not be flying out of here after all.

CHAPTER 16

The apartment that houses what is left of Maria's family sits in silence. Maria works in the office on the unit's rooftop, transmitting the last of the computer files to her father. I pace quietly in the room below, trying to decipher the events of the past days and hours, to place them in some logical order. But I cannot think past the taunting vision of Luis Rojo as he appeared on the street outside Maria's apartment, his weapon lifted skyward, pledging vengeance. Or of Rooker, as he contended with Farraday in the Golden West conference room, raising false arguments against a plot that was his own fabrication.

I find myself wishing that both of them were dead.

And I wonder, in my fatigue, if this is all that this chase has become for me: a search for retribution. Is there no longer a purpose to my actions? No remnant obligation to the millions of lost and wandering souls whose fates compelled me to help Amalfi in the first place? If retribution is my only goal, does it even matter that I learn more than I already know? Shouldn't I just leave this place and stalk Rooker and Rojo and the others until they are stopped—or I am?

I have the skills, the knowledge, and the motivation to do all of this. And I can exercise them best if I am acting alone. In fact, if I allow this woman to lead me to some unknown destination, I may never be able to exact the price that these men and their associates so fully deserve.

Yet curiosity impels me, and I decide to play the game out with Maria a little longer. As much as I want to settle accounts with those who have ended the lives of my friends, I also want to settle accounts with my confusion. I want to know why Alison and Mike had to die so needlessly after so much needless death had already occurred. If I can learn in all their richness the secrets that Rooker and Rojo and Farraday and Amalfi have killed to protect, there will be more to any payback than blind and unrequited rage. There will also be understanding. And with that understanding perhaps, one day, there will also be absolution.

Absolution for deeds I now have little reason or will to hold back.

My decision made, my actions justified, I am ready to leave when Maria finally joins me. She takes a few moments to say good-bye to Eduardo and the others. I know what she must be saying. What she must be feeling. The emptiness she must be fighting. For she can calculate the uncertainty of any reunions in these harsh and unpredictable conditions as well as I can.

I give her the courtesy of looking away as she finishes, and do not turn to her until she steps up to me.

"Let's go," she says.

We are through the apartment's courtyard and out on the streets in minutes, walking toward Van Nuys Boulevard under the cover of daylight. In the midday brightness, the area does not appear as forbidding as it did the night before. Perhaps this is because so many of the hawkers and vagrants have moved inside now that the sun has again allowed them to navigate their night-darkened quarters. Or because the bonfires and their spectral shadows have disappeared, not to return until dusk.

Or perhaps it's because I am already becoming inured to the ubiquity of death and decay, like a doctor in a trauma ward or an undertaker in the season of the dead.

Whatever the cause, I am able to take my mind off the street and its inhabitants during our walk and can focus on Maria instead. Now that we are in full view of the sun, I can see that her eyes are red. From tears, no doubt. I don't need ask the reason. But she notices my glance and volunteers an answer.

"Eduardo," she tells me softly. "Every time, it's so hard to leave him."

Of all the possible explanations, this is the one I understand the most. "I know," I hear myself say, surprised at the depth of my self-pity. It is revealing in itself.

And now *she* knows.

"You have a child." She pronounces it as a fact, not a question.

"I do." I pause, starting to say the name of my own daughter. Of Cassie. But another name comes to my lips. "Darby," I say at last. "Her name is Darby." Another pause, and now an admission. "She's at the Children's Bureau."

There is no judgment in Maria's eyes as she takes in this information, no judgment in her reply. More than Alison, more than Darby herself, Maria must appreciate the pain this separation has imposed. The humiliation that comes from being told by childless authorities that one is incapable of protecting a child. The guilt that flows from being unable to secure her return.

For no one—even in these days—relinquishes those they love to the Children's Bureau by choice.

Mercifully, Maria asks only, "Where's her mother?"

I close my eyes at this, waiting for a long time before I answer. *It is hard enough to think about Darby. Please don't ask me to remember Jeannie.*

"She died that day," is all I can say.

And now Maria is silent, the only appropriate response when a stranger recalls a loss from the Catastrophe. Perhaps she guesses about Denver. Perhaps Farraday or someone else told her. I don't know. But she doesn't inquire further, and for that small and compassionate act of restraint, I am deeply grateful.

We walk the rest of the way to the boulevard without further words. A few blocks later, Maria guides me to what used to be a corner grocery store. The broad panes of glass that once wrapped around the building have been obliterated, and the interior has been ransacked, its contents either pillaged or left in useless disarray. There appears to be no one inside, and we make our way into the bowels of the store's defiled and littered confines without interference. As Maria peers up and down the aisles, I do not ask what she is searching for. But when I hear her mutter, "It's clear," I assume she was checking to ensure that we were alone.

At last, we return to the front of the store, where we sit on the crumbling remains of a pair of checkout counters. Maria pulls a radio transmitter from her handbag, clicks it on, and says simply, "We're ready." Then she places the transmitter back in the bag and watches outside.

Expectantly.

"Where are we going?" I ask her.

"To see someone who can answer your questions better than I can."

"And who is that? Your father?"

She hesitates. "It's . . . a friend of my father. An associate." And then, more urgently, "Mr. Fall—Martin—we need your help."

I remember Fran Amalfi using the same words what seems so many centuries ago, and my first impulse is to just tell her "no thanks" and to walk away. But I've trusted Dr. Maria Maas to take me this far. A few more hours, especially when I have nowhere else to go—no other allies to whom I can turn—can't matter that much.

"We'll see," I answer.

And now I'm looking outside as well, my eyes tracking hers. Two or three blocks away, a fire truck—an old hook-and-ladder unit with a large piggyback water tank—is turning a corner and heading our way. This doesn't surprise me, with the large number of fire trucks there are on the streets, the large number of new tragedies requiring attention each day. What does startle me is Maria's next statement as the fire truck reaches Van Nuys Boulevard, slows down, and angles toward the front of the store.

"Come on," she says.

I look at her as if she's crazy.

But she's up, walking toward the store's entrance, as the fire engine clatters to a stop.

"We stole it," she explains in response to my doubtful stare. "Can you think of a better way to get around? Who's gonna stop a fire truck?"

She's right, of course. But I say nothing to this, but merely wait with her there at the front of the store while a young man dressed in a firefighter's uniform steps inside, bearing fire hats and coats for the two of us. He leaves them with Maria and resumes his position on the truck's side rail. We quickly don the proffered gear, then head outside and climb into the fire truck's front seat, next to the driver.

As the vehicle departs, I'm thinking about Maria's last comment. Now that the government has banned most road travel, only certain approved vehicles can freely drive the streets. Citizens Council cars and Council delivery trucks. Buses and food wagons and Medivac units. Power company cars and police cars. Maria's friends—whoever they are—probably could have taken any of these with less trouble than would have been involved in stealing a fire truck.

I sense, without knowing why, that there must be more to this choice of transport than the mere ease of passage it provides. If I had been thinking more clearly at the moment, I would have recognized right away what it was.

And in time I do.

But this knowledge comes to me too late. And by then I am already trapped.

▼

The ride in the fire truck takes a little more than an hour, most of it through the foothills of the San Gabriel Mountains. We are heading east on an empty freeway, and I feel like I'm traveling along a boundary line between the past and the present. To the south, spread out across the plain of the San Fernando Valley, are the teeming streets, the bombed-out buildings, the broken-down homes that I have come to know firsthand—structures pressed far beyond their capacity by the incursion of helpless and frightened immigrants.

To the north, dotting the tree-covered mountains, are their opposite. The homes of the wealthy. Perched on stilts and protected by electric security fences, they look out into the canyons and arroyos below. Amid these more hospitable environs, however, there are no people. No teeming masses. No residents whatsoever. Most of these homes, in fact, were abandoned long ago, their owners having fled to heavily guarded beachfront homes in San Diego or Mexicom or to secure tropical retreats in the booming islands of Barbados or Sint Maarten or the Grenadines. Stripped bare of their furnishings by those who once lived here, these houses now sit like ghostly sentinels, watching us pass, vestiges of a time gone by.

Evidently, it is not safe—even for the moneyed classes—to risk living above a certain altitude.

At length we leave the freeway, and find ourselves winding still higher into the mountains, past even these isolated signs of human life. Sierra Madre Avenue. Glendora Mountain Road. Glendora Ridge Road. The names are from a real estate agent's dream book, addresses that are advertisements in themselves. There are homes only every few hundred yards. Veritable mansions with hedge-row fences.

Security gates. Long curving driveways. Garages with room for eight or more cars. All of the homes, just like those in the foothills, are empty and abandoned. The splendor of natural surroundings must lose its appeal, I think, when Nature itself becomes the enemy.

And I wonder: why are we headed still higher into this desolate and lifeless region?

But I don't need to ask. In minutes, the answer appears before me. We turn into a housing development full of multi-million-dollar homes long ago made worthless, and maneuver up a steep hill that eventually ends in a cul-de-sac on the mountain's summit. The house that sits there—Tudor and stone, three stories high, with a tower-shaped entrance and sprawling, glassed-in wings—is fronted by a horseshoe driveway parked full of vehicles. A Citizens Council car. Two police cruisers. A van. A Council delivery truck. Two small fire vehicles. Several Council motorcycles. All parked in under camouflaged, protective canopies, making them invisible from the air.

If this is the residence of Dr. Alejandro Maas, I'm thinking, *he must have power and capabilities beyond anything I could have imagined.*

We move closer as the fire truck pulls into the driveway and parks. From here, I can see more clearly the contingent of guards surrounding this home. Men and women out of uniform, ragtag, unimpressive at first glance except in numbers and firepower. Automatic weapons. Stinger missiles. Handheld grenade launchers. Serious hardware.

Maas must have raided a military arsenal while he was stealing city vehicles. I am chastened by this evidence of his resourcefulness.

We strip off our fire gear and climb down to the pavement, and Maria leads me toward the front of the house. There, on the porch, stands still more protection. Two guards the size of fullbacks flank a third, who stands astride the door, blocking any entry. These men are professionals, Special Forces types, clearly well trained. Voice receivers are plugged into their ears, radio transmitters clipped to their belts, a quarry of weapons concealed beneath their bulging jackets. Standing in front of them, his back to us, is a fourth man. He is unexpectedly casual, dressed in a sport coat and slacks, his carelessly combed blond hair descending to the top of his collar. He gives instructions to the others. There is an air of familiarity about him that I can't place.

"This had better be good," I mutter to Maria.

And as I do, I look to the left and notice yet another man,

half-hidden behind a Medivac. His automatic weapon is held in position, his eyes trained on me. If my trust in Maria is misplaced, my personal odyssey is about to come to an abrupt end.

We keep walking, now only a few strides from the front door. And then, in the next instant, my world explodes. My questions are answered, my confusion replaced with understanding, My sense of caution overwhelmed by a sudden hatred, the strength of which I have never known.

For it is then that the man in the sport coat turns toward us. When I see his face—*Rooker's* face—I ignore the men at his side. I forget the marksman to my left. I forget Maria. I don't even bother to reach for my gun. I just lunge for him. My eyes in flames. My hands aiming for his neck.

My lunge ends in a scream. I am only feet from my goal, from snapping his neck and putting an end to his life, when I feel as though I have been slammed against a steel wall. My arms are seized and pinned behind me. I'm held in place, immobilized, then turned away from my prey. In seconds, the fullback guards disarm and frisk me. When they find nothing more than my revolver, they spin me back around to face Rooker, my arms still clutched behind me.

Suffocated by the strength of their grip, I can hardly speak. But I do, struggling with all the ferocity I can manage. Refusing to yield. "Let me *go!*" I shout at one guard, then the other, my rage compounding. Then to Rooker, who hasn't budged. "I'll kill you, you—" Then back to the guards: "Let me go!"

None of this does the slightest good. I am rewarded only with a tighter, more painful arm hold. I can't help tearing.

And finally Rooker speaks. "Easy!" he commands the guards.

"*You're a dead man, Rooker!*" comes my shout, laden with all of the accumulated venom of my misery. I try once more to charge him. But the guards only pull me back, and the needles of pain shoot up my arm again.

I can imagine how Mike must have felt, his arm twisted and broken, in the last minutes before he died.

But I won't give up. "You killed *them!*" I rail at Rooker. "Now what? Gonna do *me* as well!"

"I didn't kill them, Martin," Rooker says without emotion.

"I was *there!* I *saw* it!"

"It *wasn't* me."

"You lying, you—" Then I turn to the guards: "Put me down!"

"They won't *put* you down until you *calm* down," says Rooker, more firmly now. "Believe it or not, we're on the same side."

He approaches me then, and I spit at him, missing. I try to speak, but my anger is so great, I can only glare.

"I'll say it again," he repeats, coming closer and then stepping around me in a circle. My eyes try in vain to follow him, to will him dead. "I did not kill Alison and I did not kill Mesoto," he goes on. "And I didn't conspire to have them killed. I have no intention of killing you either. Of doing *any* harm to you for that matter."

He completes the circle and stands in front of me again. "I fact, I never planned to bring you into this at all. But it occurred to me, after you rescued Maria and became a target yourself, that we might be able to do each other a service." A pause, then an ambivalent shrug. "Perhaps I was wrong."

"You *were* wrong, Rooker! I don't help murderers."

And now, finally, some fire comes to his eyes. "Why don't you just stop and think a minute, pal? Why would I even *want* to kill Alison or Mesoto. Or *you*? What possible threat did you pose to me?"

I don't answer, and he goes on. "I'll tell you. If you blew my cover to Fran, I was finished. I'd *have to* leave. But when you went to the processing plant, she already *knew*. Or at least had reason enough to suspect what was going on. What could I have gained by killing any of you?"

"Everything!" I spit. "Because you didn't *know* she knew."

"And that's where you're wrong. After you met with Amalfi that morning, our friend Erthein, in his usual stupidity, asked me—not once, but twice—if I'd looked at the new delivery schedule for the food-processing plant. He wanted to make sure I saw the changes you'd made."

"*Idiot!*"

"Yes, I'm afraid he was. I checked the shipment schedule more carefully than I normally would have. Alison was good, but she made a couple of mistakes. I knew it was false."

"Then why did you go ahead and rig the processing plant?"

"I didn't," Rooker says. "Someone else did." I look at him, still enraged, not believing a word. "You've got to remember," he goes on, "Amalfi and Erthein thought Farraday was as worried about the bombings as they were. They didn't know he was getting most of the oil. But Erthein also didn't trust me to incriminate myself, even with the bait you'd set. He had to make sure. To *prove* to Amalfi that I was behind it all so he could convince her that she still needed him around." A beat. "So Barry asked for a little outside help to make sure the plant was rigged."

"From who?"

"From Luis Rojo."

He pauses, letting the name simmer in his mouth. "A dangerous man, Mr. Rojo, as you've no doubt come to know. One of few people ever to be kicked out of Special Forces for being too brutal. The man enjoys his work way too much. And what's worse, he presumes to think for himself."

Rooker stops then and offers a jeering frown. "Unfortunately, what he lacks in brains he makes up for in stupidity. *He* was the one who rigged the processing plant. And he was the one who used Farraday's codes to reprogram the drone to blow up the van. Erthein's insecurity had given him an unbelievable gift. He figured, if he could frame me and kill the rest of you in one stroke, so much the better. Farraday would have the oil, and no one would be left to link him to the bombings."

"And Farraday knew all of this?"

"Who knows? I doubt it. Farraday's a ruthless businessman and takes every advantage he can get. But a murderer? Probably not outright. But he *is* very careful about what he chooses *not* to know."

"And careful enough to pay you without anyone being able to track it."

"True," Rooker says. "I didn't really need his money, of course, but greed is a useful cover. What I did need was his trust so that I could acquire the resources for Dr. Maas that I couldn't get from the Council. And that's what he gave me. Unwittingly, of course." Rooker pauses then and flashes a look that, for him, passes for sincerity. "Beyond that, the details aren't important. All you need to know is that I never killed *anyone* in those bombings. And I had nothing—absolutely *nothing*—to do with Alison's death. Or with Mesoto's."

And then the thought strikes me. "Then what about the bar? Where Mike and I were supposed to die the first time? You were the only one who knew we were going there. That had to be you."

"I was the only one Mesoto *asked* to join the two of you. That's true. But Rojo and Farraday were both still in the room when he did. Maybe Rojo heard, or maybe he followed you. I don't know. But it wasn't me. I had far more important things on my mind."

I stare at him, the anger still there. But now it's tempered, waiting.

"None of this would have happened, mind you, if you hadn't come along," Rooker continues. "You were the unexpected element in my well-laid plans. I had no idea Amalfi would ever bring you back. Mesoto was diligent, but he lacked your insight. Your intuition. I knew he would never put two and two together in time—especially since I was able to drop enough false hints to keep him headed down the wrong path.

"But you—well, you were a different story. You muddied the waters, no question about it. Amalfi had faith in you, for one thing. She respected you. And you came in with a fresh pair of eyes. It was enough to nearly ruin eight months of work." He shrugs, as if such things once troubled him, but no longer do. "No matter," he says. "There are occasions when even the worst surprises can be turned to advantage."

He stops then, studying me, looking for some break in my resistance. When he sees nothing, he waits for a moment more and then resumes. "This operation is about to resolve itself, one way or the other. And you have knowledge and abilities that we're going to need. I'd like you to help us out."

All I can do is offer a loud mocking laugh. "Not a chance."

At that, he just gives another shrug, as indifferent as the last. "Perhaps. We'll see. I'll answer all of your questions—anything you want to ask—after you've had time to calm down. Then you can decide. If you're not persuaded, I'll impose on you only to stay here until this operation is finished, to make sure you keep out of our way. On the other hand, if what you learn causes you to feel differently, there will be plenty for you to do. I can assure you of that."

He gives me one last glance, knowing he's said all he can say. And no doubt knowing that I'm still looking at him through the red lenses of hatred.

He turns to the guards. "Let him go," he orders and then steps back inside the house, my decision no longer a cause for concern. Perhaps his confidence extends to a certainty that I *will* change my mind. Or perhaps he simply has too much else to do to worry about me anymore.

Whatever the reason, the choice has now fallen to me, and I have to decide what to do.

And to realign a world that, once again, has tilted completely off its axis.

▼

The setting: a glass-walled recreation room, looking out onto the back of the home's property, converted now into a high-tech operations center. A rear-projected electronic display at one end of the room, atmospheric maps and weather charts posted at the other. A mahogany conference table, the room's centerpiece, embedded with controls for the electronic display. A bank of computers along one wall. File cabinets, electromagnetically sealed. Rows of computer printouts, stacked neatly on shelves in the remaining openings on the wall.

And oxygen tanks everywhere. Enough for dozens of people.

Rooker and Maria sit at the conference table. Maria occupies the seat nearest the table's controls, while Rooker types on a laptop computer. I am standing off to the side, a mere observer, uninvolved. It has been three hours since my arrival. The shock of my encounter with Rooker has dissipated but not yet disappeared, and it still colors my perspective. My mind continues to wish him dead, if no longer by my own hand. The latter has ceased to be an option in any case. The armed guards lining the room—and standing at my sides—ensure it.

For the last half hour, Rooker has been burrowing through the computer files Maria brought with her—files, I gather, that she stole from Golden West's research laboratory the night I was watching her. No wonder she was so furtive upon her departure. And no wonder Farraday's henchmen were so intent on disposing of her.

There is some satisfaction, I suppose, in knowing that I wasn't alone in failing to keep computer files from her hand.

But then Rooker's expression turns into a scowl and then to angry resignation. I see at once that the trail of deceit must run both ways. "We're going to have to go back into the plant," he tells her.

She's surprised. Not understanding. "Why?"

"The bio-crystallization protocol in here is worthless. I thought you got away with it too easily."

"What do you mean?"

He reaches over to the table's controls and presses a button. Rows of chemical equations suddenly appear on the room's electronic screen. "Recognize these?"

She studies them for a moment and then frowns. "It's the same procedure Father was using a year ago."

"Dressed up enough to make us think Farraday's people had perfected it. The only energy you'd get from a solar cell made of *that*," he says, pointing toward the equations, "is the heat when the bioprocessors melted." His hits the button again, and the screen goes blank. "I'm afraid you were conned, my dear. Farraday set out the bone, and when you bit, it was '*adios, muchacha.*' Meanwhile, I suspect he has the real protocol safely stored in the computers at solar plant."

Now Maria is seething. "I can't believe—" she begins, but just lets the words trail off.

Rooker only shrugs. "You were playing him, and he was playing you. Sounds about even to me."

"Except I almost got *killed.*"

"You knew the risks when you started, Maria. So let's skip the theatrics, okay?" He looks at her hard, then relaxes. But barely. "Besides, we've got more to worry about than a maniac with a machine gun."

He slides over to the table's controls and presses another set of buttons. In an instant, an electronic map of the United States projects onto the wall screen, with what appear to be storm lines and weather symbols.

"What do you make of this?" he asks her.

She looks at the scattered markings, most of them concentrated in high-altitude areas of the West. "What are they? Pressure cells?"

"Air densities," Rooker says, adjusting the screen for a closer view of the coastal regions. "Courtesy of Farraday's atmospheric model. If I'm reading this right, our little crisis is a long way from being over."

"Meaning?"

"Meaning," he says, "that your friends at Golden West are predicting another oxygen wipeout."

This time, I'm the one who speaks up, almost without thinking. "When?"

I don't even recognize the urgency in my voice until the word is spoken.

But Rooker notices and turns to face me. "Too soon," he says bitterly and clicks off the screen. "Way too soon."

He holds the look for a moment and then stands to face me. "That's why we need your help, Martin. Perhaps, now, you're ready to talk."

▼ ▼ ▼

We long ago exited the Havasupai Reservation and took to the roads again. Echeverria promised to go with us as far as the Arizona border in order to help us navigate the back roads to that point, but said he would leave us then to return to his home at the base of the mountains outside Flagstaff. The one blessing on this terrible morning was that he was finally able to reach his wife by phone, and that all of his family were alive and safe. They were at home when the air shortage struck and had ample oxygen supplies to carry them through the crisis.

I suspect that most of the other residents of Flagstaff were not so fortunate. This assumption is confirmed later in the afternoon when our radio reception comes back. It disappeared last night when we were just north of Flagstaff and has been little more than static since then. But the announcers on the few stations that have returned sound as if they are reading from the same pool reports. They all tell the same story, and their news is uniformly grim.

An estimated three million new victims were added to the toll last night. The local governments are descending deeper into chaos. And the citizenry is verging on anarchy in several urban centers. The White House has declared most of the areas of the country above three thousand feet uninhabitable, we are told, but government officials are nevertheless urging all other residents to remain where they are, and not to panic.

But they are speaking only to ghosts. Those individuals with legs or transportation to carry them away have already departed for lower elevations

Throughout these announcements, I keep hearing references to the Federal Emergency Management Administration, a government agency originally created to help protect the citizenry from a nuclear attack and, later, to lead the country's disaster preparations and response. The agency's grievous shortcomings became clear to all during numerous weather disasters many years before, but I'm led now to a more fundamental question. If we can't protect ourselves from relatively predictable events like hurricanes—whose path can be forecast with reasonable accuracy days or weeks in advance—how can we hope to safeguard ourselves from the capriciousness of the air itself, whose movements and machinations are beyond the understanding of even the most data-laden scientists?

It is a question that has been relegated to the background by those officials charged with speaking to us. Instead, they offer us faux certainty, delivered in the temperate monotones that once characterized weary war correspondents reporting from stalemated foreign conflicts. We are still convinced that *these outbreaks are freak and isolated incidents, official after official tells us. Within days or weeks, others assure us, the government will have devised a complete and satisfactory solution.*

I know that it is a paper promise, but what else can they say? It's not their job to admit defeat.

I do not realize it then, but for the past week our collective ignorance has allowed contemplations that, before long, would become untenable. The complications of traveling notwithstanding, I have been left free to focus on my own private concerns, like caring for Darby and holding at bay the agony of losing those whom I loved. And I have spent more of our journey than I care to admit immersed in the thoughts of returning to our home in the San Fernando Valley north of Los Angeles, to the blue-and-gray split-level where Jeannie and Cassie and I lived for so many years.

In so doing, I have been able to settle on one morsel of hope. By returning to our now-empty home, I can recapture some small part of my life that was. I can salve my pain with familiarity. And I can restore to Darby at least a measure of the stability that was so cruelly taken from her on that long night in Denver. These are tiny emoluments, I know. Small perquisites of sanity. But they are something to look forward to, something to carry us through, and I treasure them more than I would a suitcase filled with gold.

I am encouraged in these thoughts as our afternoon's travel winds on across western Arizona. Despite the horrors of last night that must have sent still millions more in pursuit of lower ground, the drive is as smooth as any we've experienced since leaving Denver. Santos suggests that the lightness of the traffic may be due to the fact that so few people remain alive on the south side of the Grand Canyon, and that anyone one driving down from the north would likely be avoiding these barely accessible roads.

But that very logical explanation does little to diminish the small prayer of hope that I extract from the ease of our day's travels. Against my better judgment, I even allow myself to sketch out a reassuring conclusion: within a day or two, I tell myself, Darby and I will be able, once more, to sleep in beds of our own.

As I lay my head back against the car seat to rest, it is that small hope that shelters and sustains me.

And then, in an instant, it is extinguished.

We have just slipped north of Kingman, Arizona, barely an hour from our California crossing. The others are sleeping. Santos is driving and I am still half awake. And so I hear in unmolested silence the announcement that, in a way more profoundly than the Catastrophe itself, marks the division between the past and the future.

Scientists working at a government laboratory in suburban Maryland report that the oxygen deficits experienced both last week and last night were "unequivocally linked" to an unsustainably high concentration of carbon compounds in the atmosphere. "The mechanism by which the cataclysmic destruction of oxygen takes place remains unclear," the head of the research team asserts, "but the abnormally high carbon ratios, combined with the turbulent air current patterns of the past few weeks, track almost precisely with the trail of death."

This finding at last gives us reason for optimism, the scientist goes on. For it confirms that the recent air shortages were not some random, inexplicable occurrence. They were instead a known and therefore controllable event. This assessment is followed by a stream of peremptory endorsements from the President on down, each solemn official paying homage to the small ray of salvation that has just shown through. Each speaker endorses, with equal solemnity, the urgency that this new knowledge dictates. "We must act now—and act courageously—in the interest of our people," one Congressman after another declares. "It is the only way that we can save our beloved country.

The solution, they tell us, is nearly at hand."

As they speak, another reporter breaks in, informing listeners that the White House has just announced the creation of an emergency commission to identify appropriate governmental actions in response to the new findings. While no one knows what ultimately will be decided, the reporter notes that most of the just-selected commissioners anticipate that broad fuel-use, industrial-production, and transportation restrictions almost certainly will be part of the final package of recommendations.

But as they go on, I find that I am no longer listening to their proposals or promises. I am looking out instead across the unforgiving desert.

And wondering—once again—whether we will ever reach our home.

CHAPTER 17

We step outside through the French doors that lead to the rear of Rooker's property. The broad, autumn-brown lawn extends for twenty or thirty yards toward Big Dalton Canyon, then drops off, almost straight down, into a vast sweeping gorge. There are no fences, no railings of any kind. Only a low brick wall that looks more like a decorative garden enclosure than a protective barrier.

Whoever lived here before, I think, must not have had children.

We walk along the grounds in the shadows of the rugged hills that surround us—pristine mountainsides decorated with naked oaks and maples and a scattering of still-green pines. Rooker paces beside me, holding a quarry of small stones in his left hand. He periodically arcs them with his right into the canyon, one-by-one.

"Now that God's scared everyone out of the mountains," he remarks, "it's pretty peaceful, isn't it?"

I look around us then, but all that comes to mind is a faded image of the mountains outside Denver, so I choose not to answer.

"I know you'd rather continue thinking of me as your enemy, Martin," he tells me, taking my silence for resistance. "I can't really blame you, given all that's happened. But you'll have to trust me on this one."

This draws a doubting grunt. The man may have cleared himself of malicious intent—some of it, anyway—but he's hardly done enough to earn my trust. Even the sight of him still disgusts me. But anything is better than inaction, and so I listen to what he has to say.

"Trust you enough," I ask him, "to think we can break into the solar plant?"

Rooker replies with a wave of resignation. "Alex can't finish his work without the bio-crystallization protocol," he says. "So we have to go in. We don't have any choice. You've spent more time in the plant than I have, and you understand the layout and security better. That's why I need you to go with Maria."

"I'm not going anywhere—*if* I go—until I know what this is all about."

"Fair enough." He says it casually, and then casts another stone over the edge. "Where shall I start? With Dr. Maas?"

You'll start wherever you want to, I think, and remain silent. After a moment, he sees that I am not going to respond and goes on.

"He's a great man, Alejandro Maas. He combines brilliance with principle and compromises neither. That makes him dangerous to Farraday—who, for all his arrogance, is a brilliant man in his own way."

"And you were doing business with both of them."

"Yes. As a matter of necessity. I needed access to Farraday's suppliers to furnish Dr. Maas's lab. To get the materials and instruments he needed. Things like that. And the money helped too. Farraday was only too happy to pay my price for the extra fuel, although he had no idea where his investments were going. Besides, he gave me political cover. His protests kept Amalfi and Mesoto busy looking in the wrong direction until it was too late."

Or until I showed up, I think grudgingly, but I know that's not the point. I also know that Rooker didn't jeopardize himself by smuggling fuel from the reserve tank refueling vehicles—the trickiest part of the diversion—solely for Golden West's benefit. "Farraday didn't get all of the oil, did he?"

"He *thought* he did," admits Rooker. "But I managed to siphon off enough to keep Maas's operation going."

"Which Farraday never found out about."

"No. But he has to suspect it now—especially since he knows Maria was trying to steal the bio-crys protocol. I hear he's doubled the number of men searching for Maas. I'm sure he knows the good doctor hasn't given up."

I look at him skeptically. "Given up *what?*"

"That's the real question, isn't it?" Rooker asks. "But to appreciate what Dr. Maas has been working on, you have to understand what Farraday himself was trying to do." He tosses his last stone into the gorge, watching it disappear into a thicket of trees just below the ridge. Then he dusts off his hands and turns to face me. "You've seen the solar plant from the air, of course."

"Of course. We flew in together."

"Big monster, isn't it? Now that we've finally decided to stop burning fossil fuels, Farraday thinks the rest of the world will rush to his door begging for his solar plants, not to mention solar-powered cities like Skylight. In a few months, he'll be a trillionaire."

"Presumably," I say, seeing nothing amiss other than the man's limitless greed. "What's wrong with that?"

"Nothing at all—except it won't work. With the world in a downward spiral, most countries can't even afford to feed their people. No way they'll cough up the billions needed to buy one of Farraday's white elephants, no matter how good it might be for the atmosphere. Farraday might sell two or three of his plants—enough to recover at least some of what he spent. But he won't sell nearly enough to make a dent in carbon emissions."

"Which is why you think there might be another oxygen wipeout?"

"One reason, yes. But remember: the projections are Farraday's, not mine."

We've reached the side of the property and halt there while Rooker bends down to pick up another stone. He peers out across the gorge, then propels the rock in a long arc deep into the canyon.

"You know, no matter how hard I throw it, that stone isn't going to go more than a couple hundred feet. But next week," he says, reaching up to collect a handful of air, then blowing it away, "this air will be thousands of miles away from here. And it will be replaced by air that's over some other distant part of the world right now." A pause. "Air moves. No boundaries. Which means that everyone on the planet affects the atmosphere. Not just us."

He holds the look for a moment and then strolls on toward the ridge. In the silence, I find myself staring out into the deep expanse of a gorge that is devoid of all signs of life. I am struck again by the same sensation that I felt peering out over the darkened city a few nights ago. This could be Los Angeles as it might have looked a million years in the past. *Or*, I think morbidly, *as it might look a few years from now after the whole country has become uninhabitable.*

"Farraday's right on that point," Rooker says, picking up the thread a moment later. "We *do* spew more carbon into the air than other countries. Or at least we used to. But no matter what the United States does, for good or ill, China and Russia and India and all the billions of people in the developing world will keep using the cheapest power source they can find, no matter how it affects the environment. And do you know why?"

"Why?"

"Because that's the quickest way for them to improve their standard of living. And what's more, they'll *keep* doing it until there's an easier and cheaper way for them to have the kind of life that we used to have.

"We could shut down our whole country—wipe the United States completely off the map—and if nothing else changed, carbon levels would be back to where they were within a decade. Or sooner, more likely. This air," he says, waving toward the sky, "would be just as unbreathable then as it was during the Catastrophe. Before long, it might not be breathable *anywhere*."

He pauses and stares in at me. "And that's the greatest shame of all, Martin. None of this had to happen. If we'd really been as concerned about saving the planet as we said we were, we would have had one goal from the start: to make environmentally safe energy *cheaper* than environmentally harmful energy. No mandates, no regulations needed. Just make it less expensive to do what was right." A beat. "That was it. The whole ball game. And we didn't even play."

I watch him for a moment longer, wondering how many times he must have made this same argument to unlistening ears before, and the first twinge of empathy for Rooker comes to my mind. But I swat it away, not willing to concede even a scintilla of good will to this man I only recently had vowed to kill. And so I just shrug. "So let's say you're right. What does all of this have to do with Maas?"

"Dr. Maas," Rooker says, "has *found* the answer—a solar technology that produces high-quality power at a lower cost than ever before. *Dramatically* lower. Environmentally safe power at a fraction of the cost of fossil fuels. Not only that, but he found a way to efficiently *store* energy when the sun *isn't* shining. If his approach works on the scale that we think it can, people all over the world will be able to increase their standard of living as much as they want—but in a way that does no damage whatsoever to the environment."

I stop to consider this, suddenly confused. "And Maas did all this while he was at Golden West?"

"For the most part, yes," says Rooker. "In fact, he'd almost completed a prototype just before the Catastrophe."

"Which means Farraday owns the technology. So what does he have to complain about?"

"It was just a resource question at first. Farraday thought Maas was playing in some mental fairyland, wasting time and money—both of which he desperately needed to get the solar plants finished. He was convinced that Maas's approach was completely impractical, since it involved such a radical shift from traditional solar technologies. But when the good doctor wouldn't give up, Farraday finally took the time to study the data and schematics more closely—and he realized that Maas's idea just might work." A beat. "So he shut the project down."

"He did *what?*"

"Canceled it all. Stripped everything from Maas's lab. Put the prototype on ice. Swept every vestige of the new development out of sight. Then he ordered Maas to spend his time designing conventional solar cells for the solar plant."

"Conventional cells?"

"That's right. Not a hint of the new technology."

"And that's when Maas disappeared."

"Yes. Along with all of the notes and computer files he could retrieve. Unfortunately, the final version of his bio-crystallization protocol was not among them."

I stand there, listening to Rooker, wondering why this doesn't make sense. The director of Golden West's research division produces a dramatically more efficient solar collector—a miraculous product in itself, a godsend in the wake of the Catastrophe. Yet instead of being celebrated, he is driven into hiding by a man who has proselytized solar power for most of his life. How is it that this is all so clear to Rooker? The word *cabezón*, Mesoto's word, rings in my head. I must look as dumbfounded as I feel.

"Does Farraday's reaction surprise you?" Rooker asks me, as if reading my thoughts. "It shouldn't. Before Maas, commercial solar really never worked except in gigantic arrays like the ones at the solar plant or somewhere out in the Arizona desert. Sure, you could use it as a backup power source for home water heaters and things like that. But in terms of producing large and consistent amounts of electricity, the technology was so inefficient that only big power companies like

Golden West could afford to wait the decades it took to recoup the construction costs.

"Maas's solar cells changed all that. They proved to be more efficient than anyone ever dreamt possible. He'd actually done his job a little *too* well. Not only did his technology promise to make Farraday's huge solar plants and solar cities like Skylight economically feasible, but he also made it possible for every individual home and office building to have its own inexhaustible energy source—without the burden of monthly utility bills. And that scared Farraday to death."

"Because no one would need his solar plants."

"Not just that," says Rooker. "If Maas's solar cells made it possible to power homes and buildings and even cars and trucks with small solar arrays, people wouldn't need centralized power plants of *any* kind. They wouldn't need oil wells or gas stations or coal mines or natural gas fields. And they wouldn't need the Middle East or Venezuela or any of it. Take it one step further. They wouldn't need government agencies like the Federal Energy Pricing Board or the Citizens Councils to tell them how much they had to pay for energy or how much they could use or what they could use it for.

"So what happens if Maas's solar cell comes along?" Rooker goes on. "In one fell swoop, the world's entire energy infrastructure becomes obsolete. Trillions of dollars of investment and trillions of dollars of oil and coal reserves are instantly made worthless. What's more, all the existing political equations are turned on their heads. People are no longer dependent on the energy companies or the energy-producing nations or government agencies for the power they need. Once people have their own inexpensive solar collectors, they can thumb their noses at the utilities and the oil companies and the government regulators and everyone else. It's a revolution no one could stop. Not Farraday, even with all his billions. Not the government. No one." He looks at me hard. "You don't think Farraday would do whatever he could to keep that from happening? Or Fran Amalfi and her kind, for that matter?"

I just shake my head. Even Farraday and Amalfi, for all their terrible faults, can't be that heartless. "You make it sound like they *want* the world to die."

"Of course they don't. I'm sure they think they're doing the right thing. But they also think they're the only ones smart enough to solve this problem with energy and the atmosphere—that those poor people living in the streets or the stadiums or the tent cities popping up everywhere are either too stupid or too overwhelmed to make decisions like this for themselves. Either they'll use too much energy or the wrong kind of energy or use it for the wrong things. People need to be told exactly what to do, in other words, or else they'll make bad choices. Looked at in that way, technologies like what Dr. Maas has developed are worse than naïve. They're foolhardy, even dangerous. They have to be stopped."

And suddenly I realize where he's been heading. "But if Farraday and Amalfi can shut Maas down, the danger's gone."

"Right again," says Rooker. " Their consolidation of power is complete. No more competition. No more 'wrong' decisions. They alone will decide what's best for everyone else."

"And the only way to prevent that from happening is to go back in to the solar plant."

"Correct. Without the bio-crystallization protocol, there won't be any new solar cells. No new solar cells, no atmosphere. no atmosphere, no people. Period. End of story. Have a nice day." He peers in, fixing me with a look that's as sincere as I've ever seen on Rooker. "We *have* to get Maas's data so we can start producing the new solar cells, or we're all dead."

"And if Farraday's men get to Maas first . . ."

"If Farraday' gets to Maas first—or if he destroys the data before we can retrieve it—you might as well forget everything I've just said. We could stroll out with the entire Golden West computer system, and it wouldn't make one bit of difference."

▼

An hour later, and dusk is descending. On the far side of Dalton Canyon, left to the devices of nature and vandals, a half-finished estate reclines in a muddy clearing, glistening in the sun's dying light. The structure was once the frame of a large, sprawling home under construction—an edifice of commanding opulence—but now lies in half-completed ruin. It's joined by an abandoned bulldozer, a toppled workmen's latrine, and several piles of decaying construction supplies.

In front of these skeletal remains stands a large wood sign, proud and defiant, the last remnant of a more illustrious future. The white sign is a blur to the naked eye. But with the benefit of a long-range scope, its green and black text becomes clear. "Luxury estate," the sign proclaims.

"Spectacular views. Marble floors. Pool and spa. Private tennis court. Spacious veranda overlooking canyon. Price reduced!" The bold Futura letters are easy to read through the lenses, even from this distance.

Or they would be, if they weren't being obliterated, one small piece at a time.

A soft puff comes first, almost undetectable if one weren't listening for it. It's followed by a fist-sized hole that appears dead-on in the center of the sign. Then, after a moment, another hole opens. Then, in slow succession, another. Then another. And then more, too many to count. Soon, the sign is a Swiss cheese. And then less than that: the sign's entire face is almost completely demolished, leaving only a white weathered frame that's as ghostly as the home the sign once promoted.

On the near side of the canyon, I lie in silence, assessing my handiwork. The nearly new Kodiak Magnum rests atop the low wall surrounding Rooker's property, trained on the decimated sign. This is the first time I have shot a rifle since Ray Stanford and I used to go hunting in the Sierras, and I'm surprised that my aim has held up so well. If I go back into the solar plant—an event that even now remains highly unlikely—I'll need to be prepared for more than Luis Rojo's ragtag mob.

"That's for Alison," I say softly, after firing the last shot and retracting the rifle to insert another cartridge. It's only then that I feel the presence of another human being, who evidently stepped up behind me while I was shooting.

I don't look back.

"Was she your wife?" Maria asks.

I reload, set my aim, and fire again, skewering the right-side frame of the sign.

"Just a friend."

▼

By the time I've retreated to the upstairs bedroom that Rooker offered me as a refuge for showering and reflecting, it's no longer Alison I'm thinking of. It's Jeannie and Cassie. I've denied myself thoughts of them for so long that it's a struggle any more even to visualize their faces. It's been weeks since I've looked at the frayed and creased Christmas photograph of the two of them in their sequined holiday dresses. I ignore their memory not because I've managed to conquer their loss, but because I haven't. The pain flares inside me like a stab to a freshly opened wound or a single black dot on a canvas of white. And so I choose not to revisit their memory, fearing what I might find.

But now their memory has returned to me unbidden, and I cannot cast it away. I have been sitting for several minutes in an antique mahogany chair and plant my feet on the floor in order to stand. As I do, I hear a soft crackle and look down to see that I have crushed a brittle red leaf that I must have tracked in from outside. The sound of the leaf's crackle—the sight of its fractured pieces—pierce my mind.

They are a time machine, and I am instantly commandeered into the past.

It is autumn, the same season as now, seven years before. I am standing on the patio of our home in the San Fernando Valley, talking on my cell phone. Jeannie moves about in the kitchen, just beyond my view, preparing a late dinner. It has been a horrible workday: tedious negotiations, constant recriminations, endless contention. I don't think the telephone has left my ear for more than a few minutes since morning. And the way it looks, except for the brief planned respite for dinner, the evening is likely to be the same. I find myself speaking over the phone in tones of declining civility. In fact, I suspect I would be shouting to the unseen parties on the other end of the line if I were not within earshot of my daughter, who seems to be wandering aimlessly around our backyard.

At some point during the telephone call, four-year-old Cassie rushes onto the patio and steps up to me. Oblivious to the strife that's gutting me like a hunting knife, she wears a smile as broad as her tiny sweet face will allow. She's holding something, but I try to ignore her. I don't want to spoil the image of her incomprehensibly beautiful smile with the vile and baseless acrimony that I'm hearing over the telephone.

"Daddy!"

Not now, sweetie, I tell her in my mind. But I don't say it out loud, choosing only to shake my head.

The message doesn't get through. Her honeydew voice comes again, tinged with hints of pride and insistence. "Daddy, it's for *you!*"

I look down now to see that Cassie is standing directly in front of me, looking upward, her carefully stroked ash-blonde hair framing her quietly eager face. She is holding up a frail red leaf, many times the size of her small fist, pressing it toward me. Absently, hoping that a second's attention will send her inside, I take the leaf from her hand, gripping it between my thumb and forefinger, absently nodding my thanks. Even as I do, the contention over the telephone suddenly intensifies. Forced to silence by Cassie's continuing presence, I can vent my frustration only by crushing the leaf in my closing fist and then letting its dozens of fragments fall to the concrete below. Finally, the telephone combatants pause in their conversation, and I am able to state my own position in as measured tones as I can manage.

My comments finished, I look over at Cassie. She is standing where she was, stock-still like a statue. But her smile has inexplicably been replaced by tears streaming down her face, staining her pink checkerboard jumper like acid. Though she stands rigidly, her little body convulses with each escalating sob, her eyes riveted on the crumpled leaf lying on the patio.

"I got it for *you*, Daddy," she stammers between tears. Then she runs inside, letting the screen door slam shut behind her.

Those are the last words she says to me all night.

And then, after a nearly silent dinner, it's Jeannie's turn to scold me. "Cassie spent half the afternoon picking that leaf out for you," she says, more hurt than angry. "At least you could have held it until she came inside."

I say nothing to this, and nothing later. I stay out of Jeannie's way for the rest of the evening, and even ignore her when she heads up for bed. I've been on and off the phone the entire time, but as midnight approaches, I am sitting motionless in the darkened family room, my mind wracked by guilt and self-revulsion for my insensitivity to my precious little girl. Nothing is worth this, I tell myself. Even though she'll likely have forgotten the incident by morning, I won't have. It's a symbol of what my life has become. To her. To Jeannie. And to myself.

And it ends now.

I would rather sell my soul than ever to hurt her like this again.

Like a man crippled by an eternal loss, I spend the next two hours collecting and reassembling the pieces of the broken leaf in the dim patio light. And then, back inside, I glue them with great care onto a piece of construction paper. I tape the paper to the wall beside my desk, and when Cassie sees it a few days later, she tells me simply, "Thanks, Daddy. I knew you would like it." Her resurrected smile and the hug that follows are as recuperative as salvation itself.

In that instant, I am called back from the dead.

Thinking back on that moment now, the stray leaf from Rooker's yard lying crumpled underfoot, the past merges indistinguishably with the present. The realization shudders me with a force beyond comprehension, reminding me anew that I will never see that sweet forgiving smile again. The tears well up inside me and then flow forth for the first time since I left Denver.

I sit there for uncounted minutes in Rooker's old wooden chair, a decrepit shell of a man, sobbing miserably into my hands. At some point I cannot now recall, I make my way to the untouched bed, curling up into some long-forgotten fetal pose, yielding completely to the pain's eviscerations. In that moment, I become convinced.

Rooker, Maria, Amalfi, and all the others notwithstanding, I can fight against the pain no longer.

▼

An hour, two hours go by. I've lost track. My composure has finally returned, the protective armor of my hatred and self-pity restored. But all is not quite as it was. There are holes in the armor that were not there before, yawning gaps of vulnerability that admit connections to a world outside that I long ago disavowed. I force myself to concede that Alison was right. While Jeannie and Cassie will not be back, there are others I can help, others for whom I still might have benefit and purpose.

In time, perhaps, I will allow myself the luxury of chasing that purpose. In time.

But not now.

Now, I just want out. I'm still smart enough to know that even if Rooker is right, this battle is too big for him. Or me. Or a thousand of us. If he wants to see Dr. Maas's chimeric quest to the end, he's welcome to it.

But he'll have to do it without me.

With those thoughts marauding through my mind, I remain in the upstairs bedroom, staring out into the canyon like I have been for the past half hour or so, aimlessly pacing when I can no longer stand the solitude. And thinking. My mind has fully retreated to the present, and I am able to concentrate clearly on the matter at hand. And on my conversation with Rooker, seemingly so long ago. Intellectually at least, for what it's worth, he has convinced me. I can see his logic. The merits of his case.

But my mind, still shadowed by the pain, cripples any confidence or hope I might have. We'll all be killed before we even start. And for what? If I'm going to die, I want it to be for a purpose I can actually achieve, not just wish for.

And so, like a man drawn again to the Devil's drink, I let my mind once again focus on the more mercenary goals that Maria and Rooker had temporarily forced aside. I'm slipping again and I know it. But in this self-absorbed universe, going back into the solar plant is a pursuit of no personal relevance. It may not be suicidal, but it's still a distraction. My recklessness—going to Amalfi's, coming here—has already sent me down too many unproductive paths. If Maria needs a bodyguard, she can take one of Rooker's security men with her.

They can do the job as well as I could.

I'm prepared to walk down to the floor below to tell Rooker what I've decided when I hear a knock at the bedroom door. I grunt an answer, thinking, *It's him again*. But it's not.

It's Maria.

"We leave in two hours," she says, standing in the doorway.

"Yeah, well, good luck," I tell her.

"You're not coming?" No pleading, just surprise.

"Your father's a good man, Maria, if what Rooker says is true. I wish him the best. And you too. But this is your fight, not mine."

She just glares at me, refusing to believe what I've told her. Then her expression hardens. There's no wild anger, no flare-up of emotion. Just coldness. Bitterness.

And a hatred toward me that's a match for my own.

"You self-centered—" she begins, stepping into the room, but doesn't finish. The words catch in her throat. Then she starts again, finally expelling them. "Do you think you're the only one who's suffered?" A beat. *"Do you?"*

I say nothing, just return the glare in kind.

"The world is conspiring against you, is that it? The Catastrophe, Rojo, Amalfi. Farraday. Has all of this happened just so *you* could suffer? The world versus Martin Fall? Is that what you think? Look around you. Listen to yourself—"

"No, *you* listen," I interrupt, growling the words. My recollections of Jeannie and Cassie from hours before return with swelling fury. "What I lost—"

But she doesn't let me finish. "What *you* lost? My husband was in Tahoe when it happened. Did you know that? I didn't even find out for *five days* that he'd died. You got to hold your wife. To bury her. To tell her good-bye. By the time I reached Reno, my husband was lying in a plastic garbage bag in some stinking pit with ten thousand other decomposing bodies. And you've *seen* how the rest of my family lives. Yet you stand here, safe from it all, and tell me *you've* suffered."

Then she stops, her voice choking, and she looks away.

"I'm sorry," I say, after a moment, shaking my head. Despite a lurch toward feeling, the words come across as empty, mechanical. "I didn't mean it—"

She turns back, her eyes burning through the tears. "You're *sorry?* What does that mean? 'I'm sorry.' Of course, you're sorry. We're all sorry. So *do* something about it!"

"I plan to." I say it more harshly than I had intended. But I'm taken aback, not so much by the intensity of her response as by its desperation.

"*How?* By hiding under a rock like some wild animal and waiting for Rojo or Farraday or Amalfi to walk by? Will that make things better? You think you're going to shoot them all and that'll be the end of it? Well, it *won't* be the end and you know it. There will be a new Farraday and a new Amalfi and you'll either be dead or in a dungeon somewhere. And what good will you have done? What *good* will you have done?"

She pauses, staring at me for an eternity of seconds, and then ends it. "You can't change a thing about the past, Martin. But if you give up now, you're worse than Rojo and Farraday and all the rest. At least *you* had a chance to make a difference."

A beat, and then the emotion is gone. "Two hours. Either you're with us, or Rojo can *have* you, for all I care."

The door slams on her way out, but with less ferocity than I would have expected.

▼ ▼ ▼

arby begins to cough just as afternoon turns into evening. I think nothing of it at first. But when the coughing persists—dry, hacking, feeble—I turn around to ask if she is all right.

She replies with another cough.

I pull the van over then and trade places with Santos, who has just fallen asleep in the rear seat next to Darby. As Echeverria takes the wheel and resumes our drive, I cradle Darby in my arms, running my fingers through her long dark blonde hair. It is soaked, streaked with the dampness of a hot summer morning. I feel her colorless forehead and cheeks.

It's as if I have touched my hand to burning embers.

Her coughing goes on for several miles, more loudly, so much so that Pepper looks up from the van's floor and starts whimpering. And then, a few minutes later, Darby begins to shake again. I hold her more tightly to me, muttering an incoherent prayer to whatever gods may be listening. Or to God himself, if he can spare the time. But her shaking continues, if only a bit less intense. Her condition leaves us no choice.

Regardless of the risk or delay, we have to take her to a doctor.

I tell this to Echeverria, who nods in assent. He considers our options for a moment, and then says that he may have an answer. He knows of a clinic in a nearby town that we could try. "If it is still there," he adds. I am left wondering: is he speaking of the clinic or the town? These days, it is sometimes difficult to tell.

Echeverria turns the van around to head in the opposite direction, guiding it across the center stripes, and we leave a sporadic flow of southbound traffic for the stark and empty northbound route. We have to backtrack for almost half an hour and then take a side road that leads into the heart of a small desert town. A worn and sun-bleached sign peers from behind an overgrown cactus: "Welcome to Grasshopper Junction," it declares.

Even the name is an uncertain omen.

Presently, we reach the town's main street—a narrow, dusty passage with no stoplights and no street lamps. And no people. The town is completely deserted. The stores, what there are of them, look abandoned. Most of their plate-glass windows have been shattered. The stores themselves looted. Their shelves toppled and plundered for something to eat or sell. Even in the middle of the desert, it seems, chaos has found a home.

And in that single instant of awareness, I lose all hope of finding help or salvation. I realize that we have wasted valuable time taking this quixotic and futile side trip. Clearly, there is nothing here to help Darby. I hold her tightly again, as if my strength alone could bring her back to health.

But her coughing only goes on.

And then, all at once, we see it. Just outside the entryway to a small adobe building up on the left: a single light on this otherwise sepulchral street. We pull up in front of the building where the light shines. A hand-lettered sign hangs almost dreamlike above the doorway: Medical Clinic." But the one-word placard affixed to the door itself is the real miracle: "Open," it simply reads.

This is the clinic he was hoping to find, Echeverria says. He heads inside first in order to assess its suitability and to make the arrangements. On his signal a few minutes later, I follow him into the building, carrying Darby in my arms and leaving Santos to guard the van. The interior of the tiny windowless clinic is nearly as empty as the town itself. But the doctor is there, ready to help us. A Native American of Echeverria's tribe, he is a young man, maybe thirty, whom I assume must be schooled in the methods of modern medicine. But I am puzzled. Why would a young man of such apparent promise have chosen to remain here in this tiny desert town when only desolation looms all around?

To this question, I have no answers. But on this night of dimming hopes, I am thankful only that he is here.

As the doctor begins to examine Darby, Echeverria provides the explanation I am seeking. The young man is the son of the clinic's owner—an aging former leader of the Havasupai whom Echeverria's family has known for decades and who has recently retired from the profession of medicine. The son is managing the clinic until the father can find a new owner, and then he will head to Tucson, where the process of establishing his own practice has already begun. But I wonder, as I watch the young man's steady hands and probing eyes, whether there will be any patients left in that city for him to serve.

I suspect the same question has crossed his own mind.

Fortunately, the doctor proves to be as thorough and efficient as he seemed. Within minutes, he offers his assessment. Darby's warmth and perspiration are due to nothing more than a mild fever. It isn't serious, he assures us, and gives us some pills that will bring her temperature down and help her to sleep. The coughing and shaking, he says, are most likely a reaction to the stress of her recent traumas. He doesn't believe there will be any lasting damage. But he can't be certain, and so he encourages us to take her to a hospital for observation at our earliest opportunity. Beyond that, he says, the best we can do for her is to return her to a safe and stable environment in which she can begin to put something of her life back in order.

That, I inform him, is my plan.

As he renders his final judgment, I thank him for his time and counsel and hand him a one-hundred-dollar bill for payment, but he turns it down. In these dark days, he says, we must help each other, and this is the one contribution he can make. And with that, he bids us farewell. As we drive off, we see the clinic's sole outside light go dark behind us, as if he had been waiting solely for us.

A few minutes later, we are back on the highway, retracing our route from two hours before.

As Echeverria drives along, Darby tells me that she can sit by herself now, but asks if I will stay in the backseat beside her. I tell her I will. After a few minutes, I notice that her coughing has subsided. In fact, she has revived enough to call Pepper into her lap, and she wraps her arms around him, holding him as close to her body as I recently had held her. She takes my hand too. Squeezes it. And says softly, "Thank you for taking care of me."

I can only nod. Studying her, I see that she is still pale. I know that—even with the medicine—she will need time to recover. And rest, somewhere outside of this cramped vehicle. I suggest to Echeverria that perhaps we should drive on to Kingman and spend the night there before we head across the California border. That way, I say, Darby—all of us, really—can secure some much-needed sleep. Echeverria agrees, telling us that he knows the city well and that he is sure he can find a place for us to stay.

We crest a hill then, and are high enough in elevation that we can see Kingman shining down below us in the distance. The city is brighter than I would have expected, with a scattering of white lights surrounded by a ring of flickering ruby shadows. I think for a moment that, on this night of miracles, we have been presented with yet another. That we must be watching some grand and elaborate light show, or perhaps a late-night fireworks display.

But this proves to be only a cruel deception. For in the next instant I realize that these are not lights of welcome. They are instead phantoms of fire, bearing down on the city like a thunderstorm. Already, large parts of Kingman have been given over to flames. And the rest of the town, I suspect, will mount little resistance to being consumed by the same fate.

There will be no motels with "Open" signs in Kingman tonight.

And so we merely avert our eyes and drive on. Still, we are all tired, spent beyond strength, and we need to rest. In minutes, an option as good as any other appears before us. A trailer park rises up ahead, off to the side of the road. At length, Echeverria steers our van under its collapsing entry archway. "Desert Paradise," the sign reads. But it is an empty paradise, its occupants having long ago fled. We roll down the community's main gravel road, silenced by its emptiness. Soon, we find room to pull the van up next to a faded but well-tended double-wide. The area nearby looks safe, unmolested.

It will serve for the night.

Nevertheless, as a precaution, Santos retrieves three weapons from our cache, and he, Echeverria, and I sit with them on our laps throughout the early-morning hours, always making sure that at least one of us remains awake. To watch. And to guard.

Just in case.

CHAPTER 18

"You'll be in place by one hundred hours," says Rooker, pacing at the head of the conference table. "Enter the plant an hour later, then be out by oh-three-hundred. Is that clear?"

Maria, seated at the table with a half-dozen security men, looks up doubtfully. "That doesn't give us much time."

"If you can't find the file by then, you won't find it at all. Or they'll find *you*. It won't take that long to put out the fire."

"And how do you plan to set it?" I ask.

Rooker looks to the back of the room, where I have been standing. "A small rocket launcher with a nitro-tipped projectile. No one will see it coming."

"And the man operating the launcher? Can he hit the target?"

"He'll do the job." Rooker says this evenly, but his eyes betray his interest. When I came down to the conference room at the start of the briefing, he asked for my decision. I said I would listen to the details first. Now that I have, the time has come for answers. "You seem awfully concerned about our safety, Martin," he says.

"*My* safety," I tell him.

A pause, as he considers this response. "You're with us then." No question, just a statement. "Good. We need you."

Then he looks back to the group, recapitulating his instructions. I take the time to glance across at Maria. The anger and resentment remain in her eyes, though they're leavened now with a hint of relief.

And, perhaps, a little gratitude.

I nod toward her, a token of my concession. But she only frowns and turns away.

▼

Hours later, dressed in our firefighting gear, we reach the target site, all of us anxious to get in and get this over with. In the mist and chill of the cloudless night, Maria and I crouch on a protected ridge overlooking the solar plant. Rooker's security men position themselves on either side of us, behind boulders or clumps of shrubbery, seeking their own cover. Strange new comrades, these men. In the desperation of the moment, they accept my sudden conversion without question or protest, as they would a battlefield promotion or a recaptured POW.

But I have done the same, bowing to their companionship not out of careful calculation but of necessity. Neither Rooker nor Maria nor any single dictate of logic or circumstance has brought me to this place. I have come here, almost by default, for a complex of reasons. Obligation perhaps. Or remorse or guilt. Or some combination of these. Whatever the source, it is a choice that has not yet risen to the level of commitment. I am sure of that much. But I still have a role to play. And so I concern myself, like my new comrades, with the formidable task at hand.

I will do what I have to do.

For now, we wait. Below us, the solar plant seems as much a part of a dream as when I first saw it. The mile-long solar array, lit by dim spectral floodlights that collect in a yellow-gray haze, like the shading of an unpleasant memory. The solar panels themselves, lining the cylindrical shell, already pivoted eastward so that they're ready to catch the first rays of the coming morning's sun. And most importantly, the night-winnowed battalion of guards, stationed along the shell's length, stepping back and forth in their appointed paths like listless tin soldiers.

Our first barrier. I do not expect they will be our last.

I check my watch, and just then hear the low rumbling jolt of the launcher, coming from somewhere on a distant hillside. I follow the missile in my imagination toward the target, and then in seconds see the product of its malice. A gaping hole erupts midway along the length of the cylindrical shell, ringed at once by fire and burning plastic. Fragments of metal and concrete shoot toward the sky, chased by the whipping talons of the flames. Beneath them, waves of fire crawl outward across the side and top of the shell, igniting and swiftly consuming the huge solar panels. What's left is a rift stretching from the ground almost to the shell's peak, at least thirty or forty feet wide.

Just as planned.

The shot couldn't have been any more accurate if it had been delivered by hand.

Good work, Rooker, I think, failing to grasp the irony of my silently congratulating a man who at this time yesterday I would have killed without hesitation.

But there's no chance to pursue that thought tonight. The fire truck has glided to a stop on the winding road just below us, its headlights extinguished, and the security men are scrambling down the hill to climb on board. For an instant, Maria just kneels there, peering over the ridge, watching the spreading flames.

I touch her arm, and she abruptly looks up.

"It's time to go," I tell her.

She looks at me in silence, and then just nods.

▼

In minutes, lights flashing and sirens blaring, the fire truck barrels through the solar plant's security gate. It is waved toward the fire by the frantic plant security guards. The men welcome us—their secret enemy—without doubt or delay.

We brake within close range of the fire as smoke and heat billow out from the solar shell in great, heaving gusts. The eight of us leap from the truck, unfurling hoses, disengaging ladders, mapping out plans. Rooker's security men haul the hoses toward the blaze and proficiently go about the business of firefighting, as if they had been training for the task all their lives. Maria and I step away in the opposite direction, ordering the rubbernecking employees from the site and clearing a perimeter so that our men can work. Then we pull gas masks over our faces, breathing through the small oxygen tanks attached to our belts, and slip unnoticed through the smoke and confusion and into the cylinder itself.

"This way!" Maria shouts to me. We head down the corridor toward the main part of the complex—the administrative and research wings—half a mile to our left. She leads the way through a rainstorm of sprinkler jets, managing an ungainly trot that's hampered by the nearly floor-length fire coat and belt of fireman's tools. I pace behind her, burdened by the same inconveniences, nauseated by the smoke that curls around the ill-fitting mask.

At first the best we can do as we move along is to watch our feet, and even so can barely make out the yellow traction mat that runs the full length of the corridor. But the thick smoke gradually gives way to an acrid charcoal haze, and we begin to see the outlines of the machines and cables that fill the deep pits along the walkway's sides. Then the haze itself starts to clear, and I notice that the plant's guards have wisely opened the ventilation windows high up on either side of us that lead out onto the cylinder's roof.

By the time we are halfway to the administrative wing, the smoke is gone, leaving only the bitter taste of burning plastic. Maria and I remove the gas masks and run on, breathing the air that has started to filter in from above. At last we reach the glass security doors at the shell's end and pull up there, wiping perspiration from our foreheads. We step off to the side to study the lobby beyond. I remember it well from Farraday's tour. The broad circular floor. The exposed aluminum and white girders along the walls and upper frame. The model of the sun hanging from the high, arched ceiling.

In the center of the room sits a semicircular reception desk, occupied by a young Scandinavian-blond man talking on the telephone and making hurried, nervous notes. Four other guards stand off to the sides, looking equally concerned, watching the fire on the overhead monitors suspended around the lobby.

"Any of them know you?" I ask Maria.

"I don't think so." A beat. "Let's go."

We step into the doorway's view as she presses the entry buzzer, a silent signal that alerts the young guard at the desk to our presence. He peers out toward us, then quickly hangs up the phone and hits the button that unlocks the doors, letting us through.

This is too easy, I think.

Then the guard looks up suspiciously at Maria, as if he has seen her before. All at once I expect him to call her by name or at least to ask what we are doing here. If he does that, the game is up.

But he asks only, "Bad fire?"

"Yeah. And getting worse," Maria answers, covering her nervousness. She points back toward the doors. "Don't let anyone through. And you'd better clear this area too."

The guard's eyes go to the monitor. "You think it'll get this far?"

"I hope not. But just do it to be safe. We'll check upstairs."

And then we're rushing for the stairwell, leaving the plant's security team to spread our warnings. This diversion may buy us some time, but not much. Before long, the fire will be extinguished. Workers will be coming back inside. And a suspicious young security guard will be wondering what became of two firefighters who headed upstairs and have not yet returned.

By then, I'm thinking, we had better have the computer file well in hand, or else we can forget about leaving.

"Thirty minutes," I tell Maria as we duck into the stairwell and start sprinting up the stairs.

"I know," is her blank reply.

▼

The third floor of the administrative wing has been evacuated by the time we arrive. We walk its corridors in a hurry, our footsteps and voices lost in the keening drone of the fire alarm. At length, we reach our destination undisturbed. It's an auxiliary computer room, selected in advance for its isolation along a utility hallway lined with storage rooms. Maria runs her keycard through the slot next to the entrance, and we're in.

"At least they haven't locked me out," she says.

"Not yet anyway."

It's what we had expected. We had checked remotely from Rooker's house before leaving for the plant and had confirmed that Maria's authentication codes were still valid. Farraday must have had other things on his mind than blocking her access. Or else he didn't think she would try to return so soon.

Once in the small computer room, we immediately abandon the artifice that has brought us here, stripping off our fire gear and taking our positions like the thieves we are. Maria pulls a chair up to a computer terminal bolted to a workbench that runs the length of the room. With rapid strokes she turns it on, clears through with a password she stole in preparation for a time like this, and is soon logged into the system. I leave her to her work, standing before the thick Plexiglas window that separates the room from the hallway. My weapon is drawn as I wait, watching for intruders.

And counting the minutes.

They go by quickly. Too quickly. Even more so since I have no control over the progress of our pursuit.

Behind me, Maria carries on her search, saying nothing. The room's only sounds are the clicking of her fingers on the keyboard and the whirring of the spooler as it automatically retrieves the archived data spinning off the servers.

I check my watch repeatedly, but say nothing until we have less than ten minutes to go.

"How are we doing?" I ask.

"I found the source file. But there's a thousand and one parameter sets. And the program doesn't say which is the right one."

"Can't you copy 'em all?"

"If I had a week," she snaps. "Don't interrupt, okay?"

Okay, I think sourly, resigned to watching the computer monitor as she works. Each time she enters a code, the screen goes blank for a second and then flashes the words: "Parameters Not Found."

It's easier just to stare out into the hallway.

But more minutes pass. I look over again anxiously. The screen is still answering each of Maria's tries with blunt refusals. I don't say anything, warned off by her reply from before. But I'm thinking, *Isn't there an easier way?*

"How much time?" she asks.

I don't need to look at my watch. "Five minutes."

"This isn't going to work." A heavy sigh, and I can hear the desperation in her voice. "I can't do it. There's not enough time."

With that statement, the last shreds of the hope we held coming in disappear. I feel a wave of emptiness roll through me. All of this: effort wasted, worthless. And now, worse than wasted. Our lives are in jeopardy.

We have to get out of here.

Maria is back at work, the staccato rapping of the keys returning. But my thoughts are elsewhere, far from this room. I'm thinking back to Rooker's apartment, remembering the hard drive that Mesoto pulled from his computer. "Isn't there a disk drive or something we can take with us?"

Maria looks back, her face glowing in sarcasm. She nods toward the servers—units the size of small refrigerators—visible through the window in the locked, climate-controlled room behind us. "Think you can carry that on your back?"

But her eyes stay on the servers and then slowly shift to the right, toward the banks of metal shelves running back into the darkness for a dozen yards or so. Each shelf is filled with digital backup tapes. I stare at them. All of the tapes are labeled with a bold black date and time.

"What are the chances?" she asks with rising excitement. She swivels back to the terminal, her fingers playing over the keys like the digits of a mad pianist. She hurriedly exits the parameter file, then returns to the main menu. I stay by the window that looks out into the hallway. But even from this distance I can tell that she has called up the backup directory and is checking the archival dates. She runs her fingers down the long column of entries, correlating tape numbers with their contents.

Almost immediately, she finds what she is looking for. "We're in business," she says.

She's up from her chair in an instant. She darts across to the other side of the room and flips open the control panel mounted below the window that looks into the server room. Inside the room sits a robotic arm poised to retrieve backup tapes on command. Maria toggles on the power switch and enters the code for the tape she just identified. We wait for the robotic arm to pivot toward it.

Nothing.

She flips the power switch off and then on again, then re-enters the code.

Again, there's nothing.

She hurriedly scans the windowed area. Our eyes alight simultaneously on a small, computer-printed sign posted below the control panel.

Temporarily out of service.

Her body goes rigid in that moment, and then she slams her open palms against the glass. She holds there, but only for a second. Then she moves to the metal door that leads into the storage room. Quickly, desperately, she tries the knob.

It won't turn.

Ninety seconds.

"Isn't there another way in?" I ask.

The sarcasm again. "We could call a security guard. Wanna try that?"

But I'm not listening. I'm staring at the door. *The lock,* a voice tells me. *Just blow the lock. Of course. Idiot!* Without thinking, I rip a cushion from the room's window seat. Wedge it under the doorknob. Point my pistol upward. Pull the trigger.

There's a shot.

With a dull report, the lock shatters and the door edges open. Maria looks on in disbelief.

"Learned that from a friend," I tell her.

She doesn't move.

"Come on," I tell her. "Get the tape and let's go."

▼

Quickly, we're back in the hallway, dressed as firefighters again, the computer tape strapped to my waist. We race toward the stairs we took to this level barely half an hour before. The administrative wing's corridors are still empty, but the fire alarm has been deactivated. The pounding of our shoes against the tile floor echoes off the concrete walls like gunshots. In the silence, the blows are deafening.

I turn on my communicator, trying to raise our men on the fire truck to tell them we're on our way.

No answer.

"They must have pulled out," Maria says matter-of-factly. Which means either the fire has been contained or the real fire crews have shown up. Regardless, our primary escape route has been nullified. We'll have to use the alternate.

I knew this was taking too long.

"This way," she says in a whispered shout, leading us toward the stairwell.

We vault down the stairs, then reach the administrative wing's main floor. The lobby stands before us. We'll still have to cross it, but we've been granted one mite of good fortune. Most of the guards are gone. There's only the young Scandinavian-blond guard at the reception desk, talking on the telephone. Distracted.

We step into the lobby, feigning nonchalance as we stride across.

285

"All clear," I say when the guard looks up. "You can start letting people back in."

"Wait!"

"Is there a problem?" My answer comes with exaggerated calm. I slip may hand inside my coat, my fingers searching for my pistol.

"Plant security just called. They want this exit sealed. You'll have to wait to be escorted out."

No thanks, I'm thinking. That will take ten, fifteen minutes. By then our handiwork upstairs surely will have been discovered.

"Our truck's waiting. We've gotta go," I tell him.

"I said you'll have to wait. Mr. Rojo will be here shortly."

I ignore him, taking Maria by the arm and pulling her toward the security door that leads back out to the tunnel under the cylindrical shell.

We reach the door, and I extend my hand to open it. As I do, the guard steps around from behind the desk. He spreads his legs, standing firm, and draws his gun. "The door is locked."

I don't let him finish. Our cover's about to be blown anyway. I pull the pistol from beneath my coat, level it toward him. "Then open it."

He doesn't move.

"I said, open it."

He just stands there. Defiant. Either refusing to move or too startled to do anything. It doesn't matter. We can't wait any longer.

I shift the gun away from him and aim it toward the security door's lock. And then fire. The lock is obliterated. The shot rings throughout the lobby, loud and ominous, in one stroke marking our presence and unmasking our disguise. But there's no longer any use pretending. If they didn't know who we were before, they do now. We're left with only one objective.

Escape.

I pull the security door open and follow Maria through, taking one last glance at the guard. He's back behind his desk, frantically punching a number into the telephone. I don't need to ask who he's calling.

"Let's go!"

And we're running again. We let our fire coats slip from our shoulders, making it easier to move, and sprint down the tunnel that runs beneath the solar arrays. But the walkway stretches out so far before us that it might as well go on forever. It won't take long for the guard to finish his call.

Even the smoke up ahead that might have covered our departure has almost completely dispersed. As long as we're here, heading in a straight line from the lobby, we're a clear target for whoever might want to take aim.

"Isn't there a quicker way out?" I ask Maria, urgently.

"None that won't get us killed."

Small comfort, I think. And even that solace vanishes in the next instant. We've gone only thirty or forty yards when I hear the security door slam open behind us and a man step into the corridor. "Stop or I'll shoot!"

The same reception guard, his voice quaking with authority and the chance to be a hero. Without even looking, I can see him standing there. Legs locked. Gun held out at eye level. A nervous finger dutifully gripping the trigger. By the book, right down the line.

He'll shoot if he has to.

I rip the computer tape from my belt and hand it to Maria, then pull my weapon free.

"Go!" I command her, and she sprints ahead. I duck behind a metal stanchion and peer around its side, the long pit of gears and motors whirring at my back. My gun is aimed at the young guard, at his hands. But there's no way I can shoot without hitting him in the chest. *He's just a ten-an-hour Joe,* I'm thinking. *He doesn't deserve this.*

"Drop it!" I call out.

I'm greeted by a bullet pinging off the stanchion a few feet above my head. A warning shot or high of the mark, it doesn't matter. There's no longer room for mercy.

I edge out, taking aim for the man's chest, giving him half a second's chance. But in the last moment, his now-frightened face comes clear to me and I can't do it. So I aim my gun lower, toward his legs. And fire. He doesn't have time to get off another shot before his kneecap explodes in incandescent pain. He falls forward, his gun skidding harmlessly into the machinery pit. The sight sickens me and I turn at once, as much from revulsion as out of a need to escape.

I race back down the corridor, quickly closing in on Maria.

At least the guard will live.

"What happened?" Maria shouts, calling me back to the present.

I start to answer, but then see a shadow moving off to our left, above the machinery pit, and keep quiet. I turn to look. There is a concrete cubicle—an electrical service room—perched over the whirring machines below it. A workman is stepping through the cubicle door and onto a concrete walkway that leads out onto the corridor we're racing down. He grips a spanner in one hand, a toolbox in the other. An electrician checking for damage, accidentally wandering into the line of fire.

And then the young guard's voice comes again, crying out from far behind me. "Stop him!"

The workman—strong and solid, half a head taller than me—looks confused for a moment. Then he sees my gun and rushes toward me. I try to elbow him out of my way as I run past, but he grabs my arm. Snaps me back. Knocks my weapon to the ground with a sharp uppercut. I break free for a second, reaching out in desperation for my gun. But he pulls me back, throws me up against the front of the concrete cubicle, brings his other arm around to pin me there.

Out of the corner of my eye, I see Maria. Stopping. Looking on in shock. Her eyes go to my gun, lying a few feet from me in the middle of the traction mat, and she spurts toward it.

The motion is enough to distract the workman. He turns to look over his shoulder at Maria. In that moment I lock my leg around his. Spin him around. Lever him to the ground. But the maneuver works too well and I fall with him. We hit the walkway, then slip over the edge, tumbling into the pit below us.

A thud, and we land on the pit's concrete floor. I'm dazed for an instant. Then I look up and see myself surrounded by a forest of slowly churning black machines that move the solar panels above. Only one thought comes to me: *I have to get out.*

Shaking off the fall, I crawl unsteadily to my feet. But just as I do, I feel the workman's thick sweaty arm fold around my chest, pulling me toward him. I resist with my elbow, ratcheting back toward him, but he just grips more tightly.

I look up at the main walkway. Maria is standing there, my gun in her hand, pointed at my captor.

"Shoot him!"

There's no response.

"Shoot him! *Now!*"

But she doesn't have a clear shot and just stands there. Helplessly. Watching as the workman drags me back into a corner, trying to pull me down, to hold me until help arrives.

His arm goes around my neck, choking off my words, and only my eyes can speak. They look toward Maria, pleading for help. But she looks away instead. *Shoot him, Maria!*

My eyes follow hers to a control box on the side of the cubicle. She flips the panel open with her free hand, reaches in, pushes a button. Nothing happens.

What is she doing?

And then I see. The machines that surround us start grinding faster. The gears' slow roar becomes a demonic, high-pitched whine. Above us, atop the translucent shell, the solar panels start tilting back and forth in rapid metronomic motion as dictated by the machines' command.

The workman is as startled by the motors' burst of activity as I am. In this instant of opportunity, I shove him backward with my shoulders, twisting at the same time, and he trips, stumbling back against one of the machines. I break free from his grip then and lurch ahead, feeling his hands on my legs as he lunges to pull me back with him.

But there's a ripping sound from behind me. It's followed by a louder crackling and a muffled cry of pain, and the workman's hands slip away. The cuff of his work pants has caught in the gear shaft of one of the machines, and then his entire lower leg is entangled. He is dragged back, his leg suffering one slow grind after another. I scan hurriedly, looking for bars. Handholds. Something to lift myself out of the pit. Finally I see a pulley grommet. Grip it hard. Then pull myself up, scrambling up toward the walkway.

Behind me, the workman lies prostrate on the pit floor, clawing, trying to pull himself from the jaws of the machine. His foot is already crushed and the rest of his leg is coming next. I see his face. The violent expression that held sway while he wrestled with me has washed into a plea for help. For rescue. This man who would have brought me to my death now looks to me to be his savior.

There's nothing I can do but refuse to look back. No help I can offer and still save Maria and myself. Now fully out of the pit, I take my gun from Maria and motion her onward. Instantly we're back on the walkway, sprinting ahead. But I can't help thinking: the young guard, the workman, both crippled by my own hand. Perhaps headed now toward their deaths, innocents in the service of a cause to which they weren't even a party. Am I no better than Rooker? Or Rojo, for that matter?

Is anything worth this price?

I can't let my mind answer. Like the smoke from the missile's explosion half a lifetime ago, the thought nauseates me, and I shove it aside. We still have to escape.

"Are you all right?" Maria asks as we near the hole caused by the blast, a few hundred yards ahead.

"Not if we don't get out of here."

I don't want to guess our chances. It must be four or five minutes since the guard placed his phone call, and I'm surprised that the security men haven't surrounded us already. Some luck anyway . . .

And then the luck disappears. Up ahead, two guards—their guns fixed on us—rush through the hole in the shell and onto the walkway, charging toward us. And then from behind us come more footsteps. Quick and heavy, more than one man, distant but closing in. I don't bother to look, to gauge their positions. It doesn't make any difference.

We can't hold them off. Not an entire army.

"Stop! Don't move!" one of the guards from the front calls out.

But I'm not listening. I'm looking around feverishly instead. Searching for some exit. We can't go forward; we can't head back. No other way but—

Up! The ladder! To our left, rising toward the roof of the cylindrical shell. The night sky is visible through the open ventilation window, and it beckons.

Our only choice.

"Over here!" I bark to Maria. I take her hand, pull her off the corridor's main path. We head across a short narrow walkway and toward the ladder. I push her up first, turning to fire a couple of warning shots to cover her climb. Then I'm on the ladder myself, taking the rungs quickly behind her. We're partially hidden from the guards' view by the metal stanchions, and all that our pursuers can do for the moment is fire wildly in our direction. The shots graze the machines. Strike the stanchions. Clang off the base of the ladder. Nothing close.

A few seconds later, we both make it up the ladder and through the ventilation window, uninjured.

For now.

And then we're on the roof of the shell. Like stepping through a doorway into a new universe, the world is instantly transformed into an alien landscape. The softly glowing shell extends like a runway in front of us toward a distant bath of lights that must be the helipad. The solar panels in endless rows atop the shell tilt rapidly back and forth, flailing like flat steel trees whipping in the wind of a hostile planet. The night sky above is filled everywhere with pinpoints of light, framed by distant mountain peaks made visible only by the negative space of the stars they hide. It's a world to gaze at in wonder. If we had the time.

But we have none. It won't be long before the men behind us have reached the roof in the same way that we have.

We run on, pacing along the steel beams that form the frame of the shell's roof, dodging the tilting panels, moving as cautiously as we can to avoid slipping down the slopes of the shell. "Tell me again how we're supposed to get out of here," I ask Maria. Although I know as well as she does.

"The car. Bottom of the hill." Her words are rushed, breathless.

"Yeah. If it's still there."

I look out, off to the left, toward the perimeter of the solar complex. Trying to spot our escape. All I can see is the top of the electric fence that surrounds the facility. Rooker's people were supposed to cut a hole in the fence and have a car waiting in the brush outside, next to a gravel road leading off the mountain. *Supposed to.* Unless he and his firemen were caught, in the same way we're about to be.

In which case this will be a very short trip.

Our only blessing is a thick patch of pine trees, a few acres of forest left standing between the solar shell and the fence. In the darkness, it's impossible to distinguish the treetops, much less individual trees. If we can reach them, we'll be hidden, just long enough to—

Suddenly, running ahead of me, Maria trips. Sprawls forward. I hurry toward her. But she's back on her knees, then on her feet, before I'm there. I see that she has stumbled on a damaged section of the roof, an invisible pothole. She's lucky she didn't fall through.

"You okay?"

She answers with a quick nod and then we dart forward again. The computer tape I'd given her is still clutched securely in one hand, her pistol held in the other. Another fifty yards and the parking bay on the far side of the shell will give way to bare ground, and we can climb down from the shell and head for the safety of the trees.

But we don't get that far. Up ahead, peering through another ventilation window, is one of the guards who had been running toward us on the walkway. He has ascended a ladder further up and is on the roof in seconds, followed quickly by a companion. They're shadows against the sunburst of the helipad lights a half mile behind them, easy targets. But we are too. The generator housing looms at our backs and is lit well enough that they can take good aim.

And now, their menace is joined by other footfalls, far behind us. The other guards have reached the roof.

We're pinned again.

This time, there's no higher level to climb to.

But I can't worry about the pursuers behind us. Not yet. The guards in front of us are closer, and their guns are held ready to fire. Maria and I feint to the right, ducking behind a solar panel. Then we edge along it, take a quick careful sprint, nearing the panel's end.

Just then, one of the guards steps out, twenty feet in front of us. His aim is straight on. I have not killed a man in more than a decade, in my last year on the police force, and I do not want to do so now. But I do. Instinctively, reflexively, I opt for survival. I fire two shots. Quick, not even thinking. The guard bucks and stumbles, his gun flying from his hand and clattering down the side of the shell. His body comes next, bumping against one solar panel before coming to rest limply against another.

We rush past the body, to the end of the panel. And then back to the flat peak of the roof where the footing is surer, ready to rush forward again. We are already in the clear when I see the dead man's partner maneuvering in front of us, his gun up, pointed at our chests. He can kill us in an instant if he chooses.

It is the longest second I have ever known. My eyes lock on his, and I don't even try to move. Don't even try to pull my gun into position. Neither does Maria. *Is this the way it ends?* I wonder. I don't know if I pray. But I cry a silent wish for salvation. A wish to live through this moment. For some miracle of grace or good fortune.

And then it comes. The other guard holds his pose too long and suddenly crumples, falling forward. Pained. Unconscious. I do not understand right away what has happened, and then I see.

A tilting solar panel has struck him in the back, knocking him forward, then wedges beneath its tilting frame. His gun slips uselessly from his hand.

We're safe. For the moment.

I don't pause to celebrate.

"Come on!" I shout to Maria, when the reality of this miracle has settled in. But there's no need for words. We're both racing across the top of the shell again. Detouring around the ventilation windows. Sprinting toward an exterior ladder up ahead that leads off the roof's far side and down to the ground, a few yards from the trees. If we make it, we're home.

Almost there—

But I can't finish the thought. I feel the shot before I recognize the sound. The bullet pierces my calf, sending me careening forward. I grab for a solar panel. Catch it as it's tilting past. Just manage to keep myself from tumbling over the edge.

Another shot comes, this one right above my head.

"Get down!"

Maria scrambles behind a panel opposite me, breathing hard, peering around toward the gunman behind us. She looks to me, then back to the gunman, swinging her gun toward him. The expression that comes to her eyes in the moment is so lucid that I don't need to glance toward our pursuer to know who it is. But I do anyway, and it's just as I suspect.

Rojo.

He runs in his long, loping gait across the rooftop, arrogantly keeping himself in full view. I imagine him closer. Eyes burning. Nose flaring. Gun held out level. Disdaining caution in his unrepentant rage.

Unlike the fallen guard, he will not hesitate when he has the chance to shoot us.

"We gotta go!!" Maria says in a violent, urgent whisper, still aiming her gun at Rojo. Yet he's too far away for an accurate shot.

For her anyway. Not for me.

But I don't have the chance. My revolver has fallen from me in the impact of my collapse, out of sight. And worse, my injured leg has been wedged beneath the solar panel. Trapped. Held immobile until the panel tilts back.

"Come on!" Maria again. Now crouched on her feet, wondering why I'm still here.

"I can't move!"

Several dozen yards from us, Rojo is nearing, trailed in the distance by two other security guards. I can almost see his victorious smile.

I try to pull my leg free, but it won't budge. Not for a few seconds anyway, when the panel has shifted far enough for me to escape. But by then Rojo and his men will be here.

Too late.

Another shot comes then, announcing his approach, striking the panel behind us.

I look across at Maria. "Shoot him!"

She aims, freezes. *Hasn't she ever shot a gun before?*

Rojo and the other men are twenty, thirty yards away. Five seconds. We're within easy firing range now. Rojo will enjoy this.

"Shoot him, Maria!"

And finally her shot comes. At the same time, at the instant of the shot, Rojo stumbles, spinning forward. I look toward him and see in the next instant that he has become half a man. Dropped part way through the roof. A ventilation window? Or the same hole that Maria almost fell into? It doesn't matter. He is holding on, climbing back out. Ready to sprint toward us again.

My foot is still locked in place, for seconds more. *Too long!* I pull hard, winning only pain. No freedom. *Shoot him! Now!*

And again Maria fires. The gun rocks her back this time, and she stumbles, unable to get off another round. But she doesn't need to. I'm looking across the roof again at the place where Rojo was hanging on the moment before.

But he's no longer there. He's vanished. Fallen completely from sight. Into the hole. The guards who were with him—disoriented, frightened, unwilling to sacrifice their own lives—have dropped to the roof for cover.

They stay there, for a few brief seconds, to make sure they're safe.

The seconds are enough. In the reign of their caution, I finally manage to free my foot and Maria pulls me up. We sprint the rest of the way along the rooftop, the bullet wound in my leg throbbing. We reach the ladder on the far side. Head down. In seconds, we're at ground level, running toward the trees.

And soon we're there. Surrounded by safety.
We hope.

▼

Our car—a Citizens Council Cubic from Rooker's secret fleet—speeds along the moonlit coast highway that runs like a ribbon high up the mountainside. Maria and I can finally breathe easily. In the only uncomplicated portion of our escape from the solar plant, the promised vehicle was positioned exactly where it was supposed to be, enabling us to flee Farraday's security forces while they were still navigating the dense pine forest within the solar plant's property line. When we exited the trees minutes ahead of them, we saw that Rooker's men also had cut the hole in the fence, and we crawled through to the waiting car. There was no driver, no member of Rooker's security detail there waiting for us. But at least the key was in the car and its tank was full of fuel.

A welcome relief, after all that we had been through.

Now, a few minutes later, Maria drives along in silence. I sit in the passenger's seat, massaging my injured leg in case we have to run again. I limped all the way down the steep forested hill to the fence, and with the leg's searing pain I'm surprised I made it.

But with the terror of our escape safely left behind, we've been blessed with the first relatively peaceful moment we've had since the evening began. In fact, as we pass an access road that descends the thousand or so feet down to the beach, I find myself looking out at the ocean, the moonlight reflecting off its slowly rolling waves, imagining that I'm watching it from the relaxed vantage point of an elegant veranda. I feel as if we are somewhere far away from here—on a vacation perhaps, or in another age altogether, where there is time for such idle diversions.

I must lose myself in these thoughts—or else fall briefly asleep from the pain—because the next thing I'm aware of is Maria's voice. "Thank you for your help back there," she says. "You saved my life. Again."

I don't answer because there's nothing to say. We survived. We're alive. We're safe again.

For the time being anyway.

"How's your leg?" Maria asks.

I shake off the fog from the moment's rest. "I'd cut it off if I didn't think I'd need it," I tell her, trying for dark humor but only coming across as morbid. I shrug, recouping. "It hurts. It'll be fine."

We've come to another beach access road. This time, I see that Maria has turned the car off the main highway and down the long switchback filament of a road. I look over at her, perplexed. "Aren't we going the wrong way?"

"We don't have time to drive all the way back," she says. "Rooker called while you were sleeping. He's sending a chopper for us. They'll meet us on the beach in twenty minutes."

I look over curiously at this announcement. "Yes, he has one of those too." she tells me, answering my unspoken question.

As she says it, I realize this is the first time I've seen her smile.

But the moment doesn't last. Her words are interrupted by the rising thrum of a helicopter, emanating from somewhere in the distance. Instantly, I'm alert.

Looking around.

Trying to find it in the sky.

There! Just peeking over the mountaintops, maybe five minutes to the north.

"Either Rooker's early," I tell her, "or else we've still got company."

But even as I say it, I know the answer. Rooker's chopper would be coming from the south, not the north.

I reach into the backseat of the car for a rifle. No good at this range, of course. Maybe no good at all. But it's all we have.

"Step on it!" I call over to Maria, and she revs the car. Shortly, it reaches fifty, then sixty miles per hour, whipping dangerously around the curves of the narrow, descending road. I climb into the backseat, open the car's rear passenger's-side window, and lean out, finding what aim I can. The helicopter is in the clear now, and I can barely make out the Golden West insignia on its side. It's closing fast—faster than I would have expected. The craft's right side door slides open then and a gunman leans out, aiming an M-16.

Up front, I hear Maria start to cough, and my only thought is: *I hope it doesn't hurt her driving.*

The craft draws closer, time moving on fast-forward. The gunman is almost in range. I don't even tell Maria to speed up—I know she's driving as fast as she can. Nor am I thinking about what we'll do when we reach the beach. I don't even know whether there's another road down below. But it may not even matter. The gunman's weapon is more powerful than mine, and he'll have many long minutes to fire at us long before my rifle can reply.

Still closer.

Maria continues to cough, her breaths almost wheezy, and I start to ask her what's wrong. But in the instant before I do, I realize I don't need to.

I have my answer.

In the sky beyond the fast-approaching helicopter, shimmering lights have begun to materialize . . . then quickly mutate into cascading curtains of red and yellow, as if being blown about by the wind.

The lights aren't as bright or extensive as what I saw in Denver or Flagstaff, but their meaning is no less clear.

The gunman and the helicopter pilot are oblivious to this threat, and they should be the least of my worries. But I am not allowed that luxury. The helicopter is in range now, and the gunman has started firing. One round careens off the car's trunk and another hits the rear windshield, shattering it. I have to pull back inside the car to avoid being struck.

Another shot, another hit.

At this rate, we have seconds to live. Less, if the gunman finds his aim.

To improve his chances, he leans out further from the helicopter, almost suspended in midair, readying his coup-de-grâce . . .

. . . but it doesn't come. Before he can release the shot, he drops his weapon, and it plummets to the earth. He reaches back into the chopper, convulsing. Holds on for a second or two . . .

. . . and he then lets go, tumbling after his gun to the ground.

I know all too well what has happened, am grateful for this instant miracle. But in the urgency of the moment, I've forgotten all about Maria. Now my attention turns back to her as our car starts to weave, almost running off the right side of the road, then the left. We're descending rapidly toward the beach, maybe five hundred feet up. But with one of the car's windows open and the rear windshield shattered, the oxygen in the car has long since bled out.

I take one final glance at the sky, and see that the helicopter pilot has lost control of the craft, his own fate as certain as the gunman's.

The chopper weaves and bobs for a few seconds, then spins helplessly down toward the ocean.

Behind it, the veils of red and yellow begin to whip more furiously, their threat intensifying.

And now Maria's coughs have turned into gasps, her control over the car almost gone. I crawl over the front seat and hand her an oxygen mask that's hooked to a small canister lying on the passenger-side floor.

"Put it on!" I tell her, reaching for the car's brake and steering wheel at the same time, pulling the car back onto the road just as it veers toward a steep embankment.

The vehicle whipsaws across the road, toward a cliff wall. I pull it back again, practically sitting on top of Maria but not able to do anything about it. My own breaths are rasping now, but there's only one mask up front, and I can't stop to reach into the back.

Maria's hand appears around my right shoulder then, the oxygen mask in her hand. I take a quick breath from the mask, then steer the car back to the center of the road. After several rocky bumps the car finally stabilizes, and I'm able to slide off Maria, into the passenger's seat. She's more composed now, gradually regaining her own breaths, and the car has slowed enough that she can retake control.

As she does, I look outside, down toward the beach. I see the red and yellow curtains snake close to the shoreline, far lower than they ever reached in Denver or Flagstaff, nearly touching the ocean's waves. Then, in seconds, like a tornado that has spent the last of its force, the light show is suddenly over. The curtains disintegrate and fade back into nothing.

At once, the air is filled again, this time with sound. All around us, loud warning Klaxons blare in the distance. But their warning is useless. Too late for us, and too late for any others who might have been unprepared.

At some point during this clanging concerto, our car leaves the road, and we are bouncing down the last fifty feet or so of the hillside, running over scruff and rubble, doing permanent damage to the car's underside. The metallic clatter escalates, and I can hear parts of the exhaust system being ripped off and thrown aside.

It's a wonder the fuel tank isn't punctured.

But slowly, expertly, Maria steers the vehicle along this rough tarmac, and the car gradually settles onto the flat sands of the beach before stalling altogether, a few dozen yards from the shore.

She just sits there, the oxygen mask still strapped to her mouth. Her breath catches with each inhale. But it isn't the lack of oxygen that causes her fractured respirations, nor my own.

It is the recognition of what almost was.

And the fear of what is surely yet to come.

▼ ▼ ▼

We avoid Kingman on the way out the next morning and head northwest again, leaving the main highway for the relative isolation of the less-traveled back roads. After an hour of nearly silent driving, we come to another town, a small residential community called Arizona Village. Echeverria informs us that we have finally reached our goal. We are within a mile of the Arizona-California border, directly across from Needles, California, that state's gateway city.

We are almost home.

We are able to enjoy this victory for several minutes before it too flees from us. For as we navigate the village's narrow side streets, searching for a crossing point into Needles, we encounter yet another roadblock. One we had not expected.

And as we do, we discover one thing more.

Our options—at last—have come to an end.

Our journey's conclusion arrives as we approach a broad road called Harbor Avenue, a charming small-town thoroughfare that leads over the wide river that serves as the border between the two states. A ragtag line of cars and trucks has formed along the road. While it's only thirty or forty vehicles long—far shorter than what we experienced when we tried to merge onto I-25 on our exit out of Denver—for some vague reason this particular backup bears considerably more portent.

This unease results in part, I realize, from the fact that the number of cars departing California is almost as great as the number attempting to enter. Why, I wonder, would people be leaving the safety of California's lower elevations for the deathtraps that are the mountains and plateaus of Arizona?

We have no answers, and our confusion only grows. As we crawl further down the avenue, the border crossing a hundred yards ahead comes into view. It's barricaded by a contingent of US Army trucks parked lengthwise across the road. Whether the trucks are positioned there to enforce Arizona's tightened immigration laws or to simplify the task of screening migrants into California, we do not know. But we see the product of their work in the periodic stream of vehicles that drive past us in random moments on our left, heading back toward us. We can only assume that these cars and trucks are part of the cross-border traffic that has been permitted to pass from California into Arizona.

A few minutes later, we learn that this assumption is gravely wrong.

We pull up beside an overweight Army captain standing in the center of *the road. A rifle is held at his side, a pistol strapped to his belt. I am driving our van at this point, and so I roll down the window, allowing the stinging desert air to blast in through the opening. I wipe the grit of sand and dust from my eyes and look up at the man.*

He is a portrait in weariness. But that does nothing to diminish the power of his authority, nor the import of his words.

"You'll have to turn around," *he says.*

This makes no sense at all, yet my protest comes across more as a plea than a statement. "We have a sick child."

"I'm sorry," *he replies.* "I wish I could help. But the border is closed. I'm not allowed to let anyone pass."

"How long will it be closed?"

A sullen shake of the head. "I don't know. Days. Weeks. It's hard to say."

He then offers an explanation that I'm sure he has already rendered a thousand times. Under orders from the White House, interstate travel except by bus or special permit has been prohibited until the implications of this second air shortage can be fully assessed. When I ask why border crossings have been stopped, he says only that it has something to do with keeping carbon emissions out of other states.

As if, I think, the air could be stopped by an Army barricade.

"Please," *I tell him after he has finished his explanation.* "I know you're just doing your job. But we only want to get back home."

"I know you do," *he repeats, with what sympathy his tired frame can muster.* "But I can't let you through. You might wanna go back to Kingman and catch a bus. They've got 'em running fairly regular. Though I gotta say, I'd hold off traveling altogether if I were you."

"Why?"

"There's been twenty or thirty killings along the roads since midnight. People looking for food, fuel, that sort of thing. It's not a good place to be." *He starts to step away, then gives one final look back.* "Yeah, I'd stay in Arizona for a while if you can. Just till things settle down."

I consider this option, letting the van idle for a brief moment. But my decision is already made. All I can recall is the image of the city of Kingman ringed by fire last night. Other outbreaks will surely follow.

Remaining here—or anywhere close by—is no safer than being on the road.

We have to press on.

The Army captain is waving us away, and it's time to comply. And so I roll up the window and swing the van around, heading back up the avenue in the direction from which we have just come. As we pass the other vehicles waiting in the same line where we were sitting, I can see the drivers' faces. They are full of confusion. Full of anxiety. Full of fear.

But I greet them only with a blank stare in return.

Like those we saw driving past us while we were waiting in line, we are now among the rejected.

I look back at Darby as we pull away. She is awake now, sitting silently. Confused and uncomprehending. In this respect, she is no different from the rest of us. None of us knows what kind of future we have purchased.

None of us knows what comes next.

For now, however, our choices are few. Waiting somewhere on the outskirts of Kingman, in the vain hope that the border will soon reopen, is no hope at all. It's a course against which I have already decided. And while we could try to cross the border on foot, that also is far too risky, especially with a sick child.

More realistically, we could return to Flagstaff and remain with Echeverria for a few days. There at least we would have the protection of a home and family. Enough oxygen to support us should another air shortage occur. And ample food supplies, weapons, and ammunition. Echeverria in fact makes this offer as we drive away,\ and says that his family would welcome us as if we were their own. Then he adds a more personal motivation. "We could use the help," he says flatly.

I choose not speculate on what circumstances might make our help worthwhile.

Still, I ponder his invitation for some time while we make our way through the light traffic on the highway back to Kingman. But as we pass the convoys of Greyhounds and Trailways and yellow school buses moving toward the California border we only recently left, I realize that we can run no longer. Our chase is at an end.

If we are ever to return to Los Angeles, then we too must become one with the masses. We must take to the road under the power of others, trading our freedom for the assurance that, at last, we can reach our destination.

And so I make that decision for the three of us, and Santos concurs.

But even as I do, I silently tell myself—almost pray it really—that this nightmare must end soon. As patient as we try to be, we cannot endure these roadblocks and uncertainties for much longer.

We have to reach our home.

CHAPTER 19

"Still no answer?"

"Not a thing," Rooker tells me, shutting off the transmitter.

It is late that afternoon, and the sun is quickly sinking toward the Western horizon. Just over fourteen hours ago, Maria and I bounded onto a beach, desperately gasping for air from the brief oxygen wipe-out as Farraday's security patrol chased us from the sky. We survived both, and Rooker met us soon after, arriving by helicopter as he had promised. The only surprise was the transport itself: it was no ordinary craft, but a fully-equipped Citizens Council helicopter piloted by a renegade member of Amalfi's private security detail.

Evidently, not all of Fran's most-trusted minions were as loyal as she thought they were.

Once inside the aircraft, we were treated with the care and attention normally reserved for the chopper's most frequent occupant. A city medic tended to my injured leg, carefully removing the bullet that was lodged in my lower thigh, while a second treated Maria's scrapes and lacerations. We were fed the first real nourishment we had received in nearly a day, courtesy of Fran's private reserves. Rooker, meanwhile, ran the stolen computer tape through a portable reader. This time, our efforts were rewarded: the bio-crystallization protocol it contained was the right one.

"Nice work," he told us, although he seemed less relieved than I would have expected.

As soon as we reached his mountainside residence, Rooker transmitted the tape's contents to Dr. Alejandro Maas, and later that morning received two reports back from Dr. Maas. The first informed us that the new bio-crystallization protocol had been used to produce micro-sized solar converters of exactly the quality and performance needed, and that his staff had already begun assembling the converters into their intended parabolic arrays.

The second report—more ominous—was a summary of atmospheric readings along the Pacific Coast, relayed to Maas by a friendly source inside Golden West. "O-2 levels have been all over the map the past two days," Rooker explained when we awoke a few hours ago, showing us screen after screen of high-altitude oxygen concentrations gyrating as wildly as stock market prices on the brink of anarchy. "We aren't out of this yet," he warned. "You'd better keep an oxygen tank close by at all times."

A sensible precaution, given our elevation. Yet his anxiety about the atmosphere was eclipsed as the day wore on, replaced by a more immediate concern. By mid-afternoon, we had heard nothing else from Dr. Alejandro Maas, and had been unable to contact him. Maria could imagine only the worst. As could Rooker, despite his outward calm.

"We have to go up there," he tells us as we sit with him in the residence's conference room.

"Is it safe?" I ask.

"Does it matter?" he retorts. And then, more equably, offers an explanation. "If it *is* safe, we have nothing to worry about. And if it's not safe—if Farraday's men have discovered where he's hiding—then *we* might as well be gone too. We can't do a thing without him."

▼

Two hours later, we find ourselves snaking through the San Gabriel Mountains along a rutted gravel road, headed toward Dr. Mass's secret laboratory. Our vehicle is a purloined security van, gray and undistinguished except for the Citizens Council seal stenciled on its sides. Maria and I sit next to each other in the back, prisoners of our own thoughts. Rooker is seated directly in front of us, stationed before an imposing bank of hardware installed behind the driver's seat—computers, video monitors, communications devices. Everything a mobile executive or state-of-the-art urban guerrilla might require.

But none of this equipment, for all of its sophistication, has helped us get through to Dr. Maas.

"Haven't you ever lost contact with him before?" I ask, searching for some reason for optimism.

"Never for this long," is Rooker's laconic reply.

And so we drive on, fueled by our fears. Every vent and furrow in the road jars us, as if the van had been stripped of shock absorbers and its wheels of their rubber. I'm surprised, in fact, that the electronics can even survive this journey. If Rooker's people groomed this path to make it appear untraveled, they did a convincing job.

Beside me, Maria is gazing out a small side window, staring out at the barren trees. "I pray to God he's all right," she says softly for the hundredth time.

I respond by squeezing her hand. The hardness from before has slipped away, her pain and worry left unmasked. "Are *you* all right?" I ask her.

She turns to me then, rejecting my concern. "Look, I owe you too much already. Don't run up the bill, okay?"

She pulls her hand away and folds it into her lap, facing outside again.

A few minutes later, I look up at Rooker, "Are we almost there?"

"Another three or four miles. We should reach the point crew in a couple of minutes."

The point crew is a small team of Rooker's security men who drove to the site ahead of us as an extra measure of prudence. We were taking enough of a risk coming here in daylight, when we could easily be spotted from the air. To have ridden here as a caravan would have been suicidal.

"Have they reported any activity?"

"None," says Rooker. "The grounds are dead. No one in or out for the last hour."

As likely to be bad news as good, I realize, and I know that Rooker is making the same assessment. But we don't have to wait long for answers. In minutes, we pull up alongside the point crew, and can see for ourselves.

Up ahead, visible through an opening in the brush, stands an isolated church surrounded by dirt and cracked asphalt, the sole structure in an overgrown clearing. This sanctuary, which served the residents of the nearby hills when people used to live here, looks as though it has been abandoned since the Catastrophe. And it has been—by sectarian interests. But not by secular ones.

For nearly a year, Rooker tells me, it has housed the laboratory of Dr. Alejandro Maas.

We pull the van off the road, hiding it beneath a thicket of high pine branches, and climb out. Rooker consults with the four men of the point team, and then we step cautiously into the clearing. Now, the whole church is visible, and I can take in its full dimensions. It's a single-story building, its thick walnut beams intermixed with stucco walls adorned by long, narrow rectangles of stained glass. A wood-beamed roof, rising to an obtuse angle, stretches for the length of the church. A bell tower serves as the building's steeple, the bell long ago removed, the tower now claimed as a nesting ground for crows and blackbirds. It's a study in solemnity: a way station for the lost.

We approach it silently.

And then we are in the open, standing at the edge of the tree line, thirty yards from the building's front entrance. If anything, I am more anxious now than I was at the solar plant the night before. Then, at least, there were stanchions and solar panels to mask our passage. Here, we are completely exposed, ready targets for any snipers waiting within or without. If they have already taken Dr. Maas and have stayed behind to eliminate us as well, there is nothing that we can do to stop them.

It's time to give them their chance.

The lead point crew member confers with Rooker, then signals his men, who sprint in standard two-by-two formation across the clearing to opposite corners of the church. They take quick glances through cracks in the stained-glass windows, then return to the building's front, where three of them duck inside past the broad double doors. At the same time, the fourth man scales the bell tower to survey the surrounding terrain. Evidently seeing nothing amiss, he climbs down and takes his position at the front doors, waiting for his companions to return from their survey of the interior.

Minutes later, they do. The door opens and the team leader looks out, waving the rest of us in. *All clear.*

Rooker turns to Maria. "You really should stay here," he says, nodding toward the van. "At least until we find out what's going on."

Any trace of fear or reluctance has left her. She extracts her pistol, cocking it and checking its ammunition, as if she had been carrying a gun for years. "If they even *touched* him," she says flatly, "I'll kill them all."

Rooker only shrugs. "Just don't get yourself killed in the process."

He motions for Maria and me to follow him, and the three of us steal across the fractured asphalt. In seconds, we are through the front doors and into the narthex. The foreroom is wide and functional, cleaned of whatever furnishings and trappings it once held. Only a single bulletin board remains, and it hangs at an unintended angle from the wall, random pins and staples and the ragged corners of year-old church bulletins the only signs that people once worshipped here.

We leave the room behind us and step through a pair of stained-glass doors into the main body of the church. Although I haven't been inside a church in years, the backdrop is as I remember it. High stucco and walnut-beamed walls, a match for the building's exterior. Brass plaques bolted on the walls in every blank space, commemorating the dead and their post-mortem donations. A vaulted ceiling, an array of dark wood beams interspersed with panels of clear one-way glass, admitting the day's last rays of sun. Nothing out of the ordinary.

Except for the room's contents. Once again, I feel as though we have stepped into another world. The pews and banisters have been removed and now sit uselessly along the side walls. But unlike the narthex, emptiness hasn't taken their place. Instead, there are long rows of machinery—metalworking machines, computers, laser-like devices, large vats of some type of metallic liquid, other equipment I can't identify. This assembly of hardware runs all the way from the back of the church to the front, glinting in the pale sunlight like outcroppings of gold. Set against the churchly walls and ceiling, these artifacts of industry look odd, out of place.

But they're also undisturbed. One good sign, anyway.

We head on.

When we reach the chapel's front, two of Rooker's men are just emerging from a stairwell that leads below. A storage room, one of them informs us, full of supplies. Unmolested. Another good sign. But there are still no workers. No Alejandro Maas. No evidence of life at all.

"Anywhere else we should check?" one of the men asks.

"One more place," says Rooker. He pulls aside the carpet that runs across the front aisle, revealing a trap door carved into the hardwood floor. It's a weak disguise, easily recognized by anyone who might suspect it's there, but sufficient to block someone coming in blind. Rooker motions to two of his men, who lift the door and mount the spiral, wrought-iron staircase that leads below. Then they head downward, their guns drawn. Maria and I follow, our weapons also held ready, with Rooker trailing behind us.

As we slowly descend the stairs, I can tell that this lower floor has also been given over to an unnatural function. Perhaps it was once a reception hall or a collection of cubicles where children studied their Sunday School lessons. Now, rows of high-end data servers line its walls, and the detritus of an electronic workplace is strewn about. Computer printouts. Backup disks of various sorts and sizes. Random hand tools. Discarded circuit boards.

And then, in their midst, I see what I least expect. A solitary figure, his back to me, straddles a rough wooden bench at the rear of the room. He is hunched over a crude worktable littered with tools and electronics, silent and motionless. Behind me, I hear Rooker breathe his name with relief: "Alex."

The man turns at the sound.

I have formed no preconceptions of the physical appearance of Alejandro Maas, but I am nonetheless startled when I see him. He is a huge man, broad-backed and thick-necked, with heavy muscular arms and wide powerful hands. His hair, wavy and coal-black, is streaked with strands of silver-gray. It has been brushed to the sides, neatly framing his square, expansive forehead. Dense, bushy eyebrows crowd his eyes. His face—rugged, imposing, tired—angles down to a deeply clefted chin. *This is a laborer,* I think, *or a fisherman, accustomed to things rough-hewn and weathered, barely past his prime.*

But when he rises, it is a slow and painful ordeal. His weight is lifted by his heavy arms, and his back, even when he is standing, bends forward with obvious discomfort. His hands shake as he steadies himself, and his breaths come deep and hoarse, like a man overexerted. The debilitations of his age—and the torture of the past year—consume the man's countenance in full.

Maria is instantly at his side, embracing him. *"¡Papá!"* she cries softly, not bothering to hide her tears. She buries her head in his chest.

"*¿Porqué no nos contestasté? Hé estado tan preocupada.*" Her voice carries the sound of salvation, the phrases of a mother who has found a child lost beyond hope of reunion.

Maas takes his daughter's hand and shuffles out from behind the workbench, comforting her with words I cannot make out. Then, still holding her hand, he looks up at Rooker. "Forgive me, James, for not responding to your transmissions. We heard noises outside this morning. Helicopters. I thought it best to keep the radios silent."

"Helicopters?" asks Rooker. "Are you sure?"

"Yes, my people spotted one of them in the distance. I don't know if they saw us. I don't believe so."

"Well, if they did, they'll be back. You can count on it." A pause, as Rooker assesses the situation. "What about the others? Where are they?"

"They finished their work here," says Maas. "I sent them out . . ."

The old man's eyes go to mine in that moment. They are Maria's eyes. Dark. Determined. Probing. "You must be Mr. Fall," he says quietly, glancing to Rooker for confirmation. Then he turns back to me. "You made an old man rush."

"Mr. Fall is working with us now, Papá," Maria says, looking across at her father. "He didn't know."

Alejandro Maas hears this, but it does not dispel his doubts. He steps toward Rooker, letting Maria's hand fall away. "May I speak freely?" he asks, and Rooker nods.

Slowly, still evaluating me, Maas faces me. "You worry me, Mr. Fall. Only days ago, you hunted down my daughter. Then you saved her life. By your actions, you jeopardized all of us. Now, you risk your life so that we may finish a project that you know little about. I wonder: what kind of man can change his colors so quickly? A man of great loyalty or commitment? I do not think so. Yet I owe you my daughter's life—twice. And James tells me to speak freely in your presence. Is my suspicion misplaced? Do I judge you too harshly?"

Maria answers for me, before I can reply. "They killed his friends, Papá. Mesoto and the girl. We have the same enemy."

"I see," whispers Maas, drawing the words out as he weighs this new information. "So now we bring mercenaries into our cause, men with private vendettas?" He pauses, letting the observation settle. "And you are comfortable with this, *mi hija?*"

"There is more, Papá ... ," Maria begins, and then stops, reconsidering her response. What is it that she chooses not to say? That I survived the Catastrophe while my family did not? That I have been the victim of betrayal at every turn? That Rooker told me more than I needed to know about this man who stands before me, and shamed me with his belief and dedication? That Maria made her own impassioned plea for a purpose beyond vengeance, yet she still shares her father's unease and suspicion?

She finally says the only thing she knows to be true. "I cannot speak for his motives," she tells her father, "but I can vouch for his loyalty. That is enough for now."

Rooker, it seems, has understood that this exchange was one not suited to the tidy logic and abstractions of his intellectual domain, and has kept silent. In any case, it is only Alejandro Maas's thoughts that matter at this moment. And, for reasons known only to him, he assents.

"I will speak then," he says, and looks to Rooker. "My people are in the field, preparing our demonstration. Just as you planned. It will be ready by morning."

"All of the solar plates have been fabricated?"

"Enough," says Maas. "Enough for now."

"Good. Then we can get out of here."

"Not yet. I need an hour, maybe two, to finish archiving the files. After that, we can go."

"We can't take the risk, Alex."

"We *have to* take the risk," Maas says in a peremptory tone. "We can't bring all the machines with us. And I can't leave my files." With that, he turns back to his computer, positioning himself immovably on the workbench, and reaches for another backup disk.

"Alex, you can't—" Rooker begins, but Maria has already moved to stand over her father's shoulder, gently taking the backup disk from his hand.

"I'll do this, Papá. I'll stay behind. You go. Get out of here."

Maas looks up in protest, but Rooker speaks first. "It isn't safe for you to stay either, Maria."

"It isn't safe for *anyone*," she says. "But Father's right. We have to take all of the data we need with us. We may not have a chance to come back."

"And what if there *were* helicopters this morning?" Rooker presses. "What if *they* come back? This isn't a good idea."

"I'll stay with her," I cut in, and Rooker turns to me.

"What?"

"I said I'll stay. Just leave us the other car. By the time Maria finishes, it'll be dark and safer to travel anyway. We'll be back at the house by midnight. I promise."

I say the words calmly, but I don't feel that way. I think Rooker is right. This is foolhardy and dangerous. Besides, the good doctor should have thought ahead and already had the files backed up that he needed. But I can't judge what went on here during the last twenty-four hours, can't judge what has to be preserved. In the end, that is his call, and his call alone.

But one thing is certain: if Maria is determined to stay, she shouldn't be here by herself.

Rooker studies me and then decides. My argument must have been enough. He takes the car keys from the point crew's driver and hands them to me. "As you wish," he says flatly, barely hiding his anger at being overruled. "But I won't see you till morning. We've got about twelve hours until showtime, and I have a bit of work yet to do."

"What do you mean?"

"You'll see in the morning. And so will Farraday and Amalfi and all the rest."

Whatever Rooker has to show, I doubt either Stuart Farraday or Fran Amalfi will pay much attention. "You'll have a hard time persuading them that you're right and they're not, no matter what you show them."

"I'm not talking about persuasion," says Rooker. "If we do this right, they won't have a choice." He studies me for a moment longer, and then pulls a transmitter from his belt and gives it to me. "Keep in touch. I'll see you tomorrow." And then to Maas: "Collect your stuff, Alex. We'll meet you upstairs in five minutes."

Maas nods and watches Rooker and his security team depart. Then his eyes meet mine. "Thank you for staying with my daughter, Mr. Fall." A pause. "And now, if you'll excuse me, I'd like to say goodbye to her."

Wordlessly, I step into the hallway off the computer room, standing there beyond the sound of the hushed voices of Maria and her father.

I'm pacing in short, aimless strides when my foot bangs up against a piece of metal, sending it skimming along the floor. I reach down to pick it up. It's a small concave satellite dish the size of a large pizza pan. But its surface isn't solid steel, or aluminum, or solid anything. It's composed of shiny—almost microscopic—silver pools of liquid, each bound in tiny translucent spheres no bigger than a grain of rice that adjoin each other in concentric circles around the dish's center

Dr. Maas steps in while I am assessing this metallic mystery. "Not much to look at, is it?" he asks, almost whimsically, and it's then that I realize what I'm holding. He takes it from my hands. "Can you believe this is what Mr. Farraday finds so frightening?"

I look at him, then glance back at the solar dish. "Does it work?"

"Oh, yes, it works. What I'm holding, it could power an entire house—indefinitely. If only we have the chance to prove it."

He bends down, in his slow arthritic motion, to set the solar dish back against the wall. As he rises, he looks across at me again. "I come from a country where people had very little, even before the Catastrophe," he goes on. "I knew the misery of not having enough, and I wanted to change that. But people in your country seem to be burdened with an enormous guilt because they've grown up in the midst of plenty. 'Sacrifice' comes quickly to their lips in times like these. To them, self-denial is the highest virtue—as long as it's someone else making the sacrifice." He pauses, then says more softly, "These are dangerous people, Mr. Fall. People who are willing to trade the freedom and well-being of others for their own peace of mind. They may speak words from the heart, but they act with the sword. If I fail, in the end, at least I tried to fight them, with the only tools I had."

"And you believe you can defeat them?"

"Believe? Yes, I believe. But will we prevail? I do not know. Sometimes a sling can defeat a sword, and sometimes not. We will have to see." He halts then, the reflectiveness leaving his face. "Enough of an old man's musings," he says. "Mr. Rooker is waiting, and I've kept him too long already." He offers me his hand, broad and warm and callused. I take it, and he wraps his other hand around mine. "I entrust you with my daughter, whom you have already defended at great peril to yourself. I have not properly thanked you for that, but I do now. I owe you a great debt. Nothing compares to the love for a child, don't you think?"

Remembering Cassie, and then Darby, all I can do is nod. Even now—even after all this time—the memories are too strong to bear.

Maas is speaking again. I abandon my thoughts and return my attention to him. "Thank you again, Mr. Fall," he says, his tired eyes regarding me, no longer with suspicion, but with trust. "I wish you well. Perhaps we will have the chance to meet again, in a city where there is not so much darkness."

"I hope so," I tell him quietly, as I watch him step away.

▼

Everything in this converted church, from the equipment upstairs that churned out Maas's solar converters to the computers below, is powered by a huge, ancient generator that rumbles and stutters beneath the floorboards. The roar was intermittent when we arrived, but since Rooker and his men left it has become continuous. The sound assaults my ears like the unbroken pounding of rain on a tin roof—merely annoying at first and then intolerable.

Or perhaps it's only the feeling of being trapped in this isolated mountaintop refuge, where we are the easiest of prey, almost inviting Rojo and his men to find us. And because I have no more control over our fate now than I did then. I stand as I did in the solar plant, watching Maria while she works.

And waiting, helplessly, for the enemy to track us down.

"Are you almost finished?" I ask her.

"Two or three more minutes. I'm almost—" she starts, but doesn't finish. All at once, the roar of the generator becomes a wheeze. And then nothing. The lights flicker and fail. I tense, reacting as if the power lines outside had been cut. Except, of course, there is no outside power here, only this rickety old generator, kept alive by the fuel that Rooker was able to steal.

And then, in the next instant, the generator returns to life. The lights come back on. The roar and clatter resume, bringing a moment's relief. But the computer screens have gone dark, and they stay that way. I'm assuming the network will have to be rebooted, which will add another ten or fifteen minutes to our stay.

Maria, frayed and weary, holds her head in her hands for a few seconds, and then looks up. "Do you know anything about generators?"

"A little."

"Could you adjust the intake valve or whatever is causing this racket, and maybe I'll be able to finish without the thing stalling again."

"How do I get to it?"

She points to a slatted ground-level panel in a side wall, wedged behind a row of metal shelves. I head there, flexing open the panel to expose a narrow flight of decayed wooden stairs that lead down to a sub-basement. I take a flashlight from a nearby shelf and climb through the small opening. Then, for some reason I don't consciously realize, I pull the panel closed before descending.

The last image I have is of Maria, switching on the servers, attempting to restart the network.

As I reach the bottom of the stairs, I find myself standing in a dank and cramped cell, squeezing between a crumbling cinder block wall and a bloated, ungainly engine that looks for all the world like the one that my grandfather pampered in an old wooden shed behind his barn. By the thin light of the sub-basement's solitary bulb and the even dimmer flashlight, I go to work on the generator's intake valve amid the misty memories of childhood summers on Granddad's farm. Eventually, I become so engrossed in the chore at hand that I do not recognize the sounds of intrusion up above until it's too late.

And then I do. Low, muffled voices and abrupt movements are coming from directly overhead, barely audible over the now-muted roar of the generator. And then: harsh, angry sounds, the clatter of metal on concrete, the sliding of wood across the floor. I quickly extinguish the sub-basement's sole light. And then, pistol in one hand, flashlight in the other, I stand dead still. Listening. Thinking. Overcome again by the feeling of confinement and helplessness that gripped me mere moments before.

Except now, its source is real.

There has to be another way out, I think. With the flashlight pointed toward the rear, I scan the dim gray room, anxiously searching for an exit. There *is* a door, I see, leading to another part of the sub-basement, but it's blocked by the feed pipes from the underground oil tank. The tiny opening is impassably narrow, leaving the stairs that I descended as the only alternative. With quick quiet steps, I take them, guided by my floorward-pointing flashlight and the slivers of fluorescent light filtering in through a vent in the computer room's side wall.

And, in seconds, I'm at the top of the stairway, peering out into the computer room. I see what I feared: Rojo and four other men. Two of his men stand off to the side, automatic rifles held across their chests. The other two are positioned directly behind Maria—one man on each arm—holding her immobile while Rojo faces her. His back is toward me, and I cannot see his face, only the bandages on his arm from the injuries he must have suffered at the solar plant. Even from this angle, his posture is proud and victorious.

But victory isn't his yet. Not completely. He still doesn't have all the answers.

"He left," Rojo snarls. "Yes, thank you. I can see that he left. So I ask you again: *where did he go?*"

"I'll die before I tell you."

"*Si, chica, es possible,*" he says calmly. "*Es possible.* But it will be a slow death, And a very disagreeable one." He looks away briefly to let the threat register. Then he leans close to her face, allowing me to see the edge of his leer. "When did he leave, Doctor? Not too long ago, I think. Am I right?"

Maria says nothing. Enraged by her silence, Rojo rams her across the face with the back of his hand. Her head twists from the blow, and blood begins to drip from the corner of her mouth. The others stand watching, grimly amused.

I'm losing it now. I can rip this slatted panel away and shoot Rojo where he stands. Probably take out one or two of the others as well until I am shot dead myself. All of my being compels me to take this step. My hate and frustration and, yes, my own barely suppressed death wish nearly overcome all sense of caution. But I wait, stopped only by some last thread of reason, by the knowledge that Maria will either die or be whisked away the moment I step into view.

I can only look on, desperate, able to do nothing. "It's over, *querida,*" Rojo says, dabbing the blood from Maria's mouth with a handkerchief as if rendering her a delicate favor. "I will find your father. He will come to me—because I have his daughter." He turns away, dismissively. "*¿Qué lástima, no?* All of this because of a crazy old man."

They won't kill her now, I realize. Not yet anyway. Like Rojo said, they'll try to use her as bait to lure her father back to them.

I grope for restraint.

But Maria isn't finished with him. "You're too late," she spits at Rojo. "You and Farraday both. It's *done.* Nothing you can do will stop it.

Don't, please, I think, wishing she could hear my thoughts. *Don't provoke him, not now. Give me time. I'll find a way. Please.*

And yet I can only stand where I am. Waiting, as helplessly as ever, for Rojo's reaction.

It comes in an instant. He grimaces at Maria's outburst, clearly torn between what he has been ordered to do and what he wants to do. He raises his gun, aiming it directly at her forehead, then just laughs and shakes his head before pulling the pistol away. He turns to the guards. "Get her out of here! Now!"

The two men who have been holding Maria pin her arms behind her and shove her toward the spiral stairs, while the other two collect the backup disks that Maria had been archiving. And then they too depart.

Rojo stays back for a moment, glaring after them hatefully. Then he tosses an open lighter onto a pile of papers that quickly begins to incinerate everything in the room.

▼

"They've got Maria," I tell Rooker abruptly over the cell phone he left with me, after I'm sure that Rojo and his men have gone. It's half an hour later, and the fire that Rojo started has begun to consume the entire front quarter of the church. I barely escaped before the downstairs was overcome.

"*Who's* got her?" Rooker asks urgently. "Is she all right?"

"Rojo." I spew the name like the venom it has become. "She's all right for now. They're holding her hostage. But the two men you left outside are dead. And the building's in flames. Everything's gone."

"Stupid, stupid, stupid!" he declares over a heavy sigh, and I'm not sure whether he's referring to Maria or the two guards. Or me. "Where are they taking her?"

"I'm not sure. But there's no time for this, Rooker. Just listen to me. Don't do *anything* until you hear from me again. No announcements. No demonstrations. *Nothing.* And keep the doctor under wraps as well."

Rooker doesn't respond immediately. I can feel the tension growing on the other end of the line. "You don't understand," he says at last. "We *can't* wait. If they've got Maria, then they've got Maas's data. They scan those disks, and they'll know exactly what's going on. The demonstration takes place tomorrow morning as planned, or it won't happen at all."

"You'll *kill* her!" I erupt. "Doesn't that mean anything to you?"

"Yes, it does," he says. "It means a great deal. But so does everything else we've been working for. And that's something we *can't* give up."

"So you'll just let her die?" I ask, disbelieving.

"No," he says firmly. "I'm counting on you to save her. You've done pretty well so far." He hesitates, then says, more compassionately, "Listen, Martin. Maria, you, me—we're all expendable. But what we're doing *isn't*. If Farraday manages to crush Maas's discovery, someone else will come up with the same thing in a year. Or two. Or five. *Maybe*. But I don't want to be responsible for the millions more who will die or have their lives destroyed in the meantime." A beat. "Do you?"

I don't give an answer to this because there isn't one.

"Once the demonstration has taken place, Maria is worthless to Farraday, and they probably *will* kill her. That gives you twelve hours to find her. So think: do you have any idea where they might have taken her?"

"No," I tell him after a moment, forcing myself to accept the obligation that Rojo and Rooker once again have conspired to place upon me. "I don't know where she is." A beat. "But I know who might."

"Good," is all Rooker has to say. "Then I'll let you get to it." He almost rings off, but I hear him start and then stop. At length: "Oh, and one more thing. Those disks that Maria was working on. I'm assuming Rojo took those as well?"

"Yes, he did."

"It's imperative you get those back, Martin. Without them, there's no way we can replicate Maas's work. And so anything we do tomorrow," he says, "will be just a sideshow. Nothing more."

▼ ▼ ▼

The buses leave from Kingman every thirty minutes, but we are not the first in line. Hundreds of people wind in front of us, snaking around the tall orange cones and orange-striped barricades the workers have set up—haggard blue-shirted men and women who scurry about like refugees from an abandoned theme park. But after fourteen hours of waiting, of protecting our spot against the press of foul-smelling flesh and unwashed clothing, of holding Darby close to me while relying on Santos to stare away those who would molest or confront us, we are asked to present our travel papers to the Hispanic security agent at Gate 4B.

At length, after a long series of probing questions and all-too-personal pat downs, we are permitted to climb on board.

Echeverria left shortly after dropping us off in order to return to his home in Flagstaff. I gave him Ray's van so that he could drive by himself rather than having to endure the indignities of the buses—a perquisite for which he was deeply grateful. He promised to safeguard our meager possessions, most of which we were forced to leave behind. Like the airlines before they stopped flying, the bus lines have been ordered to limit baggage to a single suitcase and one carry-on per person. Each of us spent a considerable time repacking our belongings so that our most important items were collected into a single bag. Then Darby chose her large stuffed penguin as her carry-on, while Santos and I opted for tote bags full of food. The remainder of our clothes and supplies went with Echeverria, who said he would ship them to us whenever delivery services started operating again.

We were allowed to bring Pepper with us, but only after a heated dispute and the payment of an additional fee that may or may not have been part of prescribed policy. The baggage clerk—a tight-faced Chinese woman with an attitude as truculent as the overdose of medicinal perfume she was wearing—initially refused to consider our request, sniveling that "things like that should be euthanized so the rest of us can breathe." Even Darby's tears that burst forth at this harsh dictate did not temper the woman's belligerence, and it wasn't until a supervisor was snappishly summoned, a nonstandard-package fee was paid, and explanations were given that Darby was ill and needed the dog's companionship for her health that we were finally permitted to take him with us.

I hold Pepper's leash in my free hand as we stand waiting to board our bus. But the dog presses himself against Darby, like an eternal guardian, and I realize then what the presence of this simple animal has done to keep Darby composed when her mind must be spinning with dark and tragic *recollections. Like the too-large stuffed toy she carries with her or the seemingly random trinkets she carefully deposited in her pockets before we sent our luggage off with Echeverria, the otherwise mundane and ordinary become precious beyond measure when imbued with the magic of memory.*

I have observed this alchemy in my own life over the past several days, more so than at any time in the past. I am immersed in thoughts of my home—of our home, when Jeannie and Cassie and I shared it. The images and sensations that come to me in these moments are as real as they would be if I were physically present. I smell the intoxicating aroma of the overflowing breakfasts Jeannie would cook on Sunday mornings. Hear the bubbly sounds of preteen excitement emanating from the Disney Channel or some unrecognized cartoon downstairs. Look out the front window at neighbors tending to the final weeding or mowing of autumn. This was life—my life—and its memory is what carries me *through, when chaos and hopelessness threaten to overwhelm.*

As such recollections continue to play out in our individual minds, we are allowed to step onto our final transport home—a run-down yellow school bus that was likely removed from regular service years ago. We are systematically pushed, prisoner-style, toward the rear of the bus, where we are jammed three to a seat. Even with average-size people, the seating arrangements would be uncomfortable, but with a big man like Santos joining us, they are positively claustrophobic. He tries to sit on the edge of our seat, with half of his large frame jutting into the aisle. But every time he does this, the attendants tap his shoulder with their batons, forcing him to crowd Darby and me so closely that the only way we can breathe is for me to hold Darby on my lap while Santos holds Pepper.

It is but a small sacrifice, however, I tell myself. At least we are going home.

As the bus finally pulls out into the dead of night, headed toward Interstate 40 and then west into California, I notice that each bus is now escorted by an Army vehicle and that a military police officer has stepped on board and positioned himself in the bus's center aisle for added protection. I quickly learn to appreciate their company. It is the first time the three of us have been on the interstate since leaving Colorado Springs, and as the freeway unravels through the dry barren desert, I am witness to the catastrophic transformation that has taken place all around us.

he freeway's centermost lanes have been cleared, but the outer lanes are littered with almost unbroken chains of abandoned cars and trucks. Many are burned and charred. Most have had their windows smashed, their trunks jimmied open, their tires blown or shot out. I can imagine the backstory. Isolated and unprotected vehicles were disabled. Possessions were looted. Occupants were killed or left to die.

It is the new price, I realize, for a loaf of bread or a tankful of gasoline.

When the moonlight permits, I look beyond the freeway, and the visions revealed are no more pleasant. All around us, intermixed with the decaying corpses of dead birds, coyotes, and larger animals, I can see uneven lumps lying at the sides of the road. Some are draped with sheets or tarps and some are not. I can assume only that these are bodies that have not yet been recovered, people stranded while trying to walk or crawl for assistance or else killed by assailants while they were trying to flee. Sometimes, I catch a glimpse of a dark shadow within the vehicles themselves, and I conclude that these are other victims of circumstance who were not even able to leave their cars. Together, the dying and deceased are a feast for the vultures circling overhead, totems of darkness in an ink-black sky. Mercifully, Darby sleeps through all of this, and even her nightmares must be a welcome retreat from these obscenities outside.

And then there is the air itself. Throughout our journey, a dry, searing wind pelts the bus with sand and tiny stones, and so we keep the windows closed for protection. But there is no air-conditioning in this ancient vehicle, and the heat and stench of the confined space fills us with the sickness of fever. It is all that we can do to keep tears from our eyes, and more than once I taste a stale plug of vomit rising in my throat.

When the driver himself becomes nauseated and unable to go on, we pull over and the windows and doors are opened. Some passengers step outside to relieve themselves, but the three of us remain where we are, knowing that it isn't safe to leave our seats. Sand particles blast through the bus as we wait—stinging, blinding, scratching. But at least the hot wind blows the smell of sweat and sickness from the cabin, and we are able to fill our lungs once more with the fresh desert air.

In minutes, the driver is on board again, and grinds the engine to a halting start. I look outside at the road signs as we pull back onto the freeway and notice that, at some point during the past hour, we have at last crossed into California. It is a minor achievement, so small that it almost went by unnoticed, trapped as we have been in the desert's desolation. But it is nevertheless an event of great symbolic importance.

For we are one step closer to our goal of returning to a place that—I had begun to fear—we would never even reach.

We are almost home.

CHAPTER 20

I lean back, letting the soft leather cradle my shoulders, occupying the chair as if it were my own. The room's lights are off, as they were when I entered, leaving only the moonlight to shine across the scattered personal possessions. The jacket and scarf, draped over the side chair. The designer purse. The tablet computer, turned on but in password-protected mode. A stack of unread memos and reports. And the single item that is my own. The revolver, sitting on the desk in front of me, a symbol of my mood.

The room is quiet.

And then: sounds of entry coming from the outer office, followed by tired but careful footsteps leading to the double doors thirty feet in front of me. A person returning for what she thinks is the end of the day.

But that, for both of us—despite the lateness of the hour—is only the beginning.

The doors open, and Fran Amalfi is three strides into her office before she sees me. Though her voice is hard, she is calmer that I would have expected. "Who let you in?"

I turn the white keycard over in my hands. My answer. Without Erthein here to remind her, Fran must have forgotten to change the building's security codes or to inform the guards down the hall that I had become *persona non grata*. It wouldn't have mattered anyway. I also have Erthein's gold keycard, taken from shortly after he died. My backup plan.

While Fran considers this collection of misfortunes, I reach below her desk to press the button that I discovered while waiting for her to return. Behind her, the double doors close and lock.

"Love your toys," I tell her without emotion.

Her eyes burn, and she darts to the intercom on the corner of her desk. "Get me security!"

There's not even a hum. I hold up the disconnected phone cord. "Sit down, Fran. We may be awhile."

"What *are* you doing here? Haven't you done enough damage already?"

This is Amalfi stripped bare, I think. Naked. Combative. Trumped. So I salt the wound. "I'm trying to get my job done. You hired me, remember?"

She stares at me in rage and disbelief. "That was the biggest mistake *I* ever made. You're no better than a street thug. A million dollars' damage to the solar plant last night. Two people killed. The whole plant in disarray. I didn't hire you to do *that*. I could—"

She's ranting now, almost out of control. Then, abruptly, she stops. I'm not sure if it's because the look in my eyes has convinced her that I don't care what she thinks, or because she sees the gun, lying a few inches from my hand. She turns away, moving to the window, and just stands there. Thinking. Calculating. Collecting her thoughts. This is her pattern, I realize. She went to the same spot on the day she brought me back.

"What's this all about?" she asks after a moment, turning back to face me, composed again. "Is it Mesoto? Is that it?" She looks on, certain she is right. "You know I had nothing to do with Mike's death. Rojo works for Farraday. Not for me. I'm sorry it happened. I really am. But you can't—"

"Stop the excuses, Fran. You sound like Erthein." I return her glare. Mordantly: "I suppose you're sorry about him too."

A pause. Then harder: "What do you want?"

"I want you to tell me where Rojo took the girl."

"I don't know what you're talking about."

"You know *exactly* what I'm talking about, so let's not play games. I'll ask you again: where is Maria Maas?" I speak the words in a manner than can leave no doubt as to my state of mind. "Don't mess with me, Fran. I'm almost out of time and I'm already out of patience. Where is she?"

Finally, Amalfi seems to understand that this conversation is not going to go according to script. Whether tired or defeated, she steps over to the chairs in front of the desk, the ones with the too-short legs. She pulls one out and sits down.

"You're a fool, Martin," she says at last, shaking her head. "You could have done a lot of good. For me. For this city. For all those people you supposedly care about. And instead you turn into some two-bit terrorist. You and Rooker both. This city's on the brink of chaos, and you're threatening the only institution with even a chance of improving things." She pauses bitterly. "And do you know the worst of it? You don't even know what you're fighting for."

"Listen to me. If you don't—"

"No, you listen to *me*," she cuts in, giving no ground. "None of this would have happened if Alejandro Maas had agreed to work with Farraday in the first place. The Ventura solar plant would have been online by now. We would have already started building the plants in Orange County and Riverside. And Mike and Alison would still be alive. Those are the facts of the situation—not whatever insane nonsense that lunatic Maas has been feeding you."

Her arrogance disgusts me. I wonder how misinformed she really is. "Do you even know why Farraday drove him out?"

"Because he demanded that the solar plant be shut down, that's why. Because he walked into Farraday's office with some idiotic story about miniature bio-fueled solar collectors. And when Farraday told him the design was flawed and reminded him of his responsibilities to Golden West, he quit. Stole all of the files he could walk away with. Destroyed the ones he couldn't. And left the research lab in complete disarray. *That's* your hero, Martin. That's the man you almost died for."

Our eyes meet, and I can tell that what Fran is saying isn't pretense. It's what she believes to be the indisputable truth. "Doesn't it seem odd," I ask slowly, "that Farraday would spend so much time trying to ruin Maas's reputation—even risk keeping his daughter on the payroll—if Maas were nothing but a crackpot? Or that he would send an entire army out to bring him back?"

"How Farraday spends his time doesn't matter to me. But the way he spends his money *does*. And I'll tell you this. If he hadn't stopped Maas, I would have. I saw Maas's proposal. I read Farraday's evaluation of it, and so did several people on my staff. It's worthless. A waste of money." She pauses, striving for advantage. "I presume you've seen those tin saucers he created."

"Yes, I've seen them."

"Well, let me ask you this: Have you ever seen one of them actually work?" She presses the point, hard, and I have no response. In fact, I *haven't* seen them work. I'm relying only on Rooker's and Maas's assertions that they do. But there's no sense letting Fran know that. No sense ceding the advantage to her. "Let me assure you," she goes on after a moment. "They won't work. They'll *never* work. Not in a million years."

I nod toward the outside. "Want to put it to a vote?"

"I don't put people's *lives* to a vote," she answers coldly. "I have an obligation to this city, and I intend to carry it out. Seventy million people are going to wake up in the morning expecting this Council to feed them. And our allocation system is so screwed up thanks to your friend Rooker that we won't be able to get food to half of them. *That's* what concerns me, not the wet dreams of some crazy old man."

"And what concerns *me*," I say as my hand plays over the revolver's handle "is where they took his daughter. So tell me before I have to use this thing. Where is she?"

Firm, unyielding. "I have no idea."

I pull a computer tape from my jacket pocket and set it on her desk. "Rooker thought this might jog your memory."

She looks on, suddenly interested. "What's that?"

"The last remaining copy of the city's allocation files," I tell her flatly, spinning a few feet of the digital tape from the reel. "But you're a smart girl, Fran. I bet you knew that already." She looks on, whether in horror or in calculation, I don't know. I pull a lighter from my pocket. Flip it open. Hold it up to the end of the tape. "Wanna trade?"

The tape catches fire and burns slowly toward the reel.

"Stop it! It'll take six months to reconstruct that thing. Give it to me!"

She moves closer and I pull the tape out of reach, but say nothing.

"That's enough! Don't be a complete fool, Martin. Let's talk sense."

"Start talking."

The tape burns closer. "Put the fire out. Now!"

I just glare at her. My lack of response is her answer.

And she hesitates. Half the spun-out length of tape is melted plastic now, and in a few seconds the entire reel will be consumed.

"I'm waiting," I tell her.

At the last instant: "Maria Maas is at Skylight. Now give me the tape."

I snuff out the fire, then tuck the tape back into my jacket pocket and take my gun in hand. "Good. Let's go."

"I said give me the tape."

"I will. Once we leave Skylight. And once I have Maria and her father's files back."

"What are you talking about?"

"Oh, you're coming with me," I say with a tilted smile. "Didn't I tell you? I'm afraid I've forgotten the way."

▼

We take Amalfi's official car, a sleek Lincoln Continental with rich leather seats and smoked one-way windows, the ubiquitous Citizens' Council seal prominently displayed on both sides. I am sure Fran is accustomed to having her own personal driver. But tonight, at my order, she has taken the wheel herself. It's a mixed blessing. Although I can watch her more easily this way, the hydrogen-powered vehicle lurches haltingly down the street and she has trouble staying within the lanes.

"When was the last time you actually drove?" I ask her.

"I can't remember." Sharp, unsettled. Even her anger is less assured than before. *Good.* "It would help if you would put down the gun."

"I don't want you to forget where we're going."

She sneers at this, and I can imagine she would gladly ram the car into a concrete barricade or blast the horn to signal a passing security guard—anything to free her from my control—if she didn't think it would endanger her life. But she knows me too well.

She knows I'll shoot if I have to.

And so she sits there, my servant for the moment, not at all the same Fran Amalfi who showed me into her office a few days ago. I think back to what Mike Mesoto said on our first drive to the Council offices. Until a year ago, Fran was a normal human being like the rest of us. Tonight, that's what she is again. An ordinary human being, divested of the power to command. Stripped of the slavish attentions of staff members. Freed of the abundances of privilege that keep her far from the deadly precipice of day-to-day survival.

Now, like me and the millions of others in this city, she stands at the edge. The vast chasm of chaos that the city has become is spread out before her in a way that must be far more personal—and more terrifying—than the dream-colored views from her fortieth floor office.

One step too far, and she'll lose more than the perquisites of her office.

She drives on, these grim thoughts taking over her face as we pass through the security gates of downtown for the unguarded streets outside. This is the same journey that Alison and I took on my first night I was back, except that the visions greeting us now no longer surprise me. The desecrated buildings. The shadows in doorways. The tents and cardboard boxes lining the sidewalks. And more than anything: the darkness. Here, almost all of the streetlights have been broken or turned off. Even the moon, retreating behind a thick patch of clouds, seems reluctant to light our way. The car's headlights and an occasional oil-drum fire are our only illumination, and they too are consumed by the night.

We turn a corner, toward the westbound 10 freeway, and the darkness deepens. We've entered a human canyon, lined by rows of squat, gutted apartments and filled with people. Near us, human forms move aimlessly back and forth across the street, like guppies swimming in a stagnant and forgotten fish tank. But further on, the crowd thickens and movement of any kind becomes almost impossible. There is only the crush of bodies against bodies as the lost and the weary push along in a vain attempt to reach some imagined spot that's better than their own.

Amalfi presses the car forward, more comfortable now with the mechanics of driving. She refuses to slow down, refuses to recognize the human horror of these scenes around us, and the crowd slowly parts in order to make way for her, filling in spaces along the sidelines where there appeared to be none.

Faces peer into the car from these hostile berths. Apathetic faces. Hopeless faces. People surviving by default. A mother breast-feeds a newborn in plain view. Infants crawl unattended along the curb. An old man relieves himself in the middle of the street. Hard-eyed youths wield knives and deal drugs in the sight of hundreds of others. All of these visions are accented by the shouts and rumbles of dozens of strange and indecipherable dialects, the cacophony of indifference. A whole world tilting over the edge.

I look across at Amalfi and watch her unease transform into revulsion. These must be new images for her, I realize. She has read the field reports. Studied the statistics. Seen the faces one-by-one when supplicants presented themselves to her for her special afternoon consideration. But here, the faces are no longer sanitized by distance or isolation. Now, she sees in full the raw data of despair.

"Smile, Fran," I tell her. "These are your people. The ones you're feeding and taking care of. Look at how happy they are."

She doesn't answer. I wait for a moment and then ask, "What happens if you're wrong?"

She grips the wheel. "What are you talking about?"

I look away from her before I speak. "How long," I ask her, "do you think you can keep people in this condition before they refuse to take it anymore and you lose what little control you have?"

"What do you suggest we do? Fire up the factories again, who cares whether people can breathe?"

"No, but do *something,* for goodness' sake," I say, turning back. "I could give you this allocation tape right now and you'd be no better off than you were two weeks ago. These people want their *lives* back, not just a bigger ration card. And Farraday's solar plants aren't going to give it to them."

"And neither will Mass's tin saucers. I told you. They're worthless. They won't work."

"Maybe not. But isn't it worth at least *testing them* to find out?" A pause, and I bore in. "And if they *don't* work, isn't it worth finding something that will?"

She says nothing to this, merely stares straight on at the endless walls of people who line our way. Up ahead, off to the side, a fight has broken out. Waves of young men are piling on top of each other. Punches. Angry shouts. Spurts of blood.

On the perimeter, a few faces turn toward the sound of our car, bearing their animosity and frustration outward.

"All they need is a little light," I say to Amalfi as we press on. "A little hope. No one expects you to do the impossible. But if you worked half as hard trying to *improve* people's lives as you do trying to control them—"

"I don't need a lecture from you—" she starts. But before she can finish, her eyes go to the edge of the crowd. Several of the men have seen our car now and have broken away from the fight. They approach us with metal rods and broken two-by-fours, sensing an easier target. As they near, a pipe bomb bursts in front of us, and a flash of shrapnel clatters against the windshield. Amalfi jumps as if she has been shot. Tiny streams of perspiration begin trickling down her temples. She hunches forward, peering anxiously through the filtering haze.

"Better jam it," I tell her.

She responds without answering, flooring the accelerator. The car leaps ahead. The onlookers scatter before this metallic black beast, tripping as they rush to move out of the way. The men who were coming toward us charge.

The Lincoln picks up speed then, surging with a force the tiny Council Cubics couldn't dream of mustering. We race around our would-be attackers, assaulted by glares from faces filled with fungible hatreds. As our car roars beyond them, a barrage of rocks and bullets strike the back window, shattering it, sending shards of glass skimming across our shoulders. In the last second before the danger is past, the car bounces, rough and high, as if running over a speed bump.

I don't look back to see what we've hit.

We reach the freeway on-ramp, and the last of our pursuers gives up the chase. The road before us is clear.

"See how much they love you," I say.

Amalfi only glares at me. She barrels the car onto the freeway, her breaths coming more easily now. I watch her for several minutes. Even through the hard lines of her mask, I can tell that she's been frightened. But the fears are for herself, not for those she has left behind.

I tell her at last, in a soft low voice. "So help me, you're gonna fall."

She just drives on, as if rushing away from a bad dream.

▼

By the time we reach Skylight, it's well after midnight. Amalfi and I have not spoken since mounting the freeway. After watching her reaction to the people we passed, my disgust can be salved only by forgetting she is here.

We pull up at Skylight's security gate and are waved through without incident. She swings our car around to a graded parking area overlooking the complex's service bays. Here, as on the ridge where Farraday introduced Mesoto and me to this solar-powered city, we can see the entire valley floor stretched out below us. But the city is colored now only by shadows, and the matrices of silver buildings and silver matchbox homes have turned into nearly invisible shades of black. Only the solar panels rimming the valley and the wide four-story glass dome that stands in the complex's center are distinguishable in the weak starlight, and even these are specters at this hour, corners and edges without substance.

But the solar city's service bays are awash with light. As Fran and I climb out of the car and I guide her the few yards to an overlook, it's easy to make out the details of the activity below us. Dozens of service bays are cut into the concrete wall that marks Skylight's rear entrance, and large moving vans are backed up to each one. Uniformed workers rush about, unloading furniture, file cabinets, computers, boxes of supplies. And tiny bedroom sets and nightstands and apartment-sized sofas.

All of the accoutrements of a well-stocked office or home.

"I didn't think this place was going to be operational for another six months," I say to Amalfi, puzzled.

"The timetable's been speeded up," she answers matter-of-factly, evidently resigned to being a prisoner.

I look back toward the trucks and moving vans. Something about them struck me as odd a moment ago, and now I see what it is. Almost every one bears the insignia of the Los Angeles Citizens Council. Not of Golden West Power as I would have expected.

All at once, the meaning of the scene becomes clear.

"The timetable for *what*, Fran?" I demand. But my mind is racing back to Rooker's reports about the oxygen levels. The continuing atmospheric instability. The scare that Maria and I had on the beach—at *sea level* no less. I think about all of this, and I realize that both Farraday and Amalfi must have been just as aware of these portents as Rooker was.

And now Amalfi doesn't even need to respond. I stare in at her, wanting not to believe the obvious.

"This is your *refuge*, isn't it?" I burst out, struggling to take in the implications of this vision arrayed before me. "You couldn't do anything about the air, so now you're going to hide yourselves in here like the last survivors of World War III!"

She is silent, and a new expression comes to her face. It is not an expression of denial or defensiveness. There is only self-assurance, the certain confidence that she is right. "Farraday offered Skylight to the Council on a temporary basis, and we accepted." She pauses, evaluating my shock. "*Somebody* has to survive, Martin. Things are far worse than you can even imagine. I've seen the projections for a year, two years out, and the dead are measured in *billions,* not millions. This is an extinction-level catastrophe we're facing, and it's not even close to over. Somebody has to see it through, or our entire species will be gone. Permanently."

I don't even let her last words register. I just turn away, trying with little success to process what she has said.

And she goes on, hard and insistent, speaking to my back. "The world is dying!" she spits out. "You talk about giving people a new source of power—their own *private* source of power—as if that were a good thing. But then we're back in the same destructive cycle again. If people can do whatever they want with their lives, they'll only make things worse for everyone. Can't you see that? Are you really that blind? If it's not carbon dioxide or nuclear weapons or terrorism, it'll be something else. And next time, we may not even have the *chance* to survive."

I turn back and see that she hasn't moved. Her eyes penetrate me, challenging me. But I still can't form the words to answer. "Maas's tin saucers *won't work*," she goes on. "And even if by some miracle they did, the results would be disastrous. Think about it, Martin. As terrible as this situation is—and as catastrophic as it's likely to become—there has been one small bright spot. We've finally gotten control over the waste and greed and unbridled self-interest that brought us here. Once we get the other solar plants online, we can run this city—and this country—the way it *should* be. For *all* of the people, not just for the millionaires and billionaires. Maas's solar cells would make that impossible. *He* would hold all the cards. And everyone else would have to kowtow to him, or else they wouldn't have any energy at all." A beat. "That's not going to happen on my watch. I can promise you that."

My rage deepens the longer she speaks. She must sense it, because she takes an involuntary step backward. As she does, she loses her balance and stumbles within a foot of the hillside's edge. I reach out without thinking and catch her wrist, securing her safety, but knowing as well that her life is now at my mercy. I could let go and she would fall away into oblivion. But not now, and not by my hand. There's far too much left for her to see.

And in that instant, as I'm staring into her eyes, the words finally come to me. Cold. Hard. Beyond feeling.

"Do you want to live, Fran? I ask her."

Suddenly her fear returns. She must realize how fragile her current position is, how easily she could slip off the cliff to the unyielding asphalt below. "Is that a threat?"

"*Do* you want to live?" I repeat. Harder.

This time, there's only a moment's hesitation. "Yes, of course I want to live."

"The way you want to, in that mansion of yours? Or the way somebody else *decides* you should?"

To this, she says nothing. But the answer comes in her eyes.

"Did it ever occur to you that other people might feel the same way?"

I let the words linger, staring in at her. And then finally I pull her back from the edge of the cliff, holding her wrist at her side. Her face is inches from mine, like two lovers dancing. "Now get us in there," I tell her. "Before it's too late."

▼

Fran and I are just a few yards from the long, steep stairway that leads down to the service bays when the cell phone that Rooker gave me buzzes.

"Hold on," I command Amalfi, still gripping her wrist. I pull her down with me, kneeling behind a bush, to make sure the workers below can't see us. A beat, and I click the phone on.

"Fall, this is Rooker," comes the voice on the other end. "Are you there yet?"

I have the volume turned so low that his voice comes across as a whisper, adding unneeded urgency to his already desperate tone.

This can't be good news.

"Yes, we're here," I tell him. "Your timing's not the best."

"Screw timing," he says. "Maas is gone."

"*What?*"

He got away in one of our cars about an hour after I told him about Maria. We intercepted a call he made to Farraday. He's offered a trade—"

"He did *what?*"

"Offered a trade. He thinks they'll release Maria if he turns himself in. Farraday's sending a chopper for him now."

"Great." Now I have less than an hour or they're both dead.

"It gets worse," Rooker goes on. "Maas also thinks we have his files. I didn't have a chance to tell him, and he wouldn't answer his phone when I called him back."

"I understand," I say flatly, not wanting Amalfi to know the details of our desperation. "Are you going ahead with your plans?"

"We have to. But if Farraday has both Maas *and* the backup disks, we couldn't recreate the protocols even if we tried. He's as good as won."

A long sigh. "All right. I'll do what I can."

"You might want to tune in to channel two-three-six on the short wave," he adds lamely. "We picked up some Golden West chatter on that band earlier. May be some help."

But even as he says it, I know it's a lie. I could hear every word Farraday's people were saying and I would still be on my own. The only help I'm going to get is from the person crouched beside me.

I click off the phone and turn to Amalfi. "Let's go, Fran."

She shrugs, grim-faced, and I think for a moment that she isn't going to move. But then she stands and slowly follows along with me, carefully moving along the rocky hillside as I hold her wrist behind her back. A few steps, and I entertain the fantasy that this journey is going to go smoothly, like a moonlight walk.

But then she trips, losing her balance again, and for an instant my hand slips from her wrist. In that same moment, she's free. I'm sure it's a trick. I reach out for her other wrist, grasping it more forcefully than I intended but wanting to make sure doesn't try to leave.

"What do you think you're—" I start to ask sharply, but then stop. Despite my expectations, she hasn't tried to flee. Hasn't even feinted in that direction.

I look down now, and see that the explanation for this diversion. It *wasn't* a trick she was planning. Wasn't an intentional slip at all. Even in the distant light of the service bays, it's easy to tell what I'm looking at, easy to see why she tripped.

In that moment, I forget all about Maas. Forget all about Maria. Forget all about Amalfi. For splayed beneath her, on the ground where she just stepped, is the carcass of a freshly dead bird.

Crushed, as if having fallen from the sky.

▼ ▼ ▼

We are halfway across the desert to Los Angeles, almost to Barstow, when our travels again come to an end. For the first time in a week, the three of us have been riding along a major freeway at posted speeds. This development offers both good news and bad. The good news is that our remaining time to Los Angeles has been shrinking more rapidly than I had thought it would, giving me hope that we will arrive at the Van Nuys bus station before noon. The bad news is that, when the right front tire on the aging and poorly maintained bus suddenly blows, the tire and wheel grate across the asphalt for almost half a mile before the bus is able to come to a stop. By then, the tire and wheel are completely destroyed.

We are fortunate that the bus didn't roll over and kill us all. Instead, it skidded like an aircraft hitting the tarmac without its landing gear deployed. Now, the beleaguered bus sits along the freeway's edge, mere feet from a long narrow gully. We sit there as well, shaken but uninjured, and are told that all we can do is wait. It will be several hours, the military police officer informs us, before either medical care or a replacement bus arrives.

Darby, Santos, and I decide to remain inside the bus for the time being. Santos stands and moves to the back of the bus to stretch his legs. Most of the bus's other occupants, on the other hand, immediately flee the vehicle's tight confines for the freedom of the cool predawn air. We are thus left alone, except for an elderly couple up front and a young mother with a baby and a toddler who sits two seats up in front of us. The false peace that descends upon us then gives me the time to inspect our surroundings.

I see at once that we are in the middle of a stark and barren landscape. The ground ahead and to the north of us is flat and extends seemingly without end. To the south, the distant mountains block out the waning starlit sky, their looming peaks featureless and foreboding. The night is silent except for the broken conversations of the passengers outside and the occasional cawing of a passing crow or the baying of a random coyote. There are no electric lights anywhere, other than the dim illumination from the bus's fading headlamps.

There is a palpable feeling of loneliness—of isolation—in this desolate setting, and I find myself praying that the freeway marauders the border guard warned us about have gone to rest until nightfall comes again.

While I am looking outside, assaying our situation, I begin to sense the presence of another person. I turn and see that the young mother in front of us has stepped up beside Darby and me. She holds her now-awakened *but nearly lifeless baby in one arm, and with her free hand pulls her young daughter to her side. The woman stands there, wordlessly, and I take a moment to study her. She is African-American, probably late twenties. And while she looks as disheveled as the rest of us after our tortuous journey, she is clearly from the professional class. Her clothes, though casual, are tailored and designer-label. Her hair is cut in a manner that suggests great care and expensive hairstyling services. Even her hands mark her. They are soft and unblemished, and her nail polish—though now chipped at the ends—is an iridescent red, a color that I suspect once matched her purse and shoes.*

And yet her eyes are as lost as those of someone who had spent a lifetime in the straits of poverty and who had now been deprived of even what little she had left.

"I'm sorry, sir," the woman says in a weak and tentative voice. "I hate to ask, but could you help us? My children . . ." Tears come to her eyes then, and she chokes them back. "My children haven't eaten in two days. I have no food, no formula. And no one wants our money." A pause. She rallies, finishes. "Please, sir, if you could help us, I would . . . we would appreciate it so much."

She lets the words trail off. She looks at me then, her eyes gentle and desperate. In the middle of the silence, I realize that Pepper has started to whimper. "Pepper has to go," Darby interjects, looking up at me. Santos steps up from the rear of the bus to say that he will take Darby and the dog outside. I nod absently, now accustomed to having Darby and Pepper in Santos's charge, and return my focus on the woman and her children.

"We have some food," I tell her. "If it would help. No baby formula. But I have a few crackers and some granola bars." I reach into my duffel bag and extract more bars and cracker packages than the woman surely expected. But my mind is called back to what the doctor in Arizona told us: "In these dark days, we must help each other."

In any even, we'll all be home shortly, and Darby and Santos and I then will have far more food than we need.

Yet the woman protests the size of my offering. "No, please, not that much," she says. "One or two will be fine."

"I insist," I tell her. I retrieve a plastic grocery bag from my satchel and fill it with the food I've collected. "Your kids need it. Please." And I'm thinking: I know you need it too.

"Thank you so much," the woman says through tears, and then turns before I can say anything more. I lean forward to wish her well, even thinking to

offer her accommodations at our home if she needs them. But before I can say anything, my thoughts are interrupted by a voice coming from the outside. Shrill. Ominous. Demanding my immediate attention.

Darby.

All at once, I forget about the woman and the food I've just given her. I race past her to the front of the bus and then bound through the doorway and out onto the hard desert surface in a single motion. I look feverishly around and finally spy Darby, off to the side. Santos has her in his arms, holding her. I think for a moment that he has must have somehow acted inappropriately or tried to harm her.

Then I follow their line of sight and the cause of this commotion becomes clear. Two young Hispanic men, probably in their early twenties, have grabbed Pepper and are sprinting off into the darkness, carrying him like a stolen treasure. I have no idea why they have taken this dog, so precious to Darby but meaningless to them.

It doesn't matter. I have to get him back.

I race after the young men, who are already a good thirty yards ahead of me. But I am in shape and the ground is flat and so I make good time, closing on them quickly. Within a minute or two, the trailing man—the one holding Pepper—is near enough that I can lunge for him. I flail at his flared pants leg, catch it, pull him down. He thuds against the desert floor, releasing Pepper from his grasp in the same motion. But the man doesn't give up. He wheels onto his back and swishes up at me with an open knife blade, just missing my chest but slicing my right arm. The wound is superficial, but deep enough that it draws blood. The long cut quickly reddens my shirtsleeve, and the blood drips in large carmine drops to the desert floor below.

I grip my arm with my other hand, wincing at the pain, and stagger back. This gives my assailant enough time to climb to his feet, and he speeds after his friend, leaving Pepper behind. Soon, both of the men disappear beyond the cone of light from the bus's headlamps, and are lost from my view.

But at least Pepper is here. Safe. In our possession again. I reach down to pick him up, grateful for his salvation, grateful that he hasn't run off.

I know how relieved Darby will be by his return.

And that's when I notice that Pepper has not moved from where he fell when the young man dropped him. The dog's skin is hot to the touch. But there is no life. No breath.

I swivel his head so that I can look into his eyes. But even before I see the death within them, I feel warmth and wetness on my palm. I pull my hand away. Study it. Rub my fingers together.

More blood. Thick and fresh. But no longer my own.

At least I know that our helpless companion died instantly from the long and vindictive knife slice across his neck.

What I don't know—and never will—is why.

CHAPTER 21

Skylight's service corridor, wide enough for a pair of tractor-trailers, extends for hundreds of yards in front of us, filled with the markers of heavy use. Scarred white walls. A cracked and oil-stained floor. Cardboard and plastic wrappings swept to the sides. Farraday must have gone to a lot of trouble, I think, in order to compress six months' work into one.

If his atmospheric forecasts are correct, it's easy to see why.

I walk beside Amalfi, my gun hidden at her side. We cleared the security checkpoint and passed through the open air-lock doors with barely a nod from the guards. They obviously knew her and didn't think to question the guest she had brought with her. Besides, the guards have their hands full checking the security credentials of the hundreds of workers hauling furniture and filing cabinets into the complex. They hurry past us on motorized dollies, rushing down the corridor's steep slope with the urgency of medics on call.

In the midst of this clamor, I am momentarily anonymous. But it's a cover that won't last. How long until I am identified? Five minutes? Ten? I don't have the luxury of fallbacks. This journey has to work perfectly, or it won't work at all.

"Where is she?" I demand of Amalfi in a harsh whisper when we're out of the workers' hearing.

"No idea," Amalfi answers. "Farraday didn't tell me, and I didn't ask." She offers a condescending smile. "You really planned this down to the last detail, didn't you?" We're no longer traveling through hostile territory as we were on the streets outside downtown, and she must feel in control again.

I respond by jamming the pistol into her side. "You'd better *get* an idea," I tell her. "We don't have much time."

"Put the gun away, Martin. I was your only way in, and I'm your only way out. You're not going to shoot me."

But as she speaks the words, her smile disappears.

"I'll say this once," I go on, "so listen carefully. If Maria Maas doesn't walk out of here, neither do you. It's that simple."

We stride on. Still no answer. I press the gun more tightly. "Where is she, Fran? *Tell me!*"

She hesitates, no doubt considering the costs of staying silent. Then, resigned again: "Probably near Farraday's office. That's the only place he can keep an eye on her."

"And where is that?"

"Off the main plaza. But you step in there and you're dead. No way you'll ever get that close."

"And if I don't, then *she's* dead, so there's really not much choice, is there?"

An indifferent pause. "If she isn't dead already."

I look at her, unforgiving. "You'd better hope she's not."

▼

Seconds later, we come to a split in the passageway. The broad service corridor continues ahead, curving around to encircle Skylight. Directly to our right, a wide doorway opens onto an underground street, one of the sixteen residential spokes that leads into the heart of the underground city. I know we'll have to take one of these eventually, despite the risks of being seen. They're the only path to the plaza.

"Which way?" I ask Amalfi.

She points toward the street. "This one's as safe as any."

We duck through the portal that leads onto the street, holding close to the edge to keep out of sight. The street, a corridor half the breadth of the one we've just left, is identical to the underground street that Farraday, Mesoto, and I traversed during Farraday's showman's tour only days before. The cobblestone lane, bordered by the slowly moving sidewalks. The tiny half-finished houses, with their Norman Rockwell décor and their shingled roofs angling toward the ceiling. The images of the sky projecting continuously above us, accented by artificial breezes and the flitting of animatronic birds.

As before, scattered carpenters and electricians work inside some of the houses. But now these crews have been joined by workers who busy themselves unpacking and arranging the homes' furnishings, readying them for the arrival of Citizens Council staff. Outside the tiny homes, the moving sidewalks have been transformed into conveyor belts. Supervisors inspect the slow parade of furniture and boxes, directing handlers to remove items as they reach their destinations.

Most of this activity takes place on the left side of the street, and so I pull us over to the right, pacing inside a long row of filing cabinets that moves along the sidewalk toward the city's center. Amalfi walks beside me, hostile but obedient, perhaps recognizing at last that there's as much danger here for her as there is for me.

Or perhaps she's simply desperate for the computer tape that I still have with me in my jacket pocket.

"Farraday's office," I ask her. "What level is it on?"

"The fourth, I think."

"You *think?* Not good enough."

"I've only been there—"

But I don't let her finish. We've gone half a block, and I can clearly see the corridor that crosscuts across this one a hundred feet or so ahead of us. Rounded curbs. Painted crosswalks. Decorative street signs. All of the appointments of a real urban intersection. There's even a group of people standing at the corner, talking and sipping coffees. Two of the men—probably supervisors—I haven't seen before. But the other man, the one giving the orders, is someone I recognize at once.

Luis Rojo.

Amalfi spots him at the same moment I do.

To my right is an open doorframe, leading into one of the small unfinished houses. Before Amalfi can say anything, I grab her by the arm and push her through. I press her to the floor, one hand over her mouth and the other readying my gun. My eyes scan the home's interior, looking for workers, security men, anyone. But the house is empty. One mite of good fortune. I lift Amalfi to her knees and we crawl to the window frame. I peer down toward the intersection. Rojo and his supervisors are still there, unaware of our presence.

I remove my hand from Amalfi's mouth but keep my gun on her. "I thought you said this was safe!" I whisper harshly.

"I didn't *know* Rojo would be here!" I watch her eyes as she says this. The artifice is gone. She's telling the truth: she *didn't* know. "This isn't like the solar plant," she snaps. "You can't just put on a fire coat and expect no one will notice. They're *looking* for you."

"Then how do we—" I begin, but stop. A moment's thought, and the answer is obvious. "They aren't looking for *you*."

"What do you mean?"

The idea is still forming and I don't have time to answer. I'm taking in the contents of this tiny house. Scraps of paneling. A can of paint. Loops of electrical wire. Nothing we can use.

Then in the corner . . . *perfect*. A long heavy wrench. I retrieve it, keeping my eye on Amalfi, then return to the window. I look across to the far sidewalk, which continues to slowly port its freight away from the intersection where Rojo and the other two men are standing. As I watch, I see for the first time that the moving sidewalks are not continuous strips. Instead, they are composed of short belted blocks that feed into one another, like the sections of an assembly line. Several yards behind us, the metal belt that covers one sidewalk panel has been partially stripped away, exposing the gears beneath.

An answer.

Amalfi's eyes follow mine. "Jam it in the gears," I tell her, handing her the wrench.

There's no reaction. I hold the gun closer. "*Do it!* And remember, we *all* leave or no one does. You do anything to attract Rojo's attention, and you're history. Is that clear?"

She doesn't speak or move as I release my grip on her arm. In this instant, we both speculate as to whether I will make good on the threat. It's a life-or-death decision for her, less so for me. I wait here and I'm dead; she calls my bluff and I'm dead. Only her life is in question, and I don't know what to expect as she steps from my grasp, through the doorframe, and back out into the street.

My gun poised, I edge nearer to the window and watch as she walks the few quick strides to the conveyor belt's gear shaft. Masked from the workers' view by a six-foot-high stack of boxes that stands next to the belt, she crouches there, examining the gears, and I can't quite tell what she is doing. In the pause, I glance toward Rojo, to make sure that he hasn't moved. I'm relieved to find that he hasn't.

Then I look back at Amalfi. But she hasn't moved either. She's still there, bowed before the sidewalk.

Do it! I silently command her. *What are you waiting for?*

And suddenly I know. She must be sizing up her own escape, probing for some way to maneuver out of my line of fire. I realize with the sickness of certain death that this was not a good move after all. That the long chase has finally come to an end.

But I'm wrong. In the next instant her hand flashes to the sidewalk, and she slips the wrench into the mesh of gears. Then she's up, striding quickly toward me, back into the house. *Done.*

"Are you satisfied?" she asks sharply.

I silence her, pressing her down below the window. We wait, listening. In seconds, there is a harsh metallic screech, and the jimmied panel clatters to a stop. But the other sidewalk panels feeding into it keep moving, propelling their freight forward. Towering boxes of furniture start piling up. Glass fixtures shatter. Heavy equipment tumbles off to the side. For a moment, the sounds are no more than the white noise of a construction site. Then they're transformed into a loud and continuous cacophony, the destruction unmistakable.

One of the supervisors at the intersection is the first to look up, followed by Rojo and his men. In one swift motion, they dart toward the collision.

"¡*Idiotas!*" Rojo erupts as he runs past.

The three men pull up at the malfunctioning panel. One supervisor searches desperately for the turn-off switch while the other tries to remove boxes from the still-functioning panels before more damage ensues. Rojo looks on beside them, angrily assessing the situation, kicking debris out of the way. With all of them standing there—consumed by this momentary crisis, their backs toward us—we have a fleeting chance.

I suspect it's the last grant of invisibility we'll have.

In that instant, I pull Amalfi to her feet and out the door. We rush in the opposite direction, toward the center of the complex, away from Rojo and his men. In seconds, we move through the intersection where they stood only moments before. And then we're beyond it, entering the last long row of houses before the escalators. Here, there are no workers to watch our passage, but also no large boxes on the moving sidewalks to hide us from view. We are in the open, easy targets again. But there's no choice but to rush on.

I only hope that Rojo doesn't look this way.

I glance over my shoulder as we head on, peering back toward the pile-up, and see that someone has finally shut down the sidewalk. But it has been done abruptly, causing other boxes and pieces of furniture down the line to sway and fall over. Rojo stands there fuming, his attention riveted on the calamity at hand. He could still see us if he looked our way. But he doesn't, and soon we're out of his sight and running on.

We reach the bank of escalators that descend the remaining four stories to the plaza, overlooked on either side by the towering silver walls of offices. I pull Amalfi along and we take the moving stairs as fast as we can without attracting notice. The downward escalators are empty, a small blessing. A few workers glide up the escalators opposite us, but they are engaged in their own conversations, and pay us no heed. Still, I watch them with quick and anxious glances, looking for any security men in their midst.

I know we can't be lucky for that much longer.

I am so focused on avoiding detection, in fact, that I almost miss the first, barely audible transmission that hisses through the earpiece attached to the cell phone that Rooker gave me. I have dialed into the short wave channel he suggested, but there have been no sounds so far. Until now. What I can hear is only a murmur at first. But then, as the static dissipates, the voices become clear.

"Skylight Tower, this is Golden-Three. Do you copy?" comes one of the voices.

Static again. And then the tower: ". . . missed that. Could you repeat?"

"I say, we're about ten minutes out. Have Security to meet us at Helipad Four to escort our passenger to Mr. Farraday's office."

"Pilot," another voice interposes, and I realize that it's Farraday himself. "What is Dr. Maas's condition?"

And then it strikes me. Maas is arriving sooner than I had expected. *Much sooner.* And if he's headed for Farraday's office, the whole area will be crawling with security people, even more than it ordinarily would be.

If I don't find Maria before then, I won't have a chance.

Amalfi and I dismount the escalator as we reach the plaza level. I almost turn down the transmission but think better of it, and am still listening as the pilot goes on.

"The passenger is strapped to his seat," comes the man's voice. "We've had to go to masks, so he's been fairly coop—"

"You've had to do *what?*" Farraday again.

"Go to oxygen masks, sir. "The O-2 readings outside aren't stable, and the chopper won't hold a seal."

More static, more raucous than before, and then I lose the transmission altogether. But I don't need to hear more. What I need to do is contact Rooker, tell him about Maas, tell him about the oxygen levels. But I can't risk it. If I can eavesdrop on Farraday, he may be able to do the same with me. *For all our sakes*, I think, *Rooker had better be monitoring the channel himself.*

I turn to Amalfi. "How far is Helipad Four from Farraday's office?"

"Three or four minutes by tram. Why?"

"Don't ask," I say, recalculating our chances as I guide her along the short, wide corridor that leads out onto the plaza. We stand there for a moment in its entryway, taking in a view that I saw for the first time mere days ago. The broad circular concourse, laid out with earth-colored tiles, several hundred feet across. The ring of empty shops at ground level. The rings of equally empty apartments and offices for eight stories above that, each ring fronted by a walkway that looks down on the plaza. Leaning against the far railings, the construction derrick, unmoved since I last saw it, reaching upward toward the octagonal glass dome a hundred feet up. And, off to their right, across the plaza: the twin oxygen tanks, seven stories high. The solar city's air supply.

Farraday will need those tonight if the pilot's air readings are accurate.

But there's something else that draws my attention even more than the derrick or the oxygen tanks. Something that wasn't here the day that Mesoto and I toured the complex: a swarm of security guards encircling the main level of the plaza, standing with their rifles in hand, ready to take down anyone who should not be here.

Like us.

"Where's Farraday's office?" I press Amalfi.

She nods toward a lighted corridor leading off the circular walkway, four stories up, on the opposite side of the plaza. Two security men stand at the entrance. We'll need a miracle just to get that far, much less go beyond.

"Is there a back way in?"

"Sure," she answers, mocking me. "Straight from the helipad."

I grimace, but say nothing. I use the moment to feverishly scan the plaza, searching for another route in. We can't stroll across the concourse, and there's no time to go all the way back to the service corridor to take one of the other walkways. We'd be in clear view of the guards in either case. No problem, if they don't recognize me.

But if they do, I'm dead. I can't take that chance.

And then there's Rojo. How soon until the moving sidewalk is repaired and he returns to Farraday's office? Surely, he'll come back to meet the good Dr. Maas in person. He may already be on his way. And when he arrives, I won't need to wonder about being recognized.

There's only one answer: somehow, we have to stay hidden until we're a few steps from Farraday's office. And we have to get there in minutes, well before Rojo and the others do. Even if we ran straight across the plaza and up the nearest flight of stairs, we would be cutting the time close. And if we wait any longer—

But as I think it, my eyes go back to the opposite side of the concourse and then to the oxygen tanks. The tanks are steel silos, their surfaces unbroken except for the pipes extruding from the tanks' sides, one set of pipes per level. The pipes appear to snake behind the rows of apartments, and my guess is that they're the feedpipes for the individual units. If so, the main pipes must run along the outer circumference of the complex, which means—

That's it! I realize it with a start. The solution races through me like an electric shock. There has to be an external service corridor of some sort that provides access to the feedpipes. And then the memory comes back to me, noticed only subconsciously when I saw it before. A few steps back, just after we left the escalators, there was a metal doorway hidden in a service alcove.

I think it was open.

I turn around, pulling Amalfi with me, and rush for the doorway. It's right where I remembered seeing it. A service entrance, flush along the wall. The sign bolted to the door reads as expected: "Filtration."

But the door is no longer open. I reach for the handle, hoping that our luck will hold, but somehow knowing it won't.

And it doesn't. The door is locked.

No good! But I'm still looking around. A technician is kneeling nearby—a young Caucasian fellow with spiked red hair and tattoos all over both arms—fixing a damaged heating gauge. A loop of keys dangles from his belt. I don't even think. I have to risk it.

"Could you let us through here? We've got to finish this inspection," I tell him as casually as I can.

He looks up, assessing me. Amalfi and I are in business suits and he's in a service uniform, so his choice is easy. *Don't mess with the suits.* "Sure, man, no skin off my teeth," he says. He spins through the keys until he finds the right one and then steps to the door and unlocks it. "Just make sure it shuts all the way when you come back out."

"Gotcha," I reply, but he's already gone from my mind. Amalfi is through the doorway and I follow as the door slams behind us. We pace the twenty feet or so through the entry hall, and then I pause for a moment to get my bearings. The hall Ts to a dead-end. On either flanking side runs a narrow passageway that follows the curvature of the plaza. I look up and see that I was right about the feedpipes. Above us is a broad air duct, with smaller pipes jutting every few yards into the interior walls—presumably into the individual apartments and offices. More important, the passage widens as it goes, and I can make out an open stairway a few dozen yards to the left, connected to the upper levels.

"This way," I tell Amalfi and lead her in that direction. We reach the stairs, and I bound up as fast as I can, pulling her along with me. But she's lagging, and so I pause for a few seconds on the fourth level to let her catch her breath. In that moment's silence I am able to hear the next transmission from the helicopter.

It isn't good news.

A bristle of static, and then: "We've got a problem, Skylight."

The tower: "What's the trouble?"

"Is Farraday still in the comm room with you?"

"Negative. He's gone back to his office. What's the trouble, Golden-Three?"

A long pause. After a moment, the static again. And then: ". . . back rotor. Repeat, we've lost our back rotor. It's jammed. Something fell into it. It looks like— like a bird. A seagull, maybe. Three or four of 'em actually. It's like they just fell from the sky."

"Say again."

". . . birds of some kind. We're shutting the rotor down to do a visual—"

Amalfi, who can't hear the transmission, looks at me oddly. "What are you—"

"Shhh," I tell her, pressing my hand against the earphone. The voice is crackling, almost inaudible.

". . . can't keep it stable much longer." The pilot again, his voice calm and professional, as if the problem were routine. "Better clear the other helipads just in case. And have the fire crews stand—"

And then the sound's lost, drowned out by a piercing roar of static. My mind goes to the man on board, the passenger who volunteered for this flight. *Alejandro Maas.* I pray that he lands safely.

And then I think: not *too* safely. If the landing's a bit rough, maybe it will distract Farraday enough that he'll have to depart his office again. Maria will be left unattended or watched only by a guard or two. Easy, compared with the alternative. We could have her out of the complex before Farraday even misses her.

If he leaves his office. *If* Maria is there. And *if* we make it.

It's a lunatic's gamble.

But whatever the odds, the one certainty is time. The helicopter can't be more than two or three minutes away. We've got to hurry.

"Come on," I say to Amalfi. We race along the curving utility corridor. Past the backs of the unoccupied apartments and offices. Through the bowels of this city of Farraday's dreams. From this perspective, Skylight looks nothing like the architectural feat that it is. Just concrete and pipes and dripping water. A place for the dead, or the soon-to-be. Even the lighting is funereal. We could be running through the sub-basement of any of a thousand skyscrapers or the hidden passages of some domed city on the moon. *Or*, I think, *the service corridor of a very large morgue.*

I choose not to dwell on it. I know if anyone dies tonight, I will be among them.

I can't worry about that now.

We rush on. In seconds we reach the end of the passageway and find ourselves facing a door that's a match for the one that we entered on the main level. If my sense of direction is correct, we should be right next to the seven-story oxygen tanks. I edge the door open, peering outside, and see that my guess is a good one. The tanks are just a few yards away, across a stretch of industrial metal flooring. I open the door a few inches more, scanning the service alcove.

Empty.

We step out.

The walkway that runs in front of the apartments and offices is just ahead of us, only several steps away. Then around to the right, fifty or sixty yards further on, is the corridor that leads to Farraday's office. *If* Amalfi was telling the truth. But I have no choice but to believe her. My only concern is whether we can make the journey without being seen by the guards below.

The two guards standing at the entrance to Farraday's corridor are another matter entirely. I'll have to find a way to deal with them. No option there.

"Here's what we'll do," I tell Amalfi, thinking quickly. "We'll walk past the corridor once to see what we're facing. When we reach the derrick, we'll turn around and head back."

"And then what?" she asks, condescending again.

"And then you get us through. Make an excuse. Say something. I don't care what. Just do it." I nod toward my gun, now hidden beneath my jacket. "And remember: I'll use it if I have to."

She shrugs, and I can guess that she is calculating again whether to call my bluff. Not that she'll need to. Most likely, one of Farraday's guards will recognize and disarm me before I have the chance to do her harm, regardless of what she might say. She must know this as well as I do, and so her nonchalance isn't surprising. In fact, if I *am* caught, she'll be the hero for bringing me into Farraday's grasp, and that has to work to her benefit.

And then all at once I understand why she didn't mount more of a fight when I demanded that she bring me here. And why she has been so compliant since we arrived. It wasn't the gun. It wasn't even the promise of the computer tape. It was the chance to buy peace with Farraday, through a sacrifice that will cost her nothing.

A simple trade: me in exchange for whatever she wants.

I'm furious again, but can't let it slow me. Not now. I take only a second to cast her a hostile glance. *You still aren't going to win.*

But even as I think it, the sudden, sour taste in my mouth tells me that she almost certainly will.

"Let's go," I grumble, and we walk the few steps through the service alcove and then move out onto the fourth-level walkway. In that instant, we are completely exposed, in plain view of any guard who might happen to look up toward us. Perhaps, I'm thinking, they will see nothing amiss even if they do spot us, or will trust their counterparts outside Farraday's corridor to deal with us.

But I shut out the possibility and the portent that it brings. Shut out all sights and sounds other than our objective. I can do nothing about those chances, and so there is no use thinking about them. Now, everything has to be automatic.

We have to act.

I lead Amalfi to the right and we stride on. I feel as though we're marching through a vacuum chamber. The only sounds are the rush of our breaths and the clicking of our shoes on the concrete path, magnified against the background of the silence.

And then comes another sound, intruding above us, from well beyond the perimeter of the plaza. Soft. Rasping. Irregular. Like the roar of a distant waterfall or the beat of a dying heart when a hand is pressed against the chest.

The helicopter, I realize, on its final approach. In seconds, it will be within sight.

No time!

I quicken our pace, and we reach Farraday's corridor. And then pass it, looking straight ahead. Surprisingly, the two guards at the corridor's entrance ignore us. And down below, the same: the security men stationed around the plaza, if they see us at all, pay us no attention. I take this instant to glance down the length of the corridor that leads to Farraday's office, and like what I see. No other guards, just the light edging out from under the door that presumably leads into Farraday's suite.

Maybe, I am thinking, this will be easier than I had expected.

Maybe.

We're within a few yards of the derrick when I learn otherwise. My earpiece rages to life again, and this time there's no static. The voices are clear, so loud that if we were still walking past Farraday's corridor the guards would surely hear.

"... serious problem!" comes the pilot's voice. He's desperate now, even feverish. The professional calm from before has been completely stripped away. "*Repeat*, Tower, we have a serious problem!"

"You're coming down too fast, Golden-Three! Maintain present altitude until you're past the dome. *Repeat*, maintain—"

"That's what I'm trying to tell you! We can't control this thing anymore! The stabilizers have all malfunctioned."

"Say again," comes the tower.

"The stabilizers are gone, you idiot! The back rotor is completely out now. And the main rotor keeps stalling. It looks like another bird's dropped into it. We'll circle around, try to— There's another one! It's jammed against—"

"Divert to Helipad Two! *Repeat*, divert to Helipad Two! Fire crews are standing by. We'll put on the high-beams to guide you as soon as you're in range. We'll—"

Again, the rush of words is overwhelmed by static, and I look up through the dome. The sound of the helicopter has risen to a low hum. In the distance, I can see a point of light. Tiny but moving toward us, growing in brightness as it approaches, like a supernova about to explode against the black background of the night sky.

"I've *got* him! *Don't shoot!*"

What the— I've been so absorbed in the conversation taking place over my earpiece that for a moment I don't know what is happening. It's Amalfi's voice, right beside me, yelling toward the plaza. *But why?* I look back at her, then to the concourse. Toward the broad corridor down below where we entered. And then I know. A familiar face looms there, glaring up at me, his eyes following the line of his gun.

Rojo.

"Don't shoot, I said—" Amalfi calls out again. But it does no good. The shot comes anyway. I'm expecting it, so I duck, trying to pull her down with me. But she's hit in the shoulder. A small spurt of blood erupts, barely enough to stain her cream-colored jacket. Then a stream of red bursts forth. She spins with the impact, twisting around backward, and lands hard against the fourth-level railing where it meets the tilted derrick.

For a fraction of a second, I see Amalfi's face. It's a mask of disbelief, of utter shock. *This isn't right!* her eyes protest. *This* can't *be*.

And then I don't see her face at all. The bolting on the railing isn't finished, and the strands of metal give way with the sudden force of her weight. She falls backward, into space. I lunge for her hand, but I'm not even close. Her body thuds against the stem of the derrick, twisting around its edge. And then she slips down—limp, helplessly—to the elevated work platform affixed to the derrick's stem a few feet below. She sprawls face-first against the cold steel mesh. One arm is trapped beneath her, sprained or maybe broken, and the other slaps hard against the platform floor

She reaches up. Flailing. Grasping. Tries to pull herself up. Her hand finds a ball-tipped lever and she tugs at it. But she has only enough strength to twist it around before her arm collapses back down beside her. At first, nothing happens. And then, as if she had willed it, the eighty-foot-long crane stem swivels in response, falling away from the railing. Slowly at first and then picking up speed, like a ladder pushed away from a wall, the stem arcs through the open space just below the dome.

In seconds, its peak plunges into the apartments off to its left. With an explosion of steel and glass, the top of the stem buries itself into an unfinished apartment unit on the second level. The stem breaks through the nearby railing, snapping it and sending pieces of steel tubing flying over the edge. Midway down the stem, Amalfi is thrown against the side of the metal platform and then slides lifelessly down into its corner. She just lies there, suspended in midair, twenty feet above the plaza floor.

I think I see a flash of movement, but I'm not sure.

And I don't have time to chase it. I've dived to the fourth-floor walkway, my gun drawn. Rojo has fired two more shots, both over my head, and now he's running for the stairwell far below me. He's trailed by two other security men—all of them, I am sure, heading toward the fourth level. In this fragment of time, I look back toward the corridor where Farraday's two guards were standing. Alerted by the commotion, they have stepped out onto the walkway and see me lying there. They draw their weapons, one of them calling out for me to stay where I am. I know they're both prepared to shoot.

My only option is to fire first.

I do. The bullets strike one of the guards in the shoulder and the other in the chest, but I don't stay around to inspect the damage. I rise to my knees and barrel through the window of the apartment unit behind me, then edge back to the unit's front. In one quick motion, I replace the magazine in my pistol and peer past the window's ripped curtains toward Farraday's corridor. Both guards are lying there, bleeding. The one that I hit on the shoulder is trying to push up on his elbow. The other is not moving at all.

And then down below: Rojo and his men have reached the second level and are sprinting up the stairs. Another squad of security men across the plaza has taken note of the shots and are rushing for the stairwell near the plaza's entrance.

And then abruptly they stop. All of them. Their faces crane toward the glass dome. *The sound!* In the silence vacated by the cessation of gunfire, the helicopter's hum has become a roar, suffocating us, filling the plaza like a death knell.

And in my ear, the frantic voices of the pilot and the controller.

"Mayday! Mayday! Golden Three to—"

"Your approach vector is—"

"*Forget* the approach vector!" the pilot coughs. "We've lost— We've lost all control! We can't—"

I look up then toward these voices in the air, through the glass panels and black steel girders of the plaza's dome. The sky has become a sodium glare, illuminated by the powerful beams from multiple helipads, converging above us in an effort to lead the falling aircraft to safety. It's the negative of the image from before. Now, the helicopter is the black spot as it moves in a deathly path against the phosphorescent background of the brightly lit sky.

Behind it, dancing like curtains in some anteroom to hell, I can just make out the edges of the approaching red and yellow aurorae.

Closer. The spot resolves now, and I can see the aircraft's outlines more clearly. The front bubble. Bouncing and bobbing, as if floating on a stormy ocean. The tail. Twitching this way and that, without the barest hint of control. The whole craft shuddering as metal strains against metal.

And still it draws closer.

There are no voices come from the cockpit now, only the background sounds of chaos.

And on the stairs. Rojo, his men, the other security guards—all stopped, all staring toward the sky.

In seconds, the black spot fills the yellow beam, consuming it. I watch, unable to move, as the helicopter nears us, fighting its fatal destiny. The craft seems to fall, then catches itself, tilting wildly from side to side before falling again. As it drops, it gains a moment's stability and flies a few hundred feet more, lowering itself as if it were settling onto a gentle plain. But the spurts of stability don't last, and the craft soon begins thrashing violently back and forth again.

Seconds more. It's closer now, almost over the dome, headed toward the helipad half a mile beyond. *If the pilot can make it—*

Then, with the swiftness of a gunshot, the last of its stability is gone. A quick glint of silver shoots from the aircraft's glare—part of a rotor, broken and thrown off like excess baggage, taking with it the last of all hopes. Helpless now, the helicopter plunges forward, rolling lengthwise, headed almost straight down. Its momentum is enough to carry it a few hundred feet further, not as far as the helipad, but at least into the sky directly above the glass dome.

And then even that momentum is lost. The helicopter is a steel coffin now, plummeting in surreal motion, end over end over end.

Dropping—inescapably—toward the earth.

▼ ▼ ▼

As a soldier and police officer, I have killed dozens of men—most with the anonymity of distance, some in such close proximity that I could see their eyes and smell their fear. But I have always killed with a purpose, with dictated efficiency, and because it was my job. I have never killed in anger or for personal vengeance. But if I had been able to catch the two men last night after having learned what they had done to Pepper—and, in that same mindless act, to Darby—my restraint would have been tested as never before.

I hope enough humanity would have remained for me to have resisted that horrific impulse.

Indeed, my mind was so wrought with torment from the incident that, when we finally boarded the replacement bus just after noon, I had to ask Santos ride next to Darby for a few minutes while I sat in claustrophobic isolation on the outer edge of the seat. Since that first day following the Catastrophe, I had managed to sequester my grief and pain in the pursuit of a higher cause, that of simply returning to Los Angeles. And while the panic of loss and desperation might seep in during moments of weakness—sometimes so swiftly that I was almost overtaken before I knew it—something would always occur that would pull me back from that dark precipice and I would be in control again.

Now, I am held together only by the hope of reaching our home. I do not know how I can care for Darby—mentally, physically, or emotionally—when I can't even care for myself. But I know that I must. I know with equal clarity, however, that I can no longer discharge this responsibility amid the treachery of the road. Perhaps I have become a lost and wandering soul like so many of those who ride along with us.

Or perhaps, like a heart that has run too many races, I am merely worn down and lack the power to go on.

I am thankful in this moment for Dagger Santos, a man whom I did not even know a week ago, a man I would have likely ignored had I passed him on the street. He seems to possess an innate ability to handle even the gravest situations with courage and resolve. It may be the harshness of his own upbringing that annealed him to omnipresent pain or perhaps some natural element of his personal constitution. Whatever the source of this strength, I have come to depend upon him more than I care to admit. I would even allow myself to trust him with my life.

But that is an unnecessary concession. For in truth I already have.

Darby, for her part, spends most of the rest of our journey crying. Her *face is pressed against Santos's chest, and his firm hand gently strokes her hair. Even when Santos and I switch places and I am sitting next to her again, Darby's tears do not stop. I try to comfort her as well as I can, holding her close with one hand, taking her small hand in mine with the other.*

It is a frail comfort, I know. For my own heart is breaking for reasons not that different from her own. But it is a comfort that I also know I will need to provide to her from now on—in strength and without hesitation—beginning all too soon.

Within minutes, that time is here. Miraculously and unceremoniously, we arrive in Los Angeles. Our debarkation point is the Van Nuys bus station, only a few miles from Jeannie's and my Northridge home. In a very short while, Darby once again will have her own room where she finally can begin her recuperation. And where she can have the time alone that she surely needs in order to come to terms with her grief in a way she has not been able to thus far.

As for myself, in this moment of our travels' end, I am consumed by only one goal. All I want to do is to return to our home, to that place of pleasant memories. To bathe myself in their midst. To sleep for a thousand and one nights until I also can begin, at last, to let them go.

I realize then that this is all I have waited for during these long anguished days since Denver. Now that the time of my returning home is almost here, I am anxious, my nerve-ends exposed, my frayed and tattered mind singlemindedly focused on that one moment of salvation.

As we disembark and collect our luggage, Santos locates the appropriate city bus to take us to Northridge. I have not contacted anyone I know during these last few days, and have ignored Alison's and Mesoto's phone calls on the rare occasions across the desert when cell service was working. Now that we are in Los Angeles, I could easily summon Alison or Mike to meet us here and drive us to our house. But I prefer the anonymous transport of the city buses.

I do not want those I know to see me this way.

The bus ride to Northridge is a stark transformation from what we have experienced this past week. The long, sleek vehicle is ordinary, clean, and only half full. Were it not for the growing lines of the itinerant and frightened migrants standing along the streets, the two or three overturned cars I see, the blackened and smoldering remains of a shop or two along the way—if it were not for any of these, I would think that we had tracked back in time to the week before the Catastrophe. To a time when life was normal and, from our future perspective, calm and uncomplicated.

In the unaccustomed space of this new and freshly sanitized bus, Darby and I sit together again in the back uncrushed and alone, while Santos takes a seat across from us. The separation gives each of us time to lose ourselves in our own private thoughts. I cannot say what the others are thinking, but my own mind is filled with images of Jeannie and Cassie. Of happier times and places. Of the life that I once loved and always will. I even allow myself the luxury—one that I have steadfastly denied myself these past several days—of dwelling on these lost memories for more than seconds at a time. For at long last it soon will be safe again to embrace them, to hold onto them, in this blessed sanctuary where they were born.

The bus ride goes on. The closer we get, the more clear my memories become. I can see our house and our neighborhood in my mind long before we reach them. A quiet cul-de-sac. Modest and immaculate homes, with whitewashed siding, winged shutters, dormer windows. Minivans and SUVs are parked in driveways and along the curbs. Parents and teens wash cars and tend gardens while younger children play soccer and football on the gently sloping lawns. And then in the distance: our house, at the far end of the cul-de-sac. Blue-on-white, with the old English gas lamp that Jeannie and I installed the summer before standing proudly in front. Nearby, the first fall of brown autumn leaves are piled into a corner of the yard, waiting to be bagged and hauled away.

And then up close: Jeannie sits in our porch swing, reading or grading school papers, while Cassie kicks her soccer ball into the net at the opposite edge of the lawn. I watch these two loves of my life for endless minutes in my mind. And I think: I can't wait for Darby to join them.

Presently, that time is upon us. Of course, there is no Jeannie and no Cassie when we arrive. There is no one at all waiting to welcome our return as we disembark and walk the last block to our home. This much I had expected.

But the rest tears me apart.

There is hardly anything of our house left at all. Just a half-burnt carcass that sits before us at the end of the cul-de-sac, like an ancient ruin, or a warning. And our home is the least of the victims. Most of the other houses in the circle, the places where our friends and neighbors used to live, have been turned into hulking charcoal shells. The cul-de-sac itself is barricaded with cars and a school bus, but these too have been burned as well. The stench of rubber and sulfur floats on the air like some foul perfume.

It is Kingman in miniature, but more personal and permanent, leaving my last shred of hope gone. All of my hope gone.

I break down right there in the street, right in front of Darby and Santos. In the suffocating silence all around me, I'm kneeling on the ground and my tears and the great gasping heaves of pain won't stop. All I can do is cry out in some mad awful wail to gods unknown. The mournful blast shatters Darby so much that she has to bury her face into Santos's broad and protective arms to drown it out.

And that's when I look up and see him. A young boy, not that much older than Darby, maybe twelve or thirteen, is bounding out of the house—our house—porting random treasures. Others his same age and ilk trail behind him. They carry bags of food. Electrical appliances. Collections of DVDs. Clothes and shoes that none of them can wear. Their expressions give them away: happy, carefree, as if they have just been shopping.

I can no longer control myself. I charge after them. Grab the first boy I can catch by his shirt collar and pivot him to face me in one swift move. Glare at him as if I could kill. His happiness in his conquest transforms abruptly into terror, and his eyes burst forth with tears. "¡No me hagas daño!" *he wails.* "¡No me hagas daño!"

He's just a little boy! My mind flays me. Just a helpless, homeless, frightened little boy! And now tears come to my eyes again as well.

In that instant, I feel Santos step up behind me and grip my shoulder. I release the terrified boy's shirt collar then and he darts away toward his companions, all madly fleeing this maniac in their midst, leaving their fleeting spoils behind. Santos's other hand goes firmly to my opposite shoulder and my composure slowly returns.

But even as it does, I know that I am now a different man. A broken man. A man without place, without purpose.

A man without hope.

CHAPTER 22

The next five seconds take place in slow motion, and only after the fact am I able to sort them out.

Above the glass dome, the tumbling helicopter plummets toward the ground.

In the plaza, dozens of pairs of eyes look upward. In awe. In fear. In dread.

All around, like a sudden fog, a plague of silence immobilizes tongues and leaves mouths agape.

Footsteps die as the sprinting and sluggish alike turn to stare at the sky.

Above the dome, the spotlights' yellow glare fills with the spinning black stain descending from above.

And then: *contact.*

With the roar of a thousand bombs exploding all at once, the helicopter slaps against the steel barricade that encircles the dome, sending a shudder through the walls of the complex. Upon contact, the aircraft flips backward and the body of the craft whips toward the dome's surface. For an infinitesimal moment in time, the black bubble seems to hover above the dome, as though lying atop it. Then the thick glass panes shatter. The spider web of black girders collapses. And a shower of glass and steel storms down over the plaza.

The helicopter ricochets across the span of the girdered dome, striking the opposite side with nearly equal force. Then it plunges through the storm of glass and steel toward the far side of the concourse, as if shot from a rocket launcher. The craft's front end crashes against the second-level walkway near the toppled derrick, crushing steel and concrete alike. The resulting shock wave obliterates windows and ripples walls on every unit within hundreds of feet. The chopper's still-rotating motor coughs out the remaining rotor blade, which shoots toward the base of the oxygen tanks. It pierces the leftmost tank in the unprotected underbelly where the hardening isn't finished, puncturing it. In the same motion, the aircraft—its tail sheared and its bubble almost completely disintegrated—spins away from the point of impact, slams against the tiled floor, and rolls and skids toward the center of the concourse.

And then comes the fire. In one instant, there is nothing. And in the next, the whole craft is enveloped. A corona of flames engulfs the broken helicopter. Long crimson filaments whip skyward, followed by acrid black smoke. The sodium glare still visible through the fractured dome is reduced to fading patches and then blocked out completely. Inside the plaza the air fills with the stench of burning oil and searing flesh.

Already, even on the fourth level, it is becoming hard to breathe.

I look out over the fourth-floor apartment window, my face blackening with soot. In the moments before I move, a cannonade of sights comes to me at once.

The helicopter rolls over, the craft's skeleton outlined against the flames.

A stream of fuel leaks across the concourse, followed by a trail of fire.

The construction derrick where Fran Amalfi lay, rocked by the explosion, swivels and crashes to the floor.

Workers and security men—those still fortunate enough to be alive—rush for ground level, heading toward the exits.

And Luis Rojo, trapped by indecision, looks up at me, then looks across at the burning aircraft. The resolution comes quickly to his eyes. He'll let the flames deliver me and save himself. His decision made, he races back down the stairs and toward the corridor where he and I both entered, barking unheard commands into his radio as he runs.

In the transfixed seconds that I watch his retreat, my mind goes to the one man I know died in this crash. Alejandro Maas, an unintended victim of his own choices. If I had time, I might mourn his passing with tears. More loss, more sadness, compounding all that has gone on before.

But there is no time. I have to go.

I stand, and in the instant that I do I am jarred to the floor. The whole complex shakes with the ferocity of a small earthquake. I return to the window of the apartment and knock away the remaining shards of glass with my gun, then climb out onto the walkway. The aftershocks of the crash are immediately apparent. The helicopter had initially struck the dome on the side of the plaza by the oxygen tanks before rebounding to the dome's opposite side. The force of the collisions has now caused portions of the plaza's unfinished upper levels to buckle and collapse. In their wake, the entrance to Farraday's corridor—broad and easily passable only seconds before—has been reduced to almost nothing.

Maria!

At once, I realize she must still be there, trapped somewhere behind this rubble just a few dozen yards away. I rush to the corridor, stepping over the motionless bodies of the two guards, and pause at the corridor's shrunken opening. A triangle of space has been formed by the floor and the fallen walkway from above. It's only three or four feet wide and probably wildly unstable. But I have to risk it. It's the only way in.

I crawl through, skimming along on my knees, and in a few feet the opening widens enough that I can stand. Amazingly, I now see, the rest of the corridor beyond this mangle of steel and concrete still lies undisturbed. I race down the open passage, toward the lighted doorway that's supposed to lead to Farraday's suite.

If it's not, I have no idea where Maria is, and she's as dead as if I weren't even here.

I reach the door and pull it open, relieved that my guess was correct. But then I step into the suite, gun drawn, and the relief flees. The room is a shambles. A steel beam has crashed through the ceiling the length of the office, crushing the huge executive desk at the end of the room and flattening it atop its occupant. *Stuart Farraday.* His chair has tumbled backward with the impact, and his desk lies spread across his legs, making movement impossible. He looks up at me as he sees me, his eyes pleading for help.

Behind him, standing in neat rows against the back wall, are enough oxygen tanks to last for weeks.

"Fall, thank goodness you're here! Get me out of here!"

My thoughts come in a rush as I watch Farraday lying there.

Defenseless. Humbled by an accident of fate and trapped by his own vengeful acts. This is the man who was responsible for the death of my friends, for the near-death of Maria and myself, and for the violence inflicted on the body and spirit of Alejandro Maas. I could kill him in less time than it would take me to answer, and he knows this. I should feel triumph in this ironic reversal of fortune, in the power that has suddenly been transferred to me. But all I feel is disgust. There would be no joy in killing him nor any purpose. It wouldn't bring Mike or Alison back, and it wouldn't ease my loss.

I let him live. But he still has information I need, and so I hold onto the threat.

"Where's Maria?" I demand.

"Get me out and I'll show you. Come on!"

I ignore him, looking around the room. There are two doors along the wall to my right. One, ajar, appears to lead into a bathroom. The other is closed, and I see Farraday's eyes flash toward it in the same instant that mine do. An answer without words.

I duck under the fallen beam and dart to the door, pounding. "Maria!"

No response.

I look to Farraday, holding my gun level. "Where is she? *Now!* Or I *will* use this."

A pause, and he relents. "She's in there, but she's tied up. Get me out and I'll give you the keys—"

I don't listen to the rest, just blow away the lock with my pistol and throw open the door. There's a short hallway, leading into a darkened alcove. I step toward it, flip on the light, and see that I'm in a conference room. It's undamaged, despite the destruction outside. And then, more grace. There, on the sofa against the wall—her arms and legs roped together and tape fixed across her mouth—lies Maria.

I rush to her, removing the tape and untying the rope. "Are you all right?"

She takes a long breath before answering. "Yeah, I'm fine. What in the world . . . ?"

"You'll see soon enough. We've got to get out of here."

I pull her to her feet and lead her through the short hallway and back into Farraday's office. I glance over her. There are a few scratches, nothing more. At least they didn't hurt her.

"Okay, you've got her!" Farraday shouts when we're in sight again. "Now get this desk off me! Hurry!"

In the moment he says it, there's a rumbling from above.

Maria and I edge back under the beam and I step to the desk to see if it's even possible to free him. I know I should just leave him here. But we've got a minute or two. If we have to, we can take the rear exit, the one leading to the helipad.

I bend over Farraday and catch a glimpse of Maria's expression as she looks on. Hatred: pure and boundless. If she were the one holding the gun, she wouldn't hesitate to shoot.

"The backup disks!" she shouts.

As she says it, Rooker's comment comes back to me, that we need either Maas or his computer files if there's ever any hope of manufacture more solar collectors. We certainly aren't going to have Maas, and so the disks are our only option.

I turn to Farraday. Harshly: "Where are they?"

He doesn't answer, and his calculation becomes clear. He'll give me Maria. But not the disks. Knowing that Maas is surely dead, he also knows that these disks are all that stand in the way of the trillions he'll earn peddling his solar plants.

I couldn't care less.

"Tell me or we're gone!" I demand.

Again, there's no answer. This is a waiting game that Farraday is not used to playing, a game in which events have fallen out of his control. His slipping composure shows it. His silver hair has lost its mold, and perspiration rolls down his face. And now, even more. As I pull Maria toward the door, a whitewash of fear comes over him as if he has seen his own death.

"The safe!" he growls. "They're in the safe."

I turn back, looking toward the corner behind me. A small office safe. I should have seen it earlier. "What's the combination?"

This time, without protest, he answers. "It's unlocked. Now get me out of here!"

"Get the disks," I tell Maria, then step over to Farraday. The beam has crushed the whole left side of his desk, I now see, and the only way to free him would be to push the beam off of it. Even working together, I don't know if Maria and I could move it.

"They're all here!" Maria calls out, pulling the silver DVD-size backup disks from the safe and jamming them into a canvas utility bag that's lying on a nearby table.

"Good," I tell her. But my mind is locked on Farraday, and I step around behind the desk to see if there's any way I can free him.

As I do, the rumbling comes again from above, louder this time.

I glance at the ceiling above him. As if time had slowed to quarter-speed, I can see a long strip of acoustical tiles start to drop. Slowly. In fractions of an inch. But my mind senses what my eyes can't yet perceive, and I know that there's nothing more I can do.

I race around from behind the desk and grab Maria by the hand, then pull her toward the corridor. We hurtle through the doorway, tripping and slamming against the corridor's marble floor just as the ceiling behind us collapses—filling Farraday's office with the remains of the upper floors. Stuart Farraday's last, anguished scream is drowned out by a symphony of steel and concrete.

A moment of anguished silence passes as we lie there, immobile, waiting for the corridor's ceiling to come crashing down upon us and take our lives as well. We wait, dreading it. Expecting it. But there's nothing.

And then, all at once, the cacophony behind us ends, settling into a low roar. *We've got to get out!* I help Maria to her feet and turn to lead us down the corridor, toward the helipad. The closest exit.

Blocked.

The ceiling at the far end of the corridor must have given way at the same time the floors above Farraday's office collapsed. All that remains of this nearest exit is a mountain of girders and floorboards. If we had an hour or two, we might be able to break through. But we have minutes at best. Already I can feel the rumbling returning and taste the foul smoke as it rolls in from the plaza. And now, there's only one way we can go.

Directly toward it.

I take Maria's hand and we rush the few yards toward the opening at the plaza end of the corridor where I crawled through only moments before. It's still there, this blessed triangle of space, undisturbed by the tumult behind us. We push our way through, out of the corridor and onto the walkway.

And then stop, facing out onto the plaza, overlooking some imagined pit of hell. There's smoke everywhere. The thick, black oil-fired clouds spread out over the wide plaza and roll toward the sky. Across

363

the concourse, a broad carbon plume tumbles skyward from the helicopter, the craft reduced now to an island of ash and twisted metal. Smaller smoke clouds pour forth nearby, the signatures of combustible equipment and supply boxes given over to the flames.

Behind this charcoal curtain loom the fires themselves, dancing in shadows of red and black. All the Dantean elements come together at once. The pyre at the center of the plaza, bright and malevolent even through the haze, fueling the broadest skyward plume. Cauldrons of fires standing in random formation—luminescent pools with indistinct boundaries and uncertain sources belching their black smoke in unison. Marquees of shops and stores, melting and crashing to the ground. Bodies. Dozens of bodies. Charred, twisted, crawling. And all around, the synthetic tiles of the plaza floor are being consumed by the flames, bubbling like a molten brown lake. Through it stream rivers of fire following a train of fuel that rolls unstoppably toward the edges of the concourse.

Against this inferno, the plaza's sprinklers are useless, water guns raised against the end of the world.

My eyes go to Maria, terrified by this spectacle. And then beyond her, to the tall silver silos just visible through the gauze of smoke and fire. The heat from the flames blows over me, and then a wave of cold, as I realize what I'm staring at.

Tanks filled with pure oxygen.

At their base, the fire rolls closer, aiming straight for the slowly leaking hole near the output pipe that was opened up by the piercing rotor. The flames are mere yards away now. Even the painted lettering at the base of the tanks is beginning to burn.

"We've gotta go!" I shout over the din. I lead Maria in the opposite direction, toward the metal stairwell that Rojo had been ascending, near the point where the construction derrick had stood. How long before the tanks blow? A minute? Two minutes? It doesn't matter. There's no chance we'll be very far from here when they do. There's too much space to cross, and too many barriers along the way.

We bolt down the stairs, almost flying, taking two or three steps at a time, barely able to see where our feet are landing. The clatter of shoes against the metal is lost in the roar of the flames and in the pounding of my heart. My mouth fills with smoke as we run, and my chest responds with angry beating blows, the pain spreading in knife-edged pulses to my limbs.

But we can't stop. Can't even let up.

And now, finally, we're at ground level. Here, beneath the ceiling of the smoke, the mist is thinner—a light gray haze that stings and burns the eyes—but at least we can see. And what we're see are scenes fit only for the eyes of Satan. The bodies of workers and security guards lying in hopeless repose, burned and beyond help. The cauldrons of fire arching upward into the smoke clouds, burning more fiercely now. A filigree of red rimming the oxygen tanks like an assault force, closing in. And far across the concourse: the corridor that leads to the escalators, to the rows of tiny homes, and to the outside. Our only hope.

If we can make it.

"This way!" I yell to Maria, choking back the smoke-wrapped words as they send a spear of pain to my chest. We run on, toward the exit, leaping over bodies and piles of debris. And then up ahead lies something that we can't jump over: the fallen derrick, splayed across the floor, its yellow paint being licked by the flames. We'll have to climb over it.

We approach quickly, running toward the end where the derrick's cross-section is thinnest. And then I see her. *Fran Amalfi*. Dazed. Frantic. Choking. Desperately trying to crawl away from the flames. Her cream-colored suit is ripped and stroked with soot, her arms and shoulders splattered with blood, her leg caught in the twisted steel mesh of what used to be the derrick's platform. It's a miracle she survived the fall, even more so that she survived what happened after.

I pull to a quick stop and she sees my feet, then looks up. "Martin . . ."

My name comes out in a frail rush of breath that dies before she can finish.

I look at her, then at the oxygen tanks on the far side of the plaza. The flames are drawing closer, collecting at the tanks' edges, plying their wild victory dance. Minutes, and the tanks will blow.

I turn back to Amalfi. Her eyes beseech me, the eyes of a terrified child. Her hand reaches out to me.

"Please . . ."

A jumble of conflicting thoughts race through my mind. After all that she's done, I know I should just leave her here, to suffer the consequences that she herself brought on. It would be an excusable response to her betrayal that few would question. And I almost consider it. But I'm just as quickly chastened. No one—not even someone as venal as Fran Amalfi—deserves this fate.

"Come here!" I yell to Maria. Maria stops a few yards away and turns, anxious to move on. But she bows to my command and rushes back. We bend down to Amalfi, working hurriedly in those fractured seconds, hardly thinking about what we're doing. As we do, we keep one eye on the distant oxygen tanks, waiting for the fire to overtake them and end us all.

At length, Maria untangles Amalfi's leg from the crumpled derrick platform. I lift Fran to her feet, pulling her arm around my shoulder. She stands weakly, unsteadily. *How much blood can she have lost?* But it's a question for another time. For now, there are more urgent matters. *We have to get out!*

"Can you walk?" I ask her.

Amalfi nods weakly, still dazed.

Together, the three of us mount and climb over the recumbent derrick, then drop to the other side. The exit corridor is thirty yards ahead of us, its outlines diffuse but visible through the fast-gathering gloom. I tighten Amalfi's arm around my shoulder, then turn to Maria. "Go on! We'll catch up!"

And then to Amalfi, as Maria sprints off: "We'll have to move or we'll never make it."

". . . do my best." Pained. Barely audible. But somehow she forces herself forward.

We head on, Amalfi limping next to me but gaining a little strength. I guide her along and she struggles ahead. Her breaths are even more labored than mine, her eyes glazed.

In seconds, we pass through the corridor's entryway and into the corridor itself, leaving the inferno of the plaza behind us. We scramble the last few yards to the escalators, and our fortune holds: they're still running. Amalfi collapses on the railing as we step onto the moving stairs. It may be only my mind's embattled impression, but the escalator seems to be rising in dreamlike slowness, climbing only inches per second. *Too slow!*

We have mere seconds to live.

I look ahead and see Maria nearing the top of the second escalator flight, sprinting forward, her shoes slapping against the tiled walkway. Then she vanishes, gone from sight, moving into the residential corridor. Amalfi and I need to be there too. *Now!*

I grab Amalfi's arm. Rest time is over. "Come on!"

And we're climbing again. Slow, hard steps. Even here, away from the thickest clouds of smoke, breathing is difficult, and my chest pulses in a constant ache, spreading through me. But we've been lucky too long, and we're still not out of danger. If we're anywhere near here when the tanks explode, we're dead.

We finally reach the top of the first bank of elevators and rush to the second. After eternal seconds of climbing, we near its summit. I have to drag Amalfi up the last few steps, so close is she to collapse, and we race across the short swath of tiles before the residential corridor begins.

And that's when it happens.

From behind us comes a burst of thunder so loud that it blots out all consciousness. Then the first strokes of heat claw at our backs as the scorched air rushes up the escalators and blows through the residential passageway as if it were a wind tunnel.

I practically throw Amalfi through the open doorway of the nearest house and dive in after her, ducking below the base of the window and pulling a thick construction tarp over us, holding her there while the initial burst of the heat shoots past. Even crouched behind the wall and covered by the fireproof tarp, we're singed, and the air around us starts to boil. I look up, peering out from under the black tarp. The windowsill and doorframe are ringed by flames, as if someone had decorated them with Christmas lights.

And then, in the next instant, I'm on my feet, pulling Amalfi up with me. The heat and flames are only going to grow worse as the inferno in the plaza intensifies. *No time!* Quickly, wrapping ourselves in the tarp, I lead Fran back through the fiery doorway, into the underground street, and we peer down the length of the passage toward the corridor's exit. All of the overhead lights have been blown out, all of the workers long since cleared away. Now the street is filled with a gray translucent fog, and the supply cartons and furnishings along the moving sidewalks have turned into bonfires. Blasted by the force of the explosion, audio-animatronic birds lie scattered about, charred and blackened, having fallen from the simulated sky. All along the street, the doors and windows of the homes are encircled with wisps of red, the ornaments of the season, celebrating the Devil's holiday.

And behind us, even worse. The bottoms of the escalators have sunken into a roiling sea of fire, and the flames are riding the metal stairs the rest of the way to the top.

In seconds, they'll be here.

"Let's go!" I call to Fran, and we race off down the cobblestone path. The heat surrounds us, slowing us, and the cobblestone pavement sends sharp spikes of pain up our legs. Our breaths grow more labored with each burst of speed. We pass by the red-rimmed houses as we run, but they are beyond the ken of our consciousness, unattended scenery outside a moving train. We make it across the intersection that divides the residential spoke into two segments, and then there's only one image left in our sights: the wide doorway that leads out into the service corridor, where Fran and I entered how many millions of years ago. The air-lock doors have been blown away by the force of the blast, but the passage through them is clear.

We run on.

Closer now. Only a few dozen yards from the exit.

And then, from beyond this broad doorway, comes a scream.

We run on, faster now, and I sprint ahead of Amalfi, leaving her to her own resources. The voice of the screamer is unmistakable. *Maria.* I dread what I will see. Know all too certainly what it will be.

And I'm right. I'm into the service corridor in the next instant, spurting into the center of the passage with my pistol drawn, and I see what I expect: Luis Rojo, standing a few yards away. A gun is held to Maria's head, the backup disks she was carrying tossed on the floor behind her.

Rojo greets me with piercing eyes, consumed now by rage and vengeance. An angry smile comes to his lips despite the horrors all around us. He is burnt, black-faced, and his clothes are spotted with ash. He must have tried to come back in after all—for Farraday, for the backup disks, for who knows what.

"Now, she's mine," he says slowly. He cocks his pistol. "And you can watch!"

I do the only thing I can. I charge. Madly. Violently. The rush of a wild animal. Swing my gun into position as I go. The suddenness of the move startles Rojo, and he pulls his gun away from Maria's head and aims it toward me, toward my chest and then toward my gun hand just as I'm ready to fire. He shoots—

—and the bullet pierces my wrist. The pain races up my arm, and my gun is blown away behind me, too far to reach. Instead, I dive forward, ignoring my injured wrist. Rolling. Turning. Defusing his aim. He steps back and tries to get off another shot, but in the same moment Maria is all over him, one arm wrapped around his neck, the other clutching for his gun.

With a swift back cut of his elbow, Rojo finishes her threat, knocking Maria to the ground, stunned and helpless. He readies another shot, this one with both hands. I'm lying prone in front of him, mere yards away. Completely exposed. Looking straight down his gun barrel and the end of my life.

He steadies his aim, relishing the moment, knowing it will be my last, knowing that I am finally his. But I don't even see his face. All I see is his white shirt stained with sweat and splashes of black soot— —and then, suddenly, with red. Once. Twice. His arms fall from their position, his hands flexing apart. He staggers back. Another red spot, this one joined by the sound of an exploding bullet, and he twists backward. The gun drops from his hand, and his face is a mix of shock and confusion.

He's dead before he hits the floor.

I jerk my head around to look behind me. My gun is off the floor, in Amalfi's hands. She kneels there. Rigid. Shaking. Just now realizing what she has done. I watch her for a long second, picturing in my mind what must have happened. My eyes offer her a silent glimpse of thanks.

But she doesn't respond in kind. Her face fills instead with unease, and then with fright. She takes a deep breath. Or tries to. But it won't come.

She can only gasp.

Her look of fright transforms into terror, and I feel it too. In my throat. In my chest. Tightness. Pressure. Pounding. *How can this be? The smoke isn't that thick this far from the plaza.*

I force back the pain and hurry to Amalfi, helping her to her feet. Then I leave her and dart to Maria. She is just climbing to her knees, gathering the last of the backup disks. I give her my arm and she stands, unsteadily, but on her own. But she's breathing hard too, on the verge of choking. It *must* be the smoke.

"Come on!" I tell her. "Outside!"

Her eyes are full of denial. "It's the *air*, Martin!"

Of course! The signs were there, as clear as ever. But in my desperate rush to find Maria and then escape, my mind had blocked them out.

But now what's happening is unmistakable. And outside won't help. The deafening blasts of the klaxons, coming simultaneously from outside and all around us, confirm it.

We've got to find masks!

My thoughts go back to the oxygen tanks lined in neat rows in Farraday's office, to the hundreds of other tanks that must have been stored throughout Skylight. Gone now. Out of reach. Consumed by the flames.

But where are there more? Down the long service corridor to our right, winding around what's left of the complex? I have no idea what's there, no idea whether it's even passable. Too great a risk.

I look in the other direction, up the corridor's steep slope as it slants toward the outside, where Amalfi and I entered. *The service bays!* The edges and corners of trucks are visible past the now-vacated security station, at least a hundred yards away.

It's a long run. But it's our only choice.

I turn back to Amalfi. She has fallen again, unable to stand on her own, struggling for breath. *No time!*

"Take her and get out!" I yell to Maria. "I'll find some tanks!" And then I'm off, racing up the corridor, my eyes locked on my destination. It's Denver all over again, except this time the terror is worse because I know exactly what is happening. And if the air's disintegrating as fast now as it was then, we have three, maybe four minutes to find oxygen before we can no longer breathe. Somewhere, in one of the trucks, there have to be some tanks. *Somewhere!*

If they haven't already been stripped away by the fleeing workers.

I run on, my chest constricting, a mass of pain worse than a heart attack. I glance behind me. Maria has helped Amalfi to her feet, and they're lurching forward, then moving faster, as quickly as Fran can go.

I look away from them, my eyes once more focused ahead. The outside is closer, but still too far. *Way too far.* And my breaths are coming like fire.

Unbidden, my mind flashes back to the solar plant. Maria and I are running again, just like we did there. Now, we're being chased, not by mad gunmen, but by the threat of a more personal death, one that I can't blow away with a pistol and good aim. Our only hope is the exit. Forty yards away, then thirty. I no longer have the power to look back. I only hope the others are following.

And then, somehow, I make it, and race out into the service bay. There are dozens of trucks parked there, washed over by the whipping light of the fading red and yellow aurorae. I see a few bodies. Randomly strewn tools. Pallets of supplies tipped over. But no people. They all must have fled down the hills with the roar of the explosion or the bellow of the klaxons that continue to blast all around me.

Or at the first hint of the lightness of the air.

I rush to the nearest truck, off to my left, and swing open the driver's door, looking around frantically. *Nothing.* Then to another. Still nothing. *Where are the oxygen tanks?*

I cross back to the opposite side of the service bay, swing wide the door of another truck, look inside. *There! On the floor!* A single tank with a mask attached. I glance at the gauge. *Full.*

I take a quick gulp of air from it, savoring the sweet taste of the oxygen, take in enough to preserve my own ragged breaths for a few moments longer. Then I glance back toward the service corridor. Maria and Fran are just stumbling out onto the tarmac, their faces blanched, their breaths fading.

I leap from the truck's cab, the oxygen tank in hand. "Here, hook her up!" I tell Maria, passing the tank to her. "I'll find one for you."

Maria takes the cylinder without even the breath for words. My last vision of the two of them is of Maria pressing the mask to Fran's mouth, framed by the fire from Skylight, the flames casting russet shadows over their gray and frightened faces.

But there's no time to wait. My throat is tightening again, and now even the smallest of breaths won't come. I run past the two trucks I've already checked, to the cab of a third. *Nothing.* Then the next, and the next. *Still nothing!*

I can't breathe!

And then, as I flee another empty cab, I tumble off the truck's lip to the asphalt below. My palms and knees skid across the unyielding surface. I try to push myself up, but can't. There's no strength.

And no one here, this time, to save me.

I just lie there, gasping for absent breaths. My chest is exploding, my mind slipping away to nothing. My ears fill with a buzzing over the blare of the klaxons. It's a distant sound, like the whir of a bird's wings beating hopelessly against the air.

And with it comes one last second of cognizance. I can't stay here or I'll die. I'm up on my knees in that instant, then to my feet. Scrambling across the open space. Running like a drunken man, toward another truck that seems to loom miles away. From somewhere behind me, I hear coughs. Choking. Maria? Or Fran? I can't tell.

But their imagined image is gone from my mind as soon as it appears. I can't help them now. Can't even help myself.

I finally reach the distant truck. Climb onto the cab's footboard. Pull myself up to the door handle. After two or three flailing tries, I manage to lever the door open, barely keep from falling back to the ground.

I try to lift myself further but can't even reach the seat. I'm looking instead across the length of the cab's floor. A metal canister with a hose attached lies there. An illusion? *It can't be.*

I reach across, touch solid metal. My fingers grasp for the hose. *A mask!* I reach for it. Miss it. Then try again. Finally catch it. I pull the mask toward me, up to my face. Hold it over my mouth. And wait. But nothing comes.

No air!

I pull myself forward, sliding across the floor of the cab, trying to focus my failing vision on the tank's gauge. In the dim light, I can see it's almost empty. Then I see the airflow switch. *Off.*

With weak and trembling fingers, I switch it on, and a burst of oxygen pours forth as the tank fills my lungs with precious air.

But it's too late. My mind is racing toward unconsciousness, and the world is spinning to black. With one last gasp of effort I slip the mask's strap over the back of my head.

And then I collapse, facedown onto the floor of the cab, my tears mixing with the sand and oil and mud where a thousand pairs of boots have trod.

And then: *nothing.*

As I descend to my death, the last impressions I have are not of sight but of sound. The roar of the fire. The wheezing of the oxygen tank. And the rhythmic hum of spinning rotors from somewhere far away, uselessly closing in, beyond the gates of forever.

▼ ▼ ▼

Alison meets the three of us later that evening after our arrival in Los Angeles, driving one of the city energy office's sacrilegiously large vans. We wait for her on the main street that runs through the dusk-shadowed Northridge neighborhood so that she does not have to see the remains of my house—a place where she and various boyfriends had visited many times for office parties and barbecues over the years. I told her our situation over the telephone earlier in the afternoon, when I had sufficiently recomposed myself to call her. And so she is uncharacteristically quiet when she arrives. She gives me a quick greeting and a brief hug, nods hello to Darby and Santos, and leaves it at that.

I am grateful she doesn't say more.

Darby and Santos climb into the back of the van and I into the front, and we ride off in silence toward the Children's Hospital, where at last I will be able to find a doctor with the equipment and the training to properly examine Darby. While we wait for the physician's report, Alison finally speaks at greater length, tearfully offering her condolences. Her help. Her support. "I'm so sorry, Martin," she says, time and again, and there are no words strong enough to express the depth of the hurt that she feels.

How do you tell someone like this—someone who truly cares about you and wants to help—that it's too late? That the long downward spiral has already begun. How do you make her understand?

I don't even try.

Soon, she switches to safer terrain. Fran Amalfi would like me to come back to work, she tells me. Especially now that she is heading a new local agency called the Citizens Council that, like its cousins in dozens of other major cities across the country, was just established by federal mandate. "It's the best thing for you," Alison suggests as persuasively as she can. "You should get back into the routine. Keep busy. Work your way through it."

Sitting here now, listening and responding blankly, I am amazed that I ever thought that things could be even remotely the same. That I could be the same. I hear Alison's voice and my own as though they were sounds whispered to me through a long dark tunnel, disappearing into the air before recognition or comprehension sets in. Santos has left us by now, heading out to the streets to try to make contact with associates he once knew. I think that hiding amid the masses, as he has opted to do, may be the best choice after all. Santos promised to get back in touch with me after a few days, and I know that he meant well. But I also know that it's a call that almost certainly will never be made.

Meanwhile, I have more pressing matters to attend to than Dagger

Santos's fate or Fran Amalfi's needs. I am finally able to meet with Darby's doctor later that night, and am prepared to hear the worst. His report is not altogether positive, but it is not as bad as I had feared. He tells me that Darby will be all right but that she will need professional supervision for a while. He recommends placement at the Children's Bureau, yet another new agency assembled from parts of other organizations in recent days. It is well staffed and intended for cases just like this, he says, and he assures me that it is Darby's best hope for recovery.

At length, and without any other choice, I give my consent.

Alison tells me afterward that she knows someone at the Bureau, a former colleague who now manages one of their programs. She says that she'll make the arrangements for Darby, that I won't have to worry about it. I thank her for her assistance, doubting that I would have had the capacity to handle matters by myself anyway. She then offers to drive us to my home so that I can collect some of my belongings. But I decline, not wanting to relive my return, even in my mind. In that case, Alison suggests, Darby and I should spend our nights in a nearby hotel—courtesy of the Citizens Council—while we wait for the Children's Bureau placement to be approved.

I accept this generosity with humility, and experience the first relative peace that I have felt in a long time.

Amalfi tries to reach me several times during the next few days, but I am not yet prepared to talk with her. When I finally am, she is out of the office, and I find myself speaking with Barry Erthein.

"I need a few weeks," I tell him.

"We've got problems," comes his reply. "Huge problems. The Council. Thousands of immigrants coming into the city every day. Countless new regulations from Washington. We need you now."

"And I need time."

"Fine. Take all the time you want," Erthein says bitterly, officiously. "Just don't expect the job to be waiting for you when you happen to be ready."

I shake my head as I hang up, not caring whether the job is there or not. It really doesn't matter to me. Not anymore.

The next morning, Alison phones to tell me that the Children's Bureau has an opening and that they are ready to see us. She arrives shortly afterward and ferries us to the Bureau—a large, gothic graystone south of downtown Los Angeles. The nurse who greets us is kind and efficient, but she might as well be an executioner. She will be taking the last of my life away from me, only moments from now.

I hold Darby's hand as we tour the facility, and when we sit with the nurse to fill out the admission forms. Then I lift Darby to me, when it's time to say good-bye, and kiss her gently on the cheek. She wraps her arms tightly around my neck then, and I whisper my promise to come back for her just as soon as she's finished with her treatments.

If there is an ember of spirit or hope left in me, encased in my cell of protective isolation, in this shell of the man I once was, it turns to ash minutes later. I stand outside the Children's Bureau's play area and watch through the thick plate-glass window as Darby sits alone, clutching the big stuffed penguin that is all that remains of her life in Denver.

"Martin Fall?" *a young administrative aide with expressionless eyes and a battered clipboard says as he peers into the waiting room where I'm standing.* "I have just a few questions for you."

"How long will you keep her?" *I ask him.*

"A week. Ten days." *The young man shrugs, but his tone informs me that he doesn't have time for such inconsequential matters.* "We can't say for sure until we've examined her."

"Is there somewhere I can stay? So I can be close to her?"

"We don't have the room. I'm sorry. Look, just go home when we're done here. She'll be back with you in no time as long as you pass the screening."

At first, I don't realize what he has said. Then I do, and his words stab me like an icy sword. I feel the seed of panic growing within me.

"Come on," *the young man says impatiently.* "We have to get this done."

I close my eyes for a moment and nod, then glance back into the play area. A nurse has entered the room and has placed Darby and her penguin in a wheelchair.

Darby looks over at me through the window then and timidly waves, her eyes filled with quiet trust and love, wishing me good-bye for what she thinks will be but a brief parting, but for what I suddenly fear may be our final farewell.

CHAPTER 23

The world returns to me in random sensations. The burry dryness in my throat. The throbbing pain in undefined regions of my body. The penetrating exhaustion. The darkness. The pulsing thrum above me, like a room fan left on too high a speed.

And a storm of fractured memories. Jumbled. Disconnected. Terrifying.

I recall looking back at Skylight as though hovering above it. I can see an image of flames reaching skyward from the city's center, dark ruby shadows glinting off the silver outskirts, while the coastal mountains reclined undisturbed against the starlit background.

Did my eyes really see this, or was it only a dream?

And before that: more recollections. Scenes of destruction. Fire. Explosions. Gunshots. Running. Struggling for breath. These scenes were real, or at least I think they were. But I can't fix them in time or place. They're fragments of memories, mere pieces of reality. And after lunging into the truck, there is nothing. No memory at all. Maria? Amalfi? What happened to them? Did they die too?

I do not know.

I try to retrieve some hint or clue, but the effort overwhelms me and I fall back into unconsciousness. Some time later—minutes, hours, it's hard to tell—I awaken again, this time to voices. Male voices. Excerpts of conversation.

". . . levels returned to normal . . ."

". . . completed according to plan . . ."

". . . yeah, if it works . . ."

Skylight

I can't decipher the words, but at least I can pry open my eyes. What I see is a blur. The outlines of figures. One crouches nearby. Another sits further away, his back toward me. Both are shadows set against the sky.

Behind them, I can make out an eerie, luminous gray, as if the time were just before dawn.

Then I hear the thrumming again, more sharply now, and I realize we must be in a helicopter. Apparently, someone else was listening in on the Golden West comm line as Maas's chopper was going down. Who?

I'm not sure.

". . . do you feel?"

The voice is directed at me, and I gurgle a response. Then: *how is Maria? Did she make it?* I ask the questions in my mind, but the words must not come out, because the man's next comment is not an answer.

". . . just a while longer," he says as he turns away. "You gotta be awake for the show."

The voice is distinct now, and I recognize it.

Rooker.

I turn partway toward him, the only movement I can manage, and my head presses up against the helicopter's glass side. My vision is clearer now. I can tell that we're flying over a broad residential area. Houses, roads, and low-lying buildings spread out in the darkness for miles in every direction. There are no lights at all, not even the light of bonfires.

There is a strange sense of recognition in this view. It comes back to me slowly, but from a different, more personal vantage point than I have experienced before.

This must be Orange County, I think.

Then the helicopter banks, and I see that my impression is correct. In the distance—rising above the endless plain of houses and buildings—stands a broad concrete bowl rimmed with dead light towers and marked by a hundred-foot "A."

The stadium.

A place I used to know well.

I study the image for a moment, as if I could actually see the tens of thousands of people huddled within this dark and forgotten refuge. Gradually, my eyes move past them to the horizon beyond. A familiar sight comes into view. A sliver of glowing orange edging into the lightening sky.

The sun, peeking over the distant perimeter of the earth, bringing with it the false promise of a new day.

And then, while I watch, something miraculous happens. A mile or so east of the stadium, a pair of floodlights shine back from the ground, as if in response to the sun's first rays. The sun rises further, and again a pair of floodlights flash back in return. The sun's climb continues, and still more lights respond. Soon the lights are blinking on almost continuously, mere seconds apart, advancing like footsteps toward the stadium.

The chopper closes in, and the pattern resolves itself into two long rows of streetlights, shining with the brightness of a life gone by.

Then even these bright spots are washed into the background. A whole sea of lights awakens before us, miles upon miles of bright white, glistening like a field of untrammeled snow.

The helicopter dips into the stadium at that moment, blocking out this illunined panorama, and my eyes turn to the people below. The sleepers reclining in the hard plastic seats. The families bundled together on the ground. The merchants setting out their morning wares.

All looking up, their eyes focused on this great flying craft descending into their midst.

And then looking beyond us, to a light brighter than the sun. Dim at first, then growing brighter. The whiteness surrounds us. I peer up to see the light towers that surround the stadium flickering to life, one-by-one, for the first time in almost a year.

Then I look more closely, and I see the reason why.

Midway up each tower is attached a small silver dish, angled precisely toward the rising sun.

The helicopter slowly settles toward the ground then. The sleepers and sellers scatter, clearing a space. As they do, I glance behind me. *Rooker. Maria. Amalfi.* All awake. All alive. They kneel before these sights in silence, their thoughts held as closely as a prayer.

We land, and the helicopter's motors are turned off. The tower lights fill the stadium now, and I can see faces outside instead of just shadowed figures. For a moment, my mind goes back to Avalon Boulevard on the day when this long journey began. But this time, the people around us do not greet us with hostile and despairing stares. They look instead toward the sky. Toward the lights. And toward us. Watching this miracle for themselves.

With surprise. With wonder.

And, at last, with hope.

▼ ▼ ▼

EPILOGUE

The noontime crowd, attired in Brooks Brothers suits and Ann Taylor dresses, gathers beneath the videoscreen high up on the Citizens Council building, watching with more intent than usual as Fran Amalfi delivers her daily remarks. It is a sight I have witnessed many times in the past. But now, a week after Rooker's demonstration, it strikes me as odd, out of place. The onlooker's faces, if anything, are graver than before. The eyes are more worried, the expressions filled with more displeasure than relief. For these people are the real managers of the city—the men and women who administer the Council's energy regulations and the government's controls over essential industries. And they are listening to their boss outline a plan for their demise. They can't be happy with what they are hearing.

And I wonder, as I scan their faces, how long Fran can stand against them.

She seems, as always, determined to try. ". . . not next week nor next month," she finishes her address. "Maybe not even next year. But someday soon we will be able to reclaim the freedom and prosperity that we as Americans had before. And not just those of us here, but for people all over the world. This path won't be an easy one, and its rewards won't come without a lot of hard work and pain and adjustment. But it's a start. A start that—for the sake of our children, and their children after that—we can't afford *not* to take."

I watch her as she speaks. The lines of her face have hardened, and her accustomed sheen of self-confidence has been replaced by scars and bruises that her makeup cannot hide. She may not yet truly believe what she says, but she is smart enough not to let her personal doubts stand in the way of her political survival.

"Sure you won't consider staying?" The voice is Rooker's. He has stepped up beside me on the crowded plaza, and I glance across at him. As I do, I recall a similar question being asked of me by another friend in a place far away from here, in the days before *catastrophe* became a proper noun.

I just shake my head. Rooker has already made his own deal. Amalfi takes credit for introducing Alejandro Maas's solar collectors to the world, while Rooker becomes deputy director of the Citizens Council, with authority over all Council's operations. I'm sure he's pleased. But the spoils Amalfi set before me—my old job, or even Rooker's—will have to wait. I have a life to reassemble first.

What there is left of it.

"The job will be here when you're ready," Fran reassured me a few days ago. "I've got some other things to do for you too."

As I'm recalling her promises, Rooker's voice intrudes again. "What's that?"

"I said you'll be missed," Rooker repeats, and I look back at him. He hands me a set of keys. "Take care of the place, all right? I'll be staying down here until all the production lines are back up."

The keys are to Rooker's house in the hills, a way station until I decide I'm ready to return.

"Thanks, Jay," I tell him. I think to say more, but there is nothing left to add. I merely nod good-bye and watch him walk off into the Citizens Council building and back into the world.

I turn away a moment later, then stroll the fifty or so yards to the park that borders the Council plaza. The area is filled with the usual overflow of the noontime crowds, and for several minutes all I can see are unfamiliar faces. Then, heading toward me, I see a person whom I do know: *Maria Maas.*

She's right on time.

Maria steps into a clearing, and I notice then that she has brought her son, Eduardo, with her. Both of them greet me with smiles—his is broad and excited, hers tinged with sadness. In the instant of recognition, the boy breaks free from his mother's grasp and runs toward me, hugging my legs.

"*¡Señor Fall!*" Eduardo exclaims, offering his own small note of persuasion. Maria is returning to Argentina to dedicate a grave for her father and plans to stay with her extended family for a few weeks until she is prepared to resume her duties here. She asked me to come along—as a friend, as someone who understands. "You could use the change of scenery," she suggested. But I told her that, no, this was *her* time and *her* space, and that my presence would only be an intrusion. But I assured her I would be here when she returned.

She accepted this decision in silence and now embraces me in the same way. I have long since said my condolences for her father, and she her thanks for my help. But there remains a bond between us that was not there before, and I cherish it.

In some ways, it is all I have left.

She pulls away and looks at me, and the sadness in her eyes is joined by a strange mixture of caring and caution. She is clearly nervous, and I don't know why.

"Come with me," she says softly. "There's someone who wants to meet you."

I study her, not knowing what to make of this. "Okay."

She takes Eduardo's hand and they walk toward the far side of the clearing. I follow behind, watching these two forms recede in front of me. Maria looks straight ahead while Eduardo turns in wonder at every sight. In that quiet instant, I have an image of another time and another place, when my best friend Ray Stanford would walk with his own eager-eyed child across the old ball field behind our home.

I close my eyes for a moment, to let the memory play itself out, to recall days that never again would be. When I open them again, I see that Maria has stopped walking. She and Eduardo have moved to the side of the clearing, and in front of me stands an ancient oak tree. And, in front of it, a gray-haired woman—stout, well-groomed, a kindly social-worker type. *What is she doing—*

And then, all at once, my thoughts stop, and that's when I see her. The woman is holding the hand of an eleven-year-old girl. A girl whose face I have not seen in a very long time.

Darby.

The woman lets go of Darby's hand and steps back. Darby just stands there for a moment, her head down, and then she looks up at me. Her appraisal is filled with fear and uncertainty, and she seems to be on the verge of tears.

I take a slow step forward. Her eyes stay fixed on mine, but she doesn't move. Another step, and I kneel on one knee. I hold my arms out to her, trying to find the right words to say, to help her to understand.

But no words are needed. She's racing toward me now, faster than on any soccer field, and in seconds she's in my arms. I lift her to my chest, bury my face in the sweet autumn smell of her hair, hold her to me as if she were the last of life itself.

Somewhere amid all of this, I glance at Maria. The nervousness has left her now, and has given way to the assurance of faith. It's a lost emotion for me, and I only hope she can read its dim reflection in my worn and grateful eyes.

But this is Darby's time, and I look back at her as tears rush down her cheeks. For the moment, there is nothing else in the world but this little girl, and I lose myself in the feel and the warmth and the love of her. When my own tears come, I don't even try to wipe them away.

For they are tears of forgetting. And in the forgetting, at last, a chance to remember.

▼ ▼ ▼

ABOUT THE AUTHOR

Kevin Hopkins, an award-winning novelist and writer, served for seven years in the White House as Policy Information Director and speechwriter for President Ronald Reagan. He later was senior policy counsel to the White House Science Office and the Office of the Mayor of San Diego, and has been a senior contributing editor to Bloomberg *Businessweek* for the past twenty-two years. He is currently Director of Research for The Communications Institute, a California-based energy and environmental research center, where he delivers speeches and seminars throughout the country and has appeared as a guest commentator on national and local news programs. He lives with his wife, Mary; his son, Brandon; his cat, Layah; and his dog, Casey, in Salt Lake City, Utah.